LONELY FOR YOU ONLY

BOOKS BY MONICA MURPHY

THE LANCASTER PREP SERIES

Things I Wanted to Say (but Never Did)

A Million Kisses in Your Lifetime

Promises We Meant to Keep

I'll Always Be with You

You Said I Was Your Favorite

Lonely for You Only (A Lancaster Novel)

THE PLAYERS SERIES

Playing Hard to Get

Playing by the Rules

Playing to Win

THE WEDDED BLISS SERIES

The Reluctant Bride

The Ruthless Groom

The Reckless Union

THE COLLEGE YEARS SERIES

The Freshman

The Sophomore

The Junior

The Senior

THE CALLAHANS SERIES

Close to Me

Falling for Her

Addicted to Him

Meant to Be

Fighting for You

When Bae . . .

Making Her Mine

A Callahan Wedding

THE DATING SERIES

Save the Date

Fake Date

Holidate

Hate to Date You

Rate a Date

Wedding Date

Blind Date

THE DAMAGED HEARTS SERIES

Her Defiant Heart

His Wasted Heart

Damaged Hearts

THE FOREVER YOURS SERIES

You Promised Me Forever

Thinking about You

Nothing without You

THE FRIENDS SERIES

Just Friends

More than Friends

Forever

THE NEVER SERIES

Never Tear Us Apart

Never Let You Go

THE RULES SERIES

Fair Game

In the Dark

Slow Play

Safe Bet

THE FOWLER SISTERS SERIES

Owning Violet

Stealing Rose

Taming Lily

THE REVERIE SERIES

His Reverie

Her Destiny

THE ONE WEEK GIRLFRIEND SERIES

One Week Girlfriend

Second Chance Boyfriend

Three Broken Promises

Drew + Fable Forever

Four Years Later

Five Days until You

A Drew + Fable Christmas

THE BILLIONAIRE BACHELORS CLUB SERIES

Crave

Torn

Savor

Intoxicated

STANDALONE NOVELS

Daring the Bad Boy

Saving It

Pretty Dead Girls

NEW YORK TIMES BESTSELLING AUTHOR

MONICA MURPHY

LONELY FOR YOU ONLY

BLACK STONE PUBLISHING

Published in 2024 by Blackstone Publishing
Cover and book design by Larissa Ezell
Cover image from Adobe Stock

Printed in the United States of America
Originally published in hardcover by Blackstone Publishing in 2024

First paperback edition: 2024
ISBN 979-8-212-63095-5
Fiction / Romance / New Adult

Version 1

Blackstone Publishing
31 Mistletoe Rd.
Ashland, OR 97520

www.BlackstonePublishing.com

LONELY FOR YOU ONLY

CHAPTER ONE

SCARLETT

I enter the elevator carefully, my dress nearly taking up the entire space.

"And where am I supposed to stand?" My mother sounds amused as she studies me.

Offering her a nervous smile, I grab at my wide, layered pale-pink tulle skirts and try to pull them in closer to me. That only gives up a few inches of space, max, but it's better than nothing. "You can stand next to me."

Mom glides into the elevator, careful not to step on the tulle. She's wearing impossibly high Louboutin stilettos, and she could tear the skirt with ease. Those shoes are like weapons.

But my mother is very careful and would never do that. This is my night, and she wants me to shine. This event is being thrown for me, and it is huge. Outrageous.

Maybe even borderline completely over the top.

Okay, there's nothing borderline about it. The party is definitely going to be completely over the top, thanks to my father. He never does anything halfway. It helps to have money like our family does. When multigenerational wealth is managed correctly, like it's been for the Lancasters all these years, it's guaranteed to take care of the family forever.

As long as no one comes along and spends it all. My father comes close with his lavish ways. As the youngest of the Lancaster brothers, he's considered the black sheep of the family. The rebel. The outlier.

Sometimes, as his oldest child and only daughter, I find his reputation hard to live up to.

The moment the mirrored elevator doors slide shut, I stare at my reflection, drinking in the extravagant dress I'm wearing to my eighteenth-birthday party. I'm suddenly afraid it's far too grand, and I mentally fight the panic rising within me, desperate to remain calm despite second-guessing my choice.

"I probably look ridiculous," I say on a sigh, wishing I could go back to my suite, where I got ready earlier, and change into something less ostentatious. Why did I think such a large dress was a good idea again? I look like a little girl desperate to play dress-up in her mom's fancy clothes.

Which, I can't lie, was sort of the look I was going for when I chose the dress in the first place, but . . .

"You're beautiful." Mom's cool palm presses into my forearm, her touch gentle. Reassuring, as always. "The dress is stunning. *You* are stunning. Remember how you said you wanted to make a statement when you walked into your party?" When I nod, she continues. "Trust me, darling. In that dress, you're going to do it. No one will be able to look away from you. Not a single person, including you-know-who."

My heart beats heavier at her not-so-subtle reference. I wring my hands together, taking a deep breath, holding it in for a beat too long before I let it out shakily. I shouldn't be nervous. This evening promises to be fun. Magical.

Possibly even life changing.

"Have you spoken to Ian yet?" My mother's voice is hushed, as if she doesn't want anyone else to hear her question, which is funny considering we're the only two people in the elevator.

"We texted earlier." Just thinking about him sets my heart aflutter.

Ian Baldwin. My friend. One of my closest friends. He's smart and sweet and handsome, and he always makes me smile when I first see him.

Pretty sure he doesn't realize that I have a huge crush on him. I've had a crush on Ian for years, which seems like such a silly way to describe my feelings for him, considering our ages. Crushes are for middle school.

But that's how he makes me feel when I'm near him. Like an awkward preteen who can barely speak.

Our parents have known each other for years—Ian's father is my father's lawyer, who he keeps on retainer. Ian is twenty and will eventually go to law school, and he has his entire life planned out. Eventually he wants to work for his father's law firm. He wants to be married by the age of thirty and to live in a two-story house not far from his parents' home. He also wants two children—a boy and a girl. His biggest desire is to be respected in the same legal circles his father moves in, and he wants to handle the biggest celebrity clients he can find.

"Celebrity is where success is at," Ian told me once at a family dinner, me sitting next to him breathless and hanging on his every word. "They're always involved in some sort of scandal and need an attorney to bail them out. It would be easy money, representing actors and musicians. Celebrities who do nothing but make videos for their so-called followers." He rolled his eyes.

I tried to ignore the insulting tone of his voice when he said that, considering I'm trying my best to become an influencer of some sort. I have a small following. People listen to me. Somewhat. It helps that I come from one of the oldest, wealthiest families in the country and that my father was—still is—somewhat famous.

His infamy is sometimes to my detriment, but I work with his past—and even current—reputation as best as I can. Eventually I want to make a difference with my platform. I'm not out to just get free stuff.

While I'm still not sure what I want to do with my future, Ian has a plan firmly in place. And I want to be a part of that plan so badly I can practically taste it. Not that I would ever tell him, but I often imagine myself as his wife. The mother of his children—the perfect boy and girl. They would be beautiful, well mannered, and well spoken. The perfect representation of their equally perfect father.

My daydreams are filled with images of me attending social events by his side. Hosting dinner parties for our large social circle at our gorgeous two-story house with an impeccable green yard and beautiful garden that I tend to while wearing a large straw hat to protect my skin from the sun.

Does my secret dream make me sound like an old woman? I sort of don't care. That's what I want.

Only with Ian, though.

"Is he here yet?" Mom asks.

Here is the Plaza Hotel. My party is being held in their famous ballroom, and it's going to be epic. I visited the ballroom earlier, when everyone was still setting up for the party, and the transformation took my breath away. The flowers, the decor, the food. And don't even get me started on the planned performances tonight. Aerialists dangling from the chandeliers. Scantily clad burlesque dancers decked out in feathers and pearls while dancing in giant cocktail glasses. That's all my father's doing. He always likes pushing things to the edge, I swear.

He even hinted at a *surprise* performance, and I don't have a clue what he's referring to. I just know he never does things in a small way. He's all about the grand gestures, which is a Lancaster family trait, but sometimes? Those grand gestures make me uncomfortable and I'd rather avoid them.

Where my dad is loud and obnoxious, I'm quiet and prefer to linger in the shadows.

But tonight, I'm excited to see who he's brought in to perform. What if it's Taylor Swift? I absolutely adore her. Beyoncé, maybe? I'm all about female empowerment, but I also wouldn't mind seeing Harry Styles . . .

"Darling, did you hear me? Is Ian in the ballroom yet?" Mom asks, pulling me from my thoughts.

I blink at her, then shrug, my entire dress shifting with the movement. "I think so? I'm running late, so I'd guess everyone who's coming is already in the ballroom."

"Oh, don't worry about being late. The guest of honor should always make a grand entrance," Mom says with all that elegant authority I wish I could emulate. She's so confident in her position as Fitz Lancaster's wife.

Gloria Lancaster is the woman I'm desperate to be when I grow up. My mother is the supportive wife to one of the heirs of the Lancaster fortune, but she's also heavily involved in a variety of charities, has gobs of friends who clamor for her attention, and after all these years, she still has the love and absolute adoration of my father.

Fitzgerald Lancaster may be a force to be reckoned with, but when he's paired with my mother, they are still the it couple of high society, even now.

And then there's me. Their oldest child, their only daughter.

The quiet one who would rather stay at home and read a good book or binge-watch a series. I'm not as dazzling in the public eye as they are or even some of my cousins—not even close. Mom pushed me to become more involved on social media about a year ago, and I've grown my platform steadily ever since. Desperate to become something beyond Fitz and Gloria's boring daughter.

Fake it till you make it, right?

"I'm definitely making a grand entrance tonight. Not sure how they'll miss me in this dress." I grab at the skirts, fluffing them out, wishing I could borrow just an ounce of my mother's cool confidence for the evening.

The elevator comes to a stop, the doors sliding open with a soft whoosh, and we're immediately hit with the sound of soft music mixed with the low murmurs of hundreds of people in conversation.

My birthday party is in full swing, and I haven't even arrived yet. My mother always says that's a good sign. Taking a deep, calming breath, I close my eyes for a moment, count to five, and tell myself it's going to be all right.

It is. I know it.

Mom stays in the elevator as I make my way out, my wide skirts dragging across the floor, even with the heels I'm wearing. The dress is elaborate, constructed of layer upon layer of delicate, baby-pink tulle, with a high-low skirt that shows off my legs yet expands into a fluffy train that trails behind me as I walk.

"Darling, you are absolutely stunning," Mom says once she exits the elevator, her gaze on me. "I'm going to text your father and ask him to join us out here. We'll escort you into the ballroom and have them announce you've arrived. What do you think?"

"Okay, that sounds good." I nod, shaking out my suddenly

sweaty hands. I hate that I'm so nervous. I've been to plenty of events in my life, but not one that's only for me. And with so many people in attendance. Tonight's party is special, but it also should be fun. It's a celebration for me.

We're also taking donations in lieu of gifts to a variety of charities my family supports, including the Trevor Project and the Center for Reproductive Rights. Plus, we'll make a considerable donation as well. It's the least we can do.

Someday I want to use my own money and donate to the causes that matter to me, but for now, I'll use the family money.

"Fitz. Darling. Please come out here and help me escort our gorgeous daughter into the ballroom." Mom ends the call, and I swear within two minutes my father is striding toward us, a giant smile on his handsome face when he spots me.

"Scarlett, my God, look at you! You're beautiful." He greets me with open arms, and we hug awkwardly, the dress getting in the way. How could it not? "You're going to make quite the appearance. You and that dress are going to be splashed all over the internet tomorrow morning."

"Stop, you're making her nervous," Mom chastises before turning to look at me. "Are you ready?"

Standing taller, I square my shoulders and lift my chin. "Yes."

"Did you tell her about the surprise?" Dad asks Mom.

"Not yet," Mom says, sending him a pointed look. As if she wants him to remain quiet.

Nerves buzz in my veins, accompanied by a small dose of wariness. "What surprise?"

Dad moves to stand to my left, rubbing his hands together. "Who I arranged to perform just for you tonight."

Oh, right. How could I forget? I was thinking about it only a moment ago in the elevator. I briefly clutch his arm, staring up at him with imploring eyes. "Please tell me it's Taylor Swift."

The Lancaster fortune is vast. Dad could totally get Taylor to make a special appearance at my party. He could pay her millions and it wouldn't make a dent in the family bank account.

"I tried, but she couldn't make it," Dad says with a mock pout.

I push aside the trickle of disappointment and move on to my next favorite. "Harry Styles then?"

"Close." His grin is huge as he loops his arm through mine. Mom does the same with my right one, all three of us linked as we head for the marble stairs that lead down into the ballroom. "Take one more guess."

"Someone else from One Direction?" My brain scrambles, my footsteps faltering as we draw closer. The music grows louder, the roar of many conversations happening at once becoming more distinct. "Maybe Liam?"

Ugh, Liam. He's my least favorite.

"You'll see." The mysterious smile on my dad's face tells me he's loving this.

"Stop making her guess," Mom says, sounding vaguely irritated. "She'll find out soon enough."

We stop at the top of the stairs, my dad waving at the man with a microphone in his hand standing nearby. The heady scent of thousands of flowers hits my nostrils, rich and sweet, and I stare down at the ballroom, taking it all in. The walls are bathed in pink light just for the night, the giant chandeliers that hang from the ceiling glittering in varying shades of pink.

There's a woman on stilts moving through the crowd, wearing a white dress with a massive skirt, the bodice dripping with strings of pearls. A violin is tucked beneath her chin as she plays a delicate tune. Servers clad in pink velvet jackets move about the room, carrying trays laden with champagne glasses full of pale-pink bubbly.

I suddenly, desperately want a drink, despite my being underage. Eighteen is the legal age to drink in Europe, right?

"Attention, everyone! The birthday girl has finally arrived! Please put your hands together in welcoming our guest of honor of the evening, Miss Scarlett Lancaster!" the man with the microphone announces.

A spotlight hits us, illuminating the three of us in shimmering pink, and I blink against the brightness, unable to make out any friendly faces. The applause is polite as we walk down the stairs, a few shouts of "happy birthday" coming from deep within the crowd. All I can do is smile and nod, pretending I know who is saying what to me as we finally come off the stairs and walk past the crowds, moving deeper into the room.

I'm trembling. God, I even stumble, and thankfully my parents keep me upright so I don't fall and make a complete fool of myself. Mom murmurs words of encouragement, telling me to keep my chin up and make eye contact, and while I try, the spotlight is making it impossible.

Worse, all I can do is wonder where Ian is. Is he here? What is he wearing? He said he would be in a suit, and I'm sure he looks crushingly handsome. I don't know if my heart will be able to take it when I finally see him.

I spot a man in the near distance, tall and lean. Much like Ian. Golden-brown hair. Is that him?

The spotlight drops and I blink, my vision back to normal, and I realize the man isn't Ian. Disappointment swamps me and I push it aside.

This evening is a happy occasion. Everything is going to come together and work in my favor.

I just know it.

"We have another exciting announcement," says the man, who I'm assuming my parents must've hired to be the MC for the night. "There will be a special performance taking place in honor of Scarlett's eighteenth birthday tonight. A member of one of her all-time favorite bands will be taking the stage in just a few minutes, performing some of their biggest hits!"

I glance over at my dad, who's watching me with fondness shining in his eyes. He looks ready to burst apart with his secret.

"Who is it? Just tell me," I insist, already over the surprise factor.

I've never really been one who likes surprises anyway.

He grins, his excitement palpable as he rests his hand on top of mine, my arm still curved around his. "Tate Ramsey!"

I frown as my father's answer sinks in, glancing about the room, my gaze snagging on the dessert table, which is covered with eighteen cakes in various shapes and sizes. This party is making me feel like Marie Antoinette, I swear. And I don't know if that's necessarily a good thing.

"Tate Ramsey?" My voice is weak, my mind swirling.

Oh God. Wait a minute . . .

The has-been lead singer from that one boy band that was huge when I was, what, thirteen?

"You mean from Five Car Pileup?"

Dad nods, seemingly pleased. "One and the same. I remember how much you adored them. Him specifically."

"But I was in middle school," I remind him. "Like, the seventh grade."

Fine, it was more like the eighth grade when my friends and I all loved them.

Tate Ramsey and the rest of Five Car Pileup were huge—five years ago. One of those boy bands put together with an audition call, they even had a one-season reality show that I vaguely remember watching. They also had quite a few hits in a startlingly short amount of time. Catchy pop songs with Tate mostly on lead vocals and the rest of them harmonizing along with him. They became famous fast, always photographed on the gossip sites. Everyone wondering who they were dating, what they were doing, what they were wearing.

And then they ran into a little trouble.

Trashing hotel rooms while on tour. One of them had a sex scandal with an underage groupie that eventually got swept under the rug. They partied constantly, much to the horror of all the parents of young teenage girls. Social media started calling them bad influences, and their reputations were tarnishing bit by bit.

Tate was the only one in a committed relationship when they were a band. He'd been steadily dating his longtime girlfriend from high school, and they were portrayed as madly in love. Fans hated her for "stealing" the cutest, most popular one—and then we hated her even more when she was caught cheating on Tate.

With another Five Car Pileup band member.

Oh, that situation became ugly fast. Tate went on a drunken, drug-fueled bender and made a complete joke of himself. Their label dropped them. The band broke up. The gossip sites crucified him specifically.

No one wanted to be near Tate Ramsey.

Does anyone still want to be around him?

"And you loved him back then. You played their music over and over, especially that one song. I remember you even had his posters on your wall." Dad pats my hand again, then lets go of me completely. "Now go on! Spend time with your friends! Enjoy your party!"

Mom gives me a brief hug before she pulls away, smiling at me. "Try to act like you're excited about the performance for your father's sake, yes? He was so excited when he found Tate Ramsey."

"How did he even find him?" I never see his name mentioned anywhere anymore.

I pretty much forgot he even existed.

"Oh, he was selling personalized greetings on one of those websites." Mom waves a dismissive hand. "You know what I mean."

"Like the Cameo site?" Oh God, that's kind of humiliating.

"Yes, something like that. You pay fifty dollars, and he wishes you a personalized happy birthday. Your father sent him a private message and made him an offer he couldn't refuse." Mom shakes her head, her delicate brows drawn together.

"How much did he offer him?" I brace myself for the answer.

"One million dollars."

CHAPTER TWO

SCARLETT

"Scarlett, hey." A hand suddenly grabs at mine as I walk past, and I turn with a gasp to find Ian standing there, smiling down at me. He gives my hand a squeeze before releasing it, taking a step back, his gaze roaming over me from head to toe. "Look at you."

I duck my head for a moment, my cheeks growing warm. Pleased that he's actually checking me out for once. "Hi, Ian."

"That dress . . ." His voice drifts, and I wait breathlessly for him to tell me I look beautiful. Gorgeous even. "It's so big."

Disappointment hits. That wasn't necessarily the reaction I was hoping for.

I glance down at myself, grabbing the tulle and giving the skirt a little shake. "I wanted to make a statement on my birthday."

"You certainly did."

And that's all he says about that.

Huh.

That's my problem with Ian sometimes. It's not that he gives off mixed signals. More like he gives off . . . no signals, and that worries me. Does he like me? I don't know. I mean, I'm positive he likes me as a friend. We've known each other a long time, since we were awkward teenagers. I've nursed a crush on him for what feels like forever. I moved on from Tate Ramsey to Ian, and I've never really liked anyone else since.

My best friend, Rachel, tells me I'm wasting my time with Ian, but I can't help it. I feel a connection with him, and I just wish he saw it.

Saw *me*.

"Are you having fun?" I glance around the ballroom, waving at a woman I vaguely recognize when we make eye contact. She returns the gesture before turning away.

"Yeah, it's great." Ian shoves his hands into his pants pockets, leaning back on his heels as he's wont to do. "This is quite the production."

"You know my parents. They never do anything small."

"Like this dress?" He reaches out, rubbing the tulle fabric directly in front of my chest. My breasts. "Oops." He realizes exactly where he's touching me and yanks his hand away, his cheeks turning ruddy. "Sorry."

I keep back what I really want to say, which is, *I don't mind*.

Because I don't mind. At all. At least it would be a small clue that he likes me as more than a friend if he were trying to cop a feel. Normally when Ian and I are together, he barely touches me.

Maybe this is a bad sign. Maybe I'm wasting my time with Ian. This isn't the first instance when I've had this same exact thought.

That's why I plan on confessing my feelings to him tonight. I'm tired of being confused. The not knowing is killing me.

I'm desperate to know where he stands.

"Pretty impressive entertainment tonight," Ian muses, his

gaze focused above us, where one of the aerialists my parents hired is currently swinging from a chandelier. She's scantily clad, her pale, lithe body on full display as she contorts her arms and legs into what seem like impossible poses. She flips over, hanging upside down as she reaches out to me, a smile on her face.

"For the birthday girl," she says, a perfect white rose clutched in her fingers.

"Thank you." Smiling, I take it from her, bringing the flower to my nose and breathing in the delicate scent. When I glance over at Ian, I find him frowning at me, his usually bright-blue eyes dark and cloudy.

"I should've given you flowers. For your birthday," he says.

"But I didn't want any gifts." My heart starts to race at what he just said. The sincere way he's watching me. "The invitation said so."

"It's still your birthday, and a woman always likes flowers. That's what my mom says, anyway." He plucks the rose from my fingers, twirling it between his, the petals flaring out. "Are white roses your favorite now?"

"Are you tucking that information away for later?" I tease, trying to flirt.

He frowns, handing the flower back to me. "No. I thought you preferred pink."

I take the rose from him, fighting disappointment. He didn't respond to my flirting attempt, of course. He's always so literal. It's hard to tease him. He takes everything so seriously.

"I do prefer pink," I say with a faint smile, trying to forge on. I can't let anything deter me tonight. "But I like white too. I like all flowers."

"Clearly." He glances around the room, his expression serious. "They're everywhere."

"Thousands of them," I admit, my voice soft. And they look gorgeous. My mother went all out—she's the one behind the floral arrangements. My favorites are the giant hearts made of a variety of flowers and greenery.

"Scarlett, hey." My cousin Crew's fiancée suddenly appears in front of us, a big smile on her pretty face. "Happy birthday!"

We embrace and I squeeze her tight. Wren and Crew are a couple of years older than me, and I've loved getting to know her when she accompanies him to family functions. She's sweet and smart and heavily into art, so she's always got something interesting to say.

"Thank you," I tell her before we withdraw, glancing over at Ian, who's watching the both of us with a stoic expression. "Wren, this is Ian."

"Hi." She offers her hand and he shakes it. "Is he your boyfriend?" Her gaze shoots to mine questioningly.

My face grows hot, and I'm sure it's bright red. "We're—"

"Just friends," Ian supplies for me, offering Wren a grim smile before he lets go of her hand.

Everything inside of me deflates, and my shoulders slump. Even my smile falls, and I know Wren can see it. She smiles brightly, waving her hand at the stage, where one of those giant floral hearts is hanging as a backdrop.

"You two should go take a photo together onstage, in front of the heart," she suggests. "As *friends*."

Ah, I could hug Wren for that suggestion.

I glance over at Ian. "Do you want to?"

"I can take the photo for you," Wren says before he can answer. "Unless you want to take a selfie together."

An unspoken message passes between me and Wren. If I take a selfie with Ian, we'll have to tuck in together real close.

"Oh, I can take it," I say airily. "But thank you."

Her smile is knowing. "Have fun! We'll chat later."

She waves and takes off, probably in search of Crew.

"You sure it's okay to go on the stage?" Ian asks, his brows furrowed.

"It's my party," I remind him, my voice firm. Ian isn't much of a rule breaker. He makes my father look like a maniac. "I can go anywhere I want tonight. Come on."

Wow, I said that with a lot of confidence I don't necessarily feel, but he doesn't protest when I take his hand and practically drag him toward the stage. People part as we walk past, making room for my wide pink skirt and train trailing behind me, and once we're at the stairs, Ian is standing next to me, our hands still linked as we walk up onto the stage.

"You can see everything from here," he says as he glances over his shoulder to check out the party.

I barely look at the crowd. I'm too entranced by the man beside me. I've adored him for far too long, and I can't help but stare at his lips. Wonder what they might feel like crushed to mine. "Ian, there's something I want to talk to you about."

He meets my gaze with the slightest frown. "Everything all right?"

I angle myself so we're facing each other, grabbing his other hand and clutching them both in mine. We're standing in front of the giant flower heart on the stage, hand in hand, and I have a fleeting thought that we look like we're about to get married.

Wouldn't that be amazing? Our wedding at the Plaza. Our families so proud, so incredibly happy as they watch. Our ceremony and reception would look just like this. Hundreds of people in attendance. Flowers everywhere. Delicious food and the alcohol endlessly flowing. A massive cake that Ian would never smash in my face. Me wearing delicate antique lace and looking like a fairy princess. Ian dashing in a black tuxedo.

"Everything is great." I clear my throat, nerves making my stomach pitch and roll. "I wanted to talk to you—"

"Scarlett! Happy birthday!"

I glance out at the crowd to see my other best friend, Rachel, standing directly in front of the stage, a giant smile on her pretty face. She cups her hands around her mouth and shouts, "Get it, girl! He's cute!"

If my entire body could blush, it would be doing so right now. I let go of Ian's hand, giving her a quick wave while shaking my head, hoping she knows I'm trying to tell her to stop talking.

She doesn't get the hint.

"Is that your boyfriend, Scarlett?"

She knows exactly who Ian is.

"Ignore her," I tell Ian as I stare up at him.

"Isn't that your friend?"

"Well . . . yes." Rachel is just giving me grief, something she's tremendously good at. She's been encouraging me for months to tell Ian how I feel about him, and I'm always making excuses about why I can't say anything to him.

"Does she think we're together? Your other friend thought the same thing." He sounds amused. And this is the perfect segue . . .

"Speaking of boyfriends, like I said, I wanted to talk to you." I take a deep breath. "About me. And you."

"What about us?" Ian's frown is deep, causing his forehead to wrinkle.

The boy is clueless, I swear. "Maybe there could be an—"

"Everyone, get excited!" The MC magically appears on the stage, striding toward us. "Our special guest performer is about to take the stage, and you do *not* want to miss this!"

I glance over at the MC, scowling at him for interrupting my moment. *The* moment I've been anticipating since we started planning this party.

"We'll talk later." Ian lets go of my hands and heads for the stairs. "It can wait, Scarlett."

No, it can't, I want to tell him, but I say nothing. I just watch him go, my chest aching as I stare at his retreating back. I realize quickly that many of the guests are watching me, curiosity in their gazes, and I wonder if my feelings are written all over my face. If I'm that obvious.

Probably, yet the very man I want to notice my feelings is completely oblivious.

Rachel, though? She's giving me two thumbs up and an enthusiastic grin. I can only smile helplessly at her, my heart threatening to beat itself out of my chest at having so many people watching me.

"You want to stay onstage and meet your first crush face-to-face?" the MC asks me, waggling his brows in an exaggerated manner.

I quickly shake my head, and without answering him, I dart toward the stairs, earning some good-natured laughter. I pick up my skirts and take the steps carefully, stopping short when Rachel rushes toward me, pulling me into a hug and delivering a smacking kiss to my cheek before she pulls away.

"You look absolutely gorgeous. That dress is to die for," she gushes, her smile wide. "Oh my God, it's been too long since we've gotten together! What, since the weekend we graduated? I've missed you!"

"I've missed you too," I tell her, meaning every word. She's good for my ego. For hyping me up, which I totally need tonight.

"Who's the guest performer, huh? Please tell me your dad reunited One Direction." Rachel laughs. "Your dad always makes grand plans. That man can make anything happen."

"It's not 1D." I lean in close, my mouth at her ear. "It's Tate Ramsey."

"What? Get out," she breathes, pulling away to stare at me with wide eyes. "We *loved* him back in the day."

"I know, but isn't that kind of cringey now? He's some old, washed-up has-been," I remind her.

"Old? What is he, twenty-one, twenty-two? I haven't looked him up in ages, but I'm pretty sure he's still clean and sober. Which means he's in his absolute prime." Her smile turns faintly naughty. "I wouldn't mind a go at him."

"Rachel." I give her a gentle shove, making her laugh. "Stop."

"I'm serious! Tate was gorgeous. The tousled hair. The soulful gaze. The mischievous smile . . ."

"All right, Scarlett, are you ready for your special birthday gift?" the MC suddenly asks.

I glance up to find his gaze is just for me.

Rachel elbows me in the ribs, making me jolt. "Answer him," she whisper-hisses.

"Yes," I yell at him dutifully.

"Fantastic! All right, here tonight for a special performance is . . . Mr. Tate Ramsey, the former lead singer of Five Car Pileup!"

The crowd goes absolutely wild, their screams filling the air, which is shocking. Women young and old start hopping up and down, their enthusiastic response genuine when Tate Ramsey himself strides out onto the stage accompanied by one of the band's most popular songs playing over the speakers. I watch as party guests—mostly women—swarm closer to the stage, their bodies starting to move in tandem when the music starts.

It's a familiar refrain. A song I immediately recognize and absolutely loved when I was thirteen and in the eighth grade. When I had braces on my crooked teeth and my arms and legs felt too long for my body. I was so awkward it was painful.

My gaze snags on Tate as he walks to the edge of the stage and stops directly in the middle. Rachel wasn't wrong when she said he was in his prime. He looks even better than he did when he was younger.

And he was so cute back then. The handsome face and bright eyes. Lean body and a sexy smirk always on his face.

The smirk has turned into a genuine smile as he greets the crowd, his deep voice filling the room when he says hello. The women around me seem to swoon all at once, their bodies swaying toward the stage. Toward him.

That smile is still plastered on Tate Ramsey's face, showcasing the straight white teeth, the dimple denting his left cheek. His hazel eyes sparkle as they sweep over the audience, and I watch as he takes a deep breath, his gaze finding mine, lingering on me as he starts to sing.

The first thing I notice is that his voice is deeper than it used to be. He definitely sounds more mature. And I can't help but think, as he sings the song that launched Five Car Pileup's career, that it feels like he's singing it only to me.

Which should make me uncomfortable, right? Women are shrieking all around me, singing along with the lyrics, with him. Yet he still doesn't look away from me. He croons into the microphone, his long fingers curled around the handle, flicking his head so the dark-brown hair flopping over his forehead shifts out of his eyes.

His face is like a piece of art. Sharp cheekbones and sexy jawline. Square chin offset by full, lush lips. He's not as pretty as he used to be, but that's not a bad thing.

He's gorgeous. It's almost intimidating, how handsome he is.

"I was right. He's even better looking now," Rachel whispers in my ear. "And he can't stop staring at you."

"Please. He's *paid* to stare at me," I remind her out of the side of my mouth, never tearing my gaze from his. Despite knowing this is all a facade thanks to the million-dollar payment my father made, I'm swaying to the beat, unable to help myself.

A new song starts, and it's my absolute favorite. Their biggest hit of all.

"Lonely for You."

A small smile forms on my lips when he sings a particular couple of lines from the chorus.

She's a beautiful girl, with a
beautiful smile
One I haven't seen in a while

I finally tear my gaze from his, grinning at Rachel, who offers a little shoulder shimmy as her response. Being with her helps me forget my worry over Ian, and I let the music take over, cheering when Tate doesn't miss a beat while slipping into the next song.

And the next one.

Yet another one after that.

The crowd feels like it's grown. I glance around, confused by all the unfamiliar faces surrounding me. Are there people here who weren't invited? Maybe they heard him singing from the corridor and decided to peek inside, and now they're caught up in Tate's voice, dancing to the songs that are familiar Five Car Pileup hits.

I genuinely forgot they had so many.

When the music stops and Tate is chatting up the crowd, I hear a familiar voice from behind.

"Hey."

I whirl around to find Ian standing so close I can feel his

body heat radiating toward me, an unfamiliar expression on his face. I break out into a huge smile and throw my arms out, wrapping him up in a hug, but he disentangles himself from me quickly.

"I should go," he says tersely.

I'm frowning, confusion swirling. "What? You're already leaving? The party has barely started!"

He leans his head toward mine, and I hold my breath, anticipation curling through me at all the possible things he might say. "You know I don't do well in crowds."

The anticipation fizzles away, replaced by crushing disappointment. He doesn't do well in crowds? I've never heard him say that before in his life. He sounds like an old man.

"But they haven't sung 'Happy Birthday' to me yet," I practically shout in his ear. I'm sure he can't really hear me thanks to how loud Tate Ramsey is now singing. The chanting crowd doesn't help matters either.

"I'll take you to lunch later this week. Just the two of us." That promise, accompanied by the small smile, is enough to relight the hope that flickers deep within me.

We didn't talk tonight, but lunch alone? Just the two of us? That's filled with infinite promise.

"Okay." I try not to sound too eager, desperate to play it cool.

"Happy birthday, Scarlett." Ian glances over to where Rachel is lurking just behind me. "Goodbye, Rachel."

"See ya, Ian," she tosses out at him, rolling her eyes the minute he turns his back on us and walks away.

"We're having lunch later this week," I announce triumphantly.

"Big deal." She waves a hand, being dismissive, and while I hate it, I also understand why. "He's just going to lead you on like usual."

I pull her away from the crowd so I can hear her better. "You really think so?"

"Yes, of course I think so! He enjoys having his fan club of one and doesn't want it to end. The guy is constantly leading you on, Scarlett. Can't you see it?"

"He doesn't lead me on." I defend him all the time to Rachel. She doesn't like him. I don't think she ever will.

"He so does. He'll probably cancel on the lunch plans. Watch. And then they'll just never happen, yet he knows he's got you in his back pocket, so whenever he needs an ego boost, he'll come around and act like he's interested in you." She points at the stage, where Tate is currently doing a happy dance along to the music, his lips curled into a huge smile. "Right now I'm thinking you have a better chance with that guy than you do with Ian."

"Oh, come on, Rach." I glance over my shoulder, my gaze somehow snagging on Tate's, and he flashes one of those megawatt smiles at me right before he winks.

My cheeks hot, I turn away, frowning. Maybe my best friend has a point.

I have been chasing after Ian for what feels like years, and he's never given me a real chance. Oh, there's always the *possibility* of us. He's implied that more than once. I remember him telling me when I was sixteen, "If only you were two years older."

That sentence alone is what started my eternal crush on Ian. If only what? What would he have done if I were two years older?

That moment is finally here. I turn eighteen years old, and he leaves my party early. I don't get it.

I don't get him.

"I saw the way he just looked at you." Rachel sidles up so she's standing directly to my right, her mouth at my ear, murmuring encouraging words. "The way he can't stop looking at you."

"You already said that."

"And I mean it. I know you think he's paid to do this, but I don't know. I think homeboy is interested." When I glance over at her, she's grinning. "Wouldn't that be the best revenge? Getting with Tate Ramsey just to piss Ian off?"

"I would never." I could never. First of all, I'm sure Tate wouldn't be interested in someone like me. And second, I don't want to send Ian the wrong message. I'm not into Tate. Not like that.

I'm into Ian. And I wish he were actually into me.

Our conversation fades as we both refocus on the performance, though my mind is in other places. Like how Ian isn't here. How he just bailed on my party and Rachel basically told me I should stop wasting my time on him.

Maybe she's right. Maybe I should focus on something else.

Like myself.

My stomach growls, and I rest a hand over it, realizing that I haven't eaten a single thing since I arrived. I could do with some food. Even a piece of birthday cake.

"Do you think he's going to stop soon?" I ask Rachel, my hips still moving to the beat of the drum.

"Why would you want him to stop? He's the hit of the party!" Rachel throws her arms up in the air and shakes her head from side to side, mouthing along with the words as Tate sings.

I glance up at him as he moves to the other side of the stage, singing directly to a cluster of older women watching him with adoring eyes. Someone steps on my skirt, and I hastily yank the tulle out of the way so it doesn't get ripped. The woman is oblivious as she continuously shouts his name. "Tate! Tate! Tate, over here!"

He ignores her, which only makes her shout louder.

Everything starts to feel noisier and even more crowded, and I'm filled with the sudden urge to abandon my own party to chase after Ian. Would he like it if I just showed up at his place and declared my undying love for him? Or would he freak out?

Maybe Rachel's wrong. Maybe Ian is frustrated just like I am. Maybe he wanted to have that conversation too before we were interrupted. I need to go to him.

I need to see him.

For my eighteenth-birthday party I secretly expected Ian to announce his undying love for me. He would remain by my side the entire night, smiling proudly as I greeted my guests, as I hugged everyone and thanked them for coming to my party. He should be with me right now, standing behind me, his arms around my waist as we both dance slowly to the music, feeling each other's bodies. Tate could sing his little heart out, and I wouldn't care if he was faux flirting with me, because I would have the man that I actually care for more than anyone else wrapped all around me. Showing everyone that we're a couple.

That we're together.

Instead, I'm alone, frustrated that Ian has left me here.

This is definitely *not* what I envisioned.

CHAPTER THREE

TATE

This night is fucking unbelievable. Indescribable. I'm on a high, and I never want to come down.

I'm also sweating profusely, not that anyone notices thanks to my all-black outfit. It's been a while since I've performed in front of a crowd, and there are a lot more people at this shindig than I thought there would be. When Daddy Warbucks, a.k.a. Fitzy Lancaster, reached out to me via DM and asked if I'd perform for his daughter's birthday party, I blew him off. Figured it was someone trying to catfish my ass.

Trust that I've had a few weird interactions since I started doing these personalized greetings, but a man's gotta do what he can to survive, and I make a decent amount of cash. I've had a lot of strange requests, though. Like that one chick who keeps offering to pay me for dick pics. She started out at five thousand—definitely not enough. Her most recent offer is fifteen grand. Naturally I declined.

Though I was still tempted, can't lie. Just for one photo? Granted it would be of my dick, and that's just . . .

Not smart. Not after all the bullshit I've been through over the last few years.

Lancaster was persistent, messaging me constantly about how his daughter is turning eighteen and he's throwing her a party. I was her favorite member of Five Car Pileup, blah blah blah. I've heard it all before, a thousand times over. She probably humped her favorite stuffed animal to thoughts of me late at night while staring at a poster of the band on her wall. I get it.

This scenario isn't new to me.

He somehow got my phone number, and when he called, I picked up because I saw the name Lancaster flashing on my screen. Next thing I know, we're talking about cars and music and fashion designers—all shit I care about like the shallow asshole I can still be. An hour later, and he's got me agreeing to perform a full set of songs at his precious baby daughter's birthday party. My payment?

One million dollars.

Yeah, I could *not* turn that amount down. I thought at first he might be playing me, but after our long phone conversation, he told me he felt we had a connection, and he wanted to help me out.

Now here I am, onstage and singing my heart out in front of a live audience for the first time in years, and it feels . . . damn good.

Don't get me wrong. I prepped and practiced during the weeks leading up to this event. Hired a vocal coach I'd worked with years ago and did some vocal exercises to get ready. After a few hour-long lessons—paid for with some of the money Fitzy sent me as an advance—he told me I sounded better than I ever had. I figured he was blowing smoke up my ass, but maybe he was right, because tonight, this performance . . .

It feels *right*, being onstage, singing to all the screaming, attractive women. When the Lancasters throw a party, pretty sure they invite all the beautiful people in New York City. Well-kept older ladies and pretty young things who are screaming so loud for me, I'm pretty sure they're creaming their panties right about now. Any one of them I could take home with me. Even one of the married ones.

Especially one of the married ones.

But I'm a different person now. I don't do that kind of shit anymore. No womanizing. No drinking, no drugs. I'm clean and sober and I meditate and I've met with a life coach more often than I care to admit. I go to the gym five days a week—Planet Fitness, not a private trainer, but a guy down on his luck can only do so much. I repeat affirmations on the daily, and I've recently reduced my red meat consumption. Damn it, I'm healthy, and sometimes . . .

Sometimes I'm bored as shit.

Can't let that get me down, though. I'm striving and trying. That's all that matters.

I finish yet another song, pausing as I let the wave of cheers and applause wash over me, a big ol' grin on my face while I try to catch my breath. This running around onstage and eye-fucking a large number of women is exhausting now that I'm an old man of twenty-one.

I need to up my workout sessions, that's for damn sure.

"How are we doing tonight, yeah?" I say into the mic, grinning when they all scream at me, their hands up in the air. "Pretty good, am I right?"

I scan the screaming crowd, looking for Little Miss Pink Pouf. The birthday girl can't be missed in the dress that reminds me of an elaborate cake. Clearly, she's trying to catch people's attention, and I suppose I can't blame her considering this party is all for her. Hundreds of people in attendance, lush flowers everywhere that probably cost a fortune, and then there's that table full of cakes I noticed earlier, when her father informed me rather proudly that there are eighteen of them in honor of his precious Scarlett.

She's a spoiled-rotten princess, I'm sure. Despite the overwhelming dress that could've made her completely disappear, she still looks hot as fuck. All that long brown hair spilling down her back. The dark-brown eyes that appear fathomless. She was smiling and eating me up with that gaze earlier. Dancing front and center of the stage at the beginning of my set, but now I don't know where she went.

"Where's the birthday girl, huh? Someone going to find Scarlett for me?" I ask the crowd.

Heads start turning; phones come out. They're on the hunt for her, when she should be fairly obvious. In fact, I spot her at that exact moment, standing at one of the makeshift bars, bringing a glass of pink champagne to her lips just when the pale-pink spotlight hits her.

"There she is! Come here, birthday girl!" I wave my hand toward the stage, and she shakes her head.

Doesn't budge either.

My hand drops to my side, the mic forgotten as I shout, "Aw, come on, Scarlett Lancaster! Join me onstage!"

She glares at me.

I grin at her.

That champagne glass is drained of the pink bubbly in seconds, and then she's marching over to the stage, the tulle skirt so wide the crowd parts for her as she makes her way toward me. She never takes her gaze from mine, and I can see a tiny flicker of irritation flaring in her eyes.

It's kind of hot, how she might be a little mad. I can't stop smiling, knowing I'm aggravating the shit out of her. I don't normally get off on making a woman mad, but I gotta admit...

This is fun.

She daintily walks up the steps in sexy silver stilettos, the sides of the skirt and train clutched in her hands so she doesn't step on it. I approach her, bringing the mic to my mouth as I murmur, "Let's sing 'Happy Birthday' to Scarlett, okay? Everyone, please join me."

The small band hired to back me starts up the familiar tune, and I sing the simple lyrics, slowing the tune down, my gaze never straying from hers. Her cheeks turn as pink as the dress she's wearing, apprehension shining in her dark gaze, but she doesn't back down.

No, she takes it. I try to make the words sound suggestive, like Marilyn Monroe did so long ago when she sang "Happy Birthday" to the president, but I don't think it's working. I'm not a bombshell in a clingy, glittery dress trying to seduce the commander in chief.

Nah, I'm just an old boy band member having one night of glory at some rich girl's birthday party.

When the song is over, the crowd cheering and the drummer tapping the cymbal over and over again, I whisper to her, "Happy birthday, Scarlett Lancaster."

Her lush lips purse, looking like she's ready to spit at me, but instead she murmurs, "Thank you."

And then storms off the stage.

I watch her go, unable to take my eyes off her as she pushes through the crowd, never once turning back. The need to follow her is strong, so I say into the mic offhandedly, "Thank you. Good night," before I flick the power off and replace it in its stand.

Without hesitation I give in to my urge and go after her, striding through the parting crowd, ignoring their requests.

"Tate! Oh my God, you were amazing! Can I get a hug?"

"Can I get your autograph, Tate?"

"Will you take a selfie with me, Tate?"

"Sign my tits, Tate! Please!"

Scarlett turns right, disappearing behind a giant floral heart that matches the one on the stage, and I go after her, increasing my pace, catching up with her easily. When I get close enough, I reach for her, grabbing her by the elbow and halting her progress.

She whirls on me, her eyes widening when she sees it's me, and she yanks her arm out of my grip, rubbing the spot where I just touched her.

"You all right?" I ask with a frown.

Her gaze isn't as hostile as it first was, the more she contemplates me. "Why did you follow me?"

"I don't know." That's the honest-to-God truth. "You didn't seem too happy with my performance."

"It was great." Her voice is flat, no inflection whatsoever. Meaning I don't believe her.

"Did I . . . piss you off or something?" I rub the back of my neck, noting the way she watches me carefully, her gaze drifting.

Like she might be checking me out.

All those women screaming my name only a few minutes ago, and it was nothing compared to how I'm feeling in this moment, with the hot little rich girl contemplating me like I'm a delicious snack.

"Not at all. Though it did turn into the Tate Ramsey show tonight, don't you think?" She lifts a brow.

I drop my hand from my neck, resting both of them on my hips. "Isn't that what you wanted? For your birthday present?"

"Actually, your appearance was a complete surprise, sprung on me by my father right before you performed." She hesitates only a moment. "And I was really hoping for Harry Styles."

Ouch. Not the first time I've heard that.

"Your friends seemed into it." That was a serious high, hearing them shout for me. Singing the lyrics along with me. They were fans—of Five Car Pileup, yeah, but also of me. And that felt good.

I haven't felt this good in a long time. No way am I going to let this spoiled brat ruin my night.

"Hardly any of those people are my friends," she mutters, wrapping her arms around her waist as if she's cold.

This causes my gaze to drop, taking in her exposed legs. They're long and thin and shiny with lotion. She has on those strappy silver stilettos, and her toenails are painted a pale pink that matches the dress.

Sexy. This girl is definitely sexy. Rich as fuck and smelling sweet. I've always had a secret thing for rich girls. They take care of themselves, and they're usually not too clingy. More on the independent side.

At least the ones I've dealt with.

"For someone who's having such a big party, you're acting like you hate every single moment of it." I take a step closer, invading her space, but not too much. "Though it looked like you were having fun at first. What changed?"

She drops her arms at her sides, her expression plaintive. Like she might burst into tears at any moment. "This night isn't going like I planned at all. And your performance actually threw it completely off. And then Ian left when that was the last thing I wanted to happen, and now I want to leave too."

Okay, this woman is confusing. "You can't leave. This is your party. And who's Ian?"

I glance around, my gaze snagging on a photographer lurking behind the massive flower heart, his camera poised in front of him. Like he's sneaking photographs of us.

What the hell? Haven't had to deal with the paparazzi in a long time, and it feels rather . . . foreign.

And kind of nice too, can't lie.

Damn, I always was a massive attention whore.

"It doesn't matter. I appreciate your performance, and I know my father paid you a ton of money, but your job is done." She waves a hand. "You can go."

I'm completely taken aback by the waving hand and the vaguely snotty tone. "Are you *dismissing* me?"

She tilts her head to the side, her eyes widening with emphasis. "Yes. Now please leave."

I hear the shutter of a camera going off again and again, and I know whatever he's getting, it looks bad. And the last thing I need is bad publicity.

I've had enough of that to last me a lifetime.

Without thought I grab Scarlett by both of her arms, hauling her into me. I'm immediately surrounded by layers of pink tulle, her chest flush with mine, her scent filling my senses, heady and sweet.

Reminding me it's been a while since I've had a beautiful woman this close.

"What are you doing?" she practically screeches.

Before she can say anything else or, worse, run, I lean in and whisper in her ear, "Just go with it, okay?"

"Go with what?" Her voice is soft, her gaze lifting to mine, and I zero in on her plush mouth. It's pink. Glossy.

Tempting.

"Follow my lead. Someone's watching. A photographer." I slip my arms around her slender waist, and she doesn't protest.

More like she melts in my arms.

Hmm.

"So?" Her brows shoot up.

"So they'll publish photos of us arguing and try to make us look bad." I pause, watching the panic fill her gaze. "You don't want that, do you?"

She's quiet for a moment, contemplating me. She's about to turn her head to check out the photographer, but I touch her cheek, keeping her in place.

Keeping her gaze on mine.

"Do you?" I ask again when she hasn't answered, my voice low, my heart hammering. I think I'm allergic to photographers. I wouldn't doubt for a moment that I'm about to break out in a full-on case of hives. This shit sucks.

I need Scarlett on my side, and I send her a look, one that hopefully communicates I need her help.

Actually, I need her cooperation.

I witness the realization dawning on her face. Her gaze softens, as do her lips, and she finally shakes her head.

"No. Of course not. This is supposed to be the best night of my life." She hesitates for only a moment. "Um . . . I think I have an idea. How to make us look better in front of that guy's camera."

"You do?" I lift my brows, surprised she's the one now doing the suggesting.

"Yes." Her hand slips around the back of my neck, pulling my head down to hers. "Just . . . follow my lead."

I realize she's repeating my words back to me.

Right before her mouth lands on mine.

CHAPTER FOUR

SCARLETT

What am I doing?

I have no idea. I don't even know why I'm doing it. It's like fifteen-year-old Scarlett took over my body and took advantage of the situation.

And now I've got my lips planted firmly on Tate Ramsey's, and ohmygod, the man can definitely kiss.

He seemed so . . . desperate. As if the last thing he wants to deal with is a nosy paparazzo splashing a bogus argument between us all over the internet. In that moment, the pleading expression on his face, I felt bad for him.

Then I thought of Ian and how ridiculous he's being and had the quick realization that maybe he needs a push. The possibility of him seeing me with someone else was too irresistible. Next thing I know . . .

I'm kissing him. Tate Ramsey.

And his lips? They're soft and sweetly persistent. He takes over the moment completely, his arms tightening around me, his hand sliding up my back ever so slowly, his fingers encountering bare skin. A shiver steals over me when his fingertips glide over my spine, and I curl my fingers into the front of his shirt, my lips automatically parting for his tongue. It dances with mine, light and flickering, and I lean into him, my lips parting further, an unfamiliar sensation coasting through my body.

He pulls away before we can take it too far, and I battle with the disappointment flooding me. When I open my eyes, it's to find him watching me with a concerned expression on his handsome face.

Did I mention that he's so much more handsome than he ever was when he was in Five Car Pileup? He is all man now. Oh, the boyishly sweet smile from before was still there throughout his performance, as well as that charisma he always exuded back in the day when he was on top of the world. When you couldn't go anywhere without hearing about Five Car Pileup and their tour. Their songs. Their influence on teenage girls worldwide.

But he's different now. Older and quieter and possibly even . . . edgier?

Or maybe that's my overactive imagination. I'm not sure.

"Get enough of us yet?"

I startle at the sound of Tate's deep voice, the hostility in his tone, and I realize he's not talking to me at all.

He's talking to the photographer, who is still snapping photos of us with our arms wrapped around each other. I'm sure to him we look like a bona fide couple, and I'm tempted to pull away from Tate. Gain some distance from him.

But I remain in place, frozen. Trembling. He skims his fingers down my back once again, a reassuring gesture that has me dipping my head, suddenly shy.

Regret hits me. This probably wasn't the smartest move I've ever made. I'm not an impulsive person, not even close, but what is Ian going to think if he sees these photos?

Hmmm. Considering I'm a nobody and Tate is a has-been, I don't think we have much to worry about.

The photographer lowers his massive camera with the giant flash—how did I not notice him before?—and grins at us. "Always hoping for a little more from you, Tate. You know how it is. And let me just say that I think you two make a nice couple."

Tate crowds me, which is almost impossible thanks to the size of my skirt, and shields me from the photographer with his body as best he can. "I'm sure you snapped plenty of photos of us. Now get the fuck out of here."

I stare up at Tate while the photographer scrambles away from us, Tate glaring the entire time, his body tense, his jaw tight. Only when the photographer is gone does Tate ease up some. He loosens his hold on me, and I step away from him, hating how woozy I suddenly feel.

It couldn't be the kiss that affected me. Not like that. Maybe it was the champagne I've consumed tonight. I don't really drink. Not even at parties when I was still in high school. But maybe the few glasses I've snuck tonight went straight to my head.

"Sorry about that," Tate says grimly, running his fingers along his jaw. "I didn't think the paparazzi would care enough to snap photos of me."

Were they really here for Tate Ramsey? Or did my father let them in?

"I can't believe they snuck into my party." I bend my head, shaking out my skirts, trying to fight another wave of disappointment. My eighteenth birthday, and the only reason I kiss a guy is so we could distract a photographer.

Ian wasn't impressed by my dress, my party . . . none of it. I don't even know where he is. I've wasted a lot of time crushing on him, when clearly, he's not interested in me.

He's made that more than obvious.

"Your father spared no expense for this party." Tate smiles, and a fleet of butterflies erupts in my stomach, making me breathless. "An event like this always draws a lot of media attention."

"My parents did mention they invited a few reporters and photographers they're close to, to cover the event. Mostly from fashion magazines and sites." My parents' wedding was featured in *Vogue* and *Town & Country*. They were the chicest couple in New York City at one point during the early years of their marriage.

"I'm sure that's who the photographer was with," Tate reassures me, but I catch the worry in his gaze. "Though he did look pretty familiar. I might've met him . . . before."

"Right." I'm distracted as I glance around the massive ballroom, realizing that we're in a very dark and private corner tucked away from everyone else. The party is raging on without me. I can hear conversations flowing, accompanied by laughter. Music is playing, a slow, sensuous beat, and that's when I spot two women draped in pearls and not much else dancing across the stage, massive pink feather fans in their hands.

I vaguely remember my father mentioning he hired dancers for the party. Looks like they started their performance.

"I should go." I turn to Tate, his gaze lifting to mine rather guiltily, and I wonder what he was staring at. My butt? How could he even see it in this dress? "I'm sure my father expects me to watch the dancers."

"Looks like burlesque." When I turn to him, he explains further. "Pretty sexy stuff. They're barely dressed."

A spotlight hits the stage, revealing two scantily clad women in a giant champagne glass tossing their arms up in the air, strings of pearls covering their chests and almost revealing their nipples. In fact, I'm fairly certain I just saw a flash of pink. "Oh. This is kind of . . ."

"Scandalous?" Tate finishes for me.

I nod, turning to look at him once more. "My father likes to go a little overboard when he throws a party."

I adore my father, but he also likes to make it all about him. Such as the burlesque dancers. That's really not my kind of thing.

"Isn't this your party, though?" Tate lifts his brows questioningly, and I can only shrug helplessly, unable to explain.

"Shouldn't it be all about you?" he continues when I still haven't said anything.

"I suppose." It's never been about me.

Not that I can remember.

"I have a question." He leans back on his heels, contemplating me.

"What is it?"

"Are you mad at me that I kissed you?"

I gawk at him for about two seconds before I realize what I'm doing and snap my lips shut, shocked at his change of subject. "N-no."

"You sure?" He lifts his brows, his gaze locked on me and no one else.

I stand up a little straighter, trying to appear composed. Like the mature adult woman I now am. As if it's normal for me to be kissed by random men on my birthday.

"Positive," I say firmly.

His smile is slow, spreading wide upon his handsome face until it's a devastating, breath-stealing grin. "Good. I know I'll never forget it."

I blink at him, unsure how to answer.

"It's okay. You can admit you liked it too."

"I-I'm somewhat involved with someone else," I say, sounding absurdly prim.

And lying through my teeth.

"Really? Where's he at?" Tate glances around the cavernous ballroom.

I can't tell him Ian left, though I already did say exactly that. Even if Ian were here, I'm sure he wouldn't go along with me if I asked him to. He would probably gently correct me and insist to Tate that we're just friends.

Sometimes, Ian can be . . . annoying.

"He's around," I say, hoping I sound mysterious.

"Uh-huh." He scrubs the side of his jaw, his gaze full of doubt.

I realize I need to change the subject fast. I decide to go the polite route. "Thank you again for performing at my party."

"Thank you again for helping me out," he returns, referring to the kiss.

I just know he is.

Is he still thinking about it? I am, even though I'd be loath to admit it. He's not the man I wanted to kiss on my birthday, though my younger self would've absolutely *died* at the chance to kiss *the* Tate Ramsey.

But he's not that same teen heartthrob anymore. And I'm not that young girl anymore either.

The kiss was still good, though, as reluctant as I am to admit it.

"I'm sorry I was rude to you before. I was out of sorts and upset over something, but it's fine now," I tell him, feeling the need to apologize.

His brows draw together in concern. "What made you so upset?"

"Oh, nothing really." I shake my head, not about to go into

detail about my pathetic pseudorelationship with Ian. "It's not that important."

"You sure about that?"

"I'm very sure." I nod, trying to laugh, but I stop at how fake it sounds. "You can stay for the party and hang out if you'd like."

Oh, that sounded stupid. He must think I'm ridiculous. I'm sure he has a gorgeous woman who he calls his girlfriend and a bunch of friends he prefers to spend time with waiting for him to be done. The last thing he wants to do is hang out at some rich girl's eighteenth-birthday party.

He takes two steps closer, the warm, woodsy scent of his cologne washing over me, and I lock my knees so I don't wobble and tip over. "Happy birthday, Scarlett," he murmurs, his deep voice settling for a too-brief moment with a throb between my legs.

And then he's gone.

"There you are! Oh my God, what happened to you?" Rachel grabs hold of my hand, stopping me from blindly walking past her.

I stop short, trying to offer up a smile as she watches me with true confusion in her gaze. "Sorry, I went . . . to the bathroom."

"Ah." She accepts my answer with ease. "Well, you missed the dancers."

"No, I didn't." I incline my head toward the voluptuous women moving across the stage, their bodies moving to the slow yet steady beat. "They're right there."

"They're almost done." Rachel hooks her arm through mine, her smile bright. "They're great and all, but no one can top that performance by Tate Ramsey. My God, he was amazing! I hope you enjoyed it, or were you worrying about Ian the entire time?"

I bristle at her mentioning Ian. Or maybe that's a case of guilt washing over me. "Of course I enjoyed it. He even called me up onstage."

The knowing look on Rachel's face appears, and I brace myself for her assessment. "You looked like you wanted to kick him in the teeth."

Leave it to Rach to be totally honest with me. "I definitely didn't want to kick him in the teeth."

"Hurt him then. Just a little. Twist his arm behind his back or something." Rachel laughs, rushing right on and not letting me speak. "Uggghhhh, he was so *good* tonight. Better than he ever was. His voice was perfection. I swear my panties melted right off when he sang 'Lonely for You.'"

"Rachel!" I admonish, glancing around to make sure no one heard her say that. "Your panties did not melt off."

"They kind of did. He caught my eye at one point during the song, and the way he stared at me—I swear he was smoldering." Rachel fans herself with her fingers. "So sexy."

An unfamiliar feeling rises up within me, and I glare at my best friend, realizing only moments later that the feeling I'm experiencing is good old-fashioned jealousy. "I don't know if I would consider him sexy."

"Liar. He's hot as hell and had every woman in this room *screaming*. Even the old grandmas." Rachel glances around, her sparkling gaze meeting mine once she's done a thorough sweep. "Where did you disappear to, anyway? Please tell me you were talking to Tate. That he asked for your number or promised he was going to DM you."

I grimace. "No, he didn't ask me for anything."

Well, he did ask for a favor . . .

And I ended up kissing him, which was okay.

God, I'm such a liar. I totally enjoyed that, but I'm also dealing with a bit of guilt here. I can't go around kissing some former boy bander while I might still have a chance with Ian. Despite how he treated me tonight, how he pretty much blew me off, I still can't help but think we have a chance.

Stupid.

"That's a shame." Rachel sighs, her tone melancholy. "I was sort of hoping he'd fall madly in love with you while crooning love songs and eye-fucking you from the stage. Talk about a love story."

She starts belting out the lyrics to "Love Story" by Taylor Swift, and I have to literally slap my hand over her mouth to shut her up. When I finally drop my hand, she's laughing, shaking her head.

"Didn't Taylor go out with Tate?" she asks.

"She's much older than him," I point out. "I'm pretty sure he went out with Billie Eilish, though."

"Really?" Rachel tilts her head to the side. "She's such a mystery to me. I'd love to hear any of his Billie stories."

"I'm not going to ask him for any Billie stories," I mutter, shaking my head.

"Aha!" Rachel points an accusatory finger at me. "You *were* talking to him. Did something happen between you two? You disappeared for a long time. Did you give him your number? Did he follow you on social media? What if he slips into your DMs? You have to respond to him. What if you got the chance to actually go out on a date with freaking Tate Ramsey?"

She starts bouncing up and down, giddy at the idea.

I grab hold of her shoulders and shake her a little, her dazed gaze meeting mine. "Nothing happened. And nothing *will* happen between me and Tate. I like Ian, remember?"

The grimace on Rachel's face is almost comical. "Please don't remind me."

I ignore the insult, releasing my hold on her as I glance to the left, then to the right, wondering if Tate is still here.

But I don't see him at all.

CHAPTER FIVE

TATE

The sun is brutal as it leaks through the cracks in my bent and broken blinds, making me squint as rays of light beam upon my face, warming my skin. When I finally got home last night, I stripped out of my clothes and collapsed into bed, falling asleep immediately, not bothering to do all the things I normally do as part of my nightly routine.

Who am I? What have I become? I feel like an old man sometimes. An old man of freaking twenty-one.

At least I dreamed of a beautiful brown-haired, brown-eyed girl dressed up like a frothy piece of cake, a faint smile on her face and her eyes sparkling as she swayed to the music while I sang only to her. I snuck her off into a dark corner and kissed her, and she didn't slap my face, which I considered a win.

Wait. That wasn't a dream. That shit actually happened.

Throwing my arm across my eyes, I crack them open and immediately slam them shut, groaning. God, the sun is bright. What time is it? How long have I been sleeping anyway?

I sneak an arm out from beneath the covers and reach toward my nightstand, grabbing hold of my phone. Turning on my side, my back to the window, I hold the phone up in front of my face and check the time.

Nine twenty-six a.m.

I also just so happen to have countless—and I do mean countless—notifications. From all forms of social media that I'm on. A bunch of missed calls. Twenty-three voice mails.

Wait a minute.

Twenty-three?

Scrubbing a hand across my face, I close my eyes again and count to three before I blink them back open.

My phone immediately starts ringing in my hand.

The name flashing across the screen is familiar. Someone I haven't talked to in a long time.

"Hey, Simon," I greet our former band manager, my voice more like a deep croak. Last night's performance took everything out of me, and I thought I was in shape, physically and vocally. I need to hit the gym more. And sing more too, apparently. "What the hell do you want?"

"So hostile! Can't your old manager check up on you, make sure you're doing all right?" His tone is falsely bright. Overly enthusiastic. That thick British accent has me on edge just like the old days, and I sigh into the phone, already triggered.

"It's been years, Simon."

"And I'm looking forward to catching up." His voice is smooth, as is his demeanor.

Like usual. The man doesn't miss a beat. But why the hell is he calling me on a Sunday morning?

An ominous feeling suddenly washes over me, dark and foreboding as it settles on my skin, sinking my stomach.

"What happened?" I sit up in bed, the comforter sliding off me and pooling in my lap, the chilly air making goose bumps rise. "Did—did someone from the band . . . die?"

Or maybe it's my dark thoughts that are bringing on the goose bumps.

Simon chuckles, and I can tell he's not loving my question. "Honestly, I always figured you'd be the first one to go."

I'm immediately offended. "Gee, thanks. Yeah, can't talk right now." I lift the phone away from my face, speaking directly into the receiver. "Huh, my connection's suddenly bad. See ya never, Simon."

"Wait a minute!" Simon screams right before I hit the red button and end the call. The panic in his voice makes me pause. "Have you been on social media today?"

"I just woke up." Unease slips down my spine, and I rub the side of my neck. "What's going on?"

"I mean, have you checked *your* social media yet? Been on the internet in any capacity?"

"Stop being mysterious and just tell me what the fuck is going on," I practically growl at him.

He's completely unperturbed by my outburst. "You're blowing up, my friend."

I hate how he calls me his *friend*. Simon was never my friend, especially near the end of Five Car Pileup's too-short career. Of course, I put the entire band at risk with my wild behavior throughout our last tour, and I'm pretty much the reason the band broke up, so I guess Simon had a reason to treat me like shit. His cash cow went belly up.

"Blowing up how?" I put the phone on speaker before I go onto Instagram and check my profile, blinking twice when I see my follower number.

I had a respectable amount for a former boy bander. Almost two hundred thousand. But now I'm at over four hundred thousand. Creeping closer to the half-a-million side.

Huh.

"You've gained a lot of followers over the last twenty-four hours," Simon observes, like he knows exactly what I'm doing.

Which is fucking disconcerting, if you ask me.

"What, you keep track of me?" I sound hostile. I *feel* hostile. All those old memories come rolling back. The constant struggle between the band and Simon. The push and pull. The demands. The pressure.

God, the pressure of trying to measure up and failing miserably every single goddamn time.

"I still keep tabs on you, Tate. Besides, what's the harm in me keeping track of your follower count," Simon says, so nonchalant over the whole thing. "There are countless sites on the web that can do exactly that. And you should stop playing stupid with me. It was never a good look for you. You know exactly why you're blowing up."

"You tell me why you think I'm blowing up," I throw at him, praying no one caught me doing something stupid at Scarlett Lancaster's party.

"Your performance last night?" Simon speaks slowly, as if he's talking to a simpleminded child who has issues comprehending information.

"Right." I fall back onto the mattress, my head hitting the pillow with a thud. "At Scarlett Lancaster's birthday party."

"Yes. Why didn't you tell me you were performing for the Lancasters?"

"Are you for real right now? Give me a break. We haven't talked in years." Like I'm obligated to tell him my every business move when he's the one who dumped me. Doubt he'd care how many "happy birthday" announcements I've made and sold over the last year.

Quite the lucrative business venture, but I'm sick of that shit.

"That birthday party is *everywhere*. All over the gossip sites.

The society sites. Fashion sites. Every. Where. Scarlett Lancaster is an emerging name from a very wealthy and well-known family. They are serious old money, and her daddy is the rebel among his brothers. You singing at Scarlett's birthday party last night has gone viral. There are videos all over the web of your performance, and Tate, you sound fucking fantastic. Women of all ages posted on social media about their reactions to your singing, and they were losing their goddamn minds over you." Simon hesitates, like he's sitting on a bomb and dying to drop it. "And then there's that one photo."

His compliments have me feeling like I'm on some sort of high. When was the last time I heard someone—Simon of all people—tell me I sounded fucking fantastic? Near the end of my career, I sounded like a dying cat squalling into a microphone. It was like my balls dropped and all of a sudden I couldn't sing anymore. I couldn't hit a note, let alone hold one. "What photo are you talking about?"

"You know which one."

"I have no clue." I rack my brain, running through last night's events chronologically. Arriving. Being greeted by Fitzy Lancaster as if I were his long-lost friend, him handing me a check—*a check*—for the remaining money he owed me for my performance. Me still believing there was some sort of catch.

Who pays a has-been that kind of money?

A rich motherfucker, that's who.

Speaking of that check, I need to make sure to walk it into my bank first thing Monday morning.

"What exactly happened last night while you were at that party anyway?" Simon asks. "Did you drink at all? Snort a line? Pop some pills?"

"Of course not." I'm offended he thinks I still do that, but then I remember Simon and I haven't talked in a long time.

And the last time he saw me, I was still an addicted mess. "I arrived at the Plaza—on time, I might add—and performed for her birthday. That's it."

"What about the daughter?"

I stare at my bedroom ceiling, noting the water stain just to the right of the overhead light fixture. Need to call the super about that and have it fixed. "She was into it. I pulled her up onstage and sang her 'Happy Birthday.'"

Wasn't as into my performance as most of the other women, but I didn't let that bother me.

Not too much, anyway.

"You sure all you did for Scarlett Lancaster was perform onstage?" Simon asks. "Or was there more of a performance happening . . . *behind the scenes*?"

The memory comes hurtling back, lodging itself in the forefront in my mind. Of me and Scarlett tucked away in a dark corner, bantering.

More like arguing.

Catching that photographer watching us. How he took photos of us while we argued. Me asking for her help, which resulted in us—

"Because from what I saw, there wasn't much talking going on between the two of you. More like you had your tongue shoved down her throat," Simon continues.

I brace myself for a lecture, like I'm sixteen all over again and just got caught partying in a hotel room with empty liquor bottles strewn across the bed and the place trashed, a pair of wadded-up black panties left in the sheets. "Is it bad?"

"Is what bad?"

"Is what they're saying about me and Scarlett bad?" My voice drops to a harsh whisper, and I hate how agitated I suddenly feel. How this moment takes me back a few years, when my life was out of control and I didn't care. It was like I had a death wish. "Is the photo causing a scandal or whatever?"

Simon's quiet for a moment. Like I just stunned him silent. "You haven't really read anything that's been said about you this morning, huh."

"Not really. Like I told you, I just woke up."

"You're in for a big surprise then. People are eating this shit *up*, Tate. They're saying you two are the next it couple."

"It couple?"

"Celebrity couple. A couple the public wants to ship. Stan. Whatever terminology they're using now," Simon mutters. "Are you that out of touch with what's going on in the world? I didn't think you'd gone that far off the grid."

Relief replaces the anxious feeling almost immediately. For once, the media seems to be working in my favor, when they've been against me for years. "Doesn't seem like you're keeping up with the lingo either, Simon. You sound like an old man."

"Shut the hell up." His tone is mild, so I don't take offense. "I called you because I wanted to see if you'd like to meet."

I'm struck silent for a moment by his change of subject—and what he's requesting. "When?"

"This afternoon."

"It's Sunday, Simon."

"Every day brings opportunity, Tate. And there is no rest for the wicked."

"Are you calling me wicked?"

He's quiet for a moment, and eventually, I fill the silence with a nervous chuckle.

"You know who you are. What you are."

"And what's that?" I ask.

"From my current viewpoint, you're a man with untapped potential who's about to have another breakout moment."

I scoff. "Bullshit."

"Meet me at my office this afternoon, and I'll let you know my thoughts."

"Why, Simon?" I grip my phone tighter. "Why do you want to meet with me?"

"To talk next steps."

"Next steps for what?"

Simon sighs, like he's irritated with me. "For your career. You've just been given a second chance, mate. Looks like you need to take advantage of it."

I take a shower to clear out the cobwebs in my brain after that mind-boggling phone call. I stand under the hot spray of water for a long time, my head full of a jumble of thoughts and ideas, plus endless speculation.

Still haven't fully explored my newfound internet blowup, but once I've dried off and slipped on a pair of boxer briefs, I can't stand it anymore, and I grab my phone, settling on my uncomfortable couch before I open Instagram back up and punch my name into the search bar like an egotistical bastard.

It's been a while since I've done something like this. Searched my name or the band name, checking up on what people are saying about me. I used to do it all the time, especially after the band first broke up. When all I wanted was a glimmer of that old adulation we used to get. When we were on top of the world and seemingly untouchable.

That changed quick. The fans who once loved us turned on us. We were a disappointment, especially me, and that was hard to face.

So I took the easy way out and stopped looking myself up.

After I sulked for approximately a year and eventually got sober, I focused on my health and well-being. And part of making sure my well-being was protected included me not searching myself or Five Car Pileup on the internet.

This feels like I'm breaking some sort of personal rule, and I brace myself, waiting for the slam of insults and disappointment that I normally receive, but that's not what I'm greeted with.

Not even close.

It's video after video of me performing last night. Posts with comments that are supportive. Complimentary. Some of them even sound like stark raving lunatics.

Marry me, Tate. You're so fucking sexy!

Ohmygod did you see that smile on his face? UGH.

I'm pregnant.

And those are just the tame comments.

Some of the videos are of women at the party reacting to my performance, their expressions full of shock and awe, their enthusiasm translating to the screen. I made these women happy.

I made them scream for me. And I haven't done that since I don't remember when.

I open up other social media sites and am greeted with much the same, my phone continuing to blow up with notifications, calls from unknown numbers that I send straight to voice mail. I don't know what's going on, but maybe Simon was onto something.

Maybe—God, it's hard to admit this without getting my hopes up, something I seriously want to avoid—but maybe I actually have been given a second chance.

Once I'm dressed and primped for my meeting with Simon, I take an Uber to his office downtown—I'm going to have a fat million bucks in my bank account; I can afford it—and show up promptly at three, our agreed-upon meeting time. I'm ushered into his office by a hot little number wearing a black formfitting dress that shows off her curves. The flirtatious smile she's sending my way has me in an even better mood than I was in before I arrived.

The moment the door shuts, Simon is pointing at the chair in front of his massive desk. "Sit."

I come to a stop. "What's your problem?"

"I saw the way she looked at you." His gaze is focused on his phone as he taps out a message to someone.

"She's hot."

"She's not for you."

"Why? Because she's for you?"

Simon glances up from his phone. "As a matter of fact, yes."

My mouth hangs open for a second. "Get the fuck out."

Simon is all right looking, I guess, but I can't imagine him banging total hotties that are my age on a regular basis.

"She just so happens to be my girlfriend. How else can I get a woman who looks like that to work for me on a Sunday? So yeah. Stay away from her." Simon sets his phone on the desk, his focus now on me. "Besides, I thought you were interested in someone else."

I stare at him for a moment, drawing a blank.

"Scarlett Lancaster." He pauses, the look on his face incredulous. "Remember?"

"Right. Fuck. I'm totally hot for her." He thinks we're together? I guess I can keep up the facade.

"Looked like you were last night."

I lean back in the chair and lift my leg, resting my left ankle on top of my right knee. "Those photos of us were pretty good, huh."

"They were fucking great. Chef's kiss, as the kids say. You

know what was even better?" Before I can answer, he continues. "Your performance. Jesus. You sounded . . ."

I sit on the edge of my seat, waiting for the rest of his words. My heart is racing, my body tight with anticipation. I catch myself gripping the chair arms and try to relax my cramped fingers.

". . . you sounded pretty fucking amazing, Tate. Your voice was clear. You sounded better than you did back in the day. Deeper and more mature."

I bask in his compliment for a moment, not saying anything.

"Five Car Pileup was a bunch of teenagers playing at singing about love and relationships, shit you kids knew nothing about. Now you've got a few more years of experience in you. You've struggled, and you've come out the other side, and it shows," Simon says. "You should be proud of yourself."

I'm stunned by the sincerity in his voice. Simon was always so slick. Always mostly full of a bunch of shit too. "Thank you."

"How much did Lancaster pay you to perform?" He holds up his hand at the same time as I part my lips, ready to brag about the ridiculous amount I made. "Don't tell me. I'll be jealous I didn't make a cut."

I snap my lips shut for a moment before I say, "It was an offer I couldn't refuse."

"I'm sure," Simon says dryly, grabbing a slim folder that's sitting on his desk and opening it. He glances at the piece of paper nestled inside, his expression thoughtful when he lifts his head to study me. "This has the potential to blow up and transform your career."

"My career can't be transformed much. Pretty sure I trashed it so hard I can never bounce back," I admit with a nervous chuckle.

"I'm not meaning in a negative manner. I'm talking positive. Your life has the potential to change completely, just like last time."

"All because I kissed an heiress?"

"You did more than kiss her. You performed like you had zero fucks left in you, kid. You were on fire on that stage. I've never seen anything like it." He shakes his head as if he's in awe of me.

A normal human being would be thrilled at all this praise. Who wouldn't want constant fame, endless money, and women throwing their panties at them? For a brief, shining time in my life, that's what I experienced as a member of Five Car Pileup.

But that period in my life also left me hollow inside. A shell of the person I once was. Hell, I lost myself. I lost friends. My girlfriend. All the fame disappeared, replaced with hate. Drugs and alcohol. Eventually the money dried up. The contracts were rescinded and the band split.

It was fucking awful.

I love hearing Simon's praise. Can't lie—it builds me up, but it also terrifies me.

Not sure I can go through that again.

"All of the attention is great, but I don't know if I'm ready for the shit that comes with it, you know?" I admit.

"I'm guessing you're not," Simon says drolly. "And why should you be? The best opportunities are usually surprises. This is where I step in."

"You want to step in?" More like take over completely. When I was a kid, I had no problem with that. But now? "I never said I was going to hire you."

"Trust me when I say that you need to. You need someone to manage your career, Tate. Keep you on the right path, line up proper business deals before you get taken advantage of."

"I'm not the same dumb kid I was," I remind him, insulted.

"I'm not saying you are. I just know this kind of thing can be . . . overwhelming. And I don't want you jumping into the first opportunity you're offered. You might have some leverage here," Simon says.

Leverage? Doubtful. I'm a has-been who the ladies are raving about for a brief moment. One of those nostalgic moments because it makes them feel young again or whatever. It'll last about two seconds before the next big thing comes along.

"I drew up a business plan for you. A strategy that I'd like to put in place before Monday morning. We need to be ready for the onslaught."

"Onslaught of what?"

Simon shakes his head, making a tsking noise, like he can't believe I'm so obtuse. "Offers, mate. Have you checked your hashtag on social media? It's exploding."

I'm such a dumbass.

Opening up Instagram, I punch in my name and look up the hashtag, my eyes widening as I take in the number. As I check out the top videos, I see they're all from last night. Me in all black, crooning to the audience. Me grabbing hold of Scarlett in that poufy pink dress, pulling her in for a deeper kiss.

Fuck, that photographer wasn't the only one who captured our embrace. Looks like other people did too.

Lots of people.

CHAPTER SIX

SCARLETT

It's the day after my birthday, and I'm in a bad mood.

I hate feeling like this. Cranky and unsettled and more than anything . . . disappointed. Those three feelings swirl within me, growing bigger and bigger, until I finally give up trying to lie in bed and indulge in my weekend-morning routine, which is scrolling my favorite gossip sites. I can't enjoy it. Especially when I'm actively involved in one of the top featured headlines.

What's happening to me is so big, so completely unexpected, I'm just . . .

I don't know what to do.

By the time I'm walking into the breakfast nook connected to our kitchen, I'm desperate. Ready to ask for any sort of advice on how to navigate this unfamiliar situation. My parents—my father—will have something to say. He's been through this sort of thing before. I'm sure he'll know what to do.

I come to a stop in the vast open doorway and stare at my parents sitting at the table, their heads simultaneously swiveling in my direction.

"Good morning, darling! Want some coffee?" Mom smiles

at me, always cheerful, appearing ready to spring out of her seat and take care of me like I'm still a little girl.

The temptation to run into her arms and let her protect me is strong, but I hold myself back. I'm a grown woman of eighteen now. Officially an adult.

I can handle this.

Right?

I put on a brave smile, hating how false it feels on my face. "I'll grab it, thank you."

My mother's gaze trails after me as I go to the coffee bar and make myself a cup, carrying the mug with me to the table and settling in across from my parents. My dad has his head buried in the newspaper, while Mom watches me expectantly.

"Did you sleep well?" she asks when I remain silent too long for her liking.

A shrug of one shoulder is my answer. I don't know how to broach this. Do they know what the media is saying? Have they seen the fallout from last night?

I'm mortified. Vaguely humiliated but also . . . excited? Is that the right feeling to have after being caught kissing a celebrity?

My mother continues with her questioning.

"Have you spoken with Ian this morning?"

Scowling at the thought of Ian, I shake my head. "I didn't even get a chance to talk to him much last night. He left my party early."

A crease appears between my mother's eyebrows, her sign that she's distressed. "Oh dear."

"Oh dear, what?" I take another sip of coffee and tell myself to calm down. I didn't think it would be such a big deal to kiss Tate in front of a photographer. Who cares about us anyway?

Apparently there's not much going on in the world, because it feels like everyone freaking cares. So many articles and posts about how great Tate Ramsey sounded. How healthy he looked. How amazing his performance was, and where has he been anyway? When did he get so sexy?

And speaking of sexy, our innocent kissing moment has caused quite the . . . scandal?

It wasn't just a single photo taken by that lingering photographer, either, but all kinds of photos of us locked in an embrace, plus videos. None of them catch me making the first move, thank goodness, but we definitely look . . . into each other. I look as if I'm enjoying that kiss.

He seemed to be enjoying it too. He held me close, his fingers drifting across my back. I clung to him as if I might float away if I didn't.

There's no denying I look really into it. I'm the one who kissed him, after all, so this isn't surprising.

There are even reaction videos to our kiss. Women picking apart our body language and acting like I'm the luckiest girl alive, kissing Tate Ramsey like that. All the comments on those particular posts, I can't figure out if they're supportive or rude.

Get it gurl.

OMG I DIE FOR HIM. FOR HER. FOR THEM.

She's so lucky, ugh I wish I was her.

Who the f is she?*

*Her dress! Look at how he's touching her. *heart eyes**

I can feel the heat scorch my cheeks just thinking about it. Knowing my parents most likely saw those photos, when I'm supposed to be completely into Ian. What are they thinking? Are they disappointed in me?

"I'm sure Ian is not pleased to see you kissing another man." Dad rattles the newspaper he's holding in front of him, and I can hear the amusement in his voice, which fills me with relief. I should've known this would be his reaction.

My father loves this sort of thing. A scandal. Before he met my mother, my father was one of the most scandalous people in New York. Young, rich, and unbearably handsome, Fitzgerald Lancaster was a force to be reckoned with. He owned Manhattan in the nineties. And my parents' relationship started in scandal—Dad basically stole her from the guy she was originally supposed to marry. She was engaged to him and everything.

My dad is what my dear grandmother would call a scoundrel. I'm sure what's happening to me is giving him serious déjà vu.

I huff out an exasperated breath, trying to play it off. "That kiss between Tate and I was nothing."

Dad lowers his paper to stare at me. "Looked like something to me."

"Me too," Mom murmurs before she takes a dainty bite of toast.

"Honestly? It all feels rather . . . familiar." Dad's blue eyes sparkle with unmistakable pride. "Pretty scandalous, Scarlett. And I never thought you were the type to cause a scandal."

"Much to your disappointment," Mom says to him, her tone wry.

He sighs, resting a hand on his chest, the paper flopping forward. "My greatest wish is for my children to live their lives to the fullest. Scarlett, you've always been such a good girl. I'm proud of you for rebelling."

Rolling my eyes, I gulp the coffee down, ignoring the way it scalds my throat. Only my parents would be proud of me for causing a ruckus. Any other Lancaster would be appalled. "Hate to break it to you, but it was all fake. He needed me to help him distract the photographer."

"Who needed your help?" Mom asks with a frown.

"Tate Ramsey."

"Isn't he used to having his photo taken?" Mom asks.

"He was trying to avoid it. After everything he's been through in the past . . ." I shrug helplessly, not sure what else I should say.

"Quite an interesting way to distract the photographer, don't you think?" Dad's brows shoot up.

"I didn't realize it would blow up like this." The only person's attention I wanted from this is Ian's, and he probably didn't even notice, while the rest of the country did.

And now I have no idea how to fix this. How to explain it. There is so much speculation about my supposed relationship with Tate Ramsey, I don't think anyone would even listen to me.

"Your party has received a lot of attention," Mom says gently.

"I'm not sure if this is the sort of attention I wanted."

"You've gained so many followers too," she reminds me. "Isn't this your goal? Aren't you trying to grow your reach?"

I glance down at the table, studying my phone sitting next to me, watching as yet another notification lights up the screen. "I've been . . . afraid to check."

"You haven't even looked yet?" The shock in my mother's voice is obvious.

"I was too scared. I looked up my name and the Plaza online, and when I saw all the articles about my . . . interaction with Tate, I clicked right out of it. I haven't even gone on my social media." I was afraid of the comments on the lone photo I shared of me in my dress before I went to the party. Scared of all the photos I'm tagged in, most likely the majority of them having to do with Tate Ramsey and his performance last night.

Well, I'm sure there are plenty of posts about his performance, but the real juicy story is the kiss.

"Darling, open them up right now." Mom waves a hand. "Go on. Do it. Hurry."

I open up Instagram, going straight to my profile to find I've gained . . .

Almost a million new followers.

What?

Switching over to my tagged posts, I scroll through them. There are so many, mostly of the kiss, though there are also plenty of photos and videos of Tate performing, accompanied by photos of the party.

But yeah. It's mostly photos of me in Tate's arms. My eyes closed. Our lips locked.

I close my eyes for a fleeting moment, my heart in my throat. What is Ian going to think? My friends? Oh God, what about Rachel?

Opening my eyes, I take a deep breath and read the various captions below some of the kiss photos, all of them along the same lines.

Tate and Scarlett—the new it couple?

OMG aren't they the cutest?

There are also headlines from gossip sites.

Tate Ramsey Snags Heiress as His Latest Conquest

Following in Her Father's Footsteps, Scarlett Lancaster Is the Toast of the Town—and Has a Boy Bander as Her New Beau

"They think I'm dating him." I glance up to find both of my parents watching me with concern in their eyes. "All of these posts imply that we're together. Me and Tate."

Dad frowns. "You're not?"

"I only just met him last night," I remind him.

"And you're already dating him? That's my girl." Dad lifts his hand up like he expects me to give him a high five.

"I'm not dating him. That's the problem." I open up one of the many photos of me lip locked with freaking Tate Ramsey, and I make it bigger with my fingers, zooming in on our faces. Our fused mouths.

The kiss is extremely convincing.

"This isn't good," I mumble to myself, rubbing my temple with my fingertips. "This isn't what I expected at all."

"But isn't that the best thing about life? When an unexpected opportunity pops up, it's always good to take advantage of it," Dad says, trying his best to sound logical.

"I have no idea how to take advantage of any of this." I set my phone on the dining table face down. "I feel like it's only going to make things worse. Everyone will be talking about me being with Tate when that's not what I want."

"What do you want, darling?" Mom asks me.

"I thought I wanted Ian." A cold shiver steals through me, and I wrap my arms around myself, staring unseeingly at the table. I don't want Tate. And I can guarantee he doesn't want me. That kiss was all for show.

It was nothing.

And now Ian will think I'm with Tate and forget all about me.

"I don't want to become that random heiress who kissed Tate Ramsey that one time," I say when my parents remain quiet.

"You could never." Dad drops his newspaper onto the table, his expression indignant. "Do they know who they're dealing with? You're Fitzy Lancaster's daughter."

"Fitz," Mom tries to interject, but he ignores her.

"I will never let anyone minimize who you are. You're going to make a difference in this world, I just know it!" He thrusts his finger in the air as if he's delivering a rousing speech to his constituents.

Mom rests her hand on his arm, gently forcing him to lower it. "She doesn't just want to be known as Fitzy Lancaster's daughter either."

I appreciate her saying that. I could never utter those words out loud to him, and especially not right now. He would be hurt, and that's the last thing I want.

And there's the root of all my issues. I am tired of being stuck in the role I was supposedly born to play. The daughter of a rich man. The heiress to a vast fortune. From a prominent family that is all lumped together. There is no individuality in the Lancaster family tree, with a few exceptions here and there.

My older cousin Whit Lancaster? He stands apart.

He also terrifies me.

My cousin Charlotte? She married a man from another wealthy family and has become the new darling of New York high society. It's kind of cute, how so many people want to spend even a sliver of a second with Charlotte and her husband, Perry.

Oh, and my cousin Crew, Charlotte's little brother? He's become the toast of Europe along with his fiancé, Wren, as they travel all over to attend various art shows and make purchases from new artists, helping elevate their careers and sales.

All of that is so incredibly *interesting*, while I'm over here living a not-very-interesting life. Stuck in the shadow of my former-playboy father and my beautiful, elegant mother. That important name that's been well known across the country—the world—for centuries.

I know I'm only eighteen. My life is just beginning, and I haven't done much, but I wish . . .

That I were somebody.

I want to stand out, stand on my own two feet. I want to make a mark on this world, and I don't want my family name or history to burden me.

"You're so much more than that one girl who kissed Tate Ramsey at her birthday party." Mom settles her hand over mine, her expression and tone reassuring. When I meet her steady brown gaze that's so much like mine, I'm immediately calmed. "Don't worry about it, darling. This too shall pass."

My anxiety ratchets up at my mother using clichés to try to make me feel better.

News flash—I don't feel better. Not at all.

Dad changes the subject, talking about a couple they're friends with who attended the party last night, and I tune him out, mulling over my situation and how I can deal with it. Is it best to ignore what happened? Pretend that kiss between Tate and me never existed? The more I post, the more buried the story will get. Eventually everyone will forget that I kissed Tate Ramsey at my party.

And that's exactly what I want. This entire situation behind me.

Never brought up again.

CHAPTER SEVEN

TATE

I figured everyone would forget about me for sure by Monday. Some new scandal or celebrity war would come along and overshadow my performance, which, in the scheme of life, isn't that big of a deal.

My chance at finding fame one more time shot down within twenty-four hours. Sounds about right when it comes to my luck.

But that isn't what happens. Not even close. Monday morning rolls around, and I'm still blowing up. I have another meeting scheduled with Simon today along with someone from my old record company. The same company that fired my ass so fast my head spun.

Or maybe that was the recurring hangover I was experiencing at the time. Still not sure.

Now all the network morning shows are talking about me. Airing clips of my performance at Scarlett Lancaster's party. They always end their segments with the kiss between Scarlett and me, asking the camera if we're together.

It's like they want us to be a couple, which I get. She's gorgeous. And I can't deny we look good together.

She's not really my type.

I checked in on my video-sharing account, and the number of personalized-message requests is unbelievable. No way can I manage them all, so I had to write on my storefront that I'm no longer available and set the account to private. I will probably piss off a ton of people, and that's most likely a mistake, but right now, I don't give a damn.

I'm not about that life anymore. I'm ready to move on to something bigger.

Something better.

By the time I'm rolling into the meeting at Simon's office, I'm a bundle of nerves, but at least I look good. Went right out and bought myself a new outfit for the occasion at Gucci. Yeah, I know Harry is the face of the company and has his own line.

If you can't beat them, join them, am I right?

"Looking good," Simon's assistant tells me as she leads me to his office, her gaze appreciative. "Gucci?"

"Yeah." I run a hand down the front of the shirt I bought off the rack. I remember back when I was in the band and they would send over clothes to us before they were in stores, allowing us to choose whatever we wanted, free of charge. They'd send over a personal tailor and everything. Times have definitely changed.

But at least I can afford the good life again.

"Don't be nervous." She rests her hand on the door handle of Simon's office, glancing over her shoulder to meet my gaze. "This is all going to work out in your favor."

I lift my brows, shocked at her encouragement. "How do you know?"

"Simon told me about you last night." Her smile is small. Maybe even a little bit naughty. "He gets off on making money, and he firmly believes you're going to make him a lot. Again."

She opens the door before I can respond, and I'm left standing there for a few seconds, shocked she'd talk about her sex life with Simon and how the idea of making a bucket-load of money . . . what, makes him horny?

There's something vaguely gross about that.

"Mr. Ramsey has arrived," the assistant announces, my cue to follow her inside the office. She turns to me. "Want something to drink?"

I shake my head. "I'm good."

"Water?"

"I've got Voss," Simon calls out.

I roll my eyes. Back in the day, I was the asshole who wouldn't drink any water unless it was Voss. Such a pretentious little prick. "I'll take some water, please. Whatever you've got."

She smiles and leaves the room, closing the door behind her while I head deeper into Simon's office.

He's standing, gesturing toward the empty chair in front of his desk. "Have a seat. Roger is already here."

I glance over to see the record exec who took us on back in the day sitting in the chair next to mine, his hair a little grayer, but otherwise he appears exactly the same. "Tate."

"Roger." I nod, rearing back a little when he rises, thrusting his hand toward me. I take it, giving him a firm shake, surprised to see the sincerity shining in his gaze.

"Bloody good performance this weekend." His hand is still clutching mine, giving it a vigorous shake. "Your voice blew me away."

"Thank you." I withdraw my hand from his and settle into my chair, glancing over at Simon helplessly. I have no idea what to say next or why they called this meeting in the first place. I mean, I can assume they want to talk to me about possibly recording a new album, but maybe that's a stretch.

And then again, maybe it's not.

"Look, let's get right to it." Roger leans forward, resting his elbows on his knees, his body angled toward mine. "You sounded fucking fantastic at that party Saturday night, Tate. Have you been working on your vocals? Getting some training, lessons or whatever?"

Not really. Only a couple of sessions to get back into it prior to the performance, but I don't want to seem lazy. "Definitely. I've been working on my singing and vocal strength for a while."

"It shows." The sincerity all over Roger's face almost makes me want to laugh. "You've never sounded better. Everyone is raving about you online. On TV. You are everywhere right now. The comeback kid, sitting on top of the world once again. It's unbelievable, man."

Tell me about it.

"I'm just grateful they had a good time at the party while I performed," I say, trying for humble. Feeling, for once in my life, actually humble. I learned my lesson from the last time I had a taste of fame. Being an asshole gets you no friends. And a shitty attitude only creates enemies. "And I'm grateful that you enjoyed my performance as well."

"I more than enjoyed it, Tate. I practically jizzed in my pants, you sounded so damn good."

I say nothing, just stare at Roger blankly while Simon coughs to cover up his discomfort. That statement is so typical Roger. I forgot how grossly blunt he is and how he always tends to take things a little too far. "That's . . . awesome, Roger."

He throws back his head and laughs, pleased he rattled me, no doubt. "I mean it, kid. You have that million-dollar face, and now you've got a million-dollar voice to go along with it. Back when you were with Five Car Pileup, I knew you had potential, but you were held back by the other bandmates. Well, them, and your voice hadn't really matured yet. Plus, you epically fucked everything up with all of your . . . issues."

Always gotta remind me how I ruined everything, don't they? "I made a lot of mistakes in my past. I'd like to think I've grown up and won't act like that anymore."

Roger squints at me. "How old are you now, kid?"

I hate how he keeps calling me *kid*. "Twenty-one."

"Just a baby then." He leans back in his chair, contemplating me. "Still drinking?"

I shake my head. "I haven't had a drop in three years."

And I definitely don't feel like a baby. I've seen and done a lot more than the average twenty-one-year-old guy.

"Snorting your royalties up your nose like you used to?" He lifts a brow, the look on his face almost defiant. As if he wants to challenge me. Fluster me.

I remain as cool as a cucumber, remembering my past hotheaded ways. There's no need for me to blow up at him. "Haven't done that in a long time either. Besides, I don't have any royalties to spend anymore."

The checks went from measly to nonexistent pretty damn quick.

Roger appears pleased at my answer. "You've cleaned up your act."

"Like I mentioned, I've been sober for the last three years. I've been working out. Working on myself." I clamp my lips shut, not wanting to lay it on thick, though I could. And I wouldn't be lying either.

Nothing like a huge scandal accompanied by your entire world imploding to make you do some hard self-reflection.

"And now you're with someone on top of all that." Roger nods, rubbing his chin. "You sound good, Ramsey. You look good. No, I take that back—you look *healthy*. Much better than the drunk seventeen-year-old you once were. Doesn't hurt that you're in a committed relationship."

Simon scoffs.

A committed . . . "You think I'm in a relationship?"

"Don't play dumb, Tate," Simon says, finally cutting into my surreal conversation with Roger. "I know you're trying to keep your relationship with Scarlett under wraps since it's still so new."

My *relationship* with Scarlett?

"You are with Scarlett Lancaster, right? I saw the photos. The videos. Pretty heavy kissing going on, yet it somehow looked romantic. Even . . . sweet." Roger smiles. "Which makes all the girls her age swoon, am I right? Like their every dream come true. The pretty girl getting with the boy she had a crush on when she was a kid. The publicity team thinks this would be a great angle for us to play off. The redeemed boy band singer who fucked up his life by doing too many drugs, saved by the beautiful heiress who used to have his posters on her wall when she was younger. She did have your poster on her wall, right?"

I have no clue. Did she?

"I wonder if she has any photos from when she was younger with a poster of Five Car Pileup on her bedroom wall, where she dreamed of you at night," Roger continues, clearly on a roll. "Oh man, that would be a great post, and that isn't even my expertise, if you know what I mean. Maybe she could share it on her Instagram. And speaking of Instagram, why aren't you two posting each other on there? I didn't see the kiss photo on either of your profiles, and trust me, I checked. The publicity team thinks that would be a good idea, if you started sharing photos of each other. Together."

The look of pure disappointment on Roger's face is almost comical, the poor guy.

"We've been keeping our relationship private," I say hesitantly, deciding to play along. More like I need to do this to make this scenario convincing. "I still can't believe that one photographer caught us kissing. We were in a pretty secluded corner."

"Divine intervention, Tate. You two were meant to be splashed across the internet. Two attractive people fucking. It's like a PR dream come true. I'm repeating myself; don't call me out on it. Just let me say this—we can't pay for this type of coverage you two are currently delivering. It's all-natural. Organic. Whatever the word is. Your relationship has gone viral, and we want to take advantage of it."

I'm still grimacing over him saying Scarlett and I are fucking. She was pretty uptight when I kissed her. Yeah, she kind of got into it, but she's young. Probably hasn't even been fucked yet, and that's the type of woman I'd rather steer clear of.

"What exactly are you talking about, Roger?" Simon asks on my behalf. As my business manager, it is up to him to find out what Roger wants from me.

"We want to make an offer to Tate, and I wanted to do it in person. We'd like to sign him on for an album." Roger sits up straight, rubbing his hands together. "Thought we'd get right in here first thing so we can be ahead of everyone else. I'm guessing they're all knocking on your door, demanding a meeting with Tate?"

Simon nods, his expression impassive. "We've had some interest."

Other record companies have reached out to Simon? That surprises me.

"I don't doubt it. He's a hot commodity right now. I mean, look at him." Roger waves a hand in my general direction. "That messy hair girls wanna tug on while he's going down on them. The arrogant grin. The smooth voice and the gorgeous girlfriend. It's a sell, Simon. You're easy to sell right now, kid. Come back to the fold. Come back to Irresistible Records, and we'll put you on the map."

"Easy there with the sales pitch, Rog," Simon says with a gentle chuckle. "We need a little time to discuss the terms first. You didn't even come with a contract in hand."

"Oh, but I did." Roger picks up the suitcase I didn't notice sitting beside his chair and opens it in his lap, pulling out a thick pile of papers stapled together. He tosses it onto Simon's desk, where it lands dead center with a heavy thud. "I emailed you a contract as well. I'm sure you'll have some changes you'd like to make, and that's fine, we're agreeable, but don't dawdle like you normally do, Simon. We need to get on it. I want to get Tate out to Los Angeles so he can start recording."

"Los Angeles?" Five Car Pileup recorded in Los Angeles, and I swear to fucking God that city was the root of my downfall. All the women, drink, and drugs I could ever want are in that city. It's where dreams go to flourish and then wither away and die.

For me, at least.

Roger's nod is firm, his expression unreadable, though his eyes seem to dance with excitement. "We already have the studio picked out. The musicians. I heard the way you put your own twist on those Five Car Pileup songs. And there was a song you sang I didn't even recognize. It was damn good. Very . . . indie pop. Ghost pop? Something like that."

Again, I have no idea what he's talking about. "You liked how I changed up the beat?"

"I liked everything about your performance, and so did half the women between the ages of eighteen and twenty-five in the United States. Stop being a cocktease and just say you're willing to sign with us, Tate. We've made magic together before. I believe we can do it again."

"I'm sure we could," I say weakly, trying to wrap my head around what's happening. Before this weekend, life had settled down, and I figured this was it. My past fame and rise to the top, all of it was a one-shot deal. A has-been at twenty-one. I suppose there could be worse things, right? At least I was making some sort of career out of the personalized appearances. Messing around and writing songs on the side while strumming my beat-up guitar on a Sunday afternoon. No one cared what I was doing, and there's some freedom in that.

What Roger is proposing sounds like it will take away every inch of my freedom, and that is fucking terrifying.

But it's also fucking irresistible. No wonder they named the record label that.

"We'll discuss it." Simon rises from his chair and rounds the desk, coming to stand beside Roger. Ready to escort him right out of the office. "And we'll be in touch."

"That's it? That's all you're going to give me, Simon? How about dinner tonight? You want to go to dinner, Tate? It's on me. It's on the label. They told me whatever it takes to get you, do it. I'm here for you, Tate. I've always been here for you. You were always the one with the talent. I'll call you. Okay? Your number hasn't changed, right? Wait, I bet it has. I'd have changed it if I were you. Simon, get me Tate's number, will you?" Roger keeps talking as Simon escorts him across the room, depositing him just outside the office before he shuts the door with a not-so-gentle slam and turns to face me with a shocked expression on his face.

A look I've never seen on Simon before. Ever.

"He seems determined," I finally say just to fill the silence in the room.

"You heard him. You're a hot commodity." Simon returns to his chair and settles in, picking up the contract and giving it a quick once-over. "I haven't done an in-depth read of the contract yet, of course, but I caught a glimpse of the advance they want to offer you just now. You're going to want to consider this."

Excitement bubbles up inside of me, and I remember what it was like before. When we were just a bunch of kids grouped together on a freaking singing competition. *American Idol* came first, and then all the other copycat reality shows followed suit. We were featured on a copycat. One with subpar ratings that got it canceled after its second season.

It didn't matter. We were formed into a band during the first season, and we were considered the breakout group. The one that was going places—and it turned out we were the only ones from that particular show. We had a couple of *Billboard* hits. Hell, we were nominated for a Grammy as Best New Artist.

We didn't win, but it got us onto the Grammys, where we actually performed, which was pretty damn amazing.

"That good?"

"The terms are probably shit." Simon scans the contract, flipping one page after another, his brows drawing together in concern.

I pace around his office, unable to keep still, eventually approaching the window and staring at the city spread out in front of me.

This is where I'm from. Where I grew up. My mom took me to the audition for that reality show in Brooklyn, and I made it. Was flown out to Los Angeles, where I stayed for over two years.

Until I came home a broken, strung-out mess with hardly any money and a drug habit that cost me hundreds per day. Mom immediately shipped me off to rehab, and it actually worked.

I haven't touched drugs or alcohol in years. I'm the most clearheaded I think I've ever been.

Why would I want to go back to a world where drugs are king, the stress is high, and temptation is everywhere? I'll be dodging land mines left and right until one eventually blows up in my face.

And knowing me, that'll happen sooner rather than later.

"The terms are actually not shit," Simon eventually says, glancing up at the same time I look in his direction. "This is a good offer, Tate."

I turn fully to face him. "Yeah?"

Simon nods. "But here's the deal. There's an . . . unusual clause."

"What is it?" They probably want me to sign something where I agree to unannounced drug tests. No sweat. Or maybe they have to put insurance on me because I'm a risk and that might come out of my royalties if I flake on them or OD or whatever.

Fairly standard stuff, I think.

"They want your little girlfriend to be part of the package."

I frown. "What do you mean, part of the package?"

"They want to include Scarlett Lancaster as part of the promotional package. Like, she has to make appearances with you. Her social media has to include photos of the two of you together. They want you with Scarlett by your side as part of your image."

"She's not my girlfriend." I hesitate. "Not really."

"They don't know that. No one has to, if you get what I'm saying."

I'm incredulous. "You want me to ask her to be my fake girlfriend?"

"If you want to make this happen, I think you should."

Panic makes me break out into a sudden sweat. "And what if she doesn't agree?"

"I don't know. This looks like they want her as part of the deal." Simon's eyes narrow as he studies me. "Can you make that happen?"

"Absolutely," I say with a nod, ignoring the knot in my gut.

First, I just need to convince her.

CHAPTER EIGHT

SCARLETT

I'm staring at my phone and chewing on my lower lip, trying to come up with the courage to send Ian a text, when my phone lights up with a notification.

A text from Ian. What, he's reading my mind?

I take this as a sign that we're meant to be. Of course.

Opening the text, I ignore the nerves making my stomach twist and read his message.

> **Ian: You're going out with a boy band member now.**

That's it. That's all the text says.

I drop the phone on my bed and flop backward on it, my mind racing with possible replies. How can I tell him that kiss meant nothing without making the incident sound bad? I suppose I could tell him the truth.

Or I could try to make Ian jealous by telling him that yes, I'm definitely seeing the former boy band member and my life is fantastic thanks to him.

Sitting up, I grab my phone and start tapping away on the keyboard.

Me: We're not going out.

I hesitate for only a moment before I send the next text.

Me: Yet.

There's no response. Ian takes so long I start pacing around the room, chewing on my fingernail as I wait for his text. My palms are literally starting to sweat, and when he finally answers, I grab my phone and open the text immediately.

Ian: I thought you were saving yourself for me.

My heart drops into the pit of my stomach. Does he actually mean that?

Another text appears.

Ian: Kidding.

It's accompanied by a laughing-face emoji.

An actual growl rises from my throat, and I'm tempted to toss the phone across the room, but I hold my impulses in check.

I decide to be bold. It's so much easier, doing that sort of thing over text instead of face to face, though it has much more meaning when you tell someone in person.

But screw it. I've been chasing after this seemingly clueless guy for the last couple of years of my life, and I'm tired of waiting for him to make a move. Looks like I need to be the one to make something happen.

Me: I mean . . . I WAS saving myself for you, but you never seemed interested.

I send the text quickly, before I can second-guess myself. I try to swallow past the lump that forms in my throat, but it's like I can't. A dull throb starts at my temple while I wait for his response.

Which doesn't come for a solid five minutes.

When my phone finally dings, I almost shriek out loud.

Ian: I was always interested.

I don't bother playing the hesitation game. I respond fast before I lose my nerve.

Me: Then why didn't you do anything about it? You've had your chance for years.

Ian: First off, you were too young. And now . . .

He's typing. I can see the gray bubble in our text thread, and I wait, breathless. This could be my chance. He could finally say, *Yes, let's go out on a date. Let's spend time together, Scarlett. Real, actual time when we act like a couple and not friends.*

I close my eyes as I clutch my phone, hoping and wishing I'll receive the answer I so desperately want.

When the text sounds, I wait for a couple of beats, scared he's going to turn me down.

> Ian: I lost my chance. You're finally eighteen and look at you. You're gorgeous. You could have anyone you want, and I'm pretty sure that Tate Ramsey guy wants you.
>
> Ian: You two make a great couple.

Um . . .

That is not what I expected him to say.

There's a knock on my bedroom door, and in walks my best friend, a determined look on her face that tells me she means business.

"You kissed Tate Ramsey? Seriously? And you didn't even think to call me? Or text? Or, I don't know, send a message to me via a raven or something?" Rachel holds out her phone, that damn photo of me and Tate lip locked blown up on her screen. "Look at you two! I'm pretty sure he has his tongue down your throat. Lucky bitch."

"Uh . . ."

She doesn't even give me time to explain. "That's when you snuck off, right? You big liar! I even asked you if you hid away in a corner with Tate or whatever, and you told me no. How could you keep this from me? This is huge!"

There is not even a hint of seriousness in Rachel's tone, which tells me she's not truly mad.

"How could I tell you when I knew you'd make a complete scene in the middle of my party?" I shrug, watching as she starts pacing around my room just like I did not even five minutes ago.

"True, true. I would've screamed at anyone who was listening that you made out with *the* Tate Ramsey. How freaking exciting, Scarlett! You're seeing him again, right?"

"I don't think so," I say weakly, noting the disappointment on her face.

"Seriously? Wait a minute." I could get whiplash from the way she shifts the conversation. "What if this is just a onetime thing and that's it? What a cool thing to claim, though. On your eighteenth birthday, you made out with the lead singer of a boy band that you crushed on when you were fifteen."

"Fourteen," I correct her. "Thirteen, even."

"Whatever. Semantics." She waves her hand dismissively, then strides toward my bed and plops her butt on the mattress right next to me. "How was it?"

"How was what?"

"The kiss! Tell me. I need *all* the details. Was it good? Better than you dreamed? Better than Ian?" Rachel's eyebrows shoot up, and I'm sure she's just waiting for me to bash on Ian.

I think she believes I've actually kissed Ian before, and I've never really corrected her, because Rachel hooked up with a few guys when we were in high school, and compared to her, I always felt . . . lacking. She had a serious boyfriend for the last three months of our senior year, only to promptly break up with him the day after we graduated.

"I only wanted a guaranteed date for prom," she admitted to me after it was over, and I was in shock she was so nonchalant about it.

She had sex with that guy too. Said it was no big deal and she was relieved to finally rid herself of her virgin status. While I'm over here stuck with mine.

"Well?" Rachel asks impatiently, waiting for my answer.

"Well, what?"

"The kiss? How was it? Amazing? Life changing? Or was he bad at it." Rachel's expression turns dreamy. "I bet he wasn't bad. Not even close."

No. Not even close. "It was . . . nice."

"Nice? That's it? There was tongue, right?"

"Um, yeah." This is vaguely embarrassing to admit, even though it's just Rachel and we've shared lots of secrets together over the years.

"*Love* that for you. Seriously, I do." Rachel grabs her phone and starts tapping away at the screen. "Should you send him a DM?"

"I am not reaching out to him. Not at all." I shake my head. "This entire situation has sort of backfired for me."

"Backfired how? You have like a million more followers. Everyone is talking about you, and your dad's name isn't attached to the conversation whatsoever."

Rachel is one of the only people who know how I feel about our family dynamic. "He's mentioned sometimes."

"That can't be helped. He is your father. But Fitzy can't say he made out with Tate, so you have one up on him." Rachel laughs.

I don't laugh at all. It's like I can't. I can only think about Ian and how he believes he doesn't have a chance with me anymore because of Tate. "That photo of me kissing Tate has ruined my every chance with Ian."

"Oh, thank God. I was worried you'd end up marrying the guy." Rachel smiles brightly. "This is a good thing, Scarlett! You'll get over him once and for all, since he's not interested in you anymore."

Her words hurt. More than I care to admit. "It's not that he's not interested. Ian truly believes he doesn't have a chance because of me kissing Tate. He thinks we're actually together. He told me that we make a great couple."

"Really? He said that?"

I nod. "And he told me he was always interested in me. He just couldn't do anything about it because of my age."

Rachel makes a dismissive noise. "Please. I don't believe that. If he wanted to make a move, he could've done something about it a while ago."

"He said I was too young."

"You really think your parents would've cared if you were seventeen, dating Mr. Perfect despite him being two years older than you? Your dad probably would've loved that." Rachel shakes her head. "Though I don't recall Fitzy loving the idea of you and Ian together."

"He didn't. Though my father loves that I kissed Tate and the photos are everywhere," I admit. "He told me he didn't think I had it in me."

"What, being scandalous?" When I nod, Rachel continues, "Why does everyone think you're so boring?"

Ouch. "Gee, thanks, best friend."

"You know what I mean." Her eyes fill with sympathy. "I didn't mean to insult you. You're not boring. Not even close."

"Nice try, but no. I'm pretty boring."

"No, you're definitely not. You' re just . . . repressed. No, that's not the word for it either. You just haven't been given a chance yet to be your true self. Now's the time for you to break free and do whatever you want. You're eighteen, you just had an epic birthday party that people are still talking about, and you're the darling of the internet. You need to capitalize on that shit, stat."

My phone dings, and I check it to see I have another text from Ian. Completely unprovoked, which means he double texted me for the first time.

Giddy, I open the text to read it.

Ian: Are you saying I still have a shot? Because if that's the case . . .

Ian: Challenge accepted.

"Oh my God," I gasp.

"What? What's wrong?" Rachel asks.

"Ian just basically said he wants another chance at me." I lift my head to meet Rachel's troubled gaze. "He's still interested."

Rachel groans, throwing herself backward on my bed so she's lying across it, staring up at the ceiling. "He's lying to you. He just likes the *idea* of you pining away for him. That's it. He'll never actually get together with you."

"You don't know that," I say, mildly offended.

I refuse to let her negativity get me down.

My bedroom door swings open, my father peeking around the edge with a cheesy grin on his face. "Oh, Scarlett, you have a visitor."

Frowning, I glance over at Rachel, who immediately sits up. "Who is it?"

"Tate Ramsey."

CHAPTER NINE

TATE

Fuck, this place is unbelievable.

They live on the Upper East Side because of course they do. And they live on the top floor of the building, in the penthouse apartment. The views are spectacular, nothing but New York City skyscrapers as far as the eye can see.

If I lived here, I'd never leave. You don't have to. I'm guessing their every need is attended to, and they have more money than they could ever spend.

Wonder what that's like. Living without a care in the world about your finances. Spending however much you want, whenever you want.

Once upon a time, I was a dumb kid who had the world by the balls and spent my money like it was never going to run out. I had no clue what I was actually making. All I knew was that I'd made it.

I was rich.

Now, looking back on that period of my life, I know I was nowhere close.

Simon says I'm close to living that dream once again—and

it's possible I'll make even more money and have bigger success. After Roger left, we talked for almost two hours, strategizing. Going over the contract. Making a few changes that he sent to Roger to look over.

I haven't heard back from Simon yet, but he finally told me to go meet with Scarlett and try to convince her to be my girlfriend. Like it'll be that easy.

"Whatever it takes, Tate," he said, his voice and his expression dead serious. "In order for this record deal to happen, in order to get another chance at making music for a living, you need that girl by your side."

Don't get me wrong. I asked Simon to get that stupid clause dropped from the contract, but he said it was a risky move. And while he normally loves a challenge, he wants to stay on the safe side of this deal. Doesn't want to fuck it up in any way—direct quote.

So here I am, showing up at Scarlett's apartment like she's actually my girlfriend. I knew her dad would let me up when the security guy at the front desk of their building called him, and I was right. Fitzy likes me.

"Saw those photos of you and my daughter," Fitzy says as he drifts over to the bar in the corner of their spacious living room and starts preparing himself a drink. "Not too sure how I feel about them."

"What exactly do you mean?" I ask, my voice cautious.

"I mean, what are your intentions with my little girl?" He turns to face me, his expression downright stern. "You might look at her in a different light, but she's my baby. My firstborn. I don't need some arrogant asshole sliding into her world and fucking it all up."

"I don't plan on fucking her life up." I stand up taller. "Sir."

He contemplates me, his jaw working, his eyes blazing as

they stare me down. I don't fold under his consideration, and when he finally blinks, I realize I've pretty much got him. "That's good to know."

I sag with relief when he turns toward the bar once more, filling the crystal tumbler he just grabbed with perfectly round spheres of ice. "Want something to drink?"

"No thank you."

Fitz glances over his shoulder. "Recovering alcoholic, right?"

"Recovering addict, yes." I shrug when he continues to stare. "I was young, I did drugs and alcohol, and I grew out of control. When I came home with my tail between my legs, my mom tossed me in rehab."

"Did it work?"

"I've been sober for three years."

"Good to hear. You should be proud of yourself." He grabs a bottle and starts pouring the brown liquid in his glass. "I've always had a good handle on my liquor. And I haven't done a line of coke since I was thirty."

I nearly choke on my own saliva at his confession.

"Make it thirty-five." He chuckles to himself. "I'm not going to lie to you and say I'm perfect, because I'm not. I'm fatally flawed, yet I still love myself anyway." Fitz caps the bottle of liquor and turns to face me once more, rattling the ice in the glass he's clutching. "I don't mind you coming around. You might've fucked up in the past, but we all deserve a second chance, and I think you have potential. But if you harm a single hair on my daughter's head, if you break her heart or, God forgive you, make her cry, I will put your balls in a vise and squeeze until they pop. Understood?"

I nod once, my knees literally going weak at the threat apparent in his face. His gaze. His entire stance. The man means business. "Understood."

"Good." He nods once and takes a massive swig of his drink. Granted, it's only two o'clock in the afternoon, but if he's got his liquor under control, I'm assuming he's fine. "I'll go get Scarlett."

"Thank you."

The moment he's gone, I walk a slow circle around the room, taking note of the fine art on the walls. The sculptures on display. That fucking bar set up with every expensive bottle of alcohol you can imagine. The million-dollar view that stretches out as far as the eye can see. The Lancaster family doesn't scrimp on anything.

I run my hand across the back of the couch, the fabric soft and inviting. There are throw pillows lining the entire expanse, and I stop with my hand still resting on the couch, my gaze snagging on a photo of the very person I came to see.

It looks recent. Maybe a senior portrait? Scarlett is smiling, standing on the beach, her bare feet covered with foamy surf. Her long dark hair is blowing in the breeze, and her brown eyes are sparkling, the sky so blue behind her it almost hurts to look at.

Wait, no. That's her face. She's so damn beautiful it pains me to look at the photo for too long. I tear my gaze away from it, turning when I hear a sound, just as Scarlett enters the room, her expression wary.

She doesn't trust me. I suppose she shouldn't. I'm coming here with nefarious intentions, which sounds like something out of a historical-romance book or movie or whatever.

"What do you want?" Her voice is quiet, her entire demeanor subdued.

"No friendly hello?" When she scowls her answer, I lean against the back of the couch, crossing my arms in front of me. "I was hoping we could chat."

"What more is there to chat about? Photos were taken, you're the hit of the party, everyone thinks we're together, the end."

Ah, shit. She doesn't sound too thrilled over it.

"I wanted to talk to you about all of that. Your party. The photos." I put on my most charming smile, the one that used to get the panties to drop on just about any female I'd encounter, but Scarlett's face is immovable.

Great. Guess I need to work a little harder. Dig a little deeper.

"They're damaging to my image."

I raise my brows. "From what I could tell, you gained a shit ton of followers thanks to our little interaction."

"Not in the way I wanted. I want to earn followers on my own terms, not because I got caught kissing some has-been boy band member," she says bitterly.

I'm actually offended. "Kind of harsh, don't you think?"

"I don't know, let me tell you exactly what's happened to me since you performed at my birthday party Saturday night. I have media outlets constantly hounding me, wanting to know the status of my relationship with Tate Ramsey. My inbox has exploded. My voice mail box is full. I can't keep up with all of the comments and DMs, and I've even seen videos of girls *reacting* to our kiss video, freaking out and screaming over it. They either want to be me or kill me. And that's not even the worst of it."

She's practically panting, she's so worked up.

"The worst part is the guy I've been in love with for the last two years of my life believes he lost me to *you*. Some random guy I got caught kissing. That kiss didn't even mean anything, and I've been waiting for Ian to make a move on me for what feels like my entire life." She throws her hands up in the air. "And while he claims he's still interested in me, I don't know if he's actually ever going to do anything about it. Because he's never actually done anything about it for the last two years, so why would he now?"

Huh. Sounds like this Ian guy is an idiot, but I know now is definitely not the time to mention that.

"So no. I don't want to hear what you have to say or talk to you about any of this, because kissing you was probably the biggest mistake I've made in my life. That photo of the two of us has ruined everything for me. I'd rather forget the kiss, your performance, and my birthday party ever happened." Her shoulders slump, and she seems so damn pitiful I'm filled with the urge to go comfort her.

But I restrain myself. She doesn't want my comfort. She doesn't want me here at all.

"Ian must not want to fight for you too hard then, huh." The words come out before I can stop them, and then it's too late.

Her cheeks turn rosy at my words, and her dark eyes flash.

Damn it, now she's pissed.

"What do you know about Ian, huh? Nothing, that's what. You just barged into my life and turned it completely upside down, and you don't even care. All that matters to you is your career and your image. Well, what about me? What about my image?"

"Don't forget that you're the one who kissed me," I remind her.

It's not totally my fault that this happened. She's the one who made the first real move. I might've grabbed her, but damn it, she's the one who put her lips on me first.

She glares. Fumes. Then lifts her hand and points her finger toward the foyer and the front door. "You need to leave."

"But—"

She shakes her head, cutting me off. "Seriously. Go. Before I get my father and he kicks you out for me."

I start to exit the living room, heading for the foyer, but I stop at the doorway, glancing over to where she stands by the window. "I'm sorry."

I probably should've said that about sixty seconds ago.

Scarlett lifts her chin. “Your apology doesn’t make a difference.”

Damn, this girl is seriously mad. “You won’t hear me out?”

“No. Not at all. I don’t care. You need to go, Tate.”

I leave the Lancaster penthouse apartment without looking back. Ride down the elevator while my thoughts are a jumble of confusion. She turned me down. She’s not going to listen to what I have to say. Every time she said something mean—which was often—I said something shitty back, and I ruined everything. I need her and I lost her, all at once. Like usual, I fucked everything up.

Including my future.

CHAPTER TEN

SCARLETT

It's only been approximately seventy-two hours since my birthday party, and my life has been turned so completely upside down that I don't know how to right it again. Tate dropping by didn't help matters. Rachel lurked in my bedroom while I spoke to him, and I was so *angry* about everything. All of it. Especially at how nonchalant Tate acted about the entire situation. Everything that's happened to him since Saturday night has been great. Wonderful. He'll be able to reclaim his career and find new stardom, while I'll be that one heiress nobody he made out with the night he got a second chance at fame.

It's so unfair. But who said life was ever fair?

No one, that's who.

I sent Rachel home after Tate left, not wanting to talk about any of it with her or anyone else. I tried texting Ian, but he mostly gave one-word responses, which told me he was super busy. Or mad. I don't know which.

Fine. Whatever. I'm done waiting around for him. Oh, I've thought this before, and I'll probably continue to wait around for him like the lovesick fool that I am, but God, I really didn't need Tate to come along and screw everything up for me.

Like my entire life.

It's Tuesday night, and I'd spent the majority of my day sulking in my room when my father announced at lunchtime that his friend and lawyer, Kincaid Baldwin, was coming over for dinner, accompanied by his wife, Miranda, and their son.

Ian.

I was a frantic mess trying to get ready for this dinner. I tried on what felt like fifty dresses, every one of them disappointing me in one way or another. I straightened my hair, then curled it. Applied too much eye shadow and out of pure frustration washed my entire face before I started all over again.

I basically drove myself so out of my mind with apprehension and worry that by the time the Baldwin family showed up, I was still in my room, half-dressed and with no makeup on my face.

The first course of dinner is being served when I finally glide into the dining room, a smile pasted on my face as I approach the table where everyone is seated. The chair directly across from Ian is empty, meaning it's my seat, and for once in my life I wish my brothers were here.

And I never wish for my little brothers to be around. They make me crazy most of the time. They're twins, they're mean, and they like to play tricks on me. Dad always says they're more Lancaster than he is, whatever that means.

Okay, I know what it means. The Lancasters are mostly a ruthless bunch. My father is a gentle soul compared to the rest of his family. Even compared to his sons.

"Scarlett, there you are! Oh, don't you look lovely," Miranda greets me, her lips curved into a polite smile.

Panic swarms like a cluster of angry bees in my stomach,

and I plop into my chair heavily, offering her a smile in return. God, did she see the photos of me and Tate? Most likely. "Thank you, Mrs. Baldwin."

My father starts talking, Kincaid interjecting here and there, which allows me to retreat for a moment and gather my bearings. I run a hand through my hair, keeping my head bent so I don't blatantly stare at Ian, and I swear I feel his gaze on me.

Watching me.

Assessing.

"Still recovering from the party, Scarlett?" Miranda asks me out of the blue after the second-course plates have been taken away.

I jerk my gaze to hers, the knowing smile on her face filling me with dread. Maybe she never thought I was a good prospect for her son, and this is her chance to sink her claws into me. "There was nothing to recover from, Mrs. Baldwin."

"Not from what I saw."

"Miranda," my mother chastises, but Ian's mom completely ignores her.

"I saw the photos." She tilts her head in my direction. "Who didn't see those photos, hmm? They were everywhere. I had no idea you were seeing that Ramsey boy."

"I'm not," I start to protest, but my father talks right over me.

"I'm the one who put them together, Miranda. Thought they might make a fantastic couple," he says, chuckling. Taking all the credit as usual. "I know ol' Ian here has been dancing around my daughter for, what . . . the last couple years at least? But something needed to happen to force his hand. It was time for him to shit or get off the pot, don't you think?"

The entire table goes quiet while I try to process what my father just said.

Am I the shit? Or am I the toilet?

"Fitzy," Mom murmurs. "That probably wasn't an . . . appropriate thing to say in regard to your daughter."

"Oh, come on, we're all thinking it. I'm just the only one who's brave enough to say it." Dad turns his attention to Ian, who suddenly appears a little pale. "What are your intentions for my daughter?"

"I . . . don't have any intentions for her," Ian admits, his gaze falling to his lap.

I stare at him wordlessly, shocked he would just give up so easily. My gaze flits to Kincaid, who appears confused, before shifting to Miranda, who's smiling.

As if she's enjoying this conversation.

"You're a coward." My voice is loud. Heated. I'm speaking right at Ian, and when he barely lifts his head to look my way, he immediately glances at his mother. As if he needs her approval to . . . what? Talk to me?

Without thought I jump to my feet and exit the dining room, practically running back to my bedroom. I slam the door behind me and lock it, just before I fling myself onto the bed, clutching one of my pillows so I can cry into it.

Ian's mom is mean—and he does nothing to stop her.

My dad calls Ian out—and Ian makes it seem like he's not interested in me.

At all.

Strangely enough, Dad also takes credit for supposedly putting me and Tate together—a bold-faced lie I don't understand.

Men. That's at the root of almost every problem I'm currently dealing with. They're all ridiculous. It's like they're purposely trying to drive me crazy.

A sob escapes me, and I press the pillow harder against my face, letting the tears and frustration flow out of me. My entire body shaking with my sobs, my throat raw from the crying. When there's a light knock on the door, I sit up straight, wiping at my face, staring at the closed door almost with longing.

Is it Ian standing behind that door? Did he come to check on me? Because if he did, that would make up for everything. Even that look he sent his mother. I can't be mad at him for coming to check on me.

It's a sign that he cares.

Slipping off the bed, I pad my way across the thick rug, stopping just in front of the door and leaning my head against it, wishing I had x-ray vision. There's another knock, this one louder, and I startle, shifting away from the door.

"Scarlett, are you in there?"

I didn't think I could be any more disappointed than I already was, but I am.

Sighing, I unlock and open the door to find my father standing on the other side, an irritated expression on his face.

"Please don't tell me you're mad at me," I say as he enters my bedroom.

He shuts the door behind him and studies me, concern written all over his face. "Mad at you? Why the hell would I be mad at you? That damn kid is so freaking weak. Why can't he stand up and say he actually likes you? Is it because of his dragon-lady mother?"

My mouth drops open at my father's outburst. "I thought you liked the Baldwins?"

"I love Kincaid. He's my lawyer and my friend, but his wife? She's a bitch, and their son? He's a complete pussy." Dad rests his hands on his hips, scrutinizing me in a way I've never seen him do before. "What do you even see in that kid, huh? You've been mooning after him for years."

"I don't know." I shrug, suddenly uncomfortable. I don't want to admit this sort of thing to my father. "He's . . . cute."

Dad snorts. "You could do better."

I keep talking. "He's smart. Polite. Steady. Ambitious. I can count on him. He'd take care of me in the future, you know?"

My father's expression switches from interrogating to incredulous in a second. "He'll take *care* of you? Honey, you can take care of yourself for the rest of your life, and all of your future generations as well. You don't need a man to help you out in life, though it's nice to find someone who can be your partner, I can't deny it. Look at me and your mother."

They are the epitome of a perfect love story, and while I admire their relationship, I don't think it's the kind I'm going to find for myself. I'm built different, and they know it.

"You're too young to think like that, Scarlett. I don't want you to settle for something safe." He says *safe* like it's a dirty word. "You just turned eighteen! Shouldn't you be going out and living it up with your crazy friend Rachel?"

My father adores Rachel. I know he wishes I were more like her sometimes. "That's not my style. It never has been. I want something . . . quieter."

"What are you? A wannabe librarian? I'll tell you what happened—you've *settled* for something quieter, that's what you've done. You're far more special than that, sweetheart. I wish you could see it." He shakes his head. "You should've given that kid a chance, let him explain himself."

"Who? Ian?"

My father grimaces. "Hell no, not that guy. Tate Ramsey. I know you kicked him out pretty fast. Wouldn't even listen to what he was going to say to you. I think that was a mistake, Scarlett. That kid—he has promise."

"Dad . . ."

"Fuck that Ian guy. He's the worst. He will never stand up to his mother, so he sure as hell will never put you first. Mama will always know best. Can't you see that?"

He's wrong. People can change. Yes, Ian loves and respects his mother, but if he were to fall in love—maybe even with me—I *know* he would put his partner first. Look at my parents.

But you're built different, remember?

I shove the nagging voice inside of my head to the darkest corner of my brain.

"I'm not interested in Tate."

"Well, maybe you should show a little more interest in Tate so it would light a fire under Ian's ass and make him do something for once in his goddamn life!" My dad is roaring, he's so angry.

"Darling, please."

We both glance over to find my mother entering my room, shutting the door quietly behind her. "Our guests can probably hear you."

"I don't give a damn! Their boy is a menace." My father's tone is fierce.

"A menace?" Mom appears ready to burst out laughing. "That is not the way I would describe Ian Baldwin. You wish he was a menace."

"You know what I mean," Dad says irritably.

"Fitz. Darling. Please return to the living room and attend to our guests." Mom's gaze lands on mine, her smile reassuring. "Let Scarlett and I discuss a few things, and then we'll join you."

Dad strides toward me and hauls me into a hug, squeezing me tight. "I just want what's best for you, sweetie."

"I know, Dad." My voice is muffled against his chest.

He lets me go, reaching out to ruffle my hair, but I duck away from him at the last second, watching as he leaves my bedroom without another word.

"Your father means well," Mom starts the moment he's gone.

"I know."

"He doesn't like how Ian treats you."

No one does.

"Neither do I," she adds.

See?

"And that's why I think it might be smart of you to spend a little more time with Tate Ramsey."

My mouth pops open. "Are you serious? You really think so?"

She nods. "If you're truly interested in Ian, then this might be the best move to get him to do something about it—about you—finally."

Rachel basically said the same thing. So did my father.

Maybe they're all right. Maybe I should forget about Ian and focus on . . . Tate.

Okay, that sounds crazy. But everyone else might be onto something.

That is, if Tate is still even interested in me. After the way I treated him earlier, I wouldn't blame him at all if he rejected me as soundly as I just rejected him.

"But isn't that . . . tricking him?" I finally ask. "Tricking Ian into thinking he has to work harder to get me?"

Mom shrugs, her lips curving into the faintest smile. "Scarlett, you're going to learn that sometimes relationships—and love—are a bit of a game. We have to manipulate the situation in order to get what we want."

I'm frowning. This is the last thing I expected her to say. "Manipulate how?"

"Well, if, for instance, you're constantly texting Ian, that makes him less inclined to text you. He knows that you'll always reach out, so why should he bother?" The pointed look she sends my way hits home.

I do always text Ian, and very rarely does he text me first. I should wait for him for once, is what she's telling me.

"Acting like you're not interested in someone is also a good move," she suggests. "Oh, and when a man asks you out and you're dying to go out with him, reject him."

"What? Why?" That just sounds counterproductive.

"You want to look like you're living your very best life, right? That means you're so busy you don't have time to just pause your schedule for a man. If they think you're busy, that makes you sound even more interesting." Her laughter is nervous. "I know this sounds like a bunch of silly games, but trust me. It can work. Most of the time."

I think about what she said when we eventually leave my bedroom. As we settle back into our seats at the dining table, I ignore Ian and his mother for the rest of the evening. Eating my food and looking through them as if they don't even exist. The reassuring smiles both of my parents send in my direction throughout dinner make me feel stronger. As if I'm making them proud.

"Chin up," my dad used to always say when I was young and on the verge of tears. *"Keep your chin up, sweetheart. Don't let the bastards get you down."*

That is something he said to me time and again, and only now can I take it to heart.

I refuse to let the bastards get me down.

Even the sexy ones.

CHAPTER ELEVEN

TATE

I stew in my feelings all that evening and into the next day, pissed that I was rejected by a spoiled little rich girl. Kicked out of her penthouse apartment with the threat that she'll sic her daddy on me.

The very same daddy who hired my ass to perform at her birthday party, not that she cares.

Scarlett Lancaster. Who the hell does she think she is anyway?

I barely get out of bed, let alone leave my shitty little apartment, too worried that I've lost my shot at fame yet again. Until I can't take it anymore and hop in the shower, trying to wash off my anger and frustration over the whole situation.

Yeah, I need to get over it. Life moves on and so do I.

Feeling refreshed once I'm dressed, I order takeout from a shitty Chinese restaurant down the block and gorge myself on too much broccoli beef and chow mein, my mind wandering.

Running through what happened over and over again.

After dinner, I grab the notebook I like to scribble in. The one that is bulging with various lyrics I've written over the last few years. I flip through it for a few minutes, reading over some of the lines, mentally noting how much they've matured over the years. I guess I've evolved.

Look at me go.

Frustration rippling through me, I open up a fresh page, grab a pen, and start writing.

And don't stop for the next fifteen minutes.

By the time I'm finished, I'm breathing hard. Overwhelmed—but in a good way. I stare at the page I just filled, flipping it to read over the second side.

Well, look at me. I just wrote an entire song.

Inspired, I go on one of those SoundCloud-type sites, cruise through the samples they've got available, and zero in on a solid drumbeat that sounds good. I download it before I go and shut all the windows, but I can still hear all the outside noise that only New York provides.

The wail of a siren. The crash of something metal. Some dude yelling and a woman screaming back at him.

I pocket my phone and grab my guitar, making my way to the bathroom. It probably has the best acoustics out of any room in my tiny apartment, and that's due to it being in the center, surrounded by other rooms and with no windows.

Meaning there won't be much outside noise interfering with what I want to do.

Once I'm loaded with my bottle of water, the notebook, a pen, my guitar, and my phone, I shut the door and close the toilet lid before I sit.

And play.

Sing a little.

Write some more. Change a few lyrics, scribbling out the old words and adding new ones. I strum my guitar along with the beat of the drum sample over and over, making sure I've got the right chords, before I start to sing the song that was in my head only minutes ago in earnest. The lyrics flow out of me, and I'm smiling.

Playing.

Singing.

Until I eventually work up the courage to record what I've put together, which is a process. I do it over and over again, cursing out loud when I get something wrong. Kicking the edge of the tub when I hit the wrong chord or mess up the lyrics. It's a nasty little ordeal that ends up taking me hours, and when I'm finally finished, it's past one in the morning and I'm literally sweating.

But then I hit play on my phone and listen back to what I've got. I'm smiling. Nodding along with the beat. Singing along with the words.

I fucking love it.

It feels good, making something just for myself. Getting my feelings and frustrations out. Creating something out of nothing. Just my thoughts.

About a certain rich girl who drives me out of my mind.

I take a shower with the song playing on repeat on my phone, reveling in the sound. It goes a little harder than the stuff I've been working on currently. Not the mellow, introspective, "I need to do better" lyrics I've been writing. This is a little more . . .

Empowering.

Like, *Fuck you, Scarlett Lancaster. Just because your daddy's got loads of money, that doesn't make you better than me.*

I'm out of the shower in minutes, throwing on a pair of briefs before I take my phone to bed and mess around on it. Uploading the song everywhere I can. On every social media site I'm on. Even fucking YouTube, which is probably a mistake because someone can rip that shit off and blast it everywhere without my consent.

For the first time in what feels like forever, I don't give a damn. In my dreams this song would go viral. Last week, I wouldn't think it was possible. No one gave a shit about me.

Now? The potential is there. Though with my luck . . .

It won't happen.

I'm awakened by the sound of my phone ringing where I left it on the bed right next to me. It's covered by my comforter, so it takes me a second to find it, and when I do, I see Simon's name on the screen.

I don't even get a chance to greet him. He's talking the moment I hold the phone to my ear.

"What the fuck, man? You release a song and don't tell me about it? Roger is beside himself!"

"Good morning," I say in response, running a hand over my face. My voice is raspy and my body is sore. I feel like I've been run over by a truck.

"When the hell did you write and record a new song?"

"Last night."

Simon is quiet. I can hear him breathing, though. He sounds like an enraged bull, blowing through his nostrils. Preparing to charge.

"Last night?" I'm about to answer, but he forges on. "Where?"

I swallow hard, wishing I'd brought my water bottle with me to bed. I bet it's still on the bathroom counter. "Here. At my apartment."

"What the fuck are you talking about?"

I explain to him the process I used to make the song. How I recorded it on my phone. Then I realize . . .

"Wait a minute. Where did you hear it?"

"I woke up this morning with all sorts of notifications about you. I've got it set up so I know when media outlets are talking about you, and they mentioned you have a new song. A new fucking song, Tate! And instead of giving it to Roger, you uploaded it everywhere! To YouTube, for Christ's sakes!" Simon is yelling. I bet his face is red and his eyes are bulging and he's got that one vein in his forehead that pops every time he's pissed.

I can't even worry about it. I'm too focused on the fact that people are talking about the song.

"What are they saying?"

"Who?"

"Everyone—anyone. What are they saying about the song? Do they like it?"

My shoulders hunch up practically around my ears as I wait for the blow his words might bring.

"What are they saying? They fucking love it, of course. They want more. It's already gone viral on that clock app. Even on Facebook, and I know you didn't upload it there."

I scoff. "Who uses Facebook still?"

"Your mom. Your sweet little auntie." Simon chuckles. "Roger is dying to put it on the album. Said he'd send take-down notices right now, but he can't, since your ass still hasn't signed the contract."

Right. The contract.

I roll out of bed and shuffle to the window, pulling back the curtain to check out what's going on outside. My apartment is a fifth-floor walk-up, and it's nothing special. No doorman.

An old elevator that most of us avoid because it always gets stuck. But the rent is reasonable and the location is decent. I can't complain.

My gaze snags on a homeless man who just whipped out his dick and started pissing on the side of my building.

Great. There's one thing I can complain about.

"They're getting antsy," Simon says, his voice gruff.

"Who's getting antsy?" I play stupid on purpose because I'm stalling. I don't want to tell him I know exactly who he's talking about and that I'm fairly certain the deal might be dead in the water thanks to Scarlett kicking my ass out of her penthouse apartment.

And that definitely isn't what Simon wants to hear.

I turned that disappointment and frustration with Scarlett into a goddamn song, and look at me now. According to Simon, people are clamoring for more. I took a chance and put together something in my bathroom, recorded it on my phone, and everyone is still talking about me.

Maybe they're talking about me even more. I don't know, but I can't believe my luck.

It continues to work in my favor.

"You know exactly who. Roger. The entire Irresistible Records team. They want the contract. They're dying for the contract so they can get this deal started, especially since you released that song. I swear Roger has already bought you a one-way plane ticket to Los Angeles."

"Why doesn't he fly me on the label's private jet?" That's what they used to do back in the day, but maybe I'm not as much of a huge deal as I used to be.

"They got rid of the plane."

"Really? Why?"

"Bad publicity. Instead, they sold it and announced they

were reducing their carbon footprint. Now they look like superstars who are all for saving the environment."

I wonder at their ulterior motives, but I'm not going to question it now. "Love that they're so conscious."

"It's the right thing to do." Simon takes a deep breath. "Listen, we need to get back on track. What's going on with Scarlett Lancaster? You convince her to be your girlfriend yet?"

I'm about to say no when he keeps talking. "Come on, Tate. Don't say no. Just lay some of that charm on the girl and convince her the two of you can make magic together. It's not too far off the mark. Now you're writing songs about her and breaking the fucking internet."

Alarm makes my spine stiffen. "How do you know the song is about her?"

"It's called 'Red,' Tate. You say the word 'scarlet' in there a couple of times. 'Happy birthday.' 'Pink dress.' Shit like that. The clues are all right there in the lyrics. Everyone knows the song is about her, and they are eating it up." Simon sounds pleased. He'd much rather talk about the positive stuff, and I don't blame him. "If she hears that song and still doesn't want to be with you, then you're fucked, my friend."

Shit. When I was writing it—even secretly dreaming about it going viral—I never imagined Scarlett would hear the song and get mad over it. The lyrics don't show her in the best light. Is she going to be mad?

Probably. When it comes to dealing with Scarlett, I don't always make the best choices.

"I'm sure she loves it," I say with way more confidence than I feel.

"We can all hope, and I can hold off Roger for only so long. Just fucking sign the contract and do your best to convince her to be your girlfriend or whatever before you leave for Los

Angeles. Maybe it'll work, maybe it won't. And what are they going to do anyway if she doesn't show up in LA? Take the deal away from you?"

"Yes, that's exactly what they would do, Simon, and you know it. Those clauses are airtight. I break it, I'm done. I'm not putting my career at risk. Not again." I rub the back of my neck, my gaze still tracking the man staggering around, an empty vodka bottle clutched in one hand. No wonder he had to take a piss, if he drank that entire bottle.

"You have nothing to worry about. They want you. They're salivating over the chance to make another album with you. Roger told you himself that he jizzes his pants every time he sees videos of you singing at that party. He's got a massive hard-on for you," Simon explains.

"If you think that's going to convince me to go for it, I hate to break it to you, but that is the last thing I want to hear, Simon. I don't want to think about Roger and his giant boner for my singing." I know none of what Roger says is literal, but still.

"He's a fan. He might possibly be your number one fan, so I don't see how the little heiress being your girlfriend or not is going to actually ruin this deal."

"You're not even making sense. You just told me a few days ago that Scarlett was the only way I'd get this deal secured. Now you're like, 'Fuck it, just sign it.' No way, bro." My voice is flat. My thoughts bleak. I press my forehead against the window, staring out at my shitty little neighborhood. "I'd rather pass than lie to them. I'm not about that anymore."

Another sigh sounds in my ear, this one softer. "What, you've got morals now?"

"You're damn right, I've got morals." Even though I'm perfectly willing to participate in a fake relationship if I can still get Scarlett on board. "Can't you renegotiate this? Send them a counter?"

"I was trying to avoid that. Hoping you would just sign and we could move forward."

"I'm not signing. Not with that clause attached—Scarlett would barely listen to me, so I'm going to have to let this go." My voice is firm. I say nothing else. Simon remains quiet too, and I begin to sweat.

But I'm not backing down from this point.

"Fine, you're right. I get it." Simon pauses, and I swear I can feel his disappointment through the phone. "I'll let them know you're passing."

My heart feels like it dropped into my balls at the finality of his words, panic flaring inside of me. "*No.* Wait a minute—don't tell Roger I'm passing yet."

"Oh, come on, kid. I can't stall him for much longer. Like I said, he's getting antsy. Impatient. He wants that song. He wants the entire album to sound exactly like that song you made in your freaking bathroom."

"He told you that?" I'm incredulous.

"Yes, he told me exactly that." Simon sighs. "You got another idea to try and get her to do this? Or do you think that song will work?"

I sang about her giving me head and how she gave me scars and left me for dead. Not the most positive anthem for my so-called relationship with Scarlett. I don't bother answering his question because I'm now worried the song will work against me.

"Just give me the rest of the afternoon. I'll try and put something together." What exactly, I'm not sure, but I could probably convince her. Right? Maybe I could just call Scarlett. Text her. Go to her place—

No, I'm not going to her place unannounced. That's asking

for an ass beating from a certain Fitzy Lancaster. I bet that motherfucker would enjoy it too.

"I'll ignore his calls for the rest of the day. But I need an answer by tonight. You have to give me a firm yes or no, got it?"

"Got it."

"Call me later." He ends the call before I can respond.

A frustrated sigh leaves me, and I toss my phone onto my bed, running a hand through my already fucked-up hair. It needs a cut. And I need a shower to wake up, come up with a plan.

Showers always help me think, and I need to clear my head and eat a decent meal and figure out how I'm going to save this record deal that's landed in my lap.

I'd be an idiot to just let it go. Why do they want her as my girlfriend so badly?

Like a masochist, I pick my phone back up and refresh the Google search I have of me and Scarlett. A bunch of new photos and articles pop up, most of them about the song. Speculation about the lyrics. Are we already going through a rough patch? Did the media attention put our relationship under stress? Are we over when we've barely begun?

This is wild. We're not even in a real relationship, and they're worried we're already over.

Most of the photos are the same ones from the night of her party, though now they're appearing with different angles. All the headlines scream worry over the song, though they all praise it too. The lyrics, the rich sound of my voice, the almost tinny quality that gives the song a nostalgic sound.

That part is hilarious. Of course it sounds vaguely tinny. I recorded it in my bathroom late at night, on a creative high and believing in myself for the first time since I don't remember when.

That's a lie. I remember the last time I felt this way.

Saturday night. At Scarlett's birthday party.

Those articles and photos and the endless social media posts and tags are exactly why the execs at Irresistible want Scarlett as part of the deal. Together, we generate a lot of buzz—now more so than ever thanks to the song.

"Red." I did write it for her. For her sexy lips and her vicious heart and that beautiful face.

Thanks to that song, the media is paying closer attention to us than ever, and while it's vaguely annoying and completely over the top, it's also kind of mind blowing how easy it is to manipulate the general public. No matter what, it's publicity.

Free publicity.

And that's the key.

That's what I need to make a go of this singer career again.

I open Instagram and check my follower count—it's grown. No surprise. I'm at over 1.5 million now. I look at the tagged photos and reels and grimace at all the fuzzy, horrible photos of the two of us. Terrible angles. My mouth hanging open as I talk to Scarlett. Her eyes wide and unblinking as she stares at me. She looks like she wants to sock me in the face.

She also looks pretty damn hot in that pink dress. I still stand by that assessment.

I remember yet again how good it felt to perform onstage that night. All those women screaming for me, singing the words to my old songs. The last couple of years I looked at those songs with nothing but bitter disappointment in my heart, but Saturday night, hearing all those high-pitched female voices singing along, it made me look at my career with Five Car Pileup in a different light.

Yeah, I fucked it all up and ruined my reputation, but our

music actually touched lives. We might've released nothing but a bunch of bad pop songs, but all those girls haven't forgotten them. They freaking loved us.

And I shit all over them. I shit all over the band and our management and the record label. Though I wasn't alone in this mess. My other bandmates, my friends, my enemies, they contributed to the wreckage too.

Damn it, I want another shot. I want to prove that I can create quality music that the general public wants to listen to. I can spit out some homegrown, bathroom-recorded bullshit, and people are losing their minds over it.

I want to keep that up. I want to write songs and sing them. I want to make an album in a quality studio and show the world I can make a comeback and they're all going to want to witness it.

That's what I want. More than anything else in the world.

Without thought I switch over to my text messages and bring up Scarlett's phone number. Yeah, I had some help obtaining it, and I would never tell anyone who got it for me—it was Simon; he's a fucking magician—and I've resisted texting her since I was basically kicked out of her home.

But fuck it. I'm texting her. I need to try.

One more time.

Me: Hey. It's Tate. I know you're probably mad at me. I know you think I'm a giant fuckup and maybe you hate that new song, but if I could get just thirty minutes of your time later this afternoon and you'd give me one more shot, I'd love to talk to you.

She doesn't respond for almost twenty minutes because this girl knows just how to keep me dangling on a string. Or she might've blocked me. I suppose I can't blame her. She told me flat out to leave her alone.

Finally I receive a response.

Scarlett: Okay.

That's it? That's her response? Just . . .

Okay?

Then another text comes through.

Scarlett: Where do you want to meet? What time?

I leap off the bed and pump my fist in the air like I just won the Super Bowl.

Maybe I can make this work after all.

CHAPTER TWELVE

SCARLETT

The restaurant I'm meeting Tate at is actually in our neighborhood, not too far from where I live with my family, though I've never been here. It's small and quiet, and since we're meeting at two thirty in the afternoon, it's not very busy either. Which I suppose is good. Maybe no one will notice us.

I'm still not sure how I feel about the possibility that people could react to catching us together again.

The hype over me and Tate possibly being a couple still hasn't died down. Thanks to the song I first heard on TikTok, it's only ramped up. Speculation abounds; all the gossip sites and morning shows and social media are still asking if we're an actual couple. Wondering if Tate ruined everything between us because of the song. The lyrics.

He makes it sound like I ruined his life, which is kind of dramatic. Rachel can't get over him writing a song about me. I heard about it from her first, she was so excited. Calling me first thing in the morning screaming, "Did you hear this?"

I don't understand him. Not too sure what he wants from me. I blew him off when he came to our place, but after he left,

I felt . . . bad. I treated him terribly. Worse, I acted like a bratty little baby.

Now here he is, wanting to meet with me again, and I vow I'm not going to act like a child. I'm eighteen. Graduated from high school and ready to go on a trip around Europe in the fall. Taking a gap year because my parents both think it's a good idea I get out and experience a few things before I go on to college. They're not against higher education, even though neither of them got a degree or even took a few classes.

They want me to live my life, especially my dad. He always talks about dreams and adventures and doing something wild and crazy. Now that I went and kissed Tate Ramsey, he finally believes I have it in me to embark on something bigger than myself. Maybe he's right.

But then again, there's that tiny part of me that doesn't believe it could happen . . .

I enter the restaurant accompanied by a soft gust of wind that catches my hair, making it fly into my face. I push the wayward strands out of my eyes, glancing around the tiny café to see Tate sitting in the farthest, darkest corner of the building. The moment our gazes catch, his lips curl into a faint smile and he rises to his feet.

I forgot how tall he is. How impressively broad his shoulders are. He's dressed in black again—a T-shirt that clings to his muscular arms and flat abs in a most appealing way that has me checking him out, my gaze lingering.

Then I realize I'm just standing there like a salivating idiot, so I push myself out of my fugue state and make my way toward his table, taking deep breaths to calm my suddenly racing heartbeat. There are way too many chaotic thoughts running through my mind. My pulse is erratic in my wrist, my neck—God, even my head is pounding incessantly.

This reaction can't be from his presence or because of the way he's smiling at me—which, I can't lie, is quite nice. Almost reassuring. No, this must be nerves. And curiosity.

What more could he want from me? Daddy already paid him. Maybe he wants to apologize for the song. The response hasn't been negative, but the conversation it's drummed up about our relationship is completely over the top. Everyone has us already split.

And we were never actually together.

"Glad you made it," Tate says when I'm close enough that I can hear him, his rich, deep voice wrapping all around me. That charming smile still plastered on his face. He pulls me in for a brief hug, his arms coming around me quickly, his lips pressed against my cheek, and I'm speechless.

I don't recall ever feeling this way with Ian. Did I react like this when he touched me? Did he ever dare try to kiss me on the cheek?

No. Never.

Tate goes to the chair opposite his and pulls it out for me like a gentleman. "Have a seat."

I settle in without a word, keeping my head bent, trying to hide the fact that I'm blushing. That I have no idea what to say.

How do I even start this conversation? His mere presence has stolen all my words, leaving me speechless, which rarely happens. I may be quiet, but I usually know how to make conversation.

"Are you hungry?" he asks once he's seated across from me, his fingers curled around the edge of the menu. "I hear their sandwiches are good."

"I already ate." I finally lift my head to meet his gaze and find he's already watching me. Those deep-blue eyes are the kind a person could get lost in if they don't watch it, and I shake my head a little, leaning back.

Needing the distance.

"Have dessert then." He flips the menu to the back and gazes at the items listed. "Looks like they have a decent selection. And I'm guessing you have a sweet tooth."

"What do you mean?" Is he implying I'm . . . fat? I've always wished I were thinner, but it's just not in my genes. My mother is on the curvier side, and I inherited that from her, so I have more boobs and butt than my friends.

I wouldn't call myself overweight, but I am definitely self-conscious around my skinny friends . . .

"At your party, you had eighteen birthday cakes." His gaze finds mine once more, his expression grave. "I assumed you like sweets. Maybe I was wrong."

"No, I love cake." I clamp my lips together, hating how my answer sounded. "My parents were the ones who made sure there were eighteen cakes. Kind of a play on Marie Antoinette, you know? Let them eat cake?"

"She was murdered for saying that," Tate murmurs.

"She was a victim of the French royalty and society." I will defend Marie Antoinette until I die. That poor woman was forced to marry the future king of France, who had no interest in her whatsoever. She was the one responsible for bringing the next heir into the world, and it was supposedly her fault she had a girl first.

I know we're nothing like European royalty, but sometimes the pressures the Lancaster family faces feel as if we're descended from a royal family. The expectations, the gossip . . . it all can be a lot. My father is the youngest of his brothers and the most open minded, thank God. He pulls away from his brothers more often than not, and I think my mother is a big influence on him as well.

I'm grateful for it. I know I wouldn't want my uncle Reggie as my father. He's the worst one.

"You're right. She died a tragic death due to lies that were told about her by her own son," Tate says.

I'm impressed by his knowledge. "He was forced to say those things. They had a child in jail, and they were abusing him."

"True." Tate rests his elbow on the table and props his chin on his fist, studying me, his gaze searching as it roams over my face. "I didn't think we'd ever get into a debate over Marie Antoinette."

This is a silly conversation, he's most likely saying. "I don't necessarily think we're debating. Pretty sure we're on the same side."

"I agree." He points at an item on the menu. "They have chocolate éclairs. Maybe we should have one in honor of Marie and France."

"I don't know . . ." A chocolate éclair sounds delicious, but they're so messy.

"We could split one," he suggests.

"Okay," I agree right as the server appears tableside.

Tate orders the chocolate éclair for us, and I ask for a vanilla latte.

"I'll take one too," Tate says, handing the menus to the server, who's blatantly staring at him.

I'm sure she recognizes him. He's become so popular again thanks to the coverage from my party; I'd bet he gets recognized just walking down the street. He must be having a surreal moment from all the attention he's received, but I still don't understand why he wanted to see me.

"Why exactly did you want to meet with me yet again?" I ask once the server is gone.

"Can't a guy who kissed you Saturday night ask you out on a date?" His smile is teasing. Downright flirtatious.

"This is a date?" My eyes feel like they want to bug out of my head.

He drops his arms to his sides and leans back in his chair, sprawling his long legs out. He's wearing black trousers and a black shirt, while I'm wearing a pink dress. Not like the monstrosity I wore at my party, but I do sense a theme here. "That's what I thought it was. Maybe you misunderstood me?"

I think I'm in shock, and I can't help but feel a little . . . excited. Tate keeps coming around, so he must be interested, right?

I remember what my mom told me about playing it cool, and I decide to go with her advice. "I figured it was just two . . . friends getting together to chat. You asked for another chance, right?"

"Right." He blows out a breath and scooches closer, resting his elbows on the edge of the table. "I wanted to talk to you about the . . . song."

"The song." I nod.

"You've heard it?" His eyebrows shoot up, and he has this expectant look on his face.

"Yes. Only parts of it, though." It's currently being played on repeat all over social media. People—mostly women around my age—have created countless video montages featuring photos of the two of us together set to that song. Specifically the lyrics that go like this:

Scarlet red
Like your lips
Like your heart
Like the scars
That you left
On my skin
In sin
Head you gave
So depraved

Yeah, I bet he wishes I gave him head.

That line is mortifying, but I can't focus on it at the moment.

"And what did you think of it?" he asks.

"It was . . . good," I admit reluctantly. I can't lie to him. The song is good. He sounds great. "I thought I saw it mentioned somewhere that you recorded it in your bathroom?"

"Yeah." He chuckles, ducking his head for a moment. Like he's almost embarrassed. "I was . . . all fired up after seeing you, and I decided to write out all of my frustrations. I have a notebook full of bits and pieces. Lyrics. Lines."

"I like to journal sometimes too," I tell him, deciding to share a small piece of myself. No one really knows that I sometimes put down my thoughts in my journal. "It's a good way to get things out. Memories for later."

"I know what you mean." Tate nods, his expression thoughtful. "Anyway, I realized I was actually putting together a song, and next thing I know, I'm in my bathroom, because it has pretty decent acoustics, and I'm recording the song on my phone."

"All by yourself?"

He nods.

"Without a studio?"

"Can you believe it?" He seems pretty proud of himself. "I was exhausted by the time I was done, and I thought, 'What could it hurt, uploading the song on a few sites?' So I uploaded them and then passed out. Next thing I know, I'm waking up to my manager losing his mind and the song already going viral."

He passed out. Was he drunk? Did he do drugs? I'm not about to ask him. It's none of my business, and I don't want to offend him.

"That's a great story," I say softly.

"You know what makes it even better?" He doesn't wait for me to respond. "It's the truth. That's exactly how it played out."

"And the song. It's really about me?" My name is even said in the song, though I wondered if I was overthinking it. Maybe he's just talking about the color. The song is called "Red," after all.

"It's really about you," he confirms, his voice just as soft. He has a really nice one, by the way. His voice. It's smooth and deep, sometimes with a hint of a rasp that's . . . sexy.

Oh God. I need to watch it before I fall under his spell.

"You're not mad about the song, are you?" he asks when I still haven't said anything.

"No." I shake my head, mulling over my feelings. When I first heard it, I was vaguely offended, but the more I listened to it, the more I realized it's flattering, that he would write a song about me.

That he's thinking about me.

That I make him feel something, even if it's anger or frustration.

It's better than making someone feel nothing at all.

"I'm glad. I might've been frustrated when I wrote it, but I think it's more of a lusty tale than anything," he says, his relief apparent.

"Lusty?" There's a word I don't hear used much.

"Yeah. Like I'm longing for her and lusting after her and I wish she felt the same way." He's referring to me as *her*, and it's a little confusing.

"Is that how you really feel?" The question leaves me before I can think too much about it, and the moment the words are out there, I wish I could take them back.

I can't, though. He's watching me with a certain look in his eyes. Like he's surprised by my question but he likes that I asked it.

He likes it a lot.

Which is stupid. I know it's stupid. Ian has shown me who

he really is. And so has Tate. He's the one who keeps reaching out like he might actually be interested.

Forget my chances with Ian. Maybe I have a chance with . . . Tate?

Rachel will absolutely die if something ever happens between us.

The server chooses that moment to appear with a tray laden with our drinks and the éclair on one plate. She sets our lattes in front of us, then settles the éclair in between us, smiling at Tate.

"Do you need anything else?"

"This is perfect, thanks." He flashes that superstar smile at her, and I swear I witness her knees buckle.

I stare at her, wishing she'd talk a little more so I wouldn't have to be alone with him.

He's going to say no to my question. I just know it. And yet again, I'll be left humiliated.

Rejected.

"I just want you to know that I loved your music when I was younger. Five Car Pileup was my favorite band," the server gushes, coming to my rescue and stalling my eventual humiliation.

Tate nods, ever so humble. "Thank you."

"And I saw the videos of your performance at that heiress's party Saturday night. You were wonderful."

I sit up straight at being referred to as *that heiress*. Again, I'm relegated to nothing. She doesn't even realize I'm literally that heiress.

"I appreciate that. It felt good to perform again," Tate says.

"I hope you continue to sing. You were fun to watch. Sexy." She blushes. Smiles. Clutches the tray in front of her like a shield.

I clear my throat, now annoyed at her lingering, and she finally takes the hint, sending a quick look my way.

"Let me know if you need anything else," the server says.

"What was your name?" Tate asks.

If he asks for her number right in front of me, I'm going to lose it.

The server beams. "Callie."

"Well, Callie, it was nice meeting you."

She nods, glances over at me for like half a second, and then runs away, heading to the kitchen.

"Sorry," Tate says to me once the server is gone. "That usually doesn't happen anymore."

"I guess your circumstances have changed." I take a sip of my latte, relieved to find it's not too hot.

"She didn't realize you were the heiress." Tate smiles, picking up his fork.

"No one knows who I am. Though they know my family. Everyone has heard of the Lancasters."

"You're practically American royalty. Like the Vanderbilts or the Rockefellers."

"It's a lot," I say with a sigh.

He smiles. "Right. It's tough coming from such a prominent, wealthy family."

"It's truly not easy." I take another sip from my latte, hating how I always feel like I must defend myself. "Money doesn't buy happiness, you know."

"Oh, trust me. I know. But it definitely makes life easier." He takes his fork and lodges it right in the middle of the chocolate-frosted éclair, cutting it in half. The cream oozes out of both ends, making an absolute mess, and I'm shocked when he forks up his half and shoves the entire thing in his mouth.

I watch as he chews, wishing I could throw all those years

of proper breeding and polite manners out the window and shove my half of the éclair in my mouth like Tate. My mother would have a fit if she ever saw me do something like that.

"How's the éclair?" I ask after he swallows.

"Delicious." He points his fork at my half. "You should eat that."

I stare at the semidestroyed half left behind and reach for my fork, tugging a flaky piece of pastry across the plate. "I can't remember the last time I had one of these."

"You only live once," he suggests, and I glance up at him, realizing that he's right.

We do only live once. We need to make the most of what we've got and enjoy it while it's all happening. Instead of wasting away and wondering if someone is going to notice. Going to care. Going to make a move.

Why should I give someone else the power when I can take care of myself?

I stab my fork into the pastry and bring it to my lips, the scent of the thick layer of chocolate making me hum with approval just before I place it carefully in my mouth.

Oh my God. The pastry is flaky, buttery goodness, and the chocolate is a thick, sweet frosting that combines perfectly with the airy cream.

Pulling the plate closer to me, I start shoveling it in, just like Tate did, though with a tad more decorum. I don't stop until the éclair is gone, and I fleetingly wonder if he'd judge me for picking up the plate and licking it.

Realizing he'd most definitely judge me, I decide against it.

"I guess you liked it," he says once I'm finished and taking a sip of my latte.

"It was delicious."

He smiles, and it hits me that he never answered my

question. If he actually feels that way for me, like how he described in his song. Maybe he avoided the question because the truth is he doesn't feel that way. Not even close. It's all a show he's putting on for the public to get more likes. To make more money. To get further ahead in his revitalized career.

I guess I don't blame him. He destroyed himself, and now he's the proverbial phoenix rising from the ashes. People rarely get a second chance, so he needs to take advantage of it.

I completely understand.

I do.

"Look." His gaze meets mine when I first speak, and I offer him a weak smile. "I know you said you wanted another chance to speak to me, and I appreciate it. I do. Maybe you wanted to apologize for what happened. Or for the song. But you don't have to. I'm not mad. Hopefully we can look back at this small moment in time someday with fondness and remember how silly it all was. And you'll have your career back, bigger and brighter than ever."

I push my chair back and rise to my feet, slinging my bag over my shoulder, noting how his gaze stays locked on me the entire time. "I wish you nothing but success, Tate," I murmur to him.

Just as I turn and practically run out of the restaurant.

CHAPTER THIRTEEN

TATE

I sit there for a moment, processing what she said, before I'm spurred into action and leap to my feet, chasing after her. The server yells out a "hey" as I start to exit through the café's front door, and I stop, reaching for my wallet. Slapping a couple of twenties on the hostess stand before I hightail it out of there.

The second I'm outside, I stop in front of the café and whip my head left, then right. Then left again, squinting as I see the back of a familiar dark head walking at a pretty fast clip. I launch after her, calling her name, but she doesn't even acknowledge me.

And I know she has to hear me.

I push my way through the crowded sidewalk until I'm practically right beside her, keeping pace with her brisk walk. "Where are you going?"

"I'm trying to leave this . . . meeting with some dignity." She lifts her chin, putting on the haughty princess act.

Can't deny it—she's pretty fucking hot when she's rocking that vibe.

"Meeting? Dignity?" I'm so fucking confused. "What happened back there?"

"Absolutely nothing." She comes to a complete stop in the center of the sidewalk, and I do too, people pushing past us, annoyed that we're blocking them. "And that's fine. Really."

No, it's definitely not fine. I don't get why she keeps saying stuff like that.

"Be real with me, Scar." I reach out, lightly grabbing hold of her elbow, and electricity sparks where my fingers press into her soft skin. "What's wrong?"

She turns her head to the side, her lips pressed together. It's like she doesn't want to look at me, and she even tugs her arm out of my grip. "You didn't answer my question."

"What question?"

"If you actually felt that way about me. When you were describing the song earlier." She fully faces me once more, and she looks like she could crumple under the pressure at any moment. As if she's on the verge of tears. "It's okay if you were just caught up in an idea. I know the reality isn't as great as the fantasy."

I'm frowning. Is that what she really believes?

"Come on. You don't really like me like that." I frown. "Do you?"

She wraps her arms around her middle, as if she's cold. "No. I barely even know you."

"Exactly. I barely know you too." I duck my head a little, trying to meet her downward gaze. She reluctantly glances in my direction. "But we can get to know each other."

"What do you mean?" she asks warily.

"What if I said I had a proposition for you." I lean back on my heels, trying to play it cool, even though my heart starts to beat in double time.

"What kind of proposition?"

"A . . . business deal, if you will." I glance around before I grab her hand and tug her toward an alcove right next to a store, where we can talk and be out of the way. "Hear me out."

"What kind of business deal are you talking about?" She yanks her hand from mine, and strangely enough, I miss her touch.

"Look." I offer her a smile. Rest one hand on my hip while I run the other hand through my hair. "This is going to sound crazy."

"Life has been pretty crazy ever since I met you."

True. But not in a bad way. At least, not for me.

"This is going to be the craziest thing yet."

"Just tell me." Impatience laces her voice, and she even rolls her eyes.

"I've been offered a record deal. With my old label." I smile at her, wishing I could tell her just how important this is. But I feel like it would be a waste of words. I just need to get to the heart of it and see what she says.

"That's great." There is zero enthusiasm in her tone.

"It really is, but here's the crazy part." I hesitate. "They think we're together."

She frowns.

"You and me," I continue.

"Like we're in a relationship?" Her eyebrows shoot up. "Like what everyone else is saying?"

"Exactly. And they love it. They think we are a great story. Two kids in love, me writing songs about you. It's a total gimmick they want to use." And exploit.

"Is it some sort of gimmick you came up with first?" Her question is pointed, her eyes narrowed.

"I wasn't thinking about gimmicks the night of your party or when I wrote that song. I was just . . . feeling it."

The doubtful look on her face tells me she's not buying my explanation.

"The only way I can get this record deal is if you're a part of it." I pause. "As my girlfriend."

Her mouth drops open, and she doesn't say anything. She even looks around, as if she's searching for an opportunity to escape, and I take a step closer to her, tempted to grab hold of her so she doesn't bail on me.

"You're serious," she finally says.

"Dead serious." I nod.

"But we're not together."

"We can pretend to be. It's working out pretty well so far." I smile.

She scowls.

My smile drops.

"This is ridiculous," she mutters.

"It actually happens all the time. Fake relationships in Hollywood? That's a total thing."

"We're not in Hollywood, though," she points out.

"We could be." I try smiling again. "That's the other part of the deal. They want me to make the album at a studio in Los Angeles. And they want you to come with me."

Her mouth hangs open again. "I don't even know you."

"We could definitely get to know each other."

"What if I don't like you?"

"I'm fairly irresistible." I'm wearing a big grin, trying to be my old charming self, but Scarlett isn't having it. "What do you say?"

She crosses her arms in front of her. "I think I've heard enough."

"And you're going to say no?" I wince, bracing myself.

"I'm definitely saying no."

Damn it.

"Why?" Why can't shit ever go my way? Why can't she be completely enamored with me and willing to do whatever I say? Any other woman would be totally down. They'd kill for the opportunity to go to sunny Southern California and let me make a record while they were off frolicking at the beach and spending their money. Going out with me on occasion and letting me grope them—lovingly—for the cameras, putting on a show.

Not this girl. She'd rather run from me like I'm a flesh-eating zombie.

"This is the worst idea I've ever heard. I don't even think I like you."

Now I'm on the defensive. "I'm not too sure if I like you much either."

"Then how are we going to be believable as a couple? Did you think that part through? Doubtful." She shoves at my shoulder and then takes off again, her pink skirt fluttering in the breeze.

I jog after her, impressed by her speed. "This will help you out too, you know. Make you stand out from the crowd."

"Maybe I don't want that. I'm not a fame whore like you." She doesn't even slow down.

Ouch. She knows just where to stick me.

"I know you're trying to stand on your own two feet," I call after her.

"Please." She tosses her head, her hair flying. "I don't matter to anyone. If I were even to go through with this, they'd only pay attention to you. This is all for you and your reemerging career. I gain nothing from this. You just want to use me for the media attention."

I think about what she said to me earlier. How no one

knows who she is. How she's lost in the Lancaster family and not seen as an individual. "If we play up the fact that you're my muse and you're the only reason I actually have a career again, I think they might sit up and take notice."

Her steps slow, her gaze finding mine quickly before she looks away again. "No one will believe that."

"*Everyone* will. They'll believe anything they're fed, especially when it's a romance like ours. Come on, I just wrote that song about you, and they're all dying over it. You're totally my muse."

She sends me an incredulous look before she grabs hold of my hand and drags me through the crowd so we're standing right in front of the window of a tiny deli. The touch of her hand in mine sends an electric bolt straight up my arm, leaving me unsettled, and when she lets go of my hand to cross her arms in front of her chest once again, I'm disappointed that she's not touching me.

I rub at my chest, trying to ease the sudden throbbing of my heart.

"This is so unbelievable." A huff of laughter falls from her lush, pink-glossed lips, and she shakes her head. "There is no romance between us, Tate."

"Our fake romance then. Can't you see we can spin it any way we want? With everyone hanging on our every word, just dying to see us together again, we can portray ourselves however we want to look to the public."

"Will they actually buy it?" she asks, her voice soft.

"They'll buy it if we sell it to them. We can do this. Look at how easily they believe we're already together." Unable to help myself, I reach out and grab her shoulders, holding her gently. "This is my last shot at making something of my singing career. I've been working on some songs and writing lyrics for the last year, like I somehow knew this was coming. And for whatever reason, I'm being given another chance. They want me again. My manager. My record label. This is big, and I don't want to screw this up now. All because they want me to have a girlfriend who isn't actually mine. That's why I need you, Scarlett. When I mentioned to my manager I wanted to write the lyrics for every song on my new album, he warned me they'd tell me no. But after the immediate success of 'Red' and me letting them know you're my muse, I think they might agree."

Scarlett grimaces. "But it's nothing but lies."

"Only to you, but only because you know the truth. They don't know about you and me." Holy shit, that would make a great song title. "The real you and me. I can see it—if we're on each other's side? We can convince the world of *anything*."

She takes a step back, and my hands fall away from her arms. I like touching her. When my hands are on her, I feel . . . connected to her. And now the connection is gone, just like that. "And what do I get out of this scenario, hmm? From my point of view, you're the only one with all the benefits."

"You finally become your own person. Not just that Lancaster girl or that heiress. You become *the* Scarlett Lancaster."

"I already am Scarlett Lancaster." She rolls her eyes, obviously frustrated with me.

"But how do people refer to you? Can your name stand on its own? Or is it always 'the daughter of Fitzgerald Lancaster, Scarlett'? Wouldn't you prefer everyone forgot ol' Fitzy once and for all and focused only on his beautiful daughter instead?"

She's quiet for a moment, staring at me, and I swear the city noise fades. Until I can't hear anything but the sound of her breathing. The sweet lilt of her voice.

"You think I'm beautiful?" Her voice is barely a whisper, the doubt in her gaze . . .

Surprising.

I tilt my head, letting my gaze blatantly roam all over that beautifully etched face. The fine cheekbones and elegant nose and that damn sexy mouth. "Come on, Scar. Don't you ever look in the mirror? You gotta know you're stunning."

She shrugs. Glances around as if what I said made her uncomfortable and she can't meet my gaze. "I don't know. I've been chasing after the same guy for years, and he never really notices me. Most of the time I feel like I'm invisible."

That guy is a giant fuckup. And I'm going to take where he messed up with Scarlett and turn it into my opportunity.

"You're definitely not invisible." I take a step closer. "Forget him. Focus on me instead. Let him chase after you when he thinks you're with me."

"I doubt he'd even care." She sinks her teeth into her lower lip, looking unsure.

I'd love to ask her why his opinion of her matters so much when he doesn't seem that into her. She's young and gorgeous and rich—there should be a ton of guys chasing after her.

But if I can convince everyone she's mine . . .

Look, if she were actually taken, that guy—or girl, hey, you never know—would have been right by her side the entire time at her birthday party. I know if this girl were mine, I'd never let her out of my sight. She's too damn beautiful to be ignored.

An idea hits me out of nowhere, and I decide to shoot my shot.

"Want to make that guy jealous?"

Her answer is immediate. "How could I do that?"

"Pretend you're with someone else." I grin. "Like me."

She's quiet for a moment, hopefully contemplating my idea. I shove my hands into my trouser pockets, waiting on her answer, hoping like hell she doesn't turn me down.

"This could get messy," she finally says.

My answer is immediate, my relief just on the horizon.

"Not if we get lawyers involved. My manager has a team of lawyers. They could have papers drawn up by tomorrow morning. You can add whatever clauses you want," I suggest, feeling desperate.

Desperate for her to agree. Desperate for her to play pretend with me, just for a little while. I *need* this record deal. I want it so fuckin' bad I can practically taste it. And the only person who can help me get it is . . .

Her.

"There will be a nondisclosure included in the agreement, of course. Something that will protect us both. We wouldn't want the truth to get out, that our relationship is fake," I add, trying to reassure her.

"Right. Of course. That would be embarrassing." She nods, her gaze finding mine yet again, hers troubled. "You really think people would believe we're together?"

"They already think we're together, Scar," I say gently. "We're all over the internet. I'm tagged in photos on social media all damn day and night. As a matter of fact . . ."

I go silent, and her eyes widen slightly. "As a matter of fact, what?"

"We probably shouldn't have this sort of discussion on the street, out in public." I glance around, suddenly afraid someone is listening.

"No one is paying attention to us." She waves a dismissive hand.

"Pretty sure everyone who passes by us is paying attention." I make eye contact with a woman who walks by, her eyes lighting up as she recognizes me. *Shit.* "They know who I am."

"It's always about you, isn't it." Her droll tone would almost be amusing if I weren't close to freaking the hell out.

"I'm being serious. Watch them. They recognize me. Us."

Scarlett does as I suggest, her gaze following people as they walk along the sidewalk, the majority of them glancing over at us with recognition in their gazes. I hear giggling and glance over my shoulder to see two teenagers blatantly staring at the both of us, one of them aiming her phone right at me, taking photos.

Double shit.

"Damn it. People are going to think we're arguing," I say, fighting the panic bubbling inside of me. "A lovers' spat."

Scarlett rolls her eyes. "Please. You wish."

"I'm serious." I rest my hand on her hip, tugging her in close, and she gasps. "Play along with me."

"Last time I did that, I ended up with my photo splashed all over the internet." She's breathless, her chest rising and falling rapidly, and I study her tits. They're bigger than I remember, though the last time I was with her, she was dressed in a mountain of tulle, so it was hard to see much of anything but her legs. Which were nice, I can't lie.

"Get ready. I'm guessing that's going to happen again." Her hands fall onto my chest, and now I've got both of my hands on her hips, tugging her forward. Our bodies collide, and I bend my head, descending slowly. Slowly . . .

"I didn't agree to this yet," she warns me, her lips practically brushing against mine when she speaks.

"You want me to stop touching you, that's fine. I'll let go of you right now. But think of the headlines once these photos hit the internet. What are people going to say about us? They'll definitely say we're fighting, and the speculation will undoubtedly get worse."

Damn it, I need her on my side, not working against me.

"I don't care what they say." Her voice is weak. Even a little shaky.

I don't believe her. She's trying to pretend it doesn't bother her what people say, but I know the truth.

"It'll be all over the internet within a couple of hours," I say almost gleefully. "'Tate and his heiress arguing on the streets of Manhattan.'"

My aim was spot on. It's the "his heiress" comment that pisses her off. I see the flare of anger in her gaze, feel the way her body tightens beneath my touch.

"I'm more than just an heiress," she retorts.

I lean in close, my mouth hovering above hers once more. "Prove it."

She blinks those pretty dark eyes up at me, her brows drawn together in confusion. A soft sound leaves her as I descend, a mixture of a sigh and a . . . moan?

Those dark eyes fall shut, and I kiss her. Softly. Sweetly. Nothing too forward or out of control. I pull away slightly, studying her pretty upturned face, the way her eyes are tightly closed and her lips pursed like she expects another kiss.

So I give her another one. It's gentle and pleasant, and there's no passion in the kiss whatsoever. As a matter of fact, it feels almost like an apology kiss.

I remember what those were like. Once upon a time, back when Five Car Pileup was first formed and everything was exciting and new, I had a girlfriend. My high school sweetheart, Jessica. She was sweet and pretty, and she gave me head on a semiregular basis, which meant my teenage self was completely in love with her. We argued a lot, and I was always apologizing to her, but at the time, I was glad to have her in my corner.

Jessica was right there beside me throughout the formation

of the band. Always with me as Five Car Pileup shot straight into the stratosphere and we became bigger and bigger until no one could contain us.

We were it. The fill-in for the hole that was left when One Direction broke up. The girls went crazy for us. So much screaming and yelling everywhere we went that sometimes it stressed me out.

But at the time, I thought it was all worth it. We were on top of the world at one point. On teen-magazine covers and performing at award shows. Everyone was praising us; even harsh music critics said we filled a void.

After a year together, my bandmates had become my best friends, we had a song in the top ten on the *Billboard* charts, and we were about to start our second US tour. This one was going to be longer and at bigger venues, and I truly believed nothing could stop us.

Were we arguing among ourselves? Yes. Were Jessica and I having problems? Oh, hell yes. She was jealous of all the attention I received. The publicity team hated having her around. They wanted me to appear single so every teen girl in America could imagine that she had a chance at me. But I refused to break up with her. I was loyal.

To a damn fault.

Then I found her with my very best friend of the band. Jamie. I walked right into his bedroom at the hotel suite we shared and caught him sitting on the edge of the mattress with Jessica on her knees, showing off her blow job skills for Jamie.

I went blind with rage. Without hesitation I socked him in the face, and he went down without a fight. I screamed at her that we were through. All the crying and carrying-on didn't affect me. Those swollen lips of Jessica's were just around my best friend's dick, and I couldn't get the sight out of my head.

I wanted to destroy him. And her. Everyone.

Most of all, I wanted to destroy myself.

That was the beginning of the end, though looking back now, I can be truthful with myself. I had already started drinking. Snorting a line here and there, just to loosen up and have fun at a club. Going to clubs when I wasn't even eighteen, let alone twenty-one.

I was a hot mess. I can't go down that path again.

"I'm sorry," I whisper to Scarlett, and her eyes pop open, her dark brows drawing together in concern. "Am I forgiven?"

"For what?" She's breathless again and even appears a little dazed.

How many times has this girl been kissed anyway? I'm guessing not very often. That kiss had zero heat in it, but she's looking like I did rock her world.

"You don't remember what I did?" I grin, pulling away slightly, giving us—her—some distance. "You must've forgiven me then."

She shakes her head and yanks herself out of my grip. "You make no sense."

"Say yes, Scarlett." I put on all the charm, flashing her my million-dollar smile. The one that used to incite girls in the crowd to throw their panties at me when we'd perform. "I'm only asking for a couple of months of your time."

"A couple of months?" The alarm on her face is obvious.

"Eight weeks." That doesn't sound so bad.

"Four."

Wait a minute. Now she's negotiating?

"Six," I say firmly, my brain going haywire, trying to compute if that's enough time for me to write all the songs and put together the tracks for my album. Probably not, but if I don't have a choice . . . "Deal?"

Her expression is wary, and just when I think I've lost her completely, she whispers . . .

"Deal."

CHAPTER FOURTEEN

SCARLETT

"Thank God you're here. I need your help," I say to my best friend the moment I open the door.

Rachel's expression is serious as she pushes past me and enters the foyer. "You call, I'll always show up. You know this."

I appreciate her loyalty, and that's why it's so hard to keep such a big secret from her. Because this one is big.

Major.

And I can't ever tell her the truth.

Or . . . can I? After all, I haven't signed the NDA yet. We're meeting with the lawyers tomorrow afternoon and signing all the paperwork. I've already looked over the rough draft that the lawyer I hired sent to me earlier, and while most of it is a bunch of legal terms that I don't understand at all, I get the gist of it.

One of the things that stood out was that I'll need to post regularly about my relationship with Tate, and all the posts must be, of course, positive. They even came up with a schedule and topic ideas.

Here's the deal—I don't want to be told what to do or how to do it. Guidance is okay, but I've been on social media for quite a while now. I know how to do this, probably just as well as or even better than anyone on their publicity and marketing team. My only concern is navigating this so-called relationship and making sure my posts and my portrayal of the two of us appear real instead of fake.

It blows my mind how my social media follower count is still growing like crazy. Our very public relationship is totally working. Tate informed me he's already signed a contract just for "Red" and Irresistible is releasing it as an official single by the end of the week. Everyone loves it, and even I have to admit it's a great song.

Even if he does sing about me giving him head. Something I've never done before in my life.

I'm sheltered, what can I say?

Being seen in public with Tate, kissing Tate. Photos from our conversation out on the city sidewalk started circulating on the web before I even made it back home. Tate sent me a text with the best photo out of all of them, accompanied by a simple, one-sentence message.

Tate: We look good together.

After staring at the photo for so long, I couldn't help but agree with him.

I didn't mention the photos to my parents, but I know they knew. The suspicious looks Mom has been sending my way ever since they came out tell me she's dying to say something, but for whatever reason, she's keeping quiet. So is my father.

Very unusual for the both of them.

Thankfully, both of my parents went out earlier, leaving me all alone. The moment they were gone, I was texting Rachel and basically begging her to come over. And like the good best friend that she is, she immediately showed up, her hair still damp from a shower and with no makeup on her pretty face.

If you know Rachel at all, you understand this is an unusual circumstance. She pretty much dropped everything and came right over.

"Is everything okay?" she asks as we head toward my bedroom.

"Yes," I assure her, noting the sympathetic look she sends my way. I'm guessing from the urgency of my message and how quick she arrived, she probably thought I was devastated over this entire situation. My normal behavior is probably reassuring.

Deep down, I know I'm going to confess all to Rachel. I need to get this off my chest, and she's been able to stay quiet. Sharing it with her will ease some of this tension bubbling up inside of me. It's eating me up, and I've only held on to this secret for less than twenty-four hours.

I would never make a good poker player. Or liar. It's just too hard.

"I'll tell you everything when we get to my bedroom," I suggest, and she increases her pace, which almost makes me laugh. I know she's eager to hear what I have to say.

By the time we're in my room and I have the door shut behind me, she's practically hopping in place where she stands, she's so amped up.

"Tell me what's going on now," she demands.

I clear my throat. "Give me a minute. I need to lead up to it first."

"Oh, come on. You can't send me a cryptic text and expect me to ask you how the weather is first."

"It's hot," I say, trying to get under her skin. Also trying to extend this moment as I scramble to come up with the proper way to make my announcement. "Might have to skip going to the Hamptons in August, though."

That last part is true, after I sign that agreement.

"Ugh. You're so annoying when you have a secret." She collapses on the edge of my bed, contemplating me with a scowl. "Just *tell* me already. Oh, wait, let me guess. That's way more fun, because I can come up with some pretty wild theories. Did you finally have sex with Ian?"

"Absolutely not." God, Ian. I should probably tell him that Tate and I are official, especially before it's announced.

But how is that going to work? When will I ever get a chance? He hasn't answered my texts lately. Meaning he's probably avoiding me after that mini tantrum I had at dinner with his family, which is totally stupid on his part. No one could blame me for acting like that, thanks to his bitch of a mother.

He never even blinked an eyelash over her behavior. Never came to my defense once. Maybe Tate is right.

Ian Baldwin is a complete idiot.

"Okay, fine, so you had sex with Tate Ramsey then." I'm about to shout out a resounding no, but her eyes narrow and her mouth keeps moving. "You're lucky you reached out to me now. I saw the latest photo of the two of you *kissing* on the sidewalk, and my immediate thought was, 'That bitch didn't even tell me she was going to meet up with him!' You've been holding out on me."

"I didn't know we were going to meet up," I offer weakly. "It just sort of . . . happened."

"Yet you didn't think to call and tell me about it?"

"I did. I texted you this morning, right after my parents left," I stress.

Rachel taps her finger against her pursed lips, contemplating me. "You never denied having sex with Tate. Which is making me hope you actually did, and if that really happened, I need details, like, right now."

"Hate to disappoint you, but I didn't have sex with Tate." I look her straight in the eyes, my gaze never wavering, because I need her to know I didn't have sex with him. Not even close.

Like I would just give it up to him that easily. I barely know the guy. Not even that sure if I actually like him. He's tolerable.

I suppose.

Attractive. Can't deny that.

Kissing him isn't a hardship, and despite everyone raving over our latest photos, I have to admit I didn't really feel that much when our lips connected. Not like I did the first time. Maybe that was because it had been such a spontaneous move on my part, but the second one out on the street, when I was irritated with him?

Meh. Not impressive.

"God, I'm so disappointed, but then again, not surprised either. You're not that type of person," Rachel says just before she actually yawns.

I'm kind of offended.

And a little hurt.

"What, I'm boring?"

"You're definitely not boring," she rushes to say, reaching out to grab hold of both my hands. Like she needs to reassure me. "I've never thought you were boring. You're my best friend. Why would I want to spend time with you if you bored me?"

Valid question, but . . .

"The yawn threw me off," I admit, my voice small. "That and you having zero expectations that I would do something so wild, like, I don't know—have sex with a celebrity." I shrug, feeling stupid I just admitted all of that. "Ignore me. I'm feeling insecure."

An exasperated noise escapes her. "Only you would feel insecure when you have a hot man seemingly chasing you every chance he gets. A hot, sexy man who women are screaming over while he wrote a song about you. Like, Scarlett, get the fuck out of here with your insecurities. That man is into you, and you act like it's no big deal."

"But—"

"Every single time I go online—which is often, we both know this—there's another post about the two of you. A video. Twenty videos. New photos. More mentions of the song. The lyrics—which are all about you—though I'm guessing some of them are a lie, like the blow job mention. Did your parents ask you about that yet?"

I shake my head, miserable. I didn't even think about what they might say after hearing those lyrics. "It's not like I've ever done much."

"With Tate? Or in general?"

"You already know the answer to that." I send her a meaningful look. I keep nothing from Rachel.

Not really.

"Listen, he kissed you again out in public, on the freaking street. If that isn't a declaration of 'Hey, I like you—wanna go back to my place and do it?' then I don't know what is," Rachel stresses.

I burst out laughing. Only Rachel would put it like that.

"What?" She shrugs, her smile telling me she's pleased by my reaction. "It's true."

"Well, what if I told you that I'm actually dating Tate Ramsey?"

"I'd say you're full of shit." She's still smiling.

"What if I said I wasn't lying?"

Her smile fades, her eyes growing wider by the second. "Don't fuck with me, Scarlett. I won't take this joke well."

"I'm not messing with you. It's not a joke." I shake my head. "I'm telling you the truth. Tate and I . . . we're kind of together."

The look on her face is straight out of a cartoon. I wouldn't be surprised if her eyeballs fell out of her head, attached by springs that bounced up and down. "What did you just say?"

"Ever since the night of my party, I've been talking to Tate Ramsey." This is sort of the truth.

"You two are actually a couple?" she squeaks.

I nod, wringing my hands together, desperate to blurt out the truth. "I'm totally into him."

Rachel is quiet for a moment, as if she needs the time to absorb what I'm saying. "What does Ian think about this?"

"Who cares what Ian thinks?"

"You do. You always do. He's at the front of your mind at all times."

"Not anymore." I proceed to tell her about the dinner with Ian's family. By the time I finish, Rachel is fired up, ready to slay the dragon lady, direct quote.

"Fuck that bitch!" Rachel's face is red, she's so angry. "Why was she so mean to you? Has she always treated you that way?"

"Not to my face, though now that I think about it, she did always treat me like I was invisible." I never got much acknowledgment from his mother, and at the time, I didn't take that as a bad sign.

But now the outward hostility is telling me she's not a fan.

The sly smile on Rachel's face makes me forget all about mean mothers and their weak sons. "My God, this is just . . . crazy. Tate? Ramsey? Tate *freaking* Ramsey! I absolutely love it. You deserve all the public make-out sessions and private sex lessons that he gives you. Seriously! What a story to tell your grandchildren someday! That you had a relationship with one of the most popular members of a successful boy band!"

When she puts it like that, I don't know if it sounds that great. "Like I'd tell my grandchildren my sexual escapades from when I was a teen."

"God, you're no fun! But you did say 'sexual escapades,' so you're giving me hope." Rachel laughs, and I can't help it.

I laugh too.

"Tell me how all of this came about." When I frown at her, Rachel continues, "You and Tate. Actually ending up together. Like I said, I need every detail. Don't spare a single one."

"It just sort of . . . happened. You know? After the kiss?"

I leap off my bed and start pacing around my room, picking up a bottle of perfume my mother gave me for my birthday before I set it back down. I haven't even opened it yet. I have no idea what it smells like. I've been slowly losing my mind since the night of that stupid party, and I hate how stressed I feel. Restless and confused, the weight of the world pressing down on me, like I'm doing a very, very bad thing and I'm going to get caught.

And once I get caught, I'll have to deal with the consequences.

"Like, did he text you constantly, and were you guys sneaking around the last few days in costumes so no one recognized you? Or really him. Truly the both of you. You guys are everywhere."

"No costumes," I murmur with a slight shake of my head.

"He came over here, then, and hung out. That's how you two got to know each other."

Tate came over once. And I promptly kicked him out.

But I probably shouldn't mention that.

I remain quiet for so long that Rachel eventually lets out a big sigh, her gaze shrewd when it lands on me.

"No offense, Scarlett, and you are my very best friend in

the whole world, but I'm finding all of this hard to believe—the two of you together. That you're totally into Tate Ramsey and want to be with him."

"You said I should be into him. That he's sexy and irresistible and I should have a total fling with him," I point out.

"Right, but I *know* you. And despite my telling you that Ian is a big ol' loser who doesn't deserve you, you've still given him chance after chance. You always told me you were in love with him, and now, boom, you're with some other guy you don't even really know? Come on, be real with me for a second. This isn't like you. You were complaining about Tate the night of your party, and now you two are a couple? It's more believable that *I* hooked up with him versus you." Rachel shakes her head. "I don't believe it."

"Rachel, please." I lift my chin, trying to keep it from trembling. I'm on the verge of tears. Like I could collapse and confess my sins at any moment. "Are you calling me a . . . liar?"

"No, of course not! I just—you have to admit this is kind of wild."

"Well, believe it. There is proof everywhere. All of those photos and social media posts. They talk about us on *Good Morning America*, for God's sake." I grab my phone and bring up a gossip site that features the photo of Tate and me kissing on the sidewalk right on the front page. I hold the phone out to her so she can look at it. "See? We're together."

Rachel snatches the phone from me and brings it close to her face, her eyes narrowing the longer she studies the photo. Finally she glances up at me, her gaze locked on me, her voice serious when she says, "Tell me the truth, Scarlett. Is this for real?"

I plop onto the bed next to her, flopping onto my back so I can stare up at the ceiling. "Of course it's real."

Even I can hear how false my voice sounds. Almost like I'm trying to convince myself?

Yeah, I'm definitely trying to convince myself, and Rachel.

Pretty sure I'm failing miserably.

We're both quiet for a moment, the air becoming downright stifling the longer we're silent, and just when I'm about to break, she speaks.

"I still don't believe you."

Sitting up, I nudge my shoulder against hers. "Why not?"

"Because the last time we talked, you were still fuming over Tate being a show-off and yearning for Prince Ian to finally notice you. You were downright pissed that those photos of you together at the party were spreading everywhere, despite it bringing you all sorts of attention, which is exactly what you've been wanting for what feels like forever." Rachel rolls her eyes. "You don't switch your feelings that quick, Scarlett. You're loyal to a fault."

I put on a brave face, my smile tremulous, my eyes most likely giving me away. "I can change my mind. Look at Tate. You told me that you thought Tate was a gorgeous human being."

"He is. He's so freaking gorgeous." She sits up straighter and starts twisting a lock of blond hair around her finger. "I'm jealous of the fact that you got to him first. Do you think he's a homie hopper? Would he be interested in me?"

I can't stop blinking at her, trying to compute the words that she just said. "Um, I don't know."

"Aha!" She thrusts her index finger into my face. "If you cared about this guy at all, if you were *really* into him, you would've immediately told me to back off."

My shoulders sag. There's no use in pretending any longer. Deep down, I knew I'd give in and tell her anyway. "Fine. You're right. I'm not interested in Tate. Not like . . . that." I wrinkle my nose. "But I've agreed to be his fake girlfriend for the next six weeks."

Now it's her turn to blink at me, her lips parting as if she's trying to find the words to speak yet can't quite come up with them. "Wait a minute. That just took a serious turn."

I nod. "We're meeting to sign the paperwork tomorrow."

"Paperwork?" Rachel asks, her voice weak. "What, like an NDA?"

"Definitely an NDA. And whatever other legal paperwork they're requiring to make this agreement airtight," I tell her. "So I guess I'm not breaking it yet since I haven't signed anything, right?"

"Right." Rachel leaps to her feet and starts pacing around the room, her expression nothing short of puzzled. "Why in the world would you agree to this, Scarlett? You don't like this guy. Or at least, that was the vibe I was picking up off you during your party."

She's right. I didn't particularly care for him that night. At first. But when we ended up getting caught by the photographer, he seemed so . . . vulnerable. Like everything was riding on that performance and he just wanted one more chance for someone—lots of someones—to see him.

I understand where he's coming from. I feel it in the very depths of my soul. I just want to be seen, so I guess we have that in common.

"Sometimes I think I sort of feel . . . sorry for him." I shrug, at a loss for words.

"For big shot Tate Ramsey?"

"Don't forget he hasn't been a big shot for years. He trashed his career. Flat-out ruined it thanks to his drug problem," I remind her.

"And that ex-girlfriend who fucked Jamie." Rachel's

referring to the other Five Car Pileup band member who got caught with Tate's girlfriend. "Has he talked to you about that?"

"Of course not. I barely know him."

"But you know him well enough to agree to be his fake girlfriend for—how long did you say? Six weeks?"

I nod, hating how I have to defend my choices.

But I get it. She's worried about me. *I'm* worried about me.

"How do your parents feel about this? I'm sure Fitzy isn't down, since it's fake." Rachel grins. "He'd definitely want it to be real."

A sigh leaves me. "They don't know it's fake."

Rachel comes to a stop in the middle of my spacious bedroom, her hands resting on her hips. "He doesn't know? Are you going to tell them the truth?"

I shake my head, wincing when a yelp escapes her. "My father has a hard time keeping things to himself. I'm afraid he'd slip and tell someone the truth by accident."

"Even with an NDA?"

I nod.

"And your mom?"

"She can't keep a secret from Dad. She hates secrets. He'd definitely know eventually, and then watch out." I throw my hands up in the air. "Everyone would find out the truth, and I'd be the laughingstock of the world."

"I don't know. I think your dad would keep his mouth shut if it protected your reputation," Rachel points out. "You're his little girl. His only girl. He's rather protective of you."

"You're right. He is." A sigh leaves me. "Part of me doesn't want to say anything because I'm worried about their reaction. What if I disappoint them when I admit I'm getting involved in a fake relationship as a publicity stunt?"

"True."

"They could tell me they won't let me do it."

"You're eighteen. They can't tell you shit." Rachel rebels against her parents all the time. She's the one I'm supposed to go on the European trip with, though we haven't really planned anything yet.

"I would hate to go against their wishes," I say.

"You never like to disappoint, so I get it. Well, I love a good secret. And I know how to keep my mouth shut," Rachel retorts as she resumes her pacing. "You need to put a plan into action."

"They already have a plan."

"Who's 'they'?" She makes air quotes with her fingers.

"Tate's team. His business manager, the rep from the record label. The label's marketing and promotion teams. The lawyers. I've reviewed the contract. Looked over the schedule. It's pretty intense."

"They sent you a *schedule*?"

I nod. "It also includes a social media schedule."

Her mouth drops open for a second before she snaps her lips shut. "Of course they did. Look, all of this protects *him*. The precious Tate Ramsey. I'm sure he's getting, what? A record deal out of this?"

How did she know? "I guess his old label is interested and they're eager to sign him. They already did for the single."

"Tate already has a record deal for 'Red'?"

I nod.

"This is all because of his performance at your party? And the kiss seen 'round the world?"

"Yeah. I suppose so."

"He owes you then." Rachel taps her chin with her index finger, contemplative.

"I also think part of the reason they want to sign him is because of . . . me."

It sounds ridiculous. I know it does. But I'm pretty sure our supposed relationship is what caused the heightened interest in him in the first place. Well, that and he sang pretty spectacularly at my party.

"You?" Rachel's delicate brows shoot up. "That wouldn't surprise me. I mean, look at you. Only daughter of a Lancaster scion. Gorgeous, sweet, great personality. You're so relatable in real life, and it translates on social media."

I've worked hard to be relatable. It's hard to get past the "rich girl with no problems" vibe people like to attach to me, but I think I'm almost there. I can't help it if I was born into this life, and I do my best to help others. Give where I can.

And I also try to keep it real. If I'm having a bad hair day or a giant zit is on the tip of my nose, I share that online. No matter how embarrassing it is. Mom says that keeps me grounded so I won't get a big head, but it also helped me create content that viewers could find common ground with.

So my embarrassments have earned me a few followers. And now the man I'm supposedly dating is earning me even more followers.

Life is so weird.

"You need to post about this," Rachel declares.

My gaze jerks to her. "I don't know if that's a good idea."

"Why not? You're the relatable queen, right?"

"Me dating Tate Ramsey is the most unrelatable thing I've ever done—besides being born into a wealthy family." I actually laugh at my own words, because it's true. What's happening to me is totally unrelatable.

More like it's the stuff of dreams.

Rachel ignores my laughter. "This is straight out of a fantasy, I have to agree, but come on. This is also where you can play up the 'I can't believe this is happening to me' part. Because let's not forget, once upon a time, you had a Five Car Pileup poster on your wall and a major crush on Tate Ramsey."

"We were like . . . fourteen. Thirteen. Whatever. And you had a crush on him too."

"I always had more of a secret thing for Aaron. He was so broody."

The dark-haired, dark-eyed mystery man of the group. The oldest one, though I think he was only a year or two older than the rest, tops. He was too moody for my liking, but it doesn't surprise me he was Rachel's secret favorite.

"Anyway, who I liked doesn't matter. We need to find that picture of the poster on your wall. And you need to post on your socials a video of you talking about your birthday party and how you found unexpected love while you were there."

"I can't." I shake my head, my insides quaking at the thought of it. "Not yet."

"You can," Rachel counters. "And you're going to. I'm going to help you."

"Rachel . . ."

"Don't 'Rachel' me." She marches over to my walk-in closet and flicks on the light before entering it, immediately going through my clothes. "We're going to find you a fabulous outfit, and I'm going to do your makeup and hair. And then you're going on camera and talking about how much you adore Tate Ramsey and you can't believe he feels the same way. It's like your every early-teenage dream coming to life. Oh shit, we should find that one song by Katy Perry and play it. It fits perfectly."

I loved that song back in the day. Before I was even a teenager.

"What about the NDA? The schedule? The topics they want me to talk about?"

Rachel pokes her head out of the closet, holding up a

super-cute dress my mom found for me the last time she was in Paris. "Fuck the schedule and the topics. You haven't signed shit yet. And you're not exposing anyone or telling the truth. You're playing up your new love story for views, and they're going to love it."

She's right. What's the harm in this?

Forty minutes later I'm wearing my new dress, and my hair is curled. Rachel set up my phone with the ring light, and I'm sitting at my desk, where I have the best light in my room, ready to talk.

Fighting off the nerves, I sit up straighter, sending her a quick pleading look, but she shakes her head, her expression firm.

I'm doing this. Rachel won't let me give up. Besides . . .

I don't want to.

Here goes nothing.

CHAPTER FIFTEEN

TATE

I'm standing at the window in Simon's office, staring at the city spread out before me, while Simon talks on the phone in low murmurs and draggy vowels accompanied by the occasional growl of laughter. I don't know who he's speaking to, but I do my best to tune him out.

Like I can focus on what that asshole is saying. Yes, my former—current (still mind blowing to me that he's taken me back on)—business manager is an asshole. That isn't an insult, considering he'd most likely agree with me. But he's *my* asshole, and I want him on my side through this dream/nightmare called my career resurgence.

It's been exhilarating and exciting and terrifying all at once. I forgot how exhausting the constant attention is. Though right now, I'm terrified for a completely different reason. Like the fact that my so-called new girlfriend is almost ten minutes late to our meeting.

Ten minutes isn't much to sweat, but considering every little thing sets me on edge lately, I can't help it.

The moment I hear Simon end the call, he starts talking loudly. To me.

"I've got a deal in the works for you, and it's a good one." He sounds smug.

I whirl around to face him. "For what?"

"High-end fashion line. Up-and-coming designer. You haven't heard of them yet, but I promise you will. They're on the verge of breaking out."

It takes everything I've got to not roll my eyes and call bullshit, but if they pay well and don't cause any online scandal, I'm game. "Sounds great."

"It will be. You're going sky high, buddy. Rising straight to the top. Just wait until they see you in action."

They've seen me in action. That's why I'm having the resurgence. But now I'm starting to doubt it'll last. Everything hinges on one thing happening, and if she doesn't come through . . .

I'm screwed.

"No one is going to see me in action if she doesn't show up," I finally say, frustration in every clipped word that drops.

Simon frowns and checks the fat Rolex on his wrist. "Where is your girlfriend anyway?"

"Where's the lawyer?" I counter, slipping my hand into my pocket, my fingers curling around my phone.

I should text Scarlett. Ask her where the hell she is, but I feel like I can't come on too strong or make any demands. She'd probably bail.

I wouldn't blame her if she did.

"She's in her office. The team is in house, bud. It's the real deal here."

"The lawyer is a woman?" I'm shocked. Not because I'm a misogynistic asshole—or maybe I am; I'm not sure—but a woman lawyer handling this fake-ass deal surprises me.

Though I shouldn't let anything surprise me. Every day lately there's been a new revelation.

"I surround myself with women, Tate. Haven't you noticed this by now?"

"Yeah, I guess so."

There's a knock on the door, and it swings open before Simon can speak, Roger barging in, thrusting his phone out in front of him.

"Did you guys see the latest?" Roger waves the phone in front of Simon's face, then mine.

I catch a glimpse of Scarlett looking fucking gorgeous on his screen. Reaching out, I swipe the phone from his hand. "What is this?"

"Your girlfriend creating marketing gold, that's what. I know we gave her topics and a schedule, but she went completely off script." Roger tips his head in my direction. "Watch it. It's fucking great. You two are magical."

I play the video, and Scarlett's sweet voice fills the room.

"I know it's completely unbelievable, right? I'm still pinching myself." She lifts her arm and pinches her wrist with a slight grimace. "But it's actually happening, and can I just say that Tate Ramsey is like my every dream come true? Am I allowed to say that? I'm probably gushing too much, but I think you'd feel the same way if the guy you used to crush on when you were in middle school was now your boyfriend. Right?"

She looks at the camera, a knowing smile on her face, her eyebrows raised. I realize her face is mostly bare and she's got a makeup brush clutched between her fingers. I glance down at the caption of the video, which says, *GRWM to go c my new bf!*

"What does GRWM mean?" Simon asks, glancing over my shoulder.

"Get ready with me," I murmur, my gaze never straying from Scarlett's face as she goes through the motions of applying her makeup, the subtle cuts in the video accelerating her process as she keeps up a steady stream of one-sided yet somehow inclusive conversation. About me.

About us.

"The girl is a genius," Roger says.

"Hand that over," Simon demands, wagging his fingers at me.

I give him the phone, blown away by Scarlett's video. That she would actually make something about us, claiming that we're together, before she even signed the damn paperwork.

I'm impressed.

"She posted this almost two hours ago," Simon says, his gaze glued to Roger's phone screen. "This is good."

"Fucking great is what it is. This girl is a PR department's every wet dream." Roger is beaming from ear to ear. "Where is she? We need to celebrate. I brought champagne."

He holds up a bottle of very expensive champagne.

"She's late," I say, hating how the nerves chew at my gut.

"She'll be here any second," Simon adds, sending me a look I can't read while handing the phone over to Roger. "She made a goddamn video about getting ready to see you, Tate. Stop worrying."

"Worrying? I have nothing to worry about. Scarlett is my girlfriend." I grin at Simon, who grins at Roger.

The grin fades from Roger's face, and he makes his way over so he's standing directly in front of me, his gaze assessing. "You better not fuck this up, kid. I know you two are coming together under a binding agreement, and while I can tell she's fully on board and ready to execute her duties, I need to know that you're on board too."

This is ironic, isn't it? I practically had to beg and plead with Scarlett to get her to even agree to this in the first place, and she makes one fucking video that makes me look bad in front of Roger. I'm not pissed at her. I just find it interesting that I'm always the bad guy in this scenario.

There's another knock on the door, and this time, there's a pause before Steffi, Simon's assistant/girlfriend, is peeking her head around it, a serene smile on her face. "Scarlett Lancaster and her lawyer are here."

"Send them in." Simon waves a hand at her, and she shuts the door with a loud slam. "Why didn't she just call me?" This last bit he mutters under his breath.

Nerves jump in my stomach, making it hard to fucking breathe, but I put on a bright smile and stand taller at my spot in front of the window. The double doors swing back open, and in walks Scarlett wearing a black dress that looks more like an oversize men's blazer, followed by an uptight middle-aged guy in a three-piece navy suit.

The lawyer.

"Scarlett." Simon rises to his feet and rounds his desk, making his way straight for my fake girl. "It's wonderful to finally meet you in person."

"It's nice to meet you too." Her voice washes over me, making me feel itchy and hot, and I tug at the collar of my black shirt, unsure how to approach her or what I should say.

This girl—woman—I wish I knew what made her tick. What exactly is going on in that head of hers? I don't have a clue, but I'd love to figure her out.

Maybe spending time with her for the next six weeks will help.

"Please, call me Simon." He hugs her. Wraps her up in his thick arms and gives her a squeeze, and I swear to God, I sort of want to pop his head off his body, which is weird because I'm not the jealous type.

Then I remember how I reacted to Jess cheating on me in the past and retract that statement from my thoughts fairly quickly.

"And of course, you remember Tate." The amusement in Simon's voice as he introduces my girlfriend to me like we're strangers makes me want to sock him in the face.

Then I remember that violence gets you nowhere but an assault charge and possible jail time, and I retract that feeling as well.

"Definitely." Scarlett smiles at me, and that's when I see it. The nervousness flashing in her gaze. It matches mine. "How are you?"

I say nothing in greeting. Just reach for her hand and pull her into me, sliding my arms around her waist and giving her a quick hug, breathing in her delectable scent, noting how soft she is. She hugs me in return, and I swear to God, I can feel her trembling.

"Scarlett Lancaster, you are a mastermind," Roger announces as he approaches us from behind.

Extracting herself from me, she whips her head in his direction, her brows drawing together in confusion. "Excuse me?"

"Roger Hammersmith, Irresistible Records." He shoves his hand out toward her, and she has no other choice but to shake it. "You, my darling, are a perfect fit with the Irresistible team."

Her gaze cuts to mine, a shaky smile on her lips. "I thought I was on the Tate Ramsey team."

Roger chuckles, letting go of her hand so he can point at her. "That right there? Absolute gold. You will win over anyone with that kind of attitude."

"You're laying it on a bit thick, Rog," Simon warns him.

I move so I'm standing to Scarlett's right, slinging my arm around her shoulders. "We are definitely a team."

She stiffens beneath my arm, her entire body seemingly frozen, and I give her shoulder a gentle squeeze, trying to get her to relax. "Yes, we are."

"Should you two have a ship name?" Roger's gaze bounces back and forth between Scarlett and me. "Is that still done? I came up with one—Tartlet. Tate plus Scarlett equals Tartlet. Don't you love it?"

I fucking hate it. Scarlett is frowning.

"That's bloody awful, Roger." Simon shakes his head. "Shall we sit down and get the process started? Hope you brought your signing hand, Scarlett. There are lots of pages where we need your initials and signature."

"I'm ready." She walks away from me, my arm falling to my side, and I watch her go, my gaze latching onto her long, shiny legs.

She seriously has great ones.

"The video you posted earlier was nothing short of brilliant," Roger gushes as we all settle at the table, Scarlett's lawyer sitting directly to her right while I sit across from her. "I fucking loved it."

"Thank you. I filmed it yesterday. Thought I may as well embrace the situation, right?" She casts her gaze around the table, the worry on her face obvious. "I hope that was okay."

"It's more than okay. It's fucking amazing. You got so many views." Roger checks his phone, his expression one of pure concentration as he taps away at it. "Over seven hundred thousand views already."

"Oh, wow."

"Don't act so shocked. You know what you're doing." Roger slaps the edge of the table. "This shit is so good! I'm excited. Aren't you all excited?"

"Definitely excited," I agree, scooting my chair closer to the table.

"Then act like it! You're all so somber. Especially you." Roger points at Scarlett's attorney. "This isn't a funeral."

The lawyer sits up straighter, annoyance in his gaze. "I'm here to make sure you're not taking advantage of my client."

"She's being well taken care of. Don't worry," Roger says breezily.

"Your client went a little off script, but nothing damaging," Simon says. "If she keeps that up, it might be a problem."

"A problem? I made that video in support of Tate, and you consider it a problem?" Scarlett's cheeks flush a deep pink, and I know Simon just pissed her off. "I thought you would appreciate the video."

"We do," Simon adds hastily.

"We definitely do," Roger says, his voice smooth as he speaks right over Simon. "We just need to make sure we're all in agreement with everything that's said publicly. This is a publicity machine, you see. And every move we're about to make is carefully calculated. You need to do your part, Miss Lancaster, and then it should work without a hitch."

"Hey." Everyone glances over at me, even Scarlett's attorney. "Could we have a minute? Alone? Just the two of us?"

"Of course." Simon doesn't even hesitate as he jumps to his feet, sending a meaningful look at Roger, who also reluctantly stands.

"I don't think that's nec—" starts Scarlett's lawyer, but she rests her hand on his arm, and he immediately goes quiet.

"It's okay. Give us a few minutes," she murmurs.

Within seconds Simon's got his hand around Scarlett's lawyer's elbow and is steering him out of the office, the door falling shut behind all of them.

When they're gone, I rise to my feet and make my way around the table so I'm standing closer to where she sits. "They shouldn't have done that."

Confusion swirls in her dark eyes. "Done what?"

"Come at you for your video. What you made was good. Great," I correct when I see her little frown. "I appreciate you doing that."

"It was my best friend's idea," she admits, her teeth sinking gently into her lower lip.

I tear my gaze away from her sexy mouth, not needing the distraction. "Your best friend? You didn't tell her what's really going on, did you?"

Scarlett stands and bumps into me, she's so close. "Of course not. I would never." Panic flares in her velvety brown eyes, and I lose myself in them for a bit. I don't remember them being that big. Or that dark. "It was difficult, though. I'm not good at faking stuff like that, especially around Rachel. She knows me better than anyone else."

"I bet." I catch her scent again on an inhale, an intoxicating floral that smells expensive. "You're still good with this, right?"

She offers the tiniest nod, tilting her chin up.

"And you're okay with all the faking stuff?"

"What do you mean, faking stuff?"

"You read the contract, right?"

Another nod.

"Well, we're going to have to pretend that we're together in public. Often. Which means there's going to be a lot of physical contact. Touching." I pause. "Kissing."

"Right." She releases a shaky breath. "Kissing."

"You had no problem kissing me the other times we've been together," I remind her.

"I know. And I won't have a problem for the next six weeks either. It's not so bad." She shrugs.

I'm actually insulted. "It's not so bad? Are you referring to kissing me?"

"Well, yeah." The way she says it, I fully expect her to add a *duh* to the end of that sentence. "How bad can it be? You holding my hand. Your arm around my shoulder. Our arms around each other. The occasional peck here and there."

The occasional peck. This girl . . .

Has no idea what she's getting herself into.

"What do your parents think?"

"About you and me? They don't seem to mind." A tiny laugh escapes her, and it's the prettiest sound. "They kind of encourage it."

"Really." My voice is flat. Now I'm the one full of doubt.

"Oh yeah. My dad lives for this sort of thing. He's constantly asking me about you. He keeps up with the gossip sites more than my mom does. Pretty sure he's seen all of the photos and posts talking about us."

"And what does he think about it?"

"I'm almost positive he's enjoying every minute of it, but he's trying to play it cool. I think he's waiting for me to bring you around so they can officially meet you as, like, my boyfriend or whatever." She rolls her eyes, trying to play it off. "I probably should tell him we're not that serious. Besides, I'm sure you have no interest in hanging out with my parents."

Huh. I didn't even think about the parents, though they're the driving force she wants to rise above. My own parents live just outside the city, and they keep mostly to themselves. They're not big on celebrity, especially mine, and when I hit rock bottom, Mom eventually came and helped me get cleaned up by forcing me into rehab.

We're not that close, but our relationship is getting better with time. Pretty sure they still view me as a major disappointment.

"Your dad is into gossip?"

"If he can find a mention about him in a gossip column, his day is made." Scarlett's tone is vaguely bitter, and I realize she's not too thrilled with her dad possibly chasing fame.

"I wouldn't mind seeing Fitzy again." I stroke my chin, remembering with fondness how easy that guy is to talk to.

Well, until he was slinging a few thinly veiled threats my way, that is.

"Are you sure?" She sounds incredulous, and I have a realization.

I flash her a quick smile. "It makes sense, right? Getting in good with my girlfriend's parents."

"Sure." She nods.

"Do they think we're the real deal?"

"I didn't tell them what's really going on," she admits, her voice low. "I'm afraid if they knew, they might slip and reveal the truth. And that would ruin everything."

"Yeah, it would," I agree with a slight shake of my head. "Can I ask you one more question?"

She lifts her chin, haughty and beautiful. "Of course."

"Is there anything you're . . . worried about? With this agreement?"

Her gaze finds mine, and she stares at me for a moment, her lush lips parted, those long eyelashes fluttering as she blinks. "If I tell you what I'm worried about, you might laugh."

"I would never," I promise. "We're in this together. You and me."

Scarlett blinks again, her jaw working. "I'm afraid the deeper we go, the more lost I'll feel."

I frown. "Lost?"

"No one will care about me." She shrugs, averting her gaze. "It'll all be about you." A small laugh escapes her. "I know that sounds really selfish, and you probably think I'm a total bitch, but it's never been about me. It's always about my family. My charming father. My beautiful mother."

I remember her complaining about this already.

"I won't let anyone lose sight of who you are, including yourself. You need me to talk you up to the press? I can do it." I nod firmly.

She's quiet for a moment, as if she needs to absorb my words.

"What exactly would you say about me?" she finally asks.

"Whatever you want. All of it positive, of course."

"Of course," she adds drolly.

"That's not part of the written agreement, but we can make our own agreement, you know? Just between the two of us." I slip my hands into my pockets, the epitome of nonchalance.

I bet she has no idea my internal system is going haywire. I need this girl more than she needs me. She's loaded and completely insulated in her wealthy world, and while I just got paid a million bucks—more like six hundred thousand thanks to taxes—that money won't last forever. I'm only twenty-one. I have a lot of years left in me, and wouldn't it be great to make a go of this singing career again? On my own?

Yes. Yes, it so fucking would.

"I'd expect the same in return," I say when she still hasn't responded. "We need to lift each other up, not tear each other down."

"I'm not the type to tear a person down, so don't worry. Didn't you watch the video I made earlier?"

"I did, and I appreciate everything you said about me—about us. Roger and Simon loved it too, especially Roger."

"He sort of went on about it a little too much, huh?" Scarlett wrinkles her nose.

"He tends to do that—gets a little excited. And that was tame behavior on his part." Unable to stop myself, I reach out and touch her, tugging on a strand of long dark hair and curling it around my finger. She doesn't move. I swear she doesn't so much as breathe, she's so still. "Thank you for making that video. You made me sound like a freaking hero."

"You're welcome," she says, breathless.

"It was unexpected."

"Like I said, it was my friend's idea."

"I think I like your friend."

Scarlett smiles. "She already loves you. Especially back when you were in Five Car Pileup. Though Aaron was her personal favorite."

"Right." I wince, knowing that no matter what, I will never be able to rid myself of the boy band label.

"I really like the idea of us having this personal . . . agreement. It makes me feel better about this. You and me." She straightens her shoulders, standing taller. "Are you ready to sign all of the paperwork?"

"Before we call them all back in here, I need to make sure we're on the same page."

Her delicate brows draw together, her lips forming the slightest pout. She has a sexy mouth. Memories assail me of the moments I kissed her, and how pleasant those moments were. Nothing earth shattering but . . .

It could be. Earth shattering. Between us.

Or maybe not. She's really not my type at all.

"I thought we already were."

"Just confirming."

"What exactly do you want to confirm?"

"First, when we make public appearances, we need to look fully invested." I pause. "In each other."

"I already said I can do that." She crosses her arms in front of her chest, which makes her skirt ride up, offering me a glimpse of her slender thighs.

I rub my chin, contemplating her. My fake girlfriend is a total smoke show. "Sometimes, you can come off pretty . . . rigid."

"I am not."

"Prove it then." Jesus. Why am I picking on her?

"Prove it how?"

Oh, she looks so confused, my sweet little girlfriend. How sheltered has her life been? Can she really manage to act like the sort of confident yet mysterious woman who can snag me?

I mean, I sound like a complete asshole in my own thoughts. But considering I'm currently in demand and I was named in *People*'s "Most Beautiful People" edition at the age of only seventeen—which grossed out a lot of people, but we won't get into that right now—I am, as Simon describes me, a hot commodity.

And she's just an heiress who was born into money.

Shit. I *am* a complete asshole, aren't I.

"Show me that you can pretend to be totally into me."

"Can you do the same for me?" she challenges.

I let my gaze roam over her slowly, starting at her black-heel-covered feet, coasting up those impossibly long legs, lingering on her chest, until I finally meet her wide-eyed gaze.

"I think I can manage it," I drawl.

A soft huff of breath leaves her, and she shifts closer to me, until we're practically touching. She tilts her head back, her long, wavy hair falling down her back, her dark eyes glittering with challenge.

"Then show me."

CHAPTER SIXTEEN

SCARLETT

Heat blooms on my skin the longer he stares at me with that hungry gaze. There's something about Tate that infuriates me.

Makes me curious.

Makes me . . . hot.

A little shaky.

A lot breathless.

I can't quite put my finger on it. Every time we're together, we start squabbling. As if we annoy each other, yet we're also drawn to each other?

It's confusing. He confuses me.

My feelings for him confuse me too. I don't know what's going on in my head full of jumbled thoughts.

The air grows heavier the longer we stare at each other, and just when I'm about to say something that's probably stupid, he reaches out, his fingers featherlight as they trace the edge of my jaw.

My entire being erupts into tingles. From the top of my scalp to my toes, I can feel him. Those fingers barely touching me, drifting upward, pausing at the corner of my lips.

I swallow hard, my lips closing around his fingertip with the movement, and I swear I see an inferno ignite in his gaze.

His hand drops, and disappointment crashes through me at the loss of connection. Without thought, I rest my hand on his black shirt—we match, like we're going to a funeral—right in the center of his chest, and I can feel his heart hammer beneath my palm.

I lift my gaze to find he's already watching me, his face deathly serious.

As if he's attending a funeral.

Defeat engulfs me, and I want to sag to the floor.

This isn't going to work.

There's no warning when he slips his arm around my waist and yanks me close, my hand still on his chest. A gasp escapes me, my breasts crushed to his front, the hem of my dress riding up when he tightens his grip on my waist. Our legs tangle and our breaths mingle and slowly he smooths his hand up my back, making a cascade of goose bumps rise all over my skin.

"You can't look at me like that, Scar," he murmurs. I swear he's the only one who's ever called me Scar. No one else would dare. It sounds almost like an insult.

"Like what?" I'm breathless. All from standing too close. From having him touch me in a relatively staid manner.

So why do his hands on me feel like . . . everything?

"Like you're scared to death of me." He reaches out with his free hand and presses the spot right between my eyebrows. "This little wrinkle needs to relax."

I feel my forehead ease just from his gentle touch.

"And you should smile more."

I paste on an overly bright smile.

"Jesus, not like that." He grimaces.

I scowl at him. He laughs.

"Only use that face when we're arguing in public."

"You want to argue in public?" That doesn't sound like a good idea.

"If we make up in public too, definitely. Look what happened the last time we did," he reminds me.

Out on the sidewalk, when he grabbed me. That kiss. That photo is still getting us a lot of attention.

"We're young and in love," he continues. "And we'll need to come up with a backstory."

"A backstory?"

"How we came together, how we fell in love."

"Are we in love yet, though? That sounds so serious."

"Okay, not love yet. Complete and total infatuation," he concludes, not letting me go at all. Still running his palm up and down my back, like he's trying to soothe me.

Well, it's working. My muscles are relaxing and I'm leaning my weight into him, my fingers slightly curled into the fabric of his shirt.

"We already have a backstory," I remind him. "We met at my party."

"Right. Well, that was quick."

"When you know, you just . . . know." My father has said that to me before, and I used to think it was utter crap.

I still sort of do. I mean, look at us, with our fake relationship.

"I want everyone to believe I'm completely fucking obsessed with you," he murmurs, and the tone of his voice, the look on his face . . .

I believe him, despite the fact that we're about to sign a ton of legal documents binding us together in a fake relationship.

And that's slightly terrifying, how convincing he is.

"You think we can get people to believe that we're the real deal?" My breath hitches when he dips his head, his mouth now right at my ear. I can hear him breathing, the steady in and out, and when he speaks, I can feel his breath. Warm, with a hint of mint.

"We're going to test it out on your parents first."

Alarm sweeps through me, and I try to jerk out of his hold, but he doesn't let me go. "That might not be a good idea."

"It's the only one I've got. You need to face them eventually, right? What better time than now?"

"Now?" My voice squeaks like I'm a little mouse.

He nods. "Text them. Ask if I can come over for dinner."

"Tonight?"

"Yeah." He nuzzles the side of my face, and my knees wobble. I think he did that on purpose, to throw me off kilter. "Tonight."

I try to pull out of his embrace a little slower this time, but he still won't let me go. "I need to get my phone. It's in my bag."

We both swivel our heads to where I left my heart-shaped, hot-pink Chanel bag on a nearby chair. "You should use that purse as much as possible when we're together. The heart is a nice touch."

I had the same thought, though it feels a little cheesy and almost sordid, hearing him say it out loud.

Maybe because I'm having some guilt over this fake-relationship thing. Rachel wasn't wrong when she kept prodding me about what I'm getting out of it. I can't quite tell her what that is because I don't even know myself. And when I admit that I just want someone—anyone—paying attention to me, that sounds . . .

Pathetic.

Tate releases me, and I go to the bag, zipping it open and pulling my phone out. I can barely fit anything in that bag, which is super annoying, but it's so freaking cute, and it was a birthday gift, so I love it.

I send a quick message to the text group that consists of me and my parents.

Me: Can I have a guest over for dinner tonight?

My father answers almost immediately.

Dad: Who? Rachel? Adore her. She's always welcome.

Mom: Of course, darling. We love Rachel.

Me: It's not Rachel.

Dad: Who is it then?

Mom: Oh is it Ian?

Is she going to be disappointed I've moved on from Ian? Maybe not. She seemed frustrated with him that night during the infamous dinner. She even told me I should see Tate to make Ian regret his decisions.

Me: I want Tate to come over for dinner.

There are no texts for a few seconds. Maybe even thirty.

"What did they say?" Tate asks, rubbing at the back of his neck.

"Nothing yet." I chew on my lower lip, nerves making my blood run a little hotter.

Or maybe that's from the way Tate is looking at me. I can't tell yet.

Dad: Tate Ramsey?

Mom: We'd love to have him.

Me: Are you sure?

Mom: Absolutely. We'd love to get to know him.

Dad: Maybe we should go out. Take him to our favorite restaurant.

Oh God. Dad's favorite restaurant is also one of the busiest restaurants in our neighborhood. We go there a lot as a family, though my brothers are still at their various sports camps, so they won't be around.

Thank God.

I lift my head, my gaze locking with Tate's. "They said yes."

"Perfect." He rubs his hands together, reminding me of Roger. Or was it Simon who did that? I can't keep track of these men trying to control our relationship. It's intimidating and more than a little misogynistic. "We'll try this new relationship of ours out on your parents. If they believe us, anyone will."

A knock sounds before the double doors swing open to reveal Simon standing there in his pin-striped three-piece suit, a smile on his face, and my lawyer standing directly behind him along with a woman with a stern expression.

Thank God I went with another attorney, one that Rachel helped me find that her dad works with. The only lawyer I know is Ian's dad, and that sounds like a disaster waiting to happen.

"The lawyers are ready if you two are," Simon announces as he strides into the room, rubbing his hands together just as Tate did only moments ago. "Damn, there is nothing better than putting together a sweet deal, don't you think?"

The amused look Tate sends my way makes me smile.

Makes me feel like we're sharing a secret.

Once all the necessary paperwork is finished, Tate and I leave Simon's office together. Ride down the elevator together. We even exit the building together, because where else am I going to go? He's by my side the entire time, his tall, broad frame making me feel small. His warm, delicious scent making me want to lean into him and take a deep sniff, like he's a drug I'm desperate to inhale.

I need to get used to this. Spending time with this man, talking to him. Looking into his deep-blue eyes and bracing myself against the intensity of his smile. It won't be a hardship because he's just so pleasant to look at.

Then he opens his mouth and says things, and I sort of want to sock him in it.

Maybe that's normal? Is that what being in a relationship is actually like?

Well, that's what we are, officially. At least according to all those legal documents we just signed.

The next six weeks of my life are completely booked. I'd planned on traveling all over Europe in the fall, but that's now been postponed. I wasn't planning on attending school, which is a good thing. As Simon told Tate, "Scarlett going to college would've really cramped your style."

Guess Simon isn't big on higher education. Especially when it interferes with his new star client.

"Where to now?" Tate asks once we're standing outside on the sidewalk. It's quieter where Simon's office is located. Not so many people trying to push past us as we stand next to each other facing the street.

I turn toward him. "I guess I should go home and get ready for dinner."

He frowns. "You won't let me come with you?"

"Oh." I'm surprised he wants to tag along with me, but . . . "Okay. If you really want to."

"Are your parents home?"

"I don't know. They were gone when I left the house."

"They won't care if we're there alone?" A single brow lifts.

"Why should they care?"

"I think most overprotective parents would have an issue with their beautiful daughter being alone with her new boyfriend in their house," he drawls.

I didn't even think of that because when I look at Tate, I don't think of him as my boyfriend.

And I really, really need to start thinking that way.

This relationship is live and ready to be put on display for all the world to see. Time for me to dig in and do the work.

"My parents trust me." I flash him a smile. "They know I wouldn't do anything that might put me at . . . risk."

"They don't know me, though. Not really." He flashes me a villainous smile, and I can't help but laugh. When he joins in, his deep, rich chuckle touches places deep within me that I didn't know existed.

Yikes. Pretty sure I'm in over my head.

We climb into our family's hired car and head back to my apartment, the both of us on our phones most of the time, so not much conversation is happening. This doesn't make me feel bad or think that we're acting awkward together. This is actually the most normal I've felt in Tate's presence since we started this entire thing.

"You always have someone to drive you around the city? Anywhere you want to go?" he asks at one point. He sounds amazed.

"Yeah. I always have."

"Do you have your driver's license?"

I shake my head. "What's the point? I have my driver's permit, but I haven't gotten around to taking my driver's test yet. I always have someone to drive me around, or there's public transit."

"I doubt very much that a precious baby girl Lancaster would be seen on the subway."

"Hey, I'm not a baby. And I've taken the subway before." A couple of times with my parents when traffic was too heavy and we urgently needed to get to our destination. On a field trip once when I was in middle school and we went to a Broadway play. A couple of times with my cousins.

Just . . . not very often.

"I'd much rather take the private car around. This is nice. Though I think you should definitely get your license. With all the money your family has, you could own any car you want, which would be totally badass." He glances around the interior of the car, running his hand over the soft leather seat, a chuckle escaping him. "I've fucked up a few limos in my day."

"Really."

He shifts in his seat, his gaze focused on the window as the city passes us by. "Not my most shining moments, but yeah. When I was younger, I was pretty destructive."

"Why?"

His head jerks toward me, his brows lowered. "Why?"

"Yeah, why did you do all that? Act that way? Were you . . . high all the time? Drunk? Or just pissed off at the world?"

He appears shocked that I would actually want a reason. Has no one ever asked him that question before? "I don't know. I can't really explain."

Tate goes quiet, his expression thoughtful as he resumes staring out the window. I start scrolling on my phone, trying to keep one eye on him, wishing he would give me more. He always talks about how crazy his life was when he was with Five Car Pileup, but he never gives actual reasons *why* he behaved so badly. It has to be more than the stereotypical "sex, drugs, and rock and roll" explanation.

I'd love it if he dug a little deeper.

"I thought I was untouchable." His soft voice has me turning toward him, though he's still staring out the window. "I believed I could do no wrong. My life had completely changed and everything was being handed to me, and all I had to do was smile and dance and sing. That's it. It was easy. Until it became hard."

I'm quiet, hoping that he'll talk more, and my silence works.

"Drugs were part of it. Alcohol. I became arrogant. Mean. I didn't like myself. I treated my girlfriend like shit. Jess . . ." He exhales, finally glancing over to meet my gaze. "I did her wrong. She might've cheated on me with Jamie, but I was cheating on her all the time. Girls would throw themselves at me, and I wouldn't turn them down. Jamie knew it. Witnessed it all the time, and he did the same shit I would do. But eventually, he used all of my mistakes against me."

"I bet that hurt." His pain emanates from him, and I can tell it still bothers him, what happened back then.

That moment ruined everything. It broke up the band.

"More than I like to admit," he says, and I can't help but wonder if he still cares about her.

Still wants her.

"Are they together?" I ask.

Tate presses his head against the back of the seat, chuckling. "I don't even know. Are they? I wouldn't be surprised if they were. They went pretty much off the grid after the band broke up. I know they were together a year ago."

I'm pretty sure they are, but I don't want to say that to him. Why make him more emotional? I'm sure that was the ultimate betrayal, his girlfriend cheating on him with one of his closest friends.

"Does that still bother you? What they did?"

"It did, for a long time. But not anymore." He shrugs. "We got together when I was sixteen, right before I blew up and went on that reality show. She was there for it all, and she got sucked into the fame and the drugs and the bullshit too. It was . . . nice having her by my side, because I thought I could trust her. She was my one reminder of home, and that made me feel safe. Comfortable. She was the one person I believed I could count on, but we know how that turned out."

His smile is wistful, and my heart twinges. She hurt him deeply, and I kind of hate her for it.

Okay, I really hate her for it.

"I thought I was in love with Jess, but I don't know if I've ever really been in love, you know?"

"I don't." I offer him a smile, hoping he doesn't think I'm pathetic. "I've never been in love either."

CHAPTER SEVENTEEN

TATE

I'm standing in the middle of every teenage girl's dream bedroom, glancing around at all the shit that's everywhere, covering every available surface. Scarlett Lancaster is a collector of pretty things, and she likes to show them off by putting them on display in her room.

Guess I can't blame her. If I came from the Lancaster wealth, I'd have a bunch of useless shit in my room too. She doesn't have to clean it or dust it. I'm sure they have a housekeeper who lives in this monstrosity of a penthouse apartment. They might have an entire fleet of servants who live in their own separate quarters, ready to assist at their owners' every whim.

"You can sit if you want." Scarlett emerges from her closet wearing a pair of denim shorts and a strappy little white top that reveals a lot of skin, her arms above her head as she pulls her hair into a high ponytail. "That chair is really comfortable."

She's pointing at an overstuffed light-pink chair and ottoman that are right next to the window.

I make my way over to it, reaching out to touch the chair

arm, my fingers sinking into the velvety fabric. How much did this chair cost?

Damn. I thought I was living the high life when I was at my most successful. This family is a whole different breed.

"You should probably take your shoes off if you're going to use the ottoman, though." She points at it. "You might get it dirty."

Without a word I toe off my shoes and settle in, resting my feet on the ottoman as I sink into the comfortable chair. "This is nice."

"I told you." She retreats back into her closet, disappearing completely. I caught a glimpse of the interior of that closet when she first walked in there, and I was impressed.

It's huge. With all sorts of shelves and racks and an island in the middle of it.

"I want to see inside your closet," I announce.

She appears in the closet doorway, a panicked expression on her face. "No way."

"Why not? Whatcha hiding in there?"

"I'm not hiding anything." She yanks the door shut behind her and stands in front of it, her hands braced against the wood. "It's a mess."

"No it's not."

"It kind of is." She doesn't move from her spot, and I don't move from the chair because I think it'll take some concentrated effort to get my ass out of it—it's that comfortable.

"That can't be all. Come on, Scar. What exactly are you hiding?"

She sighs, her shoulders falling. "I have a lot of stuff, okay? And it's sort of embarrassing to show people who don't really know me."

"A lot of stuff, huh?" I raise my brows. I'm guessing that's an understatement.

"Yeah, and it keeps coming. Look at this." She turns and goes back into the closet. I hear her rustling around, and within seconds she's reappeared with a giant wicker basket full of packages. "And this is only from the day after that photo of us first appeared. There's a huge stack of boxes in my dad's office and even more boxes waiting for us in the building's mail room."

Scarlett brings the basket over to my chair, setting it on the floor with a huff, like it weighs a lot, which I'm guessing it does.

"What is all this stuff?" I lean over the chair and start rummaging through, recognizing a few of the brands on the sender labels.

Prada. Chanel. A couple of cosmetic companies.

"Gifts mostly. They want me to wear their stuff and talk about it on my socials. I've been doing a lot of 'get ready with me'–themed posts lately, and that's when I put my makeup on and do my hair. I'm getting so much makeup they want me to feature, it's kind of crazy." She laughs, the light sound smacking me right in the chest. Wouldn't mind hearing that again. "And they're giving it all to me for free! I think I might do a giveaway or something. I could never use all of this. Plus if I held a contest, I could probably gain more followers."

"You don't need to do a giveaway to get more followers. You have a lot already," I point out.

"I'd do it mostly just to get rid of some of this," she admits. "I can afford all of this, yet they send it to me for free because they want me to share it with my audience, which I'll totally do. But I definitely don't need any of it. I'd rather give it to someone else."

This girl has a heart, which I didn't think was possible considering how snippy she's been with me. I wrote her off as a spoiled rich girl when I first met her, and while that can't be denied—even she admits she has a lot of shit—there's kindness inside of her.

And that's refreshing.

"I need to see this closet." I haul myself out of the cushy pink chair and make my way toward the closet, Scarlett right on my heels.

"No, oh my God, please don't go in there!" she's practically shrieking as she wraps her hands around my arm and tries to stop me.

I'm too strong and too fast. I slip out of her grip easily, striding right through the open door and coming to a stop as I take it all in. "Holy shit."

There are clothes literally everywhere. An entire wall consists of white shelves filled with shoes. Another wall is nothing but designer bags. There's even a freaking short hallway that leads to another section of the closet.

"I know." She sounds miserable, and I look to my right to see she's standing next to me, her expression pained. "It's too much."

I can only imagine how expensive everything in this closet is. Or maybe I can't imagine—I don't know. There's probably millions of dollars in shoes and bags alone. "I mean, if you've got it . . ."

"Some of it is my mom's. Her clothes are the absolute best, and her vintage designer bags are so gorgeous and well made compared to what they sell now. They look like they came straight off the runway, they're in such good condition."

I stop at the island in the center of the closet. There are jewelry cases everywhere. Glass dishes full of rings. An earring holder, a necklace holder. The entire top surface is covered in a variety of jewelry, and it's all glittery, the majority of it pink. I'm guessing none of it is costume. Well, the designer stuff probably is, but it's some of the most expensive costume jewelry that's ever been made.

"I don't let anyone in here," Scarlett admits as I continue

wandering around, tilting my head back as I try to take it all in. "This is my private sanctuary. I barely let Rachel in here, which infuriates her."

"Do you come in here sometimes and sit with your designer bags just to keep them company?" I shove my hands in my pockets, mentally counting all the Chanel bags sitting on one particular shelf. The shelf above it is nothing but Dior. The shelf below the Chanel is full of a mixture of Louis Vuitton and Fendi. "And do you have something against Gucci?"

"Sometimes I sit with my bags. I'll hold them like a baby. Pet them and tell them they're pretty." I glance over at her, catching the cheeky smile on her face. "There aren't enough days in the year for me to use all of those bags. My collection is kind of excessive."

"Kind of?"

"You should see my mom's closet. It's even bigger."

I don't know how that's possible.

She adds, "And I don't have anything against Gucci, but my father does."

"What's he got against Gucci?"

"He was supposed to sign with them back in the nineties and be one of the faces of Gucci. But then Tom Ford took over as a designer, and my father and Tom, they clashed. My father walked away from the deal and banned Gucci from his life ever since."

"I love Gucci," I admit.

"Better not tell my father. He'll do his best to convince you it's a bad idea to wear their clothes." She's smiling.

I'm smiling.

It's . . . nice. Spending time with her in her house. Her bedroom. Maybe she's more easygoing with me because she's in her home and she's comfortable.

And I like that.

Instead of continuously wringing her hands and worrying about me being in her closet, Scarlett gives me a mini closet tour, explaining some of the items and where they came from. Mostly it's gifts from her parents, though the stores will send her stuff as a thank-you for her mom's purchases.

"Especially when I was younger. Mom would buy a jumbo-sized Chanel bag, and they'd send me a small one in the same color. My mom is a huge supporter of Chanel. I told her if social media was a thing back when she was my age, she probably would've been sponsored by them."

I stop in front of what looks like the dress section of her closet. "Where's the party dress?"

She frowns. "What party dress?"

"From your birthday." I send her a look, my memory filled with images of Scarlett in that dress. Holding her close despite all the layers of pink tulle.

A memorable dress for a memorable night.

"Oh, it's at a specialty cleaner. They'll spot clean it, preserve it, and put it in a protective bag for safekeeping." Her cheeks turn the faintest pink. "That dress is too much to wear more than once, you know?"

"It was pretty iconic," I agree.

"You really think so?" She sounds surprised.

"Definitely. A total showstopper."

She smiles. "You sound like your manager right now. Simon."

"Hey, at least I don't sound like Roger. He'd say something like 'Seeing you in that dress made me come in my jeans, you looked so hot.'"

The moment the words leave me, I realize my mistake. I probably shouldn't have said that to her. The deepening pink on her cheeks tells me she's embarrassed. Despite her looking pretty fucking hot in that dress, I'm not sure if that was her intention.

"Roger is a rather . . . unique character," she finally says, clearing her throat.

"That's one way to describe him." I contemplate telling her what I really thought of her in that dress and decide to go for it. "You did look pretty hot, though. In that dress."

Her entire body goes still, her big eyes wide as she stares at me. "You really thought so?"

I take a step closer to her, catching her irresistible scent. Damn, she smells good. "Definitely."

"It was so poufy, though."

"You carried it off."

"I needed room everywhere I walked. The crowd would part when they saw me approach."

"Yet I was still able to get close enough to kiss you." I smile. "Well, you were the one who kissed me."

She smiles as well. More like a faint curling of her lips, but I'm counting it. "I still can't believe I did that."

"I can't believe you did it either. What came over you?" I lean against the island, my elbow nudging aside a wide bracelet, and she shifts closer, reaching over to push the bracelet out of my way so I don't knock it on the floor.

Now she's even closer, her chest brushing against mine, and I swear to God, she's not wearing a bra under that strappy little shirt she has on. It's thin, made of cotton or linen, I don't even know, and it's faintly see-through. If I squint, I think I can see the outline of her nipples.

"I don't know what came over me," she admits, her voice soft. "You seemed almost . . . desperate."

"I was." There's no point in trying to hide it. I wasn't about to turn into a colossal fuckup in front of a photographer and allow him to capture the moment for all time.

"And I felt sorry for you," she adds.

Ouch. Truth hurts. And that sucks.

"Plus, I was mad. At . . . Ian." She takes a step back, as if she's suddenly shying away from me.

The mention of Ian the idiot douses any flames that were flickering between us. "Can I be real with you for a sec?"

"Sure."

"From what you've told me about him, I'm pretty sure Ian is a fucking idiot."

A myriad of emotions shines in her eyes. Surprise. A hint of irritation. A douse of pleasure. As if it pleases her that I called him an idiot. "That's probably a little harsh, don't you think?"

"Nope. I stand by my original assessment." I clamp my lips shut, stifling the emotion bubbling up in me. "The guy is an asshole."

"Why do you say that?" She tilts her head to the side, like she genuinely wants to know my reasoning.

"If I was that guy and you were crushing on me, I would've been honest with you from the start whether I liked you or not. And if I felt the same way you did, I would've done everything in my power to show you how I feel about you a long time ago. If you were mine, I'd never let you out of my sight."

She's quiet, her chest rising and falling rapidly, and my gaze drops there, skimming over all that golden skin on display. The hint of cleavage. One of the straps slips off her shoulder, falling halfway down her upper arm, and without thought I reach out and very carefully, very slowly push it back into place, my fingertips lingering on her supple skin.

Goose bumps appear where I touched her, her breath

stuttering. I don't remove my fingers from her shoulder. Instead, I let them drift down, tracing her skin, noting how soft it is.

So fucking soft.

"Scarlett! Are you in here? Darling, where are you?"

My hand drops from her arm, and we both turn to find her mother standing in her closet doorway, a knowing smile on her face.

"What are you two doing hiding away in the closet, hmm?" Gloria Lancaster arches a brow, her lips curved into a knowing smile. Her gaze flickers to mine, and she doesn't appear upset at finding me in here with her only daughter.

If anything, she looks downright thrilled.

Scarlett brushes past me, her words coming fast. "I was just showing him my closet, Mom. That's all. No big deal."

The girl needs to learn how to be chill around her mother when it comes to us. Nothing happened in here, yet she sounds guilty as hell.

"I'm just surprised, is all. You never show anyone your closet, Scarlett." Gloria studies me, and I see the curiosity in her gaze. I'm sure her mother is wondering what makes me so special compared to everyone else. For one, the beloved, idiotic Ian. "Aren't you the lucky one, Tate?"

Yes.

I most definitely am.

CHAPTER EIGHTEEN

SCARLETT

We're in the living room, the sun starting to shift lower in the sky, casting golden beams of light upon us through the uncovered floor-to-ceiling windows. My father has made us all drinks, even me, while Mom is in the kitchen ensuring the family chef is making everything to her exacting standards. I was able to convince her that we should stay home instead of going to a crowded restaurant, and thankfully, she agreed.

Tate sits uncomfortably in one of the overstuffed chairs close to the window, while I sit on the love seat opposite him. My father is still standing at the bar, making himself another drink, and I wonder how long he's going to stand there and continuously refill his glass.

"Here you go." He hands over a glass to Tate, who's the last to receive one. He takes a big gulp from it immediately, draining half of it in one go, and I'm stricken at first, until I realize it's just water.

Tate doesn't drink. He can't. And here's my dad swigging them back like it's no big deal. That's almost . . . rude, isn't it?

Poor Tate. Even I'm sipping on some sweet alcoholic drink, and I'm underage.

Determination filling me, I set the drink on the end table and remind myself to get something different later.

"Thank you," Tate says to my father after he's swallowed, clutching the glass in his big hand.

I stare at that hand, remembering the sensation of his fingers touching my arm. My freaking arm, for goodness' sakes. It should've been nothing in the scheme of things. Just a quick push of my top's strap back onto my shoulder, but everything inside of me lit up the moment I felt his fingers on my skin. I was electrified. Focused on that one spot where he touched me and nowhere else.

I don't remember ever having that kind of reaction when Ian touched me. Or when any boy has touched me.

"Have to admit to you, Tate, that I'm surprised my daughter is interested in you," my father says out of the blue.

"Dad," I groan, wanting to run and hide. God, this is so embarrassing.

He sends me a quick look, but that doesn't stop him from talking. "Admit it, Scarlett. You've been so wrapped up in Ian Baldwin the last couple of years, I thought for sure you were going to force him to marry you."

Ugh, the humiliation. I want to snap my fingers and make myself disappear. Instead, I forget all about my earlier vow and reach for my recently discarded glass, taking a deep swallow from the rum and pineapple my father made me. Now I'm actually hoping the alcohol will make my memory blurry enough to forget this conversation ever happened.

"I have to admit I'm just as shocked as you are," Tate says, his deep voice washing over me, settling my agitated nerves. "But we just clicked that night. You saw the photos."

"I did."

"I think we make a great couple." Tate flashes me a quick smile, and I smile helplessly in return.

"You do." My father examines him closely, and I'm impressed that Tate doesn't squirm. He doesn't even bat an eyelash. "I just hope this is all on the up-and-up and you aren't using my daughter for . . . something."

"What would he be using me for?" I ask, fighting the alarm rising within me.

"I don't know." Dad turns to look at me. "Your family name. The fact that you're my daughter."

Leave it to dear old Dad to make this all about him. I get why he's saying it. I do. And I know he doesn't mean it with any ill intent, but my father has always treated the world as if it revolves around him, and while he can be charming and funny and everyone usually adores him, at the end of the day, I know he's still in love with himself.

And he fully expects everyone else to feel the same.

"With all due respect, sir, my feelings for your daughter have nothing to do with you," Tate says with the most sincerity I think I've ever heard from him . . . ever.

My heart beats a little harder at his confession. If I hadn't just signed a bunch of paperwork that legally binds us to a make-believe relationship only a few hours ago, I could almost believe he's sincere.

Almost.

The room is quiet. I can hear the rattle of ice in Tate's glass as he drains it, and I clutch my own, wishing I had more.

"Scarlett is beautiful and she's smart and she's interesting," Tate finally says, breaking the silence. "And those few moments I had with her at her party, I have to admit . . ."

He goes silent, and I lean forward, anxiously waiting for him to finish that thought.

"She completely captivated me."

I stare at him, buying into his entire speech.

"My daughter is one of the best people I know," Dad says, pride filling his voice. "She's kind. Loyal to a fault. Just ask that Ian dipshit. He can tell you all about it."

They laugh, as if they're both in on the joke, and I lean back against the couch, fighting the flicker of frustration within me that wants to burst into full flame.

I'm so tired of everyone bringing Ian up like he's some sort of joke. He never was to me.

Though now that I've gained some distance and can look back some, I do realize Ian wasn't that interested in me.

Not at all.

Not like Tate is pretending to be.

"I don't think there's any point in bringing him up in conversation anymore. I'd rather keep him out of our relationship." Tate levels his gaze at me, sending a quick wink in my direction.

If anyone else had done that, I'd think it was a bit . . . cringey.

Somehow, Tate makes winking attractive.

"Wise move." Dad raises his glass in Tate's direction. "You don't buckle under pressure. I like that about you, Ramsey."

"Trust me, I've had solid training. Being on a reality show when you're barely sixteen and having people tell you to your face that you're a shitty singer is good practice for dealing with just about anything," Tate admits.

"I always thought you were pretty good from what I saw." Dad wanders back over to the bar, glancing in my direction as he pours himself another. "You want to add anything to this conversation, lovebug?"

More humiliation. He hasn't called me that in years, so of course he's going to pull out that old nickname in front of Tate. "I like him, Daddy."

"That's all you have to say?"

"Isn't that enough?" I counter.

"Well, if I could add anything to the conversation, I'd like to say that this entire thing seems to have happened terribly fast." Mom sweeps into the room, harried yet beautiful and with not a hair out of place. Her white linen pants don't have a single wrinkle, and her crisp black cotton T-shirt fits her to perfection. She's casual yet elegant, giant diamonds winking in her ears, a diamond tennis necklace around her neck. I've always wanted to emulate her style, yet here I sit in a skimpy summer top I bought last year and never wore with boring denim shorts, like I'm going to a backyard barbecue.

"Sometimes love moves quickly," Dad says, coming to our defense. "Remember those first few weeks we were together, Gloria?"

She smiles fondly as she approaches the bar, her hand out and accepting the glass my father gives her. "A whirlwind of a romance."

"How long have you two been together?" Tate asks, sounding genuinely curious.

Either he actually wants to know, or he's a terrific actor.

"Oh, how long, Fitzy?" Mom turns to him.

He smiles at her. "Almost twenty-five years."

"That's great," Tate says with a nod. "You two have been together a long time."

"It went by fast," Mom admits. "Three kids. One just graduated, two in high school. Next thing you know, we'll be empty nesters."

"We'll have plenty to do when they're gone, Glor." Dad

wraps his arm around Mom's shoulders and drops a kiss on her forehead.

He may have been embarrassing me only a few minutes ago, but there's one thing none of us can deny. My dad truly loves my mom. Their relationship is what I aspire to, though I don't know if I want to be with an egomaniac like my father.

I study Tate, who's rattling the ice in his glass again like it's a nervous tic, his gaze locked on my parents as they murmur to each other. He glances over at me, doing a double take when he realizes I'm already watching him, and he offers me a sexy little smirk that sends a zap straight to my core.

Okay. I definitely *never* felt like that when Ian looked at me.

"Promise me you'll treat her right." Dad's face is stern, his focus returning to Tate once again. He's even pointing at him. "I know I already told you this, but you better not break her damn heart or make her cry."

"I would never." Tate's expression is solemn, and he swallows hard, his Adam's apple bobbing.

Dad's gaze is hard. Focused. "This has nothing to do with our money, does it?"

"Fitzy," Mom chastises. We both hate it, yet Dad always seems to make it about money.

"Not at all." Tate rises to his feet and walks over to the bar, setting his glass on the counter before he turns his back to it. "You compensated me well for my performance. Lucky me, I just so happened to talk to your daughter that night and completely fell for her. Now we're seeing if we can make this happen."

"You want this boy, honey?" Dad's gaze finds mine. He says it like he's giving him to me.

I nod, unable to speak. I'm afraid I might say something that sounds ridiculously insincere, and I don't want to risk it.

My father smiles, seemingly pleased. "Then you can have him."

"Pretty sure your dad is treating me like a pet the family just adopted," Tate jokes with me as we make our way to the dining room.

"I'm so sorry." My words aren't nearly enough. I don't want Tate feeling like he's our new pet. "My father is very . . ."

"Interesting," Tate supplies. Politely, I might add. "He has a unique perspective."

"That's one way to put it."

We enter the dining room, and when I spot the plates on the table, I realize Mom has brought out the family china. Which means she's really trying to impress Tate, or intimidate him.

Knowing her, probably a combination.

Since there's only the four of us and the table is for at least eight and can be extended to twelve, Mom and Dad each sit at the head of the table, while Tate and I are across from each other. I give him a look when we settle into our seats, hoping he sees that I'm trying to show him I'm his ally, not his enemy, and he flashes me one of those dazzling smiles of his, the dimple out and everything.

I practically fall into my seat, grateful it's beneath me. Also grateful I didn't have a second drink. I have enough of a buzz as it is on only one.

God, I'm such a lightweight.

The first course is brought out—fresh summer salad—and memories hit me of the night we had dinner with the Baldwins and what a shit show that turned out to be. This is much more pleasant. The conversation is flowing and easy. Dad is asking Tate about his touring days with Five Car Pileup, and while that's a sensitive subject, Tate is answering Dad's questions with ease, glossing over the tough stuff.

Thankfully Dad doesn't try to dig too deep, which is what he usually does.

We talk about summer and the weather, and when the main course arrives—grilled shrimp with broccoli and risotto, yum—Tate has all of us laughing, sharing all the weird personal-video requests he's received.

"Are you still doing that? I'm sure business is booming now, considering all the attention you've received," Dad says.

Tate shakes his head. "I'm on hiatus. Other things are happening with my life right now that are much more exciting than recording happy-birthday messages to twenty-year-olds who used to love me in their teen days."

Mom arches a brow, sending me a knowing look. "That sounds intriguing. What's coming up next for you, Tate?"

"Well, I'm in contract negotiations for another record deal." I can hear the excitement in his voice, see it in his body language. He's practically vibrating in his chair, and I can't help but smile at his excitement. "Pretty sure it's going to go through and I'll be making my first solo album. They already had me come into the studio for 'Red.'"

Ah, the elephant in the room. The song that's about me with the sexual lyrics.

"Oh yes. I heard that." Mom reaches for her wineglass and takes a sip. "It's an interesting song."

"Vaguely inappropriate," Dad adds, his eyes narrowing on Tate. "Though I do get where you were going with it."

I want to roll my eyes. Or duck under the table. Anything to stop talking about that song with my parents.

"Will it be a song on your new album?" Mom asks Tate.

"I'm not sure. Probably. It's doing so well. Hopefully the rest of the album will do just as well." Tate sounds so unsure, and my heart breaks for him a little bit.

I get the sense he moves through life acting like the whole thing will collapse on him out of nowhere. Like he can't count on any of it lasting.

"That's exciting," Dad says, lifting his glass in a cheers gesture. "Glad I could help out with the reemergence of your career."

Love how Daddy just took some credit for Tate's newfound success.

Tate toasts him in return with his water glass, taking a sip before he smothers the smile on his face with his palm. "I guess I owe you one, Fitzy."

Dad laughs, loving his response. "Nah. That was all you. You were on fire that night."

"You were," Mom murmurs in agreement. "All the ladies were screaming."

"It was a fun night," I chime in when I realize they're all waiting for me to say something.

"You recording the album here in the city?" Dad asks. "I know a few producers. Some sound engineers."

Oh boy, here we go.

"Actually, I'll be recording the album in Los Angeles." Tate levels that intense blue gaze of his at me.

"Really? That's so far. What about you and Scarlett?"

"Well." He takes a deep breath, that gorgeous smile on his face yet again, flashing it at everyone. "I was hoping she could go with me."

CHAPTER NINETEEN

SCARLETT

A few days after the family dinner, unbelievably enough, I'm preparing for my trip to Los Angeles. It's all I've been doing since Tate dropped that little bomb at the dinner table. You'd think I were being whisked away to a foreign country far, far away instead of across the country, considering how my mother is reacting to the whole thing.

"I can't believe you're going to Los Angeles instead of on your trip to Europe." The disappointment in Mom's voice is obvious, and I guess that's her biggest issue—me switching up my plans and running off to LA with a guy instead of traveling around Europe with my best friend.

We're currently in my bedroom, and I'm already packing my suitcase, though I have no idea what to bring. Rachel is coming over later to help me with everything, and I know she'll figure out exactly what I need to bring. She's good at that sort of thing.

"You make it sound like Los Angeles is a terrible place," I say as I go through a stack of shorts, most of them new, the tags still attached. "Should I bring mostly shorts or dresses?"

"Dresses," Mom says absently as she settles on the edge of the bed, right next to my open suitcase. There are already a lot of clothes inside, and I'm not even close to finishing. Though I guess it doesn't matter how many suitcases I take, because we're flying there in a plane Irresistible hired for us. "I'm going to miss you so much when you're gone, darling. It'll be so quiet here without you."

"Mom." I glance up from my pile of clothes, noting the disappointment and worry on her expressive face. "I won't be gone that long. Only a couple of weeks."

"It does not take a couple of weeks to make an album, and you know it, Scarlett. He's going to keep you there for himself for months."

Months?

I swallow hard, thinking of spending months with Tate in Los Angeles while he's always working and I'm stuck in a city I'm totally unfamiliar with. I'm only supposed to be maintaining this facade for six weeks. That's it. I won't stay a minute longer than what I signed up for.

A deal is a deal.

"I'm surprised you're even letting me go with him," I admit.

"Why? You're an adult. You can handle yourself." Mom shrugs, reaching for my stack of shorts so she can go through them herself. Her nose is wrinkling already, and she's only contemplated two pairs. "We trust you to know what to do and make the right decisions."

I'm still amazed they'd let me just go across the country with a man they barely know. After all, I only just graduated high school. I might've turned eighteen, but I don't feel like an adult. Though my feelings in regard to Tate don't feel kid-like, that's for sure. "Just so you know, Tate did promise me my own bedroom at the house we're staying at."

The record label arranged a house for us to reside in while Tate records the album. There's even a small studio on the property behind the main house, which Tate was extremely excited about. When he explained it all to me last night on the phone, his voice practically vibrated with excitement.

This record deal and this trip are a game changer for him. He doesn't want anything to mess it up, and truthfully? I refuse to be the reason anything gets messed up. We signed a contract, and I'm legally bound to him for the next six weeks, and I will do my utmost to perform this so-called job as well as I can.

"Oh. So you two won't share a bedroom?" Mom holds up her hand before I can utter a word. "Never mind. Don't tell me. I don't need all the gory details."

Even if Tate and I were actually together and doing whatever it is she's trying not to think of us doing, I wouldn't share a single gory detail with her.

How embarrassing.

"No, we won't share a room. It's too soon for all that." I round the bed and sit on the other side, sighing deeply. "Everything is still too . . . new between us."

Mom is quiet for a moment before she asks, "Have you two had sex yet?"

My entire body flushes hot at her question. "No."

"Oh." Another hesitation. "Do you need to go on birth control?"

No. I'm not having sex with Tate Ramsey—ever. "Probably," I hedge.

"You should make an appointment with the gynecologist before you leave." Mom keeps her gaze focused on the clothes so she doesn't have to look at me. "And take care of that right away."

"I will," I say softly, though I won't.

I can't. We're flying out tomorrow, and I don't have the time. Besides, I don't need to.

She lifts her head, her eyes filled with concern. "Oh, darling. Please make sure Tate treats you well."

I'm a little taken aback by the worry in her voice. "I will, I promise."

"I hope he's good to you. I really, really do." A sigh leaves her, and she shakes her head. "I googled him last night. There was a lot to go through."

Dread fills me, making my stomach twist. "You googled him?"

"Of course I did. From what I read online, he went through a very rough time."

"He did, but he's a lot better now. He's sober. Doesn't drink or do drugs anymore," I reassure her.

"I'm happy to hear it, and I wish him well. In the entertainment industry, it's so hard to avoid those sorts of things. They're everywhere." The doubt on her face, in her voice, is obvious. Mom and Dad went through their "party phase," as they like to call it, and I've done my own online sleuthing regarding my parents—excessive drug use and drinking were abundant with their crowd. I'm sure my parents partook.

I've seen photos of my dad and mom during their heyday. Sometimes they looked flat-out wasted. I'm sure her concern is warranted.

Could I approach Tate with my own worries about his sobriety and warn him that temptation will be everywhere? Or is this even something I could talk to him about? I'm sure he's aware of all of that. And maybe it's none of my business. After all . . .

He's just my fake boyfriend.

"I have total faith in him," I say with all the confidence I can muster. "He'll be fine. He's stronger than everyone thinks."

Mom studies me, warmth filling her gaze. "That's so sweet, Scarlett. How much you believe in him. I think I like you seeing this boy. Even if you did originally go to him only to make Ian jealous."

My mouth pops open as I stare at her. "That's not—"

"You don't need to lie to me," Mom says, interrupting. "I understand your motives. Maybe you'll fall for this Tate character, maybe you won't, but if he helps you get over Ian once and for all, I won't complain."

I'm a little offended. "You don't like Ian?"

"Darling, I feel like you're the only person I know who *does* like him."

"You better call me every single day. No, you have to FaceTime me. I need to see the look on your face when I ask you for all the details about what you're doing with Tate and you try to lie to me."

Rachel and I are sitting in a restaurant, having an early dinner, which is totally unlike us. We don't normally eat dinner until ten at night when we go out, but my flight with Tate to Los Angeles tomorrow is at an ungodly hour, and I don't want to stay out too late. It'll be difficult enough, having to get up that early. I'm already feeling reluctant about leaving my home. My parents. My best friend.

I'm a little scared. I can't lie.

So here Rachel and I sit at one of our favorite places, eating one of their delicious appetizers, all while I'm trying to hold it together so I don't burst into tears in front of her and admit I'm terrified of leaving.

It was difficult enough trying to keep myself calm when

I was with my mom earlier. Rachel, on the other hand? She probably won't let me cry. She'll probably scare my tears away or tell me I need to get over myself, which I know she's right about. I should totally get over myself.

But I'm nervous about this entire situation. I'm leaping into the unknown, and I can only hope that everything goes . . . well.

What does that mean? I can't even answer that question. The whole plan is still so foreign to me.

"I'm not going to lie to you." I lean across the table, lowering my voice, though I know no one is really paying attention to us. "But don't forget, you're the only one who knows what's really going on besides me and Tate."

"And his business manager, the entire team at the record label, and all the suits. Got it." Rachel flashes me a thumbs-up accompanied by a shitty smile, just before she starts laughing.

"You're the worst." I shake my head and grab a fried green bean, dipping it in spicy sauce before I pop it into my mouth.

"You're going to miss me so bad you'll end up begging your little boyfriend to let me fly out to LA and hang out with you," Rachel says.

"You wish. And there is nothing little about my boyfriend," I mutter, taking a sip from my water glass.

Rachel arches a brow so high I swear it hits her hairline. "Oh, do tell, my friend. What do you know about his, *ahem*, size?"

My cheeks go hot at her words and their implication. "I know nothing about his . . . size, but he's tall and has broad shoulders and big hands."

"I bet there are other things on his body that are big." Rachel bursts out laughing when I scowl at her. "I'm just teasing. But you've gotta know the boy is probably packing. Wait, let me correct that—the man."

"Right, the man." I nod, the green beans in my stomach

curdling at the idea of being with Tate in any sort of sexual manner. My feelings aren't disgust—they're more like fear. And I can't deny it—they're also curiosity. "My mom wants me to get on birth control."

"If I were Gloria Lancaster, I would want the same for my beautiful daughter before I sent her across the country to spend a month with freaking Tate Ramsey."

"It might not be for a month. He told me it would only be a couple of weeks, max." I feel like I'm repeating the same conversation I had with my mother only a few hours before.

"When is your return flight?"

"We don't have one. They hired a jet for us, and they'll do the same when we're ready to come back," I admit, my voice small.

The knowing look on Rachel's face is obvious. "Uh-huh. Which means you could end up there the entire time he's making his album, and that could be months, Scarlett. Did you even think of that?"

"Why would he make me stick around that long?" Alarm sweeps through me at the thought.

Alarm and a heady rush of excitement. This is truly the wildest thing I've ever done in my life. And it's especially scary because I'm doing it alone, with only Tate by my side to guide me.

"I don't know. Because it looks good? Because everyone is buying the two of you as a couple? Plus, he might need you there for good luck or whatever. Inspiration," Rachel explains.

"He told his guy at Irresistible that I'm his muse," I admit.

"His muse?" When I nod my confirmation, Rachel literally fans herself. "Well, that's all kinds of hot. Do you think he means it?"

"No," is my automatic response.

"He wrote that song about you."

"He was mad at me when he wrote it."

"Mad and horny for you, more like." Rachel starts laughing, no doubt at the look on my face. "I'm teasing you, but not really. Look, I totally believe you're some sort of inspiration to him. He wrote a freaking song about you. He wants you with him."

"That's the suits talking," I remind her. "They like the idea of us together."

"Give them what they want then." She takes a sip of her soda, her bright-pink lips pursed around the straw. "And hey, if you need me for emotional support, I could be there whenever you call, since you canceled on our European tour."

"I didn't cancel. I just postponed it." I feel terrible about it too. "I wish we could still go."

"I'm not trying to make you feel guilty." Rachel reaches out and settles her hand over mine on the table. "I'm just going to miss you."

"I'll miss you too. I'm sure I'll practically die of boredom and need you out there to hang out with me."

Rachel grins. "You really think you'll get bored with Mr. Sexy Pants?"

"Sexy Pants?" I'm giggling. "Don't know how much Tate would approve of that nickname. And yes, I think I'll get bored. This is a work trip for him. Not fun. He'll be gone all day at the studio, and I'll be stuck at a house. Alone."

"You won't be stuck. You can do whatever you want."

"I can't drive."

"You can take an Uber. Hire a car and driver to be on hand. You're a freaking Lancaster—you can do whatever the hell you want."

"I should probably learn how to drive," I murmur, nibbling on another fried green bean.

"Who's going to teach you? I suppose you could hire someone."

"That sounds . . ."

Awful. I don't want to hire someone to teach me to drive. I don't want to hire a car and driver to be on hand at my every whim either, even if that's what I'm used to. I want this time out in LA to be an adventure. Something new and exciting and just for me—and Tate.

Instead I'm sitting here trying to figure out what to do to fill enough hours in the day to keep me preoccupied. A girl can only shop for so long before she gets bored.

"I'll just hire a car," I say with a sigh. "I bet the record label will provide one."

"Sounds like a tough life." Rachel smiles at me, and I can see the sympathy shining in her gaze.

She feels sorry for me, and I sort of hate that.

I return the smile, sitting up straighter. Trying to look stronger. "You know it."

A text notification sounds right as we start laughing, and I glance down to see I have a text from . . .

My new boyfriend.

Tate: Where are you?

Me: Out to dinner with Rachel.

Tate: ??

Me: My best friend.

Tate: Oh right. I forgot for a minute.

Me: You better not forget her.
She's my very best friend and she

might come out to see me when
we're in LA.

Tate: As long as she doesn't know
what's really going on I'm cool with it.

Guilt slides through me, and I mentally shove it aside. That I told her really shows how much I trust her.

"Who's texting you?" Rachel asks.

I glance up to find her watching me. "It's Tate. He's wondering where I am."

Pausing, I glance to my left, noticing a girl who looks about our age blatantly staring at me. Like she's listening to my every word. The moment we make eye contact, she hurriedly looks away, leaning into the girl sitting next to her before they start whispering furiously.

My stomach knots. I think she recognizes me. And I just said his name out loud, which, if she does recognize me, is confirmation of who I am.

"Did you tell him?" Rachel asks.

"Not really," I admit. I'm about to tell Rachel yet again how much I need her to keep this thing quiet, but I can't do that here. Not when there are too many people around us.

Too many people possibly listening to us.

My phone buzzes again and I check it.

Tate: What restaurant are you at?

I give him the name and drop a pin with my exact location.

Tate: Perfect. I'll be there in a few
minutes.

Panic joins the cocktail of emotions currently swirling inside of me, and I blink at my phone in mute shock.

"What's wrong?" Rachel's voice rises. "You look really freaked out right now."

"Tate just said he'll be here in a few minutes." I lift my head to stare at her. "He's coming here."

"What? You don't want him crashing our last girls'-night dinner?" Rachel grabs a fried green bean and points it at me like a weapon. "He better not come between us. Especially since he's your fa—"

"People are spying on us," I interrupt her, not wanting the word *fake* to be said out loud.

Rachel slowly glances around the restaurant, her eyes narrowed. It feels like practically every person in here turns their head all at once, pretending they don't notice us. I can see the realization dawn in Rachel's eyes. The mischievous smile slowly appearing on her face. "Well, well, well. Looks like you hit Fitzy Lancaster celebrity status, Scarlett. All by dating a has-been boy band member."

"He's not a has-been," I correct. Not even close. The online chatter about Tate hasn't lessened whatsoever. In the last day it's become even worse. Rumor has it the single is going to debut in the top ten on the *Billboard* charts. He's a big deal.

"If Tate Ramsey shows up here, he's going to cause major chaos," Rachel whispers, her eyes wide.

My stomach dips. "I think that's exactly what he wants."

And I'm not sure if I'm fully prepared for it.

CHAPTER TWENTY

TATE

I'm headed to the restaurant where Scarlett is, only at Simon and Roger's suggestion. Simon is currently in the car with me, driving me to the location so I can make an ass of myself at their recommendation.

"This is stupid," I mutter under my breath, staring bleakly at the endless line of stopped traffic ahead of us.

"It's not stupid," Simon reassures. "Roger says it's going to make you and Scarlett even more recognizable and endearing to the public. And I happen to agree with the asshole."

They're both assholes, if you ask me, making me do this. "What if I humiliate myself and end up looking like a total ass?"

Simon glances over at me, his brows drawn together. "You still have some lingering PTSD you're trying to cope with? I thought you were in therapy."

"I haven't gone to therapy in over a year." It got too expensive, and the piddly health insurance I have eventually stopped covering my visits, so I gave it up.

"Maybe you should start those appointments back up. I'll see to it that the label pays for them," Simon suggests, just before he lays on the horn and screams out, "Fuck you!" to some random car.

I about jump out of my skin at his aggressive tone, sending him a look. "Sounds like you need therapy more than I do."

"I see Joanie once a week, sometimes twice." He shrugs.

I'm assuming he's talking about his therapist. "And what does Joanie say about you?"

"That I'm full of rage and should stop taking it out on my clients." The sharkish grin Simon sends my way has me laughing, the fucker.

The laughter is short lived, though, and I sober right up, trying to calm the nerves jangling inside of me. Funny how a person gets performance anxiety for something that only a few weeks ago would've been no big deal.

While I know it won't be hard, what I'm about to do, there will be a lot of eyes on us. If not at the restaurant, then at least via social media.

"You're going to be great," Simon finally says to break the tension-filled silence—most of it coming from me. "Stop getting all worked up over something you used to do all the time."

"I don't remember me doing anything like this," I tell him.

He sends me a quick look. "You used to perform all the time."

"With four other people. Now I'm on my own. All eyes on me."

"You've totally got this. They're all in love with you." Simon reaches over, gripping my knee and giving it a quick shake. "Number seven! Unbelievable!"

"Thanks."

"Red" broke the top ten in its debut on the *Billboard* Hot 100. Fucking unbelievable. I never imagined for a second I could make something like that happen again.

Now the pressure is on. Hotter than ever.

"You should be feeling on top of the world, my friend."

"Easy for you to say." I shift in my seat, my phone declaring the destination is in one mile. Traffic is moving, and as we draw nearer, I realize there are a lot of people outside the restaurant.

Huh.

Simon approaches the building and pulls over to the curb, parking in a red zone. "Go ahead and get out. I'll find parking and come back."

"You're going to leave me here alone?"

"What, are you scared?" The way he says it actually annoys the shit out of me.

What's wrong with having a little stage fright?

"I'm not fucking scared," I spit out. "But there are a shit ton of people hanging around this place."

"It's a popular restaurant. Get over yourself." He hits unlock on his car, and I reach for the handle, opening the door. "Don't forget your guitar."

I climb out of the car and open the back door, pulling my guitar out and leaving the case behind. I sling the strap around my neck, the beat-up old guitar resting in front of me, and I bend my knees so I can make eye contact with Simon, still in the car. "Want me to wait for you before I start?"

"Nah. Someone will start recording the moment you start singing, so I won't miss much. See you in a few."

I've barely slammed the car door before Simon is pulling back into traffic, causing a few cars to honk at his impatient ass. Turning, I face the restaurant, realizing that quite a few people are watching me.

A young girl screams out, "Tate Ramsey!" when she spots me, ready to charge in my direction, but the man standing with her—pretty sure that's her dad—grabs her by the shoulder, holding her back.

Her yelling out my name draws plenty of attention—heads swivel in my direction, curiosity in their gazes, recognition dawning.

Shit. Looks like I'm performing for an audience.

The restaurant Scarlett is at has plenty of windows lining the front, and as I approach the building, I'm squinting, trying to find her sitting inside. Finally, I spot her, her long brown hair streaming down her back, smiling as she sits across from a cute blond I recognize from her party. Her best friend, Rachel. The one who's supposedly going to visit us in Los Angeles.

Hopefully she's a Tate Ramsey fan.

Grateful she's sitting so close to a window, I position myself directly in front of it and grab hold of my guitar, strumming it. Ignoring everyone watching me, and that's pretty fucking difficult since they all have their phones aimed right at me, capturing what I'm about to do, I clear my throat and march right up to the window, knocking on it so hard the glass rattles.

Scarlett startles, her head swinging my way, her eyes going wide when she spots me. I glance over at her friend, who's watching me with equal wide-eyed wonder, and I clear my throat one more time before I begin to sing.

She's a beautiful girl who changed my life
Oh, what a feeling, I'm on this ride
She's the prettiest thing I ever did see
What the hell does she want with a guy like me?
Red in the face, shy as can be
Maybe she'll want to run away with me
Oh, Scarlett, my Scarlett
You're a beautiful thing

Oh, Scarlett, my Scarlett
Will you make my wishes come true?
Oh, Scarlett, my Scarlett
I just want to be with you

The crowd is clapping and cheering the moment I stop singing, and I wonder if Scarlett could even hear my ass when she leaps from her seat and practically runs through the restaurant, heading toward the exit doors. She's outside in an instant, her steps slowing when she draws closer, her expression vaguely confused.

"Did you just sing me another song?" she asks.

Damn it, I knew she didn't hear me.

"You didn't hear it?"

"Not really," she admits, her expression turning shy. "But I want to."

Her friend stops just behind her, a cheesy grin on her face. "Sing it again, Tate! The restaurant was too loud for us to hear you."

I launch into the song once more, knowing that it's not the best, lyrics-wise, but I busted it out in a matter of minutes per Simon and Roger's suggestion. An addition to the "Red" song, in celebration of it breaking the top ten on its debut.

"Go sing to her," Roger said. *"Like you did for your little girlfriend back in the day. Remember how you used to do that?"*

Yeah, I definitely remember. Can't believe they actually made me recreate the moment I wrote a song for my ex-girlfriend when we were first in Five Car Pileup. That was a song I only sang a handful of times, eventually becoming too embarrassed by the simple lyrics. Yet the moment is forever captured on film thanks to the reality show I was on.

The song was called "Jess, You Make Me a Mess."

Talk about foreshadowing, goddamn.

My gaze never strays from Scarlett's as I continue to sing, hoping she can understand what I'm really trying to tell her.

That this is a complete publicity stunt. They made me do this. The words to this lame-ass song mean nothing. We're just trying to keep the interest on social media going. *Please don't think I'm a cheesy asshole.*

Scarlett's lips curl up when I get to the "Oh, Scarlett, my Scarlett" line, and I stumble over the strings of my guitar, making them twang out of tune. I find my rhythm again; it's a quick mishap, but she notices, her eyes sparkling, her body subtly moving to the music.

I could never admit to her it was the glow in her gaze that threw me off. The faint smile curling her lips. That beautiful face of hers. It's like she's actually enjoying the song, buying into the entire moment and falling for it.

Falling for *me*.

The song ends with me drawing out the last word, and I strum the guitar before clamping my hand on the strings, making the song stop. There's actual silence in the air. I don't even hear a car horn honk or the nonstop drone of a siren like usual. These last few seconds feel downright . . .

Magical.

And then the entire crowd erupts into applause. There's clapping and screaming and whistling. Scarlett's face turns the prettiest shade of pink, and her friend Rachel grabs her shoulders from behind, giving her the lightest shake.

"Come to Los Angeles with me." I release the neck of my guitar and hold my hand out toward her.

She takes a step forward, her friend's hands falling from her shoulders, Rachel bringing them up so her clutched hands are now beneath her chin as she observes us. I feel like I've just earned the best friend's approval, and I tug Scarlett as close as I can, swinging the guitar so it's behind me.

Scarlett's chest collides with mine, her breasts smashed against me as she murmurs, "Yes."

I take my opportunity, cupping the side of her face, swooping in for another kiss, fully expecting it to be like all the rest. Simple. A little on the sweet side.

It's not. Not even close. This one feels completely different, starting from that first moment our mouths connect. Her lips are soft and sweet and open, and I take advantage, my fingers sliding down to her neck, my thumb pressing beneath her jaw, tilting her head back so I can kiss her deeply. Our tongues tangle, but I'm trying to keep this classy so we don't look like two horny people making out on the street.

That's just another day in midtown Manhattan, if I'm being real.

Scarlett eventually pulls away, breathless, her cheeks even pinker. She blinks those velvety brown eyes open, and she's smiling.

I'm smiling. I can hear people shout our names, can hear the click of photos being taken, of videos being recorded, every single person watching us desperate to get our attention, but I can't focus on anything else but her. This girl.

It's at this moment I realize I might be in too deep.

CHAPTER TWENTY-ONE

SCARLETT

"Oh my gosh, it's beautiful," I say the second we enter the house that'll be our headquarters for the next few weeks.

The floors are wood, and the furniture in the open living area is oversize and covered in pristine white. The windows that line the front of the house are massive, and the fresh yet vaguely salty scent reminds me of the ocean.

Which we're relatively close to, though the scent isn't coming from the outside air but the subtle diffuser I see sitting on top of a table close to the front door.

"Yeah, it's nice." Tate closes the door behind us and locks it, not taking any chances despite the two security guys we have currently wandering around outside, checking out the yard and the neighborhood in general.

We have an entourage coming with us. Staying with us. The security team will remain on site for the entirety of our stay here. The home we're staying at is deep in the hills of Calabasas, where plenty of other celebrities live in extremely secure neighborhoods. The point of staying here is to give the illusion of celebrity, Roger explained to us during the plane ride. And while Tate is definitely considered a celebrity, his star is still faintly tarnished.

It's my job, Roger told me privately when Tate left to use the restroom, to help ensure Tate shines brighter than ever.

I just smiled and nodded in agreement with everything that Roger told me. Told us. For most of the flight I wished for Simon to be there too, because he makes an excellent buffer, but we had to endure Roger alone, which I struggled with.

The man never knows when to shut up. His mouth is big, and he says the most inappropriate things, making me kind of uncomfortable. But throughout the flight, Tate took whatever Roger said in stride, sending me apologetic looks or even rolling his eyes. He actually yelled at Roger a few times to watch his mouth, and while he'd be on good behavior for approximately five minutes, eventually it would get to be too much, and he'd say something else awful.

Thankfully we parted ways with Roger at the airport. I was afraid he'd want to see the house we're staying at, but he jumped into his own car—which was brought to the tarmac where our private plane landed, I might add—and took off with a roar of the engine and squealing tires.

The relief I felt at his departure still lingers. The man is a bit of a menace—to borrow that term from my father.

Still have to deal with the security, though, which is odd. Our family has had security off and on throughout the years, but mostly for special events or when we're traveling and my mother insists on bringing her very best jewelry. Mom wants to show it off, and Dad wants to keep it under lock and key, so they compromise with beefy security guys who tag along with Mom when she busts out the diamonds and is decked head to toe in designer goods.

It's always a scene. Kind of like how Tate and I are turning into a scene. You'd think I'd be used to this by now, but it's still a little wild.

Especially when it's happening to me.

The record label hired a private jet for us to travel in, which comes with an even more private entrance to the airport. Thanks to our little moment in front of the restaurant last night and his new single blazing up the charts, management didn't want us to cause a commotion with our arrival.

Pretty sure that's all we've been doing since our supposed story hit the internet, and that's the part they like, right?

But it's all a game, dealing with the paparazzi. That's what Tate told me. They want you, but they don't want you too much. You have to play cat and mouse with them.

I think about what happened last night. The song he serenaded me with. It wasn't as good as "Red," but it was sweet. It felt more from the heart, even though he did admit he wrote it really quick while on the way to the restaurant.

That doesn't even matter. I thought it was . . . nice. And when Tate pulled me into his arms and kissed me until I thought my legs might give out under me?

Forget it. Our faces—usually with our mouths mashed together, locked in a passionate kiss—are now everywhere. And since he faux asked me to go to Los Angeles with him, the paparazzi are on the lookout for us at every airport in Southern California.

It's crazy. We're causing serious mayhem everywhere we go, and I don't get why people care so much.

I hear a low whistle coming from somewhere and realize I'm standing alone in the living area while Tate is already in the kitchen. "Damn, this is nice."

I follow him into the massive space, silently taking in everything. There is white everywhere. The marble countertops, the cabinets, the massive island, and the walls. There's a breakfast nook with a sleek white table and chairs filling it, surrounded by windows that overlook the gorgeous backyard with what looks like a never-ending bright-green lawn and a rectangular pool that I swear must be Olympic size.

"Wow," I murmur as I go to one of the windows and stare outside. "This is beautiful."

"Roger and Irresistible never do anything half-assed," Tate says as he moves about the kitchen. I hear doors opening and glance over my shoulder to find him staring into the refrigerator. "We have a personal chef who should be here any minute. Roger texted a few minutes ago letting me know. They'll make dinner for us."

"A personal chef?" I'm used to this sort of treatment at home thanks to being a Lancaster, but I figured we would mostly be on our own out here.

Surprisingly enough, looks like I'm wrong.

"Oh yeah, there is no expense too great for me right now, according to Roger. And Simon. Thanks to the song hitting the top ten." He leans against the edge of the pristine white marble countertop, watching me. "I'll eventually be charged for all of this, though. They'll sneak it into my royalty statements, and it'll take me years to earn out."

I glance around the contemporary kitchen, wondering how much something like this must cost. "Do they own this place?"

"They rent it, I'm sure at a steep cost. Again, it's all part of the image. 'Tate Ramsey has hit it big again. His next-door neighbor is Drake. More at eleven.'" He throws his hands up in the air and makes the jazz-hands gesture, his fingers wiggling. "The more I fit the image, the more it feeds the machine, so to speak."

"What machine?"

"Oh, come on, Scar. The publicity machine." He pushes away from the counter and starts to exit the kitchen via another hallway on the other side of the room. "Come on. Let's go check out the bedrooms."

I follow him, impressed by the size of the rooms. There are two primary bedrooms on either side of the hall, and I choose the one that overlooks the backyard. I want a view of that pool. Since I've lived in the city for the majority of my life, this sort of yard feels so different to me.

And I love it.

Our luggage is brought in by one of the security guys, and I unpack the essentials. Tate meets with the personal chef once she arrives, eventually calling me into the kitchen to join them so I can discuss any dietary needs or allergies I might have. Once she starts preparing our dinner, I go back to my room and change into a bikini, donning a black sundress as a cover-up before I slather my face with SPF and then head for the backyard.

"Where are you going?" Tate's deep voice calls from within his bedroom.

I stop in the open doorway, slipping on my Fendi sunglasses, the cute ones with the *F* logos all over the frames. "To the pool."

He's standing beside his bed, his suitcase open, and when I glance at it, I can't help but think it looks like it just exploded. Clothes are literally everywhere, most of them unfolded and wrinkled. "Going for a swim?"

"Maybe." I shrug one shoulder. More like definitely. I want to lie out in the sun first on one of those big loungers that sit by the pool. Soak up those rays—with SPF on, of course. And then once I get hot enough, I'll jump in the pool and cool off. "Do you know if they have towels outside?"

"Probably. Come on, let's go check." Tate heads toward me,

and I dart out of his way, standing to the side as he strides out of his bedroom, before I fall into step behind him. We walk out onto the back patio via the kitchen's back door, and Tate finds a storage box full of towels next to a table. He props open the box lid and reaches inside, handing me a thick white towel, our fingers grazing during the exchange. "Here you go."

"Thank you." I take the plush towel, trying to ignore the tingling sensation sweeping up my arm at the innocent touch. He's watching me with a heavy gaze, absently rubbing his bottom lip with his thumb, and I have this sudden urge to fling myself at him and see if he'd grab hold of me.

I bet he would. Wait, scratch that.

I know he would.

That kiss in front of the restaurant while a group of people watched us might've been for show, but it felt like so much more. At the very least, it felt different compared to the previous ones, unlike any kiss he's given me before, and this is the third time we've done this.

The first one was a shock, and once he got into it, he teased me, almost as if he was daring me to kiss him back, which I did.

The second time, out on the street? I think he kissed me to shut me up, and it worked. That one was simpler and, thanks to my anger and frustration, fairly unmoving.

The third one, though?

If a chorus of angels had come down from the heavens and sung us a song while we kissed, I wouldn't have noticed. Everything around us faded. The audience, the cars on the street, the usual city noise. Even Rachel faded away, and all I was left with was the sensation of Tate's mouth moving over mine. His tongue gliding against mine. His hands on my body and that warm, hard wall of muscle known as his fit body pressed against me...

I haven't been able to get it out of my mind since. I don't

remember ever feeling this way when I was with Ian. Not that he ever held me or kissed me. Oh, a few times on the cheek here and there over the years, but that was it.

And he definitely never sang to me. Or wrote me a song. He most definitely never declared his feelings for me publicly, let alone privately. Not that I expected Ian to do anything like that. Tate singing for me felt cheesy and almost silly the night of my birthday. Well, with the exception of when he sang me "Happy Birthday" and there was that dark, almost sensual gleam in his eye as he watched me. Like he was thinking about me in . . . inappropriate ways.

It might've all been a publicity stunt, but I fell for it completely. I wanted to swoon. Even Rachel—who is one of the most hardened people I know—totally fell for it. She was all giddy and fluttery around Tate, and when he took a selfie with her last night so she could post it on her stories? She was giving him a moony look that left me grumpy for about a minute.

Then I remembered I was the one who was stuck with him for the next six weeks, and I forgot all about my jealousy. Because that's what it was. I was jealous. Feeling downright territorial. For the next six weeks, Tate Ramsey belongs with me. To me.

End of story.

"You already finish unpacking?" Tate asks, his smooth voice pulling me from my thoughts.

"Kind of." Not really.

He smiles. "I'm going to finish up, and then I think I'll join you."

"By the pool?" My voice turns into a squeak.

His smile grows. "Yep. See you in a few."

Tate tugs on the end of my ponytail playfully and then heads back into the house.

I stand there for a moment, gathering my wayward thoughts. Wondering how I'm going to endure the next couple of weeks at this house with Tate. I was under the assumption he would be locked away in a recording studio for hours on end every single day, leaving me alone. But he explained to me on the drive to the house that the first week or two, he'll be working at the studio that's on the property, putting songs together with a sound engineer and a keyboardist. Meaning he'll be here for the majority of the time that I'm here as well.

I know he'll be busy, but he'll also be right here, all the time. And that might be kind of weird.

Or will it?

I pull one of the heavy loungers closer to the pool, lay the thick towel across it, and take off my sundress, readjusting my bikini top so my boobs are mostly contained before I settle down. The sun is warm but not as intense as I thought it might be, and I reposition the lounger once again before I lie on it, closing my eyes and tilting my face toward the sun. It warms my skin almost immediately, lulling me into drowsiness within a few minutes, and just when I'm about to fall asleep, I feel a shadow settle over me.

"You're going to burn."

I crack one eye open to find Tate standing at the foot of my lounger, clad in black swim trunks and nothing else, dark glasses covering his eyes.

I nearly swallow my tongue as I take in all that bare skin on display. The man is in fine physical shape, his body much more developed than it was when he was a lanky teenager during his boy band days. I remember thinking he was so cute then, my body responding in unfamiliar ways to a shirtless photo shoot he did.

He looks a million times better, plus it's in person. My body is at it again, responding in all sorts of ways, and I shift my position, pressing my thighs together to stave off the sudden needy feeling racing through me.

"Am I already turning red?" I ask, glancing down at my bare shoulder.

"A little." He lifts his shades, his narrowed eyes skimming over my body, lingering in places that make me squirm again. "You put on sunscreen?"

"Only on my face," I admit, feeling silly. I should know better. Baking myself in the Southern California sun without protection? What's wrong with me? I blame jet lag, though that's probably a bogus excuse.

"I brought some." He shows me the sunscreen can clutched in his right hand. He offers it to me, and I take it. "Hold this for me, will you."

I watch as he grabs another lounger and drags it over so it's aligned with mine. He drapes his towel across it before he turns to me once more. I'm still in the same position, sitting there with the sunscreen in my hand, holding it like I'm a display model about to sell it to someone.

Yikes.

"Spray some on," Tate encourages me, and I rise to my feet, practically bumping into him, he's standing so close.

I shake the bottle and aim the sunscreen at myself before I start spraying my arms and shoulders and chest. My stomach and the fronts of my legs. I hand the bottle to Tate.

"You should do your back," he suggests as he starts spraying himself.

My mouth goes dry as I watch the sheen appear on his smooth skin. "I can't reach it."

I feel like I'm in a movie. Haven't we all seen moments like this, when the girl needs the guy to rub sunscreen or tanning lotion on her back because she can't reach? Or she does the same for him?

Yeah. I'm having a weird sort of déjà vu feeling, though I've never actually had this happen to me.

"I'll help you if you help me." He grins, and I'm left breathless at the sight of that famous megawatt smile. "Turn around."

He twirls his finger for emphasis, and I do as he says, presenting my back to him. He starts to spray, the sunscreen hitting my skin and making me shiver. When he slowly pushes my hair away from the back of my neck, his fingers brushing my nape, I bite my lip and close my eyes, savoring the feeling of his hands on me. His body so close to mine. I can feel the heat radiating from him.

One more step and we'd be flesh to flesh. I don't know what I would do if that happened.

I sort of want to know what it would feel like. To have Tate pressed up against me. His bare chest against my back, his hands on my hips, his mouth on my neck—

"Will you spray me now?" he asks, interrupting my vaguely dirty thoughts.

My entire body flushes, and I glance up at him to see he's already offering me the sunscreen. I take it from him, and he turns so his back is to me. I start spraying, covering what feels like acres of skin, silently marveling at the smooth expanse of his back, the breadth of his shoulders. The twin dimples at the base of his spine, just above the waistband of his swim trunks.

I even bend down and spray the backs of his legs, wanting to make sure every inch of him is covered, and when I'm finally finished, I whisper, "All done."

My voice is gone. My heart is hammering in my chest, threatening to fly out at any given moment, and I tell myself to chill. This is no big deal.

It means nothing.

He glances over his shoulder, his lips curved in the faintest smile. "Thanks."

"Thank you," I return, setting the sunscreen on a nearby table.

Feeling awkward, I practically throw myself back on the lounger, grateful I have sunglasses on so he can't see my eyes. He's humming as he repositions his towel, stretching it out so it covers the entirety of the lounger.

I pretend I'm not watching as he settles in on the chair, the sunglasses covering his eyes once more, his body, gleaming with sunscreen, aimed toward the sun. My gaze crawls over his skin, taking note of every little thing. His strong neck. The muscular shoulders. How he lifts his arm, running his hand through his hair and pushing it away from his face, his biceps bulging. The faint smattering of dark hair between his pecs. The same dark hair that runs in a line from his navel down his stomach, before disappearing beneath the waistband of his swim trunks.

My mouth is dry. My entire body aching. My gaze lingers on his shorts, wondering what sorts of mysteries lie beneath the fabric, and I get all flustered and uncomfortable just thinking about it.

"You okay over there?" He doesn't turn toward me. He barely moves save for his lips when he asks the question.

I look away like I've been caught staring, when there's no indication that he actually knows what I was doing. "I'm fine." I clear my throat, trying to play it cool. "Why do you ask?"

"You're rustling around over there. Sounds like you can't get comfortable." He turns his head in my direction, lifting his sunglasses so he can peek at me. "You already getting hot?"

More like hot and bothered. "It's kind of warm out here."

He faces the sky once more, dropping his glasses over his eyes. "Jump in. I'm sure the water will feel good. Cool you down."

Yeah, I definitely need to cool down. In more ways than one.

CHAPTER TWENTY-TWO

TATE

Not too sure why exactly I feel this way—let's call it intuition—but I think my fake girlfriend is having, ah, horny feelings at the moment.

And they involve me.

My entire body is relaxed. As if I don't have a care in the world, which is the furthest thing from the truth. Deep down, I'm amped up and anxious, worried about having to come up with a bunch of fucking great songs in a short amount of time, and I don't know if I can do it.

The doubt and self-loathing hit me like a freight train the moment we walked onto the plane and I saw Roger sitting there, an expectant look on his face, his gaze assessing. Scarlett was seemingly oblivious, thank God. She doesn't need to be worried about shit.

I'm the one whose entire life feels like it's riding on this moment. This time in Los Angeles, the album, the fake relationship, all of it. One wrong move, and I could potentially fuck everything up.

My entire career—life—blowing up in my face.

The need to have a drink makes my skin itchy, but there's nothing I can do about it. The bar in the family room is empty of any sort of alcohol, which I assume isn't normal. I'm positive Roger made sure there wouldn't be a single drop of liquor in this house.

Hell, I'd even roll a joint or indulge in an edible, just to get out of the fucked-up headspace I'm currently dealing with. But none of that is readily available, and deep down, I know it would be a huge mistake. I can't be California sober, as they like to call it.

I'm either completely sober or completely wasted. There's no in-between.

Glancing over at Scarlett, I let my gaze sweep over her, taking in all that smooth, shiny skin. The gentle flare of her hips. The flat expanse of her stomach. The sweet swell of her tits.

I know exactly what would help alleviate my stress and calm me right down.

Sex.

But would my pretend girlfriend want to have sex with me?

Probably not.

I really do get the sense that Scarlett is feeling some kind of way about me, though. Like maybe with the right words and a few persuasive moves, I could have her beneath me by the end of the evening.

A couple of orgasms later, and we'd both be floating in that pool by tomorrow morning with giant smiles on our faces.

Worry smacks me right between the eyes, and I look away from her, focusing on the pool. The rippling blue water. What if I try to make a move and she slaps me and tries to have me arrested for sexual assault? What then?

Fuck that.

Deciding I need to keep my hands to myself, I remain on the lounger and watch as she eventually gets up, settling her sunglasses on the tiny table next to her before she stretches her arms above her head. The movement causes her tits to appear like they might pop out of her bikini top at any moment, and I wait anxiously for exactly that to happen.

No such luck. They remain covered, though her hard nipples press against the fabric.

Jesus.

The bikini is a fucking killer. Hot-pink triangles barely cover her chest, and those little bottoms don't leave much to the imagination, though I'm still curious, not gonna lie.

Is she bare under the bottoms, or does she have a nice little landing strip? I'm guessing the latter. Only because I'm pretty certain our girl Scar here is a virgin.

A few weeks ago, that would've meant I'd avoid her at all costs. No way would I want to be responsible for that sort of thing. Dealt with it a lot during my heyday, and there was plenty of emotional damage done.

By me.

Yeah. Not my proudest moments.

But this woman and I are legally bound in our fake relationship, and what the hell is wrong with us dabbling in sex together? I'm attracted to her. Despite the original prissy attitude and the earlier obvious disdain she felt toward me, Scarlett's definitely come around. She's much more relaxed around me, and that last kiss we shared was pretty fucking spectacular.

Wouldn't mind a repeat performance—privately.

And why couldn't it happen? We're young. We're attracted to each other. Hell, she used to have a raging crush on me during her formative teenage years, and I'm fairly certain she's still interested in me. Like, I could make a move on her, and the chances are in my favor she wouldn't say no.

I felt her gaze roaming over me earlier, when I first sat down next to her. I know she was checking me out, and fuck if my dick didn't try to rise to the occasion thanks to her wandering eyes.

She turns her back to me, her feet curling around the edge of the pool. Her ass cheeks are hanging out of the bikini bottoms, and I run a hand over my mouth to smother my groan. This girl . . .

Is definitely trying to kill me.

With little warning and surprising grace, she quickly shifts into position and dives in the pool, barely making a splash. I watch as she glides under the water, her feet barely moving, her body sleek and sexy, until her head pops out of the water in the deep end, her hands rising to smooth her hair away from her face. She's treading water right in front of me, and I stare at her, noting the water droplets clinging to her eyelashes. Her lips are curved into an inviting smile as she says, "You should jump in."

Her voice is soft and seductive.

Inviting.

"Oh yeah?" I act like I'm not interested.

Her eyebrows pinch together like they sometimes do, a little crease forming in between them. "It feels really good. Refreshing."

"The water?" I'm teasing her.

"Well, yeah." Her hand cuts through the water as she tries to splash me, and a couple of droplets hit my leg. "You should get in here."

"Are you trying to splash me?" My eyebrows shoot up.

"Of course not." She hits the water harder, and this time, she splashes my feet and calves, soaking the towel beneath me. "What makes you think I am?"

"Scarlett," I say in lazy warning, enjoying this playful side to her.

"Oh, you *don't* want me to splash you?" She does it again, the water now soaking me from the waist down. "Sorry."

She doesn't sound sorry at all. And from the expression on her face, I'd say she doesn't appear sorry either.

"You're asking for it." My voice is still mild, my body relaxed. She has no idea I'm coiled tight and ready to spring on her at any given moment.

"Oooh, I'm so scared." Another splash, and that's it.

I'm up and off the lounger in seconds, jumping into the pool directly in front of her, making as big a splash as I possibly can. She's squealing, trying to get out of my way, but I hook my fingers around her upper arm, pulling her in close, our bodies colliding.

Sparks fly between us despite the cool water, the undeniable attraction we share almost unbearable, yet it feels so damn good. Her silky legs tangle with mine, and without thought, I back her against the wall of the pool, pinning her there with my body so she can't escape.

"See what happens when you keep splashing me?" My voice sounds extra deep even to me, and I give in to temptation, my hands resting lightly on her hips.

Scarlett playfully shoves at my chest with both hands, but I don't budge. "You're no fun."

"I'm no fun?" I run my hand down her hip. Around her ass, teasing the leg of her bikini bottoms, my fingers streaking along the underside of her ass cheek. It's plump and perfect. "I can think of a few ways we can have fun."

The mood between us shifts at my words, her body going still. She keeps her head bent, so all I can see is her wet hair falling around her face, and I slip my other hand under her chin, tilting her head up so she has no other choice but to face me.

She blinks, water still clinging to her long lashes, and I'm filled with the need to kiss her.

Like the impulsive asshole that I still am, I do exactly that, pressing my mouth to hers.

She doesn't resist. Doesn't even so much as put up a fight. If anything, she gives in, her hands gliding up my bare chest, setting off sparks wherever she touches me. When her lips part beneath mine, allowing my tongue entry, I press more firmly against her. Wanting to feel her.

Needing her to feel me.

Scarlett sighs in surrender, and I swallow the sound, circling her tongue with mine, my hands playing with the waistband of her bikini bottoms. She lifts her legs up, wrapping them around my waist, and I slide my hands down, gripping her ass, ready to pull her in even closer—

"There you kids are! Oh shit, sorry to interrupt."

I slump against Scarlett for a moment at the sound of Roger's familiar cackle, closing my eyes for the briefest second before I gently push away from her and turn to face him. "What are you doing here?"

"Thought I'd stop by and check in with you two." Roger is grinning, his gaze only for Scarlett. I glance over my shoulder to watch her submerge herself so the water covers her from the chin down.

Smart move. Now Roger is leering almost in disappointment thanks to his view being cut off. I tread water in front of her, cutting him off from seeing her at all.

"We're doing good," I reassure him, glancing over my shoulder to meet Scarlett's gaze, mouthing to her, *Are you okay?*

She nods, her lips curved into the smallest smile.

"I can see that. You two seem pretty cozy." Roger's tone is knowing.

Irritating.

Reluctantly I leave Scarlett where she is and make my way across the pool, into the shallow end.

"Just trying to cool off," I say nonchalantly. I climb the stairs and exit the pool, heading for the lounger and grabbing my half-soaked towel. "Considering we're together, wouldn't you assume we're already pretty cozy?"

He draws near when I pick up the towel and start absently wiping water away from my chest. "Cut the shit, kid. I know you two aren't for real."

The paperwork Scarlett and I signed is an entirely different document than the contract I signed with Irresistible. But of course Roger knows. Who the hell told him? "Just trying to give you what you want."

"And we appreciate it, Tate. We really do. The scene you two made, with you singing to her in front of that restaurant? Pure magic, kid. Fucking social media gold. She looked like she wanted to run away with you, and you looked like you wanted to tear her clothes off and fuck her right there in the street. Couldn't ask for anything better," Roger says, rambling dirtily as he usually does.

"Thanks," I say, wondering if he can even detect the sarcasm in my tone. "Why are you here, Rog?"

He glances over at where Scarlett is still treading water in the pool before he tilts his head toward the house, indicating he wants to talk to me inside. "I need to go over a few things with you."

"Let's go in the house," I tell him before I check yet again on Scarlett, who's watching us with those big doe eyes, a trace of worry in her expression. I know Roger makes her a little uncomfortable, and I can't blame her for feeling that way. "I'll be right back," I tell her.

She nods. "Okay."

Roger and I head for the house, and the moment the door is closed behind us, I'm talking. "You need to watch your mouth around Scarlett."

Roger appears taken aback at my demand. "What's wrong with my mouth?"

"It says some really inappropriate shit." I rub at my chin, hating that I'm trying to be fucking serious while I stand here in my swim trunks and Roger is fully clothed. I should've at least pulled on a T-shirt. "And I don't like the way you were staring at her either."

"I can't stare at a pretty girl when her tits are out in that bikini she's wearing?"

Even hearing him talk about Scarlett's tits infuriates me. "Not with Scarlett, you can't. Back off."

Roger studies me for a moment, slowly shaking his head. "You're taking this boyfriend role of yours seriously."

"I like her—I *respect* her," I tell him. "And if that means I need to tell you to check yourself when you're around her, then I will."

Roger throws his hands up in defeat, though he's got a grin on his face, the fucker. "Noted. I'll watch myself."

That was easier than I thought. "Thank you."

He drops his hands. "But that means you also need to watch yourself. I'm the one who gave you this record deal, and if you do something I don't like, I have the power to take it away from you. Don't forget that."

Anger simmers in my blood at his obvious threat. There's the Roger I remember from near the tail end of Five Car Pileup. The one who would kiss our ass one minute and then kick it the next. This guy had a serious Jekyll-and-Hyde thing going on back then, and it looks like that hasn't changed. "I'm not here to fight with you, Roger. I just want to make sure you respect Scarlett."

"Right, the hot little eighteen-year-old with more money than anyone else on this planet who can have whatever she wants as long as Daddy buys it for her deserves *my* respect." Roger rolls his eyes. "How about your little girlfriend show me a little respect? I got you this record deal, this fucking sweet-ass house with a studio. When I showed up here, I fully expected to find you in the studio already trying to lay down some tracks. Maybe you'd be holed up somewhere writing lyrics, I don't know. But instead, I find you playing grab-ass in the pool, looking ready to fuck her when she isn't even your actual girlfriend. Like, what the hell, Tate?"

I'm flabbergasted the man thinks I'd be productive enough that I'd be ready to lay down tracks already. "We only just got here."

"And time is money, my friend. You need to get on it. You have a month to get your shit together."

"A month?"

"We need to strike while the iron is hot. You know this. In three months, your ass could end up yesterday's news. Justin Bieber could get his hot wife pregnant or, I don't know, Britney could finally come out with a tell-all book. A new album. Shit, maybe Bieber breaks up with wifey and gets back together with Selena. What I'm trying to say is, anything could happen and the public would forget all about you, just like that."

Roger snaps his fingers for emphasis.

That anxious feeling returns, thumping hard in the exact part of my chest where my heart resides, and I rub at the spot, hating how Roger's words make me feel. Like I'm already behind and it's going to be impossible for me to catch up. "I'll start working first thing tomorrow."

"Might I suggest you start working tonight? Take your girlfriend out to dinner, and go someplace popular, where you'll be seen. I'll have my assistant text you a few restaurant suggestions." Roger reaches into his back pocket and grabs his designer wallet, opening it up and pulling out a few hundred-dollar bills. "Dinner is on me, kid. Make sure she wears something hot and tight, and I want you to keep your hand firmly planted on her ass anytime you're in public. Got it?"

I take the money from him, fighting the disgust that swirls within me at his demands. "Got it."

The back door opens and in walks Scarlett, her hair twisted up into a wet bun on top of her head, that black sundress covering her voluptuous body, thank Christ. "Oh, sorry to interrupt," she says when we both turn to look at her.

"You're not interrupting anything, baby doll." Roger approaches her, all smiles and softness as he leans in and plants a quick kiss on her cheek. "As a matter of fact, we were just talking about you."

Scarlett looks like she wants to rub the kiss he left off her face, she's so disgusted. "Why were you talking about me?" Her questioning gaze finds mine.

"I was just telling your boyfriend how I want you two to go out to dinner tonight. Show her the town, kid. Let her see all your old haunts." Roger stands next to Scarlett and smiles that sharklike grin of his aimed right at me, pleased with himself.

All my old haunts. Please. Is he talking about the clubs where I got kicked out for being a belligerent drunk? The restaurants where I would throw a scene after I got caught doing coke in the bathroom? One time, I almost got arrested and had to be escorted out of the building. Oh, maybe I should show her the back alleys where I'd meet my old dealer.

No thanks.

"I should get going," Roger says when neither of us says a word. "You two crazy kids try to keep your hands to yourselves, okay? Don't do anything I wouldn't do!"

He's gone in a matter of seconds, sailing through the house

and out the front door and disappearing as if he were never here.

"I'm guessing he'd do just about anything we can think of, so that isn't the best warning," Scarlett says after he's left.

"You're speaking nothing but straight facts." I run my hand through my damp hair, messing it up thoroughly but not really giving a shit. "Want to go out to dinner tonight?"

"Not particularly." She tilts her head to the side. "I thought the chef was making us dinner tonight."

"I think plans have changed." My phone buzzes, and I check it to see it's a text from Roger's assistant with a list of restaurants they're recommending. "Actually, it looks like we don't have a choice."

"Why not?" She's adorably confused.

"Roger wants us to make an appearance. Can't let anyone forget we're a couple, right?" I'm trying to sound like I'm joking, but I fail miserably, so I let the smile fall from my face.

"Right," she echoes, nodding. "Are you all right?"

"I'm great." My voice is overly enthusiastic, and I should probably tone it down, but it's like I can't. "How are you?"

Her gaze returns to mine, and I swear it feels like she can see right through me. "What exactly did Roger say to you?"

I exhale loudly, grabbing the back of my neck with both hands. "He's pissed that I'm not toiling away in the studio and writing songs already."

Scarlett frowns. "What? But we just got here."

"That's what I told him, but I don't think he cares." I don't bother telling her that he knows our relationship is fake. I don't need to add that stress on her too. "Pretty sure he wasn't too happy to see us together in the pool either."

Her frown deepens. "What? Why not? I thought he believed we were a real couple."

"He says I should stop fooling around with you and start working."

"Oh." She pauses. "So now I'm a distraction."

"You're not." I start to approach her, and she takes a step backward, like she needs the distance from me. "Trust me."

"I probably shouldn't have splashed you."

"Scarlett . . ."

"I'll leave you alone. Tell me when you want to leave for dinner, and I'll go get ready, okay?"

Before I can say a word or reassure her that she's not at fault . . .

She's gone.

CHAPTER TWENTY-THREE

SCARLETT

I'm an idiot.

I thought Tate was into me, but maybe I read him all wrong. Or maybe he knew Roger was going to stop by, so he put on a little show just for his benefit, and it backfired. I'm supposed to be his fake girlfriend, but instead I've become his real distraction, and this whole plan is freaking stupid.

I want to go home.

Instead, I take a long, cool shower and mentally try to convince myself that I did nothing wrong. I'm not at fault here. Deep down, I know I'm not. I just got caught up in the moment. Caught up in ogling Tate's body and giving in to my urges to tease him.

Flirt with him.

Oh, how it worked. He was in that pool and on me within minutes, and for a moment there, it all felt so incredibly real. The tension between us was thick. The heat. The hunger. His body pressed against mine, his eyes on my mouth, staring at me like he wanted to devour me whole.

And when he kissed me? I reacted without thinking,

allowing him in, tangling my tongue with his. His hands on my body. My legs automatically wrapping around him, his hands on my butt . . .

It was amazing. It was hot.

Until Roger had to show up and ruin everything.

I absently rub my cheek, still trying to rid myself of the lingering sensation of Roger's lips on my face when he gave me that brief kiss.

Gross.

After my shower I blow-dry my hair, standing in the bathroom in a pair of panties and nothing else, seriously contemplating my body and finding nothing but flaws. No guy has been interested in me before, not even the one who I basically threw myself at for the last two years of my life. Why would I think someone like Tate—who has been with numerous women in the past and could probably get anyone he wanted right now with a snap of his fingers—be interested in me? Whatever happened out at the pool was a one-off. A moment that will most likely never occur again.

He's got work to do. An album to make. Songs to write. I need to stay out of his way and be there like a good little devoted girlfriend when he needs me. That's it.

End of story.

Once my hair is dry, I slip on a pale-yellow strapless dress, liking how the color makes my lightly tanned skin glow. My phone buzzes with a notification, and I glance down at where I left it on the counter, realizing that I haven't posted for a couple of days.

I decide to do a "get ready with me" video and keep it real.

When I crack open the blinds on the window, plenty of sunlight pours in, and I set up my phone, propping it against a lamp. This is good enough.

"Guys, I'm in sunny Southern California, and I feel a little in over my head." I stare into the camera, hoping they can see the genuine fear and apprehension I'm currently experiencing. "I know none of you will feel sorry for me. 'Oh, poor little rich girl getting to travel across the country and spend the next few weeks with her hot, famous boyfriend while he makes an album.' I get it. I do. But guys." I lean in closer, my goal always intimacy. "My hot boyfriend is extra hot out here, and I think I'm a total distraction."

As I put on my makeup, I ramble about my presence being an issue when all I want is to support and even inspire him. I even talk about my life feeling like a movie, right down to the Southern California location and how none of this seems real, blah blah blah. It feels good to get my feelings and worries off my chest. Like I just called up Rachel and unloaded on her.

I watch a few minutes of my video once I'm finished filming and decide . . . screw it.

I'm posting it right now, before I chicken out. Despite management or whoever coming up with a recording schedule and topics for me to discuss on my social media, I'm doing my own thing. Most of those ideas seemed incredibly phony anyway, and that's the last thing I want to do. I've been at this for a while, and I'm pretty sure I know what my followers want.

Me being as raw and real as possible.

With shaky fingers I hit post on a few different sites, then breathe out a shuddery sigh of relief once I'm done. Too late to take it back now.

The moment after I post, there's a knock on my door, and I go to open it to find Tate standing there. Looking gorgeous as usual in a pair of khaki shorts and an untucked white button-down shirt that's open at the neck with the sleeves rolled up. "Ready to go to dinner?"

"Is it already time?" I go to my bed to grab my bag from where I left it and then get my phone before I return to where he waits at the door. "I'm ready."

"You look . . . nice." He sounds as if he just forced himself to say that, and I want to wilt under his too-brief inspection.

His word choice isn't great either. Nice? Okay.

"You do too." I paste on a bright smile and sling my purse strap over my shoulder, ready to walk past him, but he stops me with a gentle brush of his fingers on my arm. I see the look on his face, and everything inside of me starts to tremble. "What's wrong?"

"Just . . . don't feel bad about what Roger said to me earlier."

My fake smile slips back into place. "I don't."

"You don't have to lie to me, Scar. I know it bothers you. You're not a distraction." His fingers slip down my arm, featherlight and leaving a trail of goose bumps in their wake. "More like an inspiration."

"Oh." We stare at each other for a moment before I blurt, "I made another 'get ready with me' video."

His brows draw together. "Oh yeah?"

I nod. "I forgot to follow the script, though. Think they'll be pissed?"

"I'm not sure. Depends on what you said." A slow smile curves his lips, the sight of it absolutely devastating. Will I ever get used to that smile of his? "Funny how you keep doing that at certain moments."

"I couldn't help it. And I kind of went on a tangent about this entire surreal experience of being here and how I feel like I'm living in a fantasy," I explain. "A Netflix movie or series or whatever."

"I need to see this." He pulls his phone out of his pocket, and I stop him, resting my hand on top of his.

"Watch it later. When I'm not around."

"Why? Does it make you uncomfortable?"

"You watching me rattle on about you being my fantasy boyfriend while I'm standing right here?" Nervous laughter escapes me. "Yes."

He shoves his phone back into his pocket and offers his arm to me. "Shall we go to dinner?"

I curl my arm through his with a faint smile. "Let's."

The sun is starting to set by the time we make it to our destination. Southern California freeways are no joke, and the restaurant we had our reservation at was only seventeen miles away, yet it took us over an hour to get there, thanks to rush hour traffic.

But the location is absolutely beautiful, filled with equally beautiful people dressed casually to the unknowing eye, though I recognize almost everything they've got on.

Designer clothes everywhere. Both subtle and obvious labels letting people know that they've got major money. Diamonds on the women's fingers sparkling in the dim light of the restaurant, their hair perfect, their faces giving me serious filter vibes—and they all start to look the same. As in they've been Facetuned to the max. Chanel and Hermès bags are everywhere I look, and the scent of expensive perfume mixed with men's pricey cologne lingers in the air.

I can tell this is a place to see and be seen. The lighting is dim, and there's an entire outside deck that faces the ocean, which is packed with people. There's also a massive bar on the other side of the restaurant that appears crowded as well.

"Did you pick this restaurant out?" I ask Tate once our server has seated us and left to get water for the table.

"It was Roger's suggestion," Tate admits.

Makes sense. He wants us visible and creating content. I noticed a few people inconspicuously taking our photos before we entered the building. Paparazzi? Were they informed of our location? I imagine it'll become a little more chaotic by the time we leave.

"Have you eaten here before?" I open the menu, surprised by the lack of options. This must be one of those restaurants with a renowned chef who only makes a certain number of dishes each night.

"No, I haven't." Tate scans the menu. "They don't have much."

"I'll have the shrimp salad." I shut my menu. "I'm surprised Roger didn't tell me I needed to lose weight."

"Why the hell would he say that?" Tate practically growls, his gaze lifting to mine.

I'm surprised by the hostility in his tone. "I could stand to lose a few pounds. I'm sure I'll be judged, out here in the land of the beautiful plastic people."

"You don't need to lose weight." His voice has a firm finality to it that tells me he's not interested in arguing with me about that particular subject. "And you can't let being here give you a complex. If you do, you might need therapy by the time we leave."

He speaks as if he has experience.

"There was something about the way Roger looked at me, though," I admit, hating that I'm going there. The last person I want to talk about tonight is Roger. "Like he didn't approve of me."

Exhaling loudly, Tate closes his menu and sets it on the table, studying me intently. "If you ask me, Roger approves far too much of you. I told him to quit with the vulgar comments when he's in your presence."

I'm shocked. "You did?"

He nods. "I'm tired of his big mouth. He says the worst shit, and I don't want him making you uncomfortable."

Aw. That's the sweetest thing. "He is kind of . . . odd sometimes."

"More like he's a total prick, but if you want to be kind and call him odd, okay." Tate smiles at the server when he appears at our table once more with two glasses of water, setting them on the table. "Can we get the crab cakes, please?" He shoots me a quick look. "You can eat crab cakes, right? You're not allergic to shellfish or anything like that?"

"I have no allergies that I know of." I smile at the server. "The crab cakes sound lovely."

"I'll get them started and come back in a few to get the rest of your order." He pauses, glancing between us. "Unless the two of you would care for a drink from the bar?"

Tate hesitates, and I see a flicker in the depths of his gaze. Like he might be tempted. "Water is fine," he bites out.

"I'm okay, thank you," I tell the server, who nods at us both before taking off.

"Is it difficult still? Consciously choosing to not drink?" I ask Tate.

I think of my father, who drinks a lot. Who, as he calls it, "likes to party." I know in his twenties he often drank to excess. But he seems to have it under control now.

Mostly.

"Lately? Hell yes," Tate admits, his voice raw. Like it took a lot for him to admit that. "Guess the pressure is already getting to me."

My heart hurts for him, and I'm a little baffled by my internal reaction. This is a man who I found arrogant and irritating when I first met him. As I get to know him, I'm starting to realize he's got vulnerabilities—lots of them. And he has feelings too.

Emotions that I feel protective of. He is, after all, a human being, but I never thought of him being vulnerable and a little shaken, not when he puts on such a confident, sometimes even arrogant act for the world to see. I've seen the mask slip more and more lately, and I worry about him.

I want to protect him.

"Is there anything I can do to help?" I ask.

The relief on his face is evident. "Just making that offer is enough, Scar. Seriously."

"This is a lot." I wave a hand around the restaurant. "Being here. Being in Los Angeles, knowing the expectations the label has on you."

"Want to know the truth?" When I nod, he continues, lowering his voice as he says, "I'm scared out of my mind I'm going to produce nothing but shit. And that they're going to hate it and drop my album from their release schedule completely. Cancel the contract. Forget the deal ever even happened. I've done this sort of thing before, but always with other people involved. My bandmates. Other songwriters. They provided us with the songs and the production and the musicians. We just showed up and recorded them like they wanted us to. I look back on that and realize how fucking easy we had it."

"Still sounds like a lot," I admit.

"Oh, it was. I can't deny that it was, but compared to now?" He leans back in his seat, slowly shaking his head as he rubs his jaw with his fingers. "This is a whole other level of stress."

"I want to help you in any way that I can," I tell him, resting my arms on the edge of the table. "Whatever you need from me, just please . . . let me know."

"You don't have to—"

"I want to," I say, interrupting him. "Please. I want to help."

CHAPTER TWENTY-FOUR

TATE

There are all sorts of things I can think of that Scarlett can help me with.

Relieving some of this sexual tension that's been brewing between us pretty much since the day we met? Yep.

Helping me relieve some of this stress that I've been carrying with any sort of sexual favor, preferably a blow job? Most definitely.

I sound like a sex-obsessed pervert in my own thoughts. It was bad enough before I saw her in the bikini, but now that I've caught a glimpse of that bangin' body of hers? Held her close while in the pool and been just about to do God knows what with her before Roger so rudely interrupted us? It's all I can think about.

Her. She's all I can think about.

Then she has to go and be sweet too.

The server shows up before I can say anything to her, bringing with him our crab cakes and delivering them onto the table with a flourish. He offers me a particular look that says, *I know who you are, and if you're lucky, I'll keep it to myself.*

But I'm not too sure if I trust the dude. This restaurant's clientele is made up mostly of people who want to see or be seen, and I'd guess the employees are paid to reveal who's dining inside to whatever media outlet wants to know—for a price. Roger chose this location with purpose—he wants Scarlett and me being seen out together. I wonder if there will be paparazzi outside waiting for us when we leave.

Probably. And that just ups my stress level another couple of notches.

"These look delicious," Scarlett says, eyeing the crab cakes like she wants to fuck them.

I scrub a hand over my face, mentally telling myself to calm down. Not everything has to do with sex, right? "Yeah, they do."

She grabs one of the small plates the server brought us and forks up a crab cake, then passes the plate over to me before she gets one for herself. I watch her eat, my senses on high alert when I hear her murmur a low "mmm."

Damn it, I'm starting to sweat.

"Are you not hungry?" Her soft voice brings me out of my sexual trance, my gaze meeting hers almost guiltily. "I'm starving. We haven't eaten anything since the plane."

"Yeah. I'm hungry. Just . . . distracted." I cut off a piece of crab cake and pop it into my mouth, emitting my own low groan when the flavors burst on my tongue. "That's good."

"Right? So delicious."

We continue eating, the occasional low hum of approval leaving one of us—mostly her—and we polish off the appetizer quickly. When the server returns, we order our main entrées, and once he leaves, Scarlett leans over the table like she wants to tell me a secret, her lips barely moving when she speaks.

"People are staring at us."

I glance around as subtly as I can, noting the way people

are blatantly checking us out. I make eye contact with a guy at the table across from ours, and he straight-up lifts his phone and takes a photo of us. I send him a snarling glare, but he only shrugs and resumes his conversation with the woman sitting at his table.

"That guy just took our picture," I complain.

"There are other people in here who already took our photo," Scarlett says, her voice hushed. "Isn't this restaurant famous for celebrities wanting attention?"

I groan. How could I forget?

"Yeah, it is." I run a hand through my hair, already annoyed. "Maybe we should leave."

"Roger arranged this dinner, though, right? This is what he wants." She winces. "I hate to say it, but we should probably give him what he wants."

She's right. As Roger would so kindly point out, he's paying for all of this. The least we could do is make our appearances and smile for the cameras, playing the madly-in-love couple.

This is exactly what we signed up for, but it still feels . . . what? Awkward? Weird? Like a giant lie?

All of the above.

"Okay, then we won't leave." I reach across the small table, grabbing her hand where it rests and interlacing our fingers. "Let's give them what they want."

"What do you mean?" The confusion on her face is adorable.

"They want to see us all over each other, so let's deliver."

The panic in her gaze is obvious, and she sits up straighter, her eyes shifting right, then left. Like she's trying to see if people are still staring at us. "Um . . ."

"You said you'd help me out in any way you could," I remind her, feeling like a shit for using her words against her. "And this would be a big help, Scar."

Her face relaxes somewhat. "Do you know you're the only person who calls me Scar?"

"Really?"

She nods. "My mom tried calling me Lettie when I was little, but I hated that."

"I hate that too. Sounds like a little old lady's name." I squeeze her hand in mine, sending that slow, intimate smile in her direction. The one that set a million teenage girls' hearts aflutter when I used to flash it toward the camera when we filmed music videos.

Her cheeks flush, and I know it worked. I'm not trying to make her squirm. I'm just trying to give the masses what they want. Me and Scarlett so wrapped up in each other, the outside world just disappears.

"Do you mind that I call you Scar?" I ask her.

"Not at all." Her smile is small. "I kind of like it."

I bring her hand to my mouth, dropping the lightest kiss on her knuckles. Like we're having an intimate moment in one of the most-talked-about restaurants in the area. If people actually fall for this shit, they're naive as hell. "I like you."

"Tate . . ."

"Scarlett . . ." I grin at her, like we're playing a game, which I suppose we are.

She gently pulls her hand from mine, and I let her go, never taking my eyes from her. "Why did you kiss me in the pool earlier?"

Her question knocks me off balance, my smile fading quickly. "You didn't like it?"

"I never said that." She doesn't tear her gaze from mine, though her cheeks are pinker than before.

"Did I overstep my boundaries?"

"You didn't answer my question." She rests her elbow on

the table, propping her chin on her curled fist. "What was that in the pool earlier?"

"I think you know what it was."

"Why did it happen, though? There wasn't anyone around. No audience. We didn't have to put on a performance like we're doing now." Her eyes sparkle in the dim light, and I get the distinct sense that she's fucking with me. Or just flat-out trying to get me to admit to something. "So why?"

"You want the truth?"

"Definitely." She nods.

I lean in close, mimicking her posture, my fist curled beneath my chin just like hers. "Because you looked hot as fuck in that pink bikini and I wanted to get my hands on you. That's why."

Her expression doesn't so much as waver, which I give her props for. I was trying to throw her off like she just did to me, but I don't think I was successful. "That's what I thought."

"Did you mind?"

Scarlett slowly shakes her head, seemingly trying to hide the smile that wants to curl her lips.

"Want me to do it again? Because I can." I sit up straight, rubbing my chin. "I don't need the bikini excuse either."

"What do you mean?"

"You look hot in whatever you're wearing, and you know it." I hold up my hand when she starts speaking. "And don't give me that 'I need to lose weight' excuse either. I'm not falling for it. You don't need to lose weight. You're gorgeous. You can have whatever you want, whoever you want, whenever you want it, yet you chose to chase after some asshole who didn't have enough sense to figure out that the hot rich girl wanted him. Which tells me that all things sexual might actually . . . scare you."

She sits up straighter as well, her expression turning pissy in an instant. "Is that how you think of me? As the hot rich girl? I'm more than that, you know. Despite what everyone says."

"Oh, I definitely know. And no, that's not how I think of you, but you have to admit, that's what you are. At least, that's how you present yourself to the public eye."

Her eyes blaze with anger. "That's not true and you know it. I try my hardest to be relatable in my videos. And what do you know about my relationship with Ian, hmm? Not a thing. You don't know him. You don't really know me either."

I watch her, entranced. She's beautiful when she's angry. "Tell me you're not still hung up on him."

She hesitates. I catch it, though she probably thinks I don't notice. "I'm over him."

Frustration builds. I hate that Ian still has some sort of hold on her. He doesn't deserve her. He never did.

Hell, I don't deserve her either.

But I know one thing.

I want to make her forget that asshole was even a part of her life.

"You completely avoided the crux of my statement, you know," I tell her, digging in a little deeper.

"What exactly are you referring to?" she asks warily.

"The 'scared of anything sexual' comment. You completely blew past it," I point out.

That familiar determined expression of hers appears, and she lifts her chin, trying to look tough. "You don't scare me."

"I'm not talking about me. I'm talking about sex." I pause. "Does it scare you?"

She's quiet for a moment, allowing me the opportunity to blatantly stare at her. She's so damn beautiful. Despite us being in this so-called fake relationship, I'm starting to have a very real attraction toward her.

I need to be real with myself—I've always been attracted to her. From the moment I first laid eyes on the birthday girl at her party, I thought she was beautiful. When I spoke to her? Sassy. Determined, but with that hint of innocence about her that I'm drawn to. She's sweet. And most women I've been with in the past, there was nothing sweet about them.

My life has left me jaded, and no one could blame me for feeling that way. It's just facts. And Scarlett is about the least jaded, most pure person I've ever been around. I like that about her. That she's not cynical and doesn't look at everything like an attack.

Just because I have thoughts about corrupting her—and I do, especially lately—that doesn't mean it's all I notice when it comes to Scarlett. There's so much more to her. I might annoy her and make her mad, and I think I'm the only person who does that.

Makes her feel . . . other things.

"I don't think we should have that particular discussion right now," she says rather primly, her soft voice interrupting my thoughts.

I glance around the room before I return my attention to her. "No one is listening to us. They might be looking at us, but they can't hear our conversation. So tell me, Scar."

"Tell you what?" Her eyes are wide and unblinking.

"Are you scared of sex?"

She leans back from the table as if she needs the distance. "Are you trying to dig into my sexual history?"

I shrug, deciding to be completely honest with her. "Yeah. I am."

She stares at me for a moment, that mind of hers processing my answer. "It's really none of your business."

"I'm curious." I shrug. "And I want to know more about you. It'll help bring us closer, don't you think?"

Okay. I'm full of horseshit. I just want to know if she's actually done the deed or not. Or if she's done anything.

My guess is no.

"Ask me my favorite color and movie. Or what I like to eat. You need to lead up to the sex life questions." She laughs nervously.

"So you do have a sex life."

Scarlett remains quiet.

"Right?" I prod.

A sigh leaves her. "This is embarrassing."

"We're two adults here."

"I'm barely an adult."

"Talking about your sex life while we're in a relationship shouldn't be too daunting."

"It is when what we're doing isn't . . ." She lowers her voice to a whisper. "Real."

She's right. What we're doing isn't supposed to be real, but why does it feel like that?

This is a date. I don't know what else to call it. And here's what's funny—I haven't gone on a lot of dates in my life. I didn't need to. I went from being with Jess to getting with a plethora of women. There was no dating going on. Just hookups.

One after another.

"Be real with me, Scar. Tell me the truth. How far have you gone?" She visibly squirms in her seat, and I'm just warming up. "What do you like doing? What do you like done to you?"

Her lips part, and I swear to God she's breathing heavier. "Tate."

"Just tell me. You don't have to hold back. I'm not going to judge you. Besides, we have legal documents in place, so I can't spill all of your secrets." I grin at her, enjoying myself. I'm a sadistic fuck if I'm getting off on making Miss Scarlett uncomfortable with this conversation. "Tell me what you want from a sexual partner."

"Someone who's thoughtful and . . . affectionate." She sinks her teeth into her lower lip, like she's afraid to say more.

"That's what you want from a *relationship*." I wave a hand, dismissing her answer. "What are your kinks? What are you into? I mean, I know you're only eighteen, so if your kink is doing it with you on top, I get it. You've barely dipped your toe into the sexual pool, so to speak."

"You're giving me serious Roger vibes right now," she accuses, her gaze narrowed as she watches me.

I rest my hand on my chest, wounded. "Damn, Scar. That hurts. The last thing I want is to be compared to him."

"You keep this up, digging for info about my sex life, and that's exactly who you remind me of," she mutters, her brows lifting.

"Just trying to get to know you." I shrug, playing it off.

I'm being an asshole. I know I am. But it's like I can't help it. I feel antsy. Worked up. In the past, I would've eased this feeling with a combination of alcohol and drugs, topped off by sex.

Now, the only option is sex. And I want to know if I have a chance with Scarlett.

More than anything, I'm trying to figure out what she likes. What does she want? Me worshipping her body? I can do that. Going down on her? I've never been afraid of licking pussy, though I know a few guys who don't like it.

Seriously. What the hell is wrong with them?

I could fuck her from behind, against a wall, in the shower—whatever she wants, I'm game.

Yeah, I'm also horny. This is why my thoughts are filled with images of Scarlett naked. Tits swaying while she sucks my cock. Tits swaying while she rides my dick. Moaning while I fuck her hard.

Reaching up, I brush my fingers against my forehead and realize that I am indeed sweating.

"I didn't think getting to know me would include an in-depth interrogation into my sex life." Her haughty rich-girl voice is downright arousing, which means I have a deeper problem than I thought.

"All right, let's switch it up then. Since you asked me what I was trying to do when we were in the pool, now it's my turn." I smile at her, just before I hit her with, "What did you want me to do to you when we were in that pool?"

CHAPTER TWENTY-FIVE

SCARLETT

Things are shifting between Tate and me. I was trying to bait him with that question about the pool, and now he's baited me right back. Over and over again, because he's much better at this game than I am. To the point that I'm flustered and embarrassed by his questions.

I have zero experience with situations like this. Boys at school, they never really noticed me. Or they left me alone because of who I am. Most Lancasters rule Lancaster Prep, thanks to our family owning the school. Though I preferred to stay in the background, a role I've lived my entire life.

Now I have a man paying attention to me, and not in a fake way either. We may have signed an agreement to pretend to be together, but there's nothing phony about what's happening between us.

How do I answer him when he asks what I like? How can I tell him I have no idea, considering I've never done anything before, so I have no idea whether I like it or not? While I'm sure he's done everything possible and has all the expertise to prove it.

We are complete opposites in every way I can think of. This man shouldn't be interested in me—and I shouldn't be interested in him either. Not at all. Yet there's something about him . . .

Something about the two of us. Together. A magnetic pull I can't help but feel when I'm with him. It's the way he looks at me when he speaks. As if he's thinking of doing . . . *things* to me. Sexual things.

I'm intrigued, though I probably shouldn't be. And really? I'm also flattered. I practically threw myself at Ian, and he acted like I was just some sweet little girl he barely knew and was most definitely not interested in. Oh, he said a few things here and there that made my heart trip over itself, but only recently. Like when he told me he'd lost his chance after seeing me and Tate together. I thought he was finally going to make a move. But in the end, he didn't follow through.

He never follows through.

Forget Ian. Actually . . .

I pretty much already have.

"I feel like we're going 'round and 'round with this conversation," I finally tell Tate, because it's true.

"We are. Though that's mostly your fault. If you would just answer my questions, Scar, we'd be a lot farther ahead." He's teasing. I can tell by his bright smile. The way his eyes sparkle. He really has the most expressive face.

A sigh leaves me, and I'm propping my elbow on the table again, resting my chin on top of my curled fist while I watch him. "You want the truth?"

He nods, looking eager. "Definitely."

I push past the nerves that suddenly swamp me. "Well, so far I've done . . . absolutely nothing."

Tate stares at me for a moment, like he needs to absorb what I just said. "Nothing?"

He sounds shocked.

"Not a single thing." I slowly shake my head.

"You've never hooked up with anyone?"

"What constitutes hooking up for you?" I lift my brows.

"Kissing. Feeling each other up, getting each other off with fingers, oral sex," he ticks off rapidly. "Actual sex counts too."

"The only person I've ever really kissed is . . ." Oh, this is embarrassing. "You."

"Get out," is his automatic reply.

"I'm serious."

"I don't believe you." He shakes his head, his voice firm.

I knew he wouldn't believe me.

"It's true," I insist. "And I've never done anything else either. No feeling each other up, getting each other off with fingers, oral sex, or actual sex." I repeat his words back to him, refusing to be embarrassed over it.

Though my face is burning hot. And my stomach is twisting, making any appetite I still had disappear.

"My untouched girl," he murmurs, his brows shooting up the moment the words leave him. "That's a good song title."

Like magic his phone appears in his hands and he's tapping at it, frowning at the screen.

"What are you doing?"

"Adding that to my title list. It's a good one." He swipes his finger across his phone screen and pockets it. "Can I be real with you? If you'd admitted to me a few weeks ago that you were a virgin, I'd run screaming from the room."

I'm vaguely hurt.

"But now, for whatever reason . . . I'm curious." He tilts his head to the side, contemplating me. "Do you think of me like I think of you, Scarlett?"

"How do you think of me?"

"You probably don't want to know." The grin on his face is rather naughty.

"Now I definitely want to know," I tell him without hesitation.

"I imagine the two of us . . . together."

"Sexually?" My voice is hushed.

He nods. "Definitely. I'd been wondering what you look like naked, but now I have a pretty good idea of that, thanks to the bikini you wore earlier."

He wonders what I look like *naked*? Fine, I've wondered about him too. The pool moment didn't help matters—just made my thoughts even more chaotic. "Do you think I showed too much skin?"

I sound like a naive little baby—which I guess I sort of am when it comes to this type of stuff.

While Tate has probably done everything. Experienced things I've never even imagined.

"You didn't show enough," he stresses. "And fucking Roger had to show up at the worst time."

Right. When Tate had me pinned against a wall, our mouths fused and his hands kneading my butt. "His timing was awful."

Tate's eyes flash. "So what you're saying is, you didn't mind me feeling you up in the pool."

Busted. "Well, when you phrase it like that . . ."

He laughs, reaching out to snag my hand again, curling it in his. "You're a lot more . . . easygoing than I thought you'd be."

"How did you think I'd be?" I ask, almost not wanting to know.

"You were very uptight the night we met at your party. And you continued that uptight attitude for a while."

"A while?" I arch a brow, knowing exactly what he's talking about.

"Every time we were together, for the most part."

"From what I remember, you seemed to enjoy antagonizing me," I remind him. "Then you had to go and ask me to be your"—I lower my voice—"fake girlfriend, and I really thought you'd lost your mind."

"Yet somehow, here you sit in a restaurant after traveling clear across the country with me." He kisses the back of my hand again, this time his warm lips lingering on my skin, his gaze never straying from mine.

Deciding I might as well play along—I am contractually obligated to, after all—I stretch my fingers out, reaching for his face, my fingers skimming along his jaw. His eyes light up with surprise, and I'm proud of myself for making a move.

For willingly touching him.

I've got a long way to go if I want to be considered bold.

The server appears by our table, interrupting the moment. "Just checked with the kitchen, and your entrées are almost ready. Would you care for something more to drink?"

I drop my hand from Tate's face, quiet as he takes over and asks for refills, though his gaze is still on mine. I smile back at him, and the moment our server is gone, I murmur, "I need to use the restroom."

Tate frowns. "You sure that's a good idea?"

"Why wouldn't it be?"

"Someone might follow you in there, Scarlett. And want to talk to you. Dig for information. Or worse, take your photo." His tone is dead serious, as is his gaze. "You need to be careful."

"I'll be fine. There are all sorts of celebrities in this restaurant right now." I glance around, trying to spot one, but I don't recognize anyone sitting nearby. "At least I think there are."

Tate's concerned gaze tracks my movements as I rise to my feet. "Want me to escort you there?"

"I'm a big girl," I reassure him. "I'll be right back."

"Okay." The doubt is thick in his voice, and I feel his gaze on my back as I walk away. By the time I'm in the bathroom, I'm breathing a sigh of relief, telling myself Tate was completely overreacting.

When I'm in the stall taking care of business, I hear someone enter the restroom, her heels clicking on the tile floor. The person washes her hands, the water running for what feels like forever, and by the time I'm slipping out of the stall and about to approach an empty sink, I realize Tate wasn't overreacting at all.

"Scarlett Lancaster, right?" The woman standing in front of me is tall and extremely thin, wearing a black pantsuit with a bright-pink tank underneath the jacket, her heels the same pink color. Her dark hair is cut into a severe bob that hits right at her chin and swings back and forth as she talks, her head moving animatedly. "You're Tate Ramsey's latest piece."

The word slips from my lips without thought. "*Piece?*"

How freaking insulting.

The woman laughs. "Sorry. That sounds incredibly rude. Tate's latest *girlfriend*. Hookup. Whatever you want to call yourself." She hesitates. "You are Scarlett, correct?"

I turn on the water and wash my hands, hating how they're shaking. She watches me quietly while I try to play it cool, doing everything as quickly as possible so I can get out of here, but once I shut the water off, I realize she's standing directly in front of the paper towel dispenser.

"Excuse me," I say, my voice trembling. It's taking everything inside of me to try to keep it together. I don't want her thinking that what she's doing is bothering me, but I'm completely unsettled by her presence.

God, if I can't handle a little confrontation in a restaurant bathroom, how am I going to be able to maintain this facade for the next six weeks?

She doesn't so much as budge away from the towel dispenser. "Agree to let me interview you and Tate on camera, and I'll move out of the way for you."

Sighing, I dodge around her, shaking my still-dripping-wet hands as I flee the bathroom. The woman is on me in an instant, crowding me from behind, her hand grasping for my wrist. I yank my arm away from her, whirling on her.

"Don't *touch* me."

The woman laughs in my face. "Stupid girl. Where's your security detail? Where's your boyfriend? Why isn't he running to your defense?"

"What is wrong with you?" I ask, watching as her face morphs and changes into an angry, almost ugly mask.

"Must be nice, being a rich-as-fuck Lancaster and never having to worry about money your whole life. Some of us have to work for a living," she practically spits in my face.

"Hey."

We both turn to see Tate standing a few feet away in the hall that leads to the restrooms, his deep voice sharp and demanding. "Get the fuck away from her."

The woman immediately pulls out her phone and starts filming us both. "Tate, tell us about your new little flavor of the month. Or is it week? Chasing after heiresses now, huh? At least you're moving up in the world instead of messing around with broke groupies."

"Scarlett. Come here," Tate commands.

I rush toward him, grateful when he wraps his arm around my shoulders and presses me close to his side, guiding me through the restaurant as he curses under his breath. The woman follows us the entire way, filming our escape, barraging us with endless questions and comments.

"She's cute, Tate, but can she handle your style of violence? Don't forget, honey, he lashes out and destroys everything in his path when he has too much to drink. He's been arrested before too, though his team covered that all up."

What?

I had no idea Tate had been *arrested*.

"Ignore her," Tate murmurs close to my ear. "We're almost out of here."

A man in a three-piece suit appears out of nowhere, approaching us, concern mixed with irritation written all over his handsome face.

"Please, follow me, Mr. Ramsey," the man says, his voice deep and calm as he guides us toward a swinging door that leads into the kitchen. The woman is stopped by a beefy-looking guy who comes from the front of the restaurant, blocking her path.

"Come on, lady," I hear him say as we keep walking. "Time for you to go."

Once we're in the kitchen, we finally stop, and I pull out of Tate's embrace, needing the distance. I rest a hand on my chest, breathing deep and trying to calm my racing heart as the man in the suit apologizes profusely.

"We are so sorry. That sort of thing usually doesn't happen here," the man explains. I assume he's the manager or owner of this restaurant, and he's visibly sweating. "We pride ourselves on running a restaurant where celebrities can be out in the open with the public, yet never harassed. I don't know where she came from, but I assure you she will be banned from the premises, effective immediately."

"Thank you. We appreciate it," Tate says, grabbing hold of me once more and hauling me closer. I stay locked by his side, my gaze still going to the door, afraid that horrible woman might burst in at any moment.

"I've never seen anything like that. She was horribly persistent." The man offers me an apologetic smile. "I'm so sorry, Miss Lancaster."

I'm shocked he knows who I am, but I need to get used to that. Lots of people know who I am now thanks to all the media attention from being with Tate.

"Guess I bring out the worst in people," Tate jokes, but I can see the hurt in his gaze. It's there, buried deep, and I wish I knew who this woman was.

And who sent her into the bathroom to basically attack me.

"We can find you another table, Mr. Ramsey, if you and Miss Lancaster wish to stay and finish your dinner," the man continues. "And this meal is on us. Again, my apologies."

"It's okay. It's not your fault," Tate reassures, remaining calm, which is impressive.

I'm guessing the Tate of old might've blown up and thrown a fit. I'm not sure.

"Thank you, sir. We can also pack your food up to go and call your car up. Whatever the both of you are more comfortable with." The man offers me another apologetic smile, and I pull myself out of Tate's hold, turning toward him.

"What would you rather do?" Tate asks, his voice low.

I release a trembling breath, tucking a few strands of hair behind my ear with shaky fingers. "I'd rather leave, if you don't mind."

I'm too rattled to stay here, too wary that she'll pop up again. I don't want to risk it.

"We'll take the food to go," Tate tells the manager, who smiles and nods, just before he moves deeper into the kitchen, shouting orders to the kitchen staff.

Tate pulls me back into him, his arm going around my waist, his hand resting possessively on my hip. “Are you all right?”

I shake my head, on the verge of tears just from the concern in his voice, the way he’s looking at me. Like he cares about my well-being. “Not really.”

“Shit, Scarlett, I told you not to go in there—” He clamps his lips together, cutting himself off, gazing at the kitchen door like he’s imagining that woman busting in here too. “It doesn’t matter what I told you. I didn’t think someone would come for you that aggressively. It’s clear that from now on, we’re going to need security with us wherever we go.”

I didn’t like the idea of those two big guys trailing us everywhere earlier, but now I wish they’d accompanied us to dinner. “All right,” I say with a nod, trying to pull away from him yet again, but he doesn’t let me go.

“Come here.” He wraps me up in a big hug, and I cling to him, breathing in his spicy male scent, closing my eyes and savoring the warmth of his chest. How firm he is. How strong.

I’m in over my head here. Not just with Tate and my newfound feelings for him but with all the craziness that surrounds him too.

I wanted a different life. I was desperate for people to pay attention to me, but now?

Now I’m not too sure if this is what I want.

Or if it’s even worth it.

CHAPTER TWENTY-SIX

TATE

After we wait a few minutes and I text the driver to come meet us, I escort Scarlett out the back door of the restaurant, my arm around her shoulders as I guide her to the waiting vehicle. She presses herself against me, hiding her face like someone is going to spot us. I try my best to ignore the fury coursing through my blood, but it's difficult.

I'm pissed that the confrontation happened. Mad at myself for not insisting that the security team accompany us. I didn't think it would be that big of a deal, showing up unannounced at a restaurant known for celebrity clientele.

Looks like I was wrong.

Once I've gotten Scarlett into the car, I glance around the parking lot, making sure no one is nearby, before I crawl into the back seat with her. The moment I shut the door, the driver pulls away from the building, maneuvering his way through the parking lot with a few sharp turns that have the brakes squealing, causing Scarlett to practically fall into me. Within minutes we're back on the freeway, the traffic a lot lighter than it was when we drove here.

Our dinners are in to-go boxes sitting on the passenger seat by the driver, but I'm so furious my appetite has completely left me. I knew Scarlett shouldn't have gone to the bathroom by herself, but damn it, I'm not her daddy. I can't tell her what to do. I also couldn't trail after her and stay in there to make sure she was safe. She would've told me I was overreacting, and I would've agreed with her.

But something felt off from the moment she left the table. I noticed a woman—*the* woman—heading for the restroom soon after Scarlett did, and just seeing her gave me an uneasy feeling.

It felt like Scarlett took too long. Or maybe she didn't. All I know is that I had this sensation I couldn't ignore that something was wrong, and I needed to go investigate.

Only to find Scarlett being cornered by some thirty-year-old former Five Car Pileup fangirl slinging insults at her.

Okay, maybe it's a stretch that the woman was a former FCP fan, but she was definitely at least thirty. And rude as fuck, practically screaming in Scarlett's face, demanding that she answer her questions. About me. About us. The look of pure panic and terror I glimpsed in Scarlett's expression—shit.

I scrub a hand over my face, trying to push it out of my mind. She was scared.

And it's all my fault.

It's always my fault. Everywhere I go, something happens. Something big. Something bad. I'm destructive. My dad told me that when I was a kid. Mom always called me impulsive. I realized later that was a nice way to say that sometimes I do really dumb shit.

Coming to this restaurant tonight with no one escorting us is an example of dumb shit I do.

Scarlett inhales deeply, and I can feel her gaze on me, heavy and questioning. I finally dare to glance over at her, prepared to see the hatred in her eyes, all over her face, but all I notice is . . .

Gratitude.

"Thank you for getting me out of there," she says, her voice soft.

"I'm the reason all of that just happened to you, so it's the least I could do." I want to touch her. Cup her face and ask if she needs anything—if she needs *me*—but she'll most likely tell me no.

So I keep my hands to myself.

"I appreciate it." Her smile is small, her eyes watery, and I swear if she starts crying, I don't know what I'll do.

Tears freak me out. A pretty woman's tears especially.

"Scarlett." I give in to my urges and touch her face, skimming my fingers across her cheek. Her eyelids flutter, and a single tear drops from the corner of her right eye, slowly making its way down her face. I catch it with my thumb. "You're crying."

"I know. I'm sorry. She was awful." Her voice is a hoarse whisper. "I didn't know what to do."

"Damn it." I pull her into my arms, grateful she didn't put her seat belt on yet as I cradle her close to me. She rests her cheek on my shoulder, a soft sigh escaping her, and I settle my hand on her hair. Tangle my fingers in the soft strands as I slowly begin to stroke. "I'm so fucking sorry."

"It's okay." I glance down at her to see her eyes are closed, another tear sliding down her cheek. I catch that one too. "I'm okay."

"We won't let that happen again. Security is going with us everywhere from now on," I say firmly, working my jaw.

I've never been tempted to hit a woman before in my life, but that bitch tonight . . . What she did was completely un-fucking-called for.

My phone rings, and I check the screen to see that it's Roger. I answer immediately, not in the mood to deal with him, yet knowing I can't ignore him either. "What?"

"I just spoke to Leonard. He said that there was some trouble at the restaurant?" At least he has the decency to sound appalled.

"Who's Leonard?"

"The restaurant manager. What happened? He didn't give me much detail. Just said you two ran into some trouble."

"And what, he called you to let you know?" That's some weird shit.

"He's an old friend. Wanted to reach out and let me know before I heard it somewhere else."

"So you already know what happened. That a woman attacked Scarlett in the bathroom," I tell him, my voice flat.

"Attacked? As in physically assaulted her?" Roger is practically screaming.

The panicked look on Scarlett's face makes me feel bad for phrasing it that way. "It wasn't that bad," she whispers.

"More like the woman interrogated her and cornered her in the restroom," I explain.

Roger mutters a few choice curse words under his breath. "What sort of operation is Leonard managing over there? He mentioned there was a little run-in, but he glossed over all the fine details. Please tell Scarlett I'm sorry. I thought it would be good exposure to get you kids out on the town and showing yourselves off at the hottest restaurant in Santa Monica, but that backfired."

"We probably should've gone to the other restaurant in Beverly Hills," I tell him, though, shit, it's probably bad over there too.

"When I put this together, I didn't imagine something like

this could happen. Again, please apologize to Scarlett for me." Roger at least sounds contrite.

"I'll let her know." I glance over at Scarlett to find her still watching me.

"How's she handling it?"

"She's good. She's strong." I smile at Scarlett, who returns a small smile in my direction.

"Good to know. And hey, I'm coming by your place tomorrow. I'd like to see what you've been working on so far."

My stomach sinks. We haven't even been here for twenty-four hours.

"Okay, great," I say through clenched teeth.

Shit. I have barely anything. Some lyrics in the Notes app on my phone. A few song titles. That's about it.

"I'll pop in around noon. Give you some time to sleep in and get some rest. Expect to hit it hard tomorrow, kid. Lots of late nights coming your way."

He ends the call as usual, not giving me a chance to respond.

Whatever.

"Is he mad?" Scarlett asks me.

"Pissed that it happened, yes. Mad at you or me? No."

"Did he mention my video?"

"Which one?"

"The 'get ready with me' video I filmed earlier. Just before we left the house. I wanted to show people that we were together in Los Angeles." She winces. "He wasn't mad about it, was he?"

"He loves it when you do that." I stare at her for a moment. "Even if you go off script."

The helpless look on her face is almost amusing. "I don't mean to. I just get into filming, and I forget I'm supposed to stick to a plan. Script. Whatever."

"You just love to mess with their schedule, don't you?" She's brave that way, I'll give her that. I figured she'd be the perfect little rule follower, never wanting to do anything to rock the boat or cause trouble.

And look at her, constantly making waves.

"Their topics are kind of . . . awful. Besides, I know what I'm doing online," she says assuredly, just as she lifts her head away from my shoulder. I immediately miss the weight of her leaning against me. "And I really don't think they do."

"As long as Roger or Simon don't complain, I think you're good."

"I said some things about you, though." She bites her lower lip, appearing unsure. "So you could complain. Possibly."

"Nothing too horrible, I hope."

"Oh, I would never say anything horrible. That would be breaking the contract."

Disappointment fills me at her remark. I kind of wish she didn't want to say anything horrible about me because she actually likes me. Not because of the stupid contract.

But what do I expect? We're locked into a contract together.

She's just doing her job.

"I mostly went on about having a massive crush on you when I was much younger, and now my life is like a dream and I can't believe my earlier wishes came true," she further explains.

I stare at her for a moment, absorbing her words. "You really had a massive crush on me?"

She nods. "Well, yeah. I thought you knew this. Something about Five Car Pileup seemed so much more . . . accessible than One Direction. Like we had a chance to get with you guys."

"For one, we weren't nearly as famous."

"True." She smiles. "Plus you were a little closer to our age. Rachel and I firmly believed we could use that to our advantage."

"And look, you actually did."

"I did." She leans her head against my shoulder, and it feels as if all is right in the world, holding her like this. "I didn't think it would be like this, though."

"Like what?" I thread my fingers through her hair once again, eager to touch her.

"It's a little terrifying. The fame. The recognition. Yet kind of exhilarating too, you know? It's hard to describe."

"I get what you mean." I stroke her hair for a moment, loving how soft it is, how fragrant. Every single part of her smells good. "I'd forgotten how out of hand it can get. Even a little scary."

"What happened in the bathroom earlier was really scary. That woman wouldn't leave me alone." She shivers.

I wrap my other arm around her shoulders, pulling her in as close as she can get. "I won't let something like that happen to you again. I've got you."

Another great song title. *I've got you.*

I need to write that down later for sure.

"Thank you." She lifts her head, those shining eyes meeting mine, and I drown in them for a little bit, getting lost. It's easy to do with Scarlett, when she looks at me like that. As if I can do no wrong. As if I'm her fucking hero.

No woman has looked at me like that before. Ever.

My throat is clogged with an emotion that I can't describe, and I give up on trying to speak. Instead, I kiss her.

The spark is there, lighting up between our lips the moment they connect, and when she parts hers easily for me, I take advantage and slip my tongue inside, sliding it against hers. She returns the kiss, her hands curling around my shoulders as she clings to me. I cup the back of her head and drink from her lips, my tongue stroking, a growling sound rumbling deep in my chest.

Fuck, she tastes good. Somehow even better than when

we kissed in the pool. Those soft little pants of breath get right under my skin, and when I pull away to tease at the seam of her lips with my tongue, her soft moan makes everything inside of me tighten up.

We kiss for long minutes, the car hurtling down the freeway, the driver completely ignoring us. It's as if I can't stop kissing her, pulling on her arm so she has no choice but to practically collapse on top of me, her knees coming around to rest on either side of my hips, straddling me.

She rises above me, and I open my eyes to watch. Her hair falls around her face, her lips red and swollen, her eyes heavy lidded as she studies me. Her chest rises and falls with every quick breath, and my gaze drops to it. The dress she's wearing exposes the tops of her breasts. Smooth, pale skin on display. A little hint of cleavage.

Again, I give in to my urges and press my face to her chest, right in between her breasts. I breathe in her scent deeply, my lips pressed against her soft skin, wishing I could push her dress out of the way so I could see all of her.

"You got a bra on?" I lift my head to meet her gaze.

She slowly shakes her head, and I feel like I hit the fucking jackpot.

Reaching out, I trace the edge of her neckline, noting the gooseflesh that rises with my touch. Her skin pebbles, her nipples poking against the fabric, and without warning I tug on the fabric, exposing her more, though not all the way.

I lean in before she can say a word or stop me, sucking on her lush flesh, laving it with my tongue before I pull away, studying the red mark I leave behind.

"Tate . . ."

Once again our eyes meet, hers wide and unblinking. "Tell me to stop and I will."

"I—"

"I won't push myself on you, Scar. And just to let you know, this isn't part of the contract."

"But—"

I cut her off. "I want you. So fucking bad. I've wanted you since the moment in the pool."

Liar.

I've wanted her since before that. Hell, since the night of her birthday when she was fuming after I pulled her up onstage and sang "Happy Birthday" to her like I was trying to emulate Marilyn Monroe, which was ridiculous. Despite the way she looked at me as if I were supposed to be singing for someone else, it didn't matter. I wanted her then.

I want her even more now.

"I refuse to push you, though. Or make you uncomfortable. If you don't want to do this, I'm okay with it. I'll let you walk." I release my hold on her, spreading my arms out wide, but she doesn't move from her spot on my lap. Instead, she leans in closer, her eyes locked on mine, her lips so close I can feel the heat of her breath fanning across my mouth.

"You'll let me walk? From everything?" she whispers, sounding incredulous.

That is the last thing I want, but . . .

"Yes. From everything."

That would be a huge mistake on my part. Letting her break the contract would most likely kill my record deal. I'd be an idiot to let her go. I'm on the verge of changing my entire life, and so much of it hinges on this girl.

Scarlett Lancaster holds so much power over me in the palm of her hand, it's downright scary.

She's quiet for a moment, and so am I. The traffic goes rushing by, the light from the streetlamps coming through the window and flickering on her face, and I don't think I've ever seen her as beautiful as she looks right now. In this fucking moment.

"What if I told you I don't want to walk?"

Hope rises within me, and I mentally tamp it down. "You don't want to?"

"No. We signed a contract. And I won't break my promise to you."

She sounds so solemn, so endearing. If she only knew how this entire city and all the other cities that surround it are full of people who stab each other in the back and break deals all the damn time. She's the only one who's soft and sweet, surrounded by a bunch of jaded sharks.

Including me.

"Just . . . don't move too fast, okay? Be patient with me." She bites her lip again, and I groan like I just got stabbed in the dick, burying my face in her cleavage once more.

"You're going to be the death of me," I murmur into her tits, meaning every word I say.

It's true. If I have to be patient and wait for her, she's going to straight-up kill me. And she doesn't even realize the hold she has on me.

Scarlett slides her fingers into my hair, holding me to her as she rests her cheek on top of my head. "I understand, though, if you don't want to wait."

"I'll wait," I say without hesitation. This girl . . .

I have a feeling she'll be worth it.

CHAPTER TWENTY-SEVEN

SCARLETT

"Shit."

I lurk outside the den where Tate is working, going still when I hear him curse. He's been tense since our first night here, after the incident at the restaurant. The moment in the back of the car. I figured it was sexual frustration at first, but he's been working in this room nonstop since we arrived in Los Angeles. Sometimes I'll go to bed and he'll be in here, only for me to wake up and find him in the same position.

Like he didn't even bother going to bed.

He's currently muttering under his breath and scribbling words inside of a journal, which is what I keep seeing him do every time I walk past the open door. Or he's having meetings with Roger, or on Zoom with Simon.

But when Roger comes over, it's worse. He always leaves Tate even more tense than before he arrived.

It's been . . . difficult, the last few days. Not for me but for him.

Tate begins to hum, his deep, smooth voice washing over me, and then he starts to sing.

"I've got you no matter what, but you don't put your trust

in me . . ." His voice drifts, the melody over. "No. That's pure shit."

Deciding to make my presence known, I appear in the doorway, waving at him awkwardly. "No it's not. I liked it."

He glances over at me, his expression flat, his eyes dull. Clearly the man is exhausted. And stressed. "Hey. What are you up to?"

Noticing how he didn't acknowledge my compliment, I let it go.

"Nothing." I wander into the room, approaching him slowly. He's kicked back on the overstuffed white couch, that ever-present worn-out notebook in his lap, the lines he's written on it looking more like angry slashes. Lots of scribbling and words that have been crossed out so hard the paper is dented. "I'm kind of bored."

"We've only been here three days."

"I know. And like I said, I'm already bored." I sit on the edge of the coffee table, just to the left of him. "I haven't left the house since the first night we got here."

"You have a nice tan to show for it." His gaze warms as it skims over me.

I glance down at my arms, then my legs. They're golden from the sun, like the majority of my body is. "I can only lay out by the pool for so long."

An aggravated exhale leaves him, and he leans his head back on the couch, staring up at the ceiling. "If you're looking for me to entertain you, I'm the wrong guy. I need to focus and work on these songs."

"How are they coming along?" I already know the answer.

"Fucking terrible." He chucks the pen he was holding across the room, and it lands on the bare floor with a clatter, rolling underneath the love seat. "I think I have serious writer's block."

"You don't have any songs finished? Not one?" I've overheard enough snippets of conversation between Roger and Tate to know that Roger has high expectations. He wants a list of songs for an album in like . . . less than two weeks. More like one.

"I have a couple of titles. No actual lyrics. Lyrics that are any good, that is." He jumps to his feet and starts pacing the length of the room. "Honestly? I'm fucking frustrated. Nothing is coming to me—like, nothing. I think it's the pressure. Knowing the expectations that they've put on me—I'm buckling. Drawing a complete blank."

I watch him walk back and forth across the room, his gaze on the floor as he grips the back of his neck. He's wearing black sweatpants and a white T-shirt that stretches across his broad chest, and despite the casual outfit and the disheveled hair, he is still mouthwateringly gorgeous.

"Maybe you need a change of scenery," I suggest.

He stops in the middle of the room, throwing his arms out wide. "That's exactly what this is. I'm in a whole new location with a fucking studio at my fingertips and all the fucking sunshine I could ever ask for, and I can't even take advantage of it. I'm not getting shit done."

"I haven't seen you go to the studio at all," I say, referring to the small studio that's on the property, not too far from the pool.

"Because that place intimidates the hell out of me. I went out there a couple of days ago, in the middle of the night when I couldn't sleep, and the moment I walked inside, I froze up. All sorts of old feelings came at me, one after the other." He's got both hands in his hair now, sliding down to grip at the back of his neck as he turns to face me. "I want a drink."

Alarm fills me, and I stand, panicking, unsure of what to say. "You can't drink."

"I know. And I won't." He hesitates. "But I want one just the same." He blinks, gazing at the floor. "'Just the same.' That's a great song title too."

Tate dashes over to the coffee table and picks up the discarded notebook, glancing around in search of his pen. I assume he remembers he threw it because he grabs his phone instead and taps some information into it before he shoves it into his pocket.

"Let's get out of here," I suggest. "We can, I don't know—throw on a hat and some sunglasses so no one will recognize us, and we can just drive. Stop somewhere and grab some food. You need to get out of your head and out of this house."

"I haven't driven a car in a while," he admits, looking sheepish. "What if I wreck it?"

"That's what insurance is for. Come on, Tate. We need to get out of here and do something on our own. Escape this atmosphere for a bit, because instead of helping you, it feels like it's stifling you."

"It totally is," he agrees.

"Or maybe you should go by yourself." I was sort of hoping I could get out of here too. I feel like I'm climbing the walls, and I have almost six more weeks of this monotony.

I'm over it. There's only so much scrolling online and lying out by the pool I can do. I want to explore. Check things out. I'd even go to Disneyland for the day if I could. I've been to Disney World in Orlando, but I've never checked out the California park.

"If I go by myself, I'll end up even more in my head, and that's not where I want to be." He levels that intense blue gaze on me. "You need to come with me."

"I'll go with you." I glance down at myself. "I should change."

"Hurry up and go do it before I leave without you." He's grinning. That's the first time I've seen him smile in days, so I take it as a good sign.

"Do we have a car?" I ask.

"There's a couple in the garage that Roger provided. Remember?"

Oh, that's right. We have everything we need at our fingertips, yet we've barely left the house, much to Roger's annoyance, I'm sure.

"I'll go change too," Tate says as he starts to exit the room.

I follow after him, darting into my room and shutting the door. I go through my clothes, deciding on a cute floral-print dress, shedding my T-shirt and shorts quickly before I yank the dress into place. After brushing my hair and applying a little mascara, I slip on some white Nikes and go out into the hall to find Tate already waiting for me.

"Ready to go?" He's got car keys in his fingers, twirling the key ring around, and I nod, eager to leave.

We walk out to the garage, and Tate hits a button so the door slides up. Two men from the security team appear in the driveway, frowns on their faces and sunglasses covering their eyes.

"Where are you two off to, Mr. Ramsey?"

"Going on a drive." Tate opens the passenger-side door of the Porsche 911 for me, and I slip inside.

"Don't you think we should accompany you?" The man is tall and broad and incredibly imposing, but Tate seems completely unfazed.

"Nope. We don't plan on stopping anywhere." He leans against the still-open door.

"Just driving?"

"Just driving," Tate agrees with a nod before he glances down at me and winks.

He slams the car door, cutting me off from whatever conversation they continue having, and by the time he's slipping into the driver's seat, both men have entered the house. "Did you bring a hat?"

I shake my head, glancing toward the door that leads into the house. "Should I go grab one?"

"No. I brought one for you just in case." He reaches into the narrow back seat and holds up the sun hat I like to use when I'm out by the pool. I see his black baseball cap sitting next to it on the seat. "You got sunglasses?"

I nod, holding up my Prada straw tote. "In here."

"Perfect." He starts the car and presses on the gas, the engine roaring to life, and then hits a button. The top of the car slowly lifts away from us, turning the Porsche into a convertible, and I can't help it.

I laugh.

"Your laugh is like a song," he tells me, his voice as serious as the look on his face, and my heart catches, I swear.

"Is that a good thing or a bad thing?" I ask, teasing him.

He smiles, shifting the car into reverse. "It's a really good fucking thing."

Tate backs the car out of the driveway and pulls out onto the street, taking off with a loud squeal of the tires as he shifts the car into a higher gear. He drives like a maniac through the neighborhood, and I reach out to brace my hand against the inside of the passenger door, yelping at every corner he takes.

The man drives like a demon, and when he finally notices the look of pure terror on my face, he starts to laugh. "It's okay, Scar. I've got you."

We come to a squealing stop at a red light, the engine rumbling, a sleek black BMW convertible stopping directly beside us. I glance over to find two beautiful blond women blatantly checking Tate out. One of them even slides her sunglasses down the bridge of her nose to see him better.

"Damn it." Tate turns his head toward me so they can't see his actual face, his expression one of pure panic. "I forgot the hat."

"And the sunglasses." I reach into the center console and hold up the pair he brought with him, and he takes them from me, slipping them over his eyes.

"Maybe they don't recognize me," he murmurs.

"Hey, Tate!" one of the women yells.

He winces, and I can't help it—I smirk at him. "I think they might."

Ignoring them, he leans over the center console and presses his lips to mine, stealing my breath with one kiss. The light turns green, the car behind us honks with impatience, and within seconds Tate is facing forward once more, gunning the engine and zooming past the BMW. I turn and grab our hats from the back seat, plopping my sun hat on my head firmly so it won't fly off before I hand the baseball cap to Tate.

"Put it on me," he says with a grin as he slows down and turns right, onto the on-ramp for the freeway.

I flip it so the bill is backward and shove it on his head, leaning over and pressing my lips against his cheek. As I pull away from him, he grins, and something bubbles in my chest.

Happiness.

I like seeing him like this. Carefree and smiling. It's as if the second he got behind the wheel of the sports car, he forgot all his troubles. And we've barely left the neighborhood.

"This was a good idea, Scar," he says as he presses his foot on the gas, the speedometer close to eighty in seconds. "Getting away for a little bit."

"Where are we going?" I lean my head back against the seat, watching him. The man from a few minutes ago with the dull eyes and sullen expression is gone. Now he's smiling, that dimple in full view, his hair flipped up at the ends and blowing with the wind, barely contained by the ball cap.

I like this version of Tate much better.

"I don't know." He hits the blinker and glances in the rearview mirror, changing lanes. "How about the ocean? We could walk along the beach."

I wrinkle my nose. "Not any of them close by, don't you think? They'll be so crowded. People will recognize you."

"Us," he corrects, glancing over at me quickly before he returns his attention to the road. "And that's a valid point."

"Something we're trying to avoid," I remind him. "Especially if we don't have security with us."

"Are you worried?"

"Not at all. I only wanted you to relax for a bit." I smile at him, pressing my hand on top of my head to keep my hat in place. The floppy brim is waving so much I'm worried it's going to fly off. "Just take me far away from here, and we're good."

"You're right. Maybe we should go to Newport. Laguna. Oceanside?"

"We'll need to eat." My stomach growls to remind me. I swear I wasn't nearly as hungry back home as I am all the time here in California. I blame the endless blue skies and sunshine.

"We can find a restaurant."

"And I might get thirsty."

"Are you led by your gut, Scarlett?" He sends me a look.

"Maybe." I laugh, dropping my hand, and just like that, the wind takes my hat, making me squeal. "Oh no!"

"Too late." He glances in the rearview mirror again, like he can see it being whisked away. "Bye-bye, hat."

"I loved that hat." I pout for a moment, then glance over my shoulder, but it's already gone.

"It's okay. I'll buy you another one." He reaches over and

settles his hand on my knee, his fingers inching up my leg until they're resting on my thigh. His palm is warm and broad, and his touch feels like a brand.

Claiming me.

There's no one around to see our supposed act. What's going on between us doesn't feel like an act at all.

More like it feels terribly, wonderfully real.

CHAPTER TWENTY-EIGHT

TATE

We end up in San Clemente and walk around downtown for a little bit, peeking into the cute shops before we stop at a restaurant and have lunch. Both Scarlett and I are ravenous, ordering a bunch of seafood and sharing it between ourselves. Eventually we waddle out of the restaurant almost two hours later, the both of us groaning over how full we are.

It's . . . fun, spending time with Scarlett. Especially after being so caught up in my own damn head the last few days. I know it hasn't been fun for her. I'm stuck in that damn makeshift office pretending to get work done while she's hanging out by the pool, bored out of her mind. Tiptoeing around the brooding security guys, who stand around and scowl wherever they are.

It sucks. The vibe at the house was bringing me down, even though I was mostly responsible for it.

A quick getaway was just what I needed.

After lunch we go to a nearby surf shop, and I buy a couple of large towels before we head to the beach. The sun is out and the wind is strong, bringing with it a slightly chilly ocean breeze. We try to lay both towels on the sand, but the wind keeps making one of them slip out of our fingers. We end up sitting close together on the one towel, Scarlett taking the other and draping it over herself like a throw blanket while we stare at the water, watching the waves roll in.

People are everywhere. Small families sitting on the beach, children digging up sand with their bright plastic shovel-and-pail sets. Plenty of laughter fills the air. The occasional frustrated cry from a child. Lots of couples out walking their dogs. An older gentleman with a shock of white hair and a bright-red sun visor sitting jauntily on his head approaches us with a metal detector, his movements slow and methodical.

"You ever find anything?" I ask the man as he scans the sand surrounding us.

"You'd be surprised by all the things I find," he says rather cryptically, walking away.

Scarlett sends me a look once the man is out of earshot. "He must have a lot of patience."

"If he's helping people look for their valuables, I think he's doing a great service," I say softly, my gaze stuck on the old man as he walks farther and farther away from us.

Until I can't see him at all.

We're quiet for a long time, lost in our thoughts, and for the first time in days, I don't mind being in my head. All the clutter and garbage and Roger's insistent words leave my brain, clearing it completely, and I take a deep breath, letting it out slowly.

"This is nice," Scarlett murmurs, her focus still on the ocean.

"Yeah, it is. I can't remember the last time I felt like this."

She turns toward me. "Like what?"

"Like my normal self," I admit.

"I know how long it's been. Since the day before my party," she says.

She's right. Everything turned upside down the moment that kiss was caught on camera. I haven't been the same since.

"Do you miss it?" When I give her a confused look, she explains, "Feeling like your normal self."

"Sort of. I don't know. Things were pretty mundane in my life before this all blew up. I remember thinking a couple of months ago, 'Is this it? Is this all I've got to give? Selling birthday greetings online for fifty bucks a pop?'" I kick off my slides and nudge my toes into the cold, wet sand. "I didn't know what to do. I considered going to college, but for what? I didn't like school. We were all still in high school when the band was first put together, but they had us doing classes after we finished our recording sessions, and I graduated when I was barely seventeen."

"Do you regret missing out on a normal high school experience?"

"Hell no." I make a face, thinking of my past high school life. "I wasn't anybody special in high school. Definitely not a part of the popular crowd, so when I got this chance to actually be somebody, I took full advantage of it."

I wasn't a loser in high school, but I definitely wasn't popular either, and deep down, I always wanted to be. The idea of fame, of being in the entertainment industry, whether through acting or singing or whatever, appealed to me ever since I was a little kid.

"I didn't like high school either," she admits, tracing her fingers through the sand. The hem of her dress keeps fluttering in the wind, exposing her slender thighs, and I remember how I grabbed her there earlier. As if I own her. She didn't push me away either. "I was so glad when I finally graduated. I just wanted out of there."

"Wasn't that long ago," I point out.

"A couple of months." She shrugs, her gaze stuck on the sea. "Feels like a lifetime ago."

I totally agree.

"Were you planning on going to college, or did I ruin that?" Pretty sure I didn't ruin any college plans. I remember her telling me about the gap year she was planning on taking.

"You definitely didn't ruin anything. I just—I don't think I knew what I wanted to do. I still don't. I sort of had the gap year planned with Rachel, but we hadn't made any real concrete plans, you know what I mean? And my parents were insisting I go to college after I took that year off, but . . ." Her voice drifts and she wrinkles her nose. "I don't know if I'll go. That might not be for me."

"What is for you then, Scarlett?" My tone is teasing, but I'm dead serious. I'd love to know what her future goals are.

I mean, she's young. I get it. My future goals at eighteen went up in smoke. I blew them up with my shit behavior.

"I don't know. Turn into a famous influencer and travel the world?" She shrugs. Giggles even, her cheeks turning pink. "That sounds ridiculous."

"Not if it's what you really want to do," I say, nudging her shoulder with mine. "And nothing sounds ridiculous to me. I'm over here being given another chance, which just goes to show that anything is possible. Even if I do feel like I'm on the verge of fucking everything up."

"You have a very self-defeating streak within you, Tate." When I glance over at Scarlett, I find her already watching me, her brows lifted expectantly. "What? It's true."

"What exactly do you mean?" I readjust my feet, burrowing my toes deeper into the sand so I can't even see them.

Kind of like how I bury my head in the sand sometimes and pretend I don't see what's really happening around me.

"You've been given this *amazing* opportunity to change your whole life for the better, to get a second chance, like you just said. You're able to sing again and reach potentially millions of people with your words, and all you can do is stress about how much pressure this is and how you can't come up with any lyrics for your songs." She presses her lips together when she's done, wincing when our gazes meet once again. "It's true, Tate. Instead of looking at it like such a negative, you need to convince yourself this opportunity you have is a positive."

What she's saying is right, but it's easier said than done.

"But how?" I stare out at the water once more, focusing on a fishing boat in the distance, watching as it bobs in the water. "I don't think you understand the pressure I'm under, Scarlett."

"I'm trying to. I can sort of relate to it."

I glance over at her. "How?"

"I have to deal with my dad and mom's fame day in and day out. And my dad wants me to be just like him, causing a scandal, or more like a big ruckus everywhere I go, and I'm not built like that." She grabs a handful of sand and throws it aggressively, the sand scattering all over her feet. "I've lurked in the shadows of my parents and my family's legacy my entire life. I finally get a chance to stand on my own two feet, and I'm still tied to someone. You."

Guilt hits me like a sock to my stomach. "Is that such a bad thing?"

She shrugs. "It is what it is. And this is nothing against you. I understand what you're doing and why you're doing it. I just hate that I'm getting dragged along like I always do with someone else."

I remain quiet, absorbing her words. She just wants to be her own person. Viewed for her own name and not her family's. I get that. I do. I want to stand on my own two feet, instead of always being referred to as that drunk guy who used to sing with Five Car Pileup. I'm only known for the band, and I want to prove to people that I'm more than that. That I'm more than just a stupid teenager who made some dumbass mistakes on a public stage.

"I sound like a whiny baby," she finally says, her voice quiet.

"No you don't," I immediately reassure her.

"And I made this all about me, when really this is about you." She reaches out, her hand resting on my knee as she gives it a squeeze. I feel her touch to the depths of my soul—truthfully, the fucking depths of my balls. And I never want her to remove her hand from my leg again. "You can do it, Tate. You just need to believe in yourself."

"It's just really fucking hard sometimes, you know?" I admit, my voice low. I feel like I'm revealing a deep, dark secret, confessing my struggles. "But you're right. I need to get over my shit and believe in myself."

"I believe in you," she says with an encouraging smile.

My heart cracks wide open for her. I don't think anyone has ever said those actual words to me before.

I believe in you.

"I believe in you too." I rest my hand over hers, skimming my thumb across her knuckles. "If you want to be a social media influencer and document your travels all over the world, you can fucking do it, Scar. Not like money is holding you back."

"Yeah, well, my own mental state can hold me back sometimes." She shakes her head. "But I need to let go of those negative thoughts just like you do and believe in myself too, right?"

"Right."

We stare at each other, the sun casting golden beams of light across her face, and I lean in, giving in to my urges as usual, and brush her mouth with mine. She kisses me back, our lips clinging, parting.

A phone starts ringing.

"Damn it," I mutter against her lips. "That's my phone."

Scarlett pulls away, flushing prettily. "Always interrupted."

I glance at the screen, seeing it's fucking Simon this time around, and I answer his call. "What's up?"

"You left the house?" He sounds like an angry parent.

"I needed to clear my head."

"Where are you now?"

"At the beach."

"Well, you need to get back home and change. You're going to a movie premiere tonight."

"Tonight?" I sit up straighter, Scarlett's hand falling away from my knee. "Like, *tonight* tonight?"

"Yes. I had some clothes sent over for you two to wear. Designer stuff on loan. You know the drill." He yawns, like he's bored. "Red carpet starts at eight, and movie kicks off at nine. I'll have Steffi text you the details. Hope you're not too far from the house."

The line goes quiet, and I realize he ended the call, cursing under my breath when I note the time on my phone screen. "We need to get going."

"Did I hear him correctly? We're going to a movie premiere?"

"Yeah. Love the heads-up he gave us."

I help Scarlett stand and shake off our towels before we fold them and put them in the giant straw bag she bought at the surf shop. We trudge our way up the beach toward the parking lot where the car awaits us, our steps slowed thanks to the heavy sand, and she doesn't pull away when I grab hold of her hand.

Like we're an actual couple.

"He said he had clothes sent to the house for us to wear tonight," I tell her.

"I hope he sent options." The worried look on her face says it all. She doesn't trust Roger's or Simon's decisions, and I can't blame her.

"I'm sure he did." I open my text messages to see the details are already there for tonight's premiere. "But we'll need to race back to the house. Traffic is going to be hell."

"As long as you don't wreck the car, we should be good. We'll have time, right?"

"Right." I smile at her, marveling at how just hearing her voice, seeing that smile on her pretty face, eases my soul.

Yet it feels like everyone else in my life just makes it more difficult. I'm starting to realize that I depend on this girl.

More than I probably should.

CHAPTER TWENTY-NINE

SCARLETT

Taking a deep, cleansing breath, I run my hands down the front of the sleek white Louis Vuitton dress, staring at myself in the full-length mirror in my bedroom. This is the first time I've ever worn something designed by them before, and the dress fits so perfectly you'd think they'd made it just for me.

The moment Tate and I returned to the house after our busy—and fun—afternoon at the beach, I jumped right into the shower and then went over my outfit options for tonight's movie premiere, finally FaceTiming my mother to get her opinion.

Gloria Lancaster has the best style of anyone I know. I trust her taste completely, and when she audibly gasped upon seeing me in the white dress, I knew that was the one I had to wear tonight.

"The photographs of you in that dress will be everywhere tomorrow," she gushed like she always does. "You're stunning, Scarlett. Absolutely *stunning*."

She also asked me how it was going, and I gave her a vague reply, which she accepted. I'm sure she thinks we're having filthy sex in every room of this house, the two of us alone all night long together. Which is the furthest thing from the truth.

Unfortunately.

I'm curious about sex—specifically sex with Tate—but I'm also nervous. And while I'm not 100 percent ready to do the actual deed yet, I am definitely interested in doing some . . . things.

Hookup-type things, like the ones he described when he was questioning me that night at the restaurant. Before everything took a drastic and somber turn.

I didn't tell my mother about that night, and she's never brought it up either, so I assume she didn't see the video of the woman chasing after us through the restaurant, saying horrible stuff. The video didn't go viral like I'm sure that woman wanted. In the end, she's the one who looked terrible, not us.

I take a step closer to the full-length mirror, angling my face first left, then right, checking out my makeup. I didn't do too bad of a job. Even got my vaguely winged black eyeliner on perfectly the first time around, which is pretty amazing. I grab a lip gloss from the little desk in my bedroom and uncap it before carefully applying the shiny pink shade to my lips, filling them in completely. Rubbing them together, I take a step back and examine myself in the mirror from head to toe.

My wavy hair is pulled up into a high ponytail. The dress fits to perfection, with little cutouts at the waist.

Well, more like big cutouts. And the top of the dress fits so tightly I decided to forgo a bra completely, but the fabric isn't thick enough to completely hide my nipples.

I can see them.

Oops.

There's a knock on my door, and I reply, "Come in."

The door swings open, and there's Tate, taking my breath

away completely in a stark black two-piece suit accompanied by a dark-pink button-down shirt, the first couple of buttons undone at the neck, exposing some of his chest. There's a thin silver chain around his neck, scruff on his face, and now he's the one who's golden from the sun, thanks to our afternoon by the ocean.

Our gazes meet in the mirror, and I see the approval shining in his eyes. "You look gorgeous."

I turn to face him, letting him get the full effect of the dress. "So do you."

"Black and white." He enters the room, slowly walking toward me. "Opposites attract, maybe?"

"Good cop, bad cop," I correct. "Though I don't think I've seen the bad cop wear pink before."

"I'm starting a new trend." He glances down at his shirt before meeting my gaze once more. "Is the pink too much?"

"No, I love it." I smile when he stops directly in front of me, towering over me despite the silver stiletto Louboutins on my feet. Simon went all out with the clothes and accessories he had sent over for us. "Is it Gucci?"

"Prada. Harry has got the Gucci market cornered." Tate slips his hands into his pockets, his gaze lazily roaming over me from head to toe. "Damn, Scar. I don't know if I want to take you out tonight."

I'm immediately frowning. "Why not?"

"I don't want anyone to know what a snack I've been keeping." He laughs when I scowl at him. "What, you don't like being referred to as a snack?"

"I don't think I've ever been called that before." I'm trying to look like it offends me, but I give up and let the smile free.

I don't mind being called a snack at all.

He crowds me, staring at himself in the mirror, and I turn so I'm standing right next to him, contemplating the both of us. He slips his arm around my waist, his hand resting loosely on my hip, fingers brushing the cutout in my dress just above my hip bone. "I like the holes."

"It's called a cutout," I correct him.

"Whatever. I like them. You're utterly elegant, and also a little naughty." He smiles at me in the mirror, tilting his head toward mine. "What do you think?"

It's been such a whirlwind of planning and meetings since the moment I whispered the word *deal* to Tate on the sidewalk. I've barely had a moment to really focus on me and him. On us.

As a couple.

"I think we look good together," Tate continues when I still haven't said anything. "I think the paparazzi are going to lose their damn minds when they see you tonight."

"When the ladies see you in the pink, they're all going to scream," I tease him.

His face falls ever so slightly. "Tell me the truth. You hate the pink."

I turn so I'm actually facing him, not staring at our reflection in the mirror. "I don't hate it. I love it." I touch his chest, let my fingers drift down the front of his shirt, savoring the heat of him beneath the soft fabric. "It looks really good on you."

He settles both of his hands on my hips, his expression turning serious. "This is a big night tonight."

I blink up at him, remaining quiet.

"We've been sort of playing at this couple thing, but this is our first official appearance. They'll photograph us on the red carpet, take a bazillion photos, and probably ask us a ton of invasive questions. You'll be tempted to answer."

I part my lips, ready to speak, but he keeps talking.

"You can't answer them. You just smile and nod and wave, and we keep walking the red carpet. I'll do the same.

The minute you give them any information, they'll take it and twist it to fit their agenda."

"No one has an agenda when it comes to me," I reassure him, but he's already shaking his head.

"They *all* have an agenda, and right now, it involves you and me and 'How long will those two crazy kids last?' That's what they're focusing on. I'm sure there are plenty of publicity people out there who don't believe we're even in an actual relationship."

Oh. I never thought about that. And they would be correct.

"So I'm warning you—I'm going to be all over you tonight. Be prepared." He leans in and presses his lips to my temple, breathing deep. "I'm going to kiss you and hold you all damn night. I'm going to make it look like I can't get enough of you. As if I'm obsessed with you."

Every part of my body is tingling in anticipation at his words.

"Okay," I whisper, my voice shaky.

"Do you have a problem with that?" His hands shift to my shoulders, holding me away from him at arm's length, his head bent, his gaze at my level.

I shake my head. "Not at all."

"Perfect. I'll need you all over me too then."

My mouth goes dry. We've been building up to this. I knew it would happen eventually. I can do this.

I know I can.

"That won't be a problem," I reassure him.

His smile is faint and even full of pride. "I knew you could. Roger and Simon will both be watching. They'll have expectations, and we need to meet them."

"You won't buckle under the pressure?" I ask, suddenly concerned. It was his use of the word *expectations* that did it.

"I won't. I swear." He drops his hands from my arms and slowly backs away from me. "Are you ready to go? Simon sent a private town car for us to use."

"I'm ready," I say with a little nod.

Once I find the tiny white bag that accompanied my dress, we climb into the car and are on our way to the movie premiere. Traffic is relatively light—a rarity in Southern California—and by the time we arrive in front of the theater where the premiere is happening, I'm a nervous wreck.

"Do I look okay?" I ask as we wait in line behind the many other black cars and SUVs dropping people off for the event.

Tate glances over at me, his gaze downright smoldering. "Good enough to eat, Scar."

I take that as a compliment, but I'm still nervous, tucking my hair behind my ears, my hands fluttery with nerves. By the time it's our turn to get out, our driver about to open the door, Tate murmurs, "You do realize you're getting out first."

And I'm so incredibly grateful the dress isn't short. "And you're following right after me, right?"

"Absolutely." The door swings open, and Tate gives me an encouraging smile. "Go ahead. I'll be directly behind you."

Taking a deep, fortifying breath, I climb out of the car, my hand clutching one side of my skirt. I rise to my full height, startled by the many people screaming my name.

"Scarlett!"

The bulbs flash what feels like hundreds of times. All these giant cameras aimed right at me, taking photos of me standing there frozen next to the car.

Tate miraculously appears beside me, slinging his arm around my shoulders and tugging me in close to him. "Smile," he says out of the side of his mouth.

I jerk my gaze toward him, noting how at ease he seems,

his smile in place, his gaze scanning the crowd. "How can you see anyone?"

"I can't. Just smile for the camera." He faces me, leaning in and kissing me before I can even paste on a fake smile.

The crowd goes wild, most of them chanting for Tate now. They want his attention—our attention—and act like they will do whatever it takes to get it.

"Come on," Tate murmurs as he withdraws from me slightly, taking my hand and leading me down the red carpet. Past the barricade that contains the photo corps, ignoring their shouts and questions.

"Tate! Tate! Look over here, Tate! Scarlett!"

"Tate, is it true you're going on tour next spring?"

"Tate, how's the album coming?"

"Are you two engaged yet, Scarlett?"

"How's Tate in bed?"

"Word on the street you're reuniting with your Five Car Pileup bandmates!"

Tate stops at that question, frowning at the guy who asked it. "Where did you hear that?"

The man shrugs. "Saw it somewhere on the internet. Reddit?"

Tate groans and keeps walking, my hand still firmly in his. "Reddit," I can hear him muttering. "You can't trust that site."

All I can do is smile and look pretty, feeling like a doll. A blind doll who can see nothing thanks to the constant shutter of the flashes.

We enter the building and are greeted by publicity people who are wearing headsets, and they murmur our names into the tiny speakers, not even having to ask who we are.

Weird.

Once we're checked in, we stand in front of a promo screen

for the movie and take a few photos together, Tate's hand always resting on my waist, his fingers brushing against my exposed skin thanks to the cutouts. A shiver steals through me every time, and I know he knows. I can tell by the way he smiles.

The way he looks at me.

Once the last of the photos are taken, we go to the concession stand, where all the items are free for the night. I order a bucket of popcorn and a Coke in the largest size they have.

I was too nervous to eat when we were getting ready, and now I'm starving.

"You going to share that with me, or should I order my own?"

Turning to my right, I find Tate smiling at me, standing in front of the counter as the concession employee gazes at him with wide-eyed wonder.

I'm probably her age. She might even wish she were me, just for the opportunity to be with Tate tonight.

"I'll share," I tell him teasingly. "Though I wouldn't mind if you got some M&M's."

"You heard my date," Tate tells the employee, flashing her that devastating smile. The poor girl. I can barely withstand it myself.

"Are you really going to eat greasy, buttery popcorn in that gorgeous white dress?" the publicity woman asks me, her tone snide.

I glance over at her, frowning. She looks to be in her midtwenties, maybe even late twenties, with a pinched expression and overly bleached blond hair. She's clearly not impressed with me.

Well, that's just great. I'm not impressed with her either.

"I am." I take the bucket from the concession worker and lift it toward the publicity woman in a sort of cheers gesture. "This is my dinner."

"Better make sure you take some napkins," the woman says as I grab my giant cup.

"What, are you her mother?" Tate slides his arm around my waist and guides me away from the concession counter. "What the hell was her problem?"

"I don't know. Maybe she's tired of dealing with celebrities." I carefully nudge my elbow into his waist. "Did you get the candy?"

He holds up the familiar brown box. "Sure did. You going to share that drink with me?"

"And the popcorn," I reassure him.

"You're so generous," he says as we enter the darkened theater and follow a gentleman who takes us to our seats. Once we're settled in, Tate leans over and whispers in my ear, "Think you'll let me make out with you back here?"

We're in one of the farthest-back rows. And who's going to be watching us? They'll all be focused on the movie.

"If you're lucky." I toss some popcorn into my mouth.

He rubs his hands together, then reaches over and grabs the soda from where I left it in the cup holder between us. "Pretty sure I'm going to get lucky tonight."

Maybe even in more ways than one.

CHAPTER THIRTY

TATE

After the movie—a full-on hanging-on-the-edge-of-your-seat action thriller that was pretty decent—some of the younger members of the cast approach us, making easy conversation that leads into them inviting us to go to dinner at a nearby restaurant.

I of course accept, and Scarlett doesn't seem to mind, so we hop in our town car and make our way down the street to a tiny Italian restaurant tucked behind a wall of ivy. The moment we walk inside the restaurant, the atmosphere is warm and welcoming, every single table full save for a long one in the back that has a tiny folded card set up in the center that says *Reserved*.

"Oh my God, it smells delicious in here," Scarlett practically groans, and I glance over at her, giving her hand, which is still in mine, a squeeze.

"You're still hungry after all that popcorn you consumed?" We've been teasing each other all night. The more we spend time together, the easier it is with her. Nothing feels fake or forced between us.

I actually like her. I'm fairly certain she likes me. And the closer we get, the more I want her.

Scarlett rests her other hand against her flat stomach, smiling almost apologetically. "I didn't eat that much."

She ate a lot, but I'm not going to give her shit for it. I ate a lot of popcorn too. And the candy.

Shit, I'm going to have to go for a run every morning for the rest of the week to burn all of these extra calories off. And we're having a late pasta dinner on top of it?

It's like I'm trying to sabotage myself. Roger keeps harping on me about how I need to stay in shape, and he's right. I need to be physically ready for a tour, which is already tentatively scheduled.

Fucking terrifying, how I'm handing over my life to my record label and they're just making shit happen and consulting me after the fact. I'm expected to say yes to everything they do, and normally I do. But when does it ever stop?

At the rate it's going, it feels like never.

The hostess takes us to our table, and the six of us settle into our chairs, Scarlett sitting right next to me. We all glance over the menus and discuss our options, Scarlett remaining quiet as usual, and I wish she weren't so shy. Though I know it's hard for her to make small talk with other people. She claims she's better behind a camera than in person, and I've come to realize that with strangers, she's not wrong.

One of the actresses from the film, Katrina, sits on my left side, her gaze knowing when mine meets hers.

"We met once, you know," she tells me as the server is on the other end of the table, starting to take all our drink orders.

I frown, scrutinizing her face, but it's not familiar. "We did?"

Katrina nods, her lips curved into a smug smile. I can't deny that she's gorgeous. Icy-blond hair that hangs in a straight line at her shoulders, her full lips covered in bold red lipstick. The dress she's wearing is a shimmery gold and clings to her curves. I'd peg her as a little older than me, but then again, maybe I'm wrong.

Hollywood, celebrity—it hardens a lot of us. Makes us seem older than we are. Only because we've seen so much and done so much compared to the average person that's our age.

"A few years ago," she says vaguely. "Before you had your public meltdown."

Everything seemed to happen to me before my meltdown. "So a lifetime ago then."

"Yes." Katrina leans in a little closer, her gaze falling to my lips. "We met at a club."

"Okay." Where is she going with this?

"I was a dancer." Her laugh is sultry, and I'm immediately uncomfortable. Nothing good ever came out of a club back in our heyday. "I gave you a lap dance. You slipped me an extra five hundred, and we met back up so I could give you a blow job later that evening. You were drunk off your ass. Had a hard time coming."

Oh fuck. Embarrassment coats my skin, and I swallow hard, wishing I could forget that ever happened.

Unfortunately, I remember that night. Not one of my prouder moments.

Katrina is watching me, waiting for my reaction, and I swear it seems like she's enjoying this. Seeing how uncomfortable her words make me feel.

"Well, it looks like you're doing great now," I say, trying to steer the conversation away from the fact that we've had a sexual encounter.

I remember the night. I barely remember the girl. Just that she had a good mouth and all I could think about was her sucking my dick. It was right after I caught Jessica with Jamie, so I was feeling especially down in the dumps.

Eager to lose myself in alcohol. Drugs.

Someone else.

"I am." Katrina scoots closer, and I catch the strong, almost overwhelming scent of her perfume. "I slept with a lot of producers to get this role, and I'm not about to fuck it up now. I have some jobs lined up."

I'm literally starting to sweat, and my gaze goes to the server, who's drawing closer, thank God.

I hate Los Angeles. Hollywood. It's all the same. Everyone's a shark. Or a snake.

And they're all out to get you.

"That's great," I tell her. "Good for you."

I'm saved by the server, who interrupts us to take our drink orders. Katrina orders some overpriced alcoholic drink, while I ask for an ice water before I turn my focus on Scarlett, who's watching me with a slight frown on her face, a hurt glow in her gaze.

Shit. She probably overheard my conversation with Katrina.

Leaning in toward Scarlett, I murmur, "You all right?"

"Do you know her?" She inclines her head toward Katrina.

"Barely." I shrug, desperate to play it off.

"I thought I heard her say you two met once."

"We did." I don't want to go into too much detail with Scarlett when it comes to Katrina. "The typical Hollywood thing, you know? Back in my Five Car Pileup days."

"Uh-huh." The shrewd look Scarlett sends my way has me squirming in my seat, but thankfully, we're interrupted by the server, who requests her drink order.

Once the server leaves, Scarlett keeps her back toward me, starting up conversation with the actor who's sitting on her other side. He's probably in his early thirties, and he's been in a few movies. She knows exactly who he is but is playing it cool.

Ignoring me.

And leaving me with no choice but to talk to Katrina, since the people sitting directly across from me are involved in a hushed, serious-looking conversation.

"Your new girl is real cute." Katrina's voice is laced with sarcasm.

I send her a cool look. "I think so."

"Kind of young, though." Katrina flashes me a smile. "You into that sort of thing?"

"What are you referring to?"

"Young girls who are barely eighteen and have never sucked a dick before? Because that's what she looks like." Katrina laughs, the sound annoying the shit out of me. "She's just a baby, really. Especially compared to you."

"I'm not that much older than her." I glance over at Scarlett yet again, but her back is still to me, tension radiating off her.

Like she's mad.

"I'm not talking about your ages. I know what you're all about, Tate Ramsey, and you have no business entertaining a cute little innocent thing like that heiress." Katrina inclines her head toward Scarlett. "Send her home to Daddy and end this charade for good. Find yourself a real woman."

Her charade remark hits home, but I ignore it. Ignore the wave of unease that sweeps over me. She has no idea what's going on between me and Scarlett.

No one really does.

"A real woman, huh? Like you?"

Katrina's smile is sharp. "You catch on fast. I'm sure I can inspire a few songs for you to sing."

I frown. "You been keeping up?"

"We've all been keeping up with your story, Tate. It's a good one." She rests her hand on my arm, her nails pressing against my skin, even through my suit jacket. "We could make a better one. Hollywood actress on the rise and popular singer given a second chance? A classic story."

"How's your follower count?" I raise my brows at her, and she removes her hand from my arm, sending me a disgusted look.

"Is that all you're doing it for, then? Because she has a solid follower count and makes those idiotic 'get ready' posts?" Katrina rolls her eyes. "I'm a *serious* actress. Not some dumb high schooler trying to make it as an influencer."

"First of all, I'm not a high schooler anymore, and I'm definitely not dumb. I graduated valedictorian of my class." Scarlett's cool voice has us both turning in her direction. "And how serious of an actress can you be when you're in a franchised action film and say all of . . . what? Five lines?"

Katrina glares, her lips thinning as she contemplates Scarlett. "Ten. I have ten lines."

Scarlett's amused. I can see it in her eyes. The way her lips curve, like she might burst out laughing at any second.

And I'm . . . proud. Proud that she stood up for herself to Katrina. Scarlett looked her right in the eye and called her out.

That was kind of hot.

"You wouldn't understand." Katrina pushes her chair back and rises to stand. "Spoiled little princess."

With a huff she takes off, headed to the bathroom, no doubt. Another actress from the film goes to follow her, and I wonder if they're going to do drugs in the bathroom.

I wouldn't doubt it. Taking a hit of something eases the sting of taking an insult from a well-spoken and freakin' gorgeous eighteen-year-old.

I angle myself more toward Scarlett, my back now to Katrina's seat as I slide my arm around the back of Scarlett's chair. "You popped off."

Scarlett straightens her shoulders, her expression serious. "She was totally coming onto you. And insulting me in the process."

"You put your back to me, talking to that actor," I remind her. "I thought you were mad at me."

"I sort of was, but I realized you didn't make me mad. She did." Scarlett's posture relaxes. "It felt good, saying that."

"You were impressive." I shift my arm closer to her, my fingers sliding over her upper arm.

She smiles. "I don't do that enough. Voice my opinion. Defend myself."

"You're pretty good at it. Maybe you should do that more often."

"In the situation we're currently in, I have a feeling I'm going to need to," she admits, dipping her head.

"Hey." I slip my fingers beneath her chin and tilt her face up, her gaze meeting mine. "You have nothing to worry about. I wasn't interested in her at all."

Her smile is tremulous. "Is that because of—" She waves her hand, and I know what she's referring to.

The contract. The agreement we're locked into.

"No." I shake my head. "I'm not interested in anyone else."

"Oh yeah?" she breathes.

"Yeah." I dip my head, brushing her lips with mine. "I'm only interested in you."

CHAPTER THIRTY-ONE

SCARLETT

During dinner, things shift between Tate and me, which has become a common theme with us. One I'm enjoying.

Appreciating.

I was infuriated, listening to that actress try to come for my boyfriend. I don't care if he's my fake boyfriend—the woman clearly had no boundaries and treated Tate like he was readily available.

Spying on their conversation, I also figured out that he definitely had a previous run-in with her before in his boy band days. A sexual encounter, from what I could tell. And while normally that would send me running away from him screaming, I don't feel that way now.

I've learned a lot about Tate in the last few days while we've been in California. Some of it has been a struggle—he can be very frustrating. But some of it is also . . . enlightening.

Thrilling even.

There's no way I can ignore that he has a past, and I accept it. What he did before me doesn't matter. I can't let it bother me, and I'm not thinking this way only because our relationship is supposedly fake.

The more time I spend with him, the more real everything feels.

It's also so . . . sweet, how patient he is with me. He doesn't push. Even when I can tell he wants to. He gets a certain look in his eyes, like he wants to pounce on me. Devour me. Every time I see that particular gleam in his gaze, my body responds.

I want to know what it's like, to have him . . .

Consume me.

The food is delicious and the conversation interesting throughout dinner. Once Katrina returns to the table with her friend, they swap seats and ignore us for the rest of the meal, which is fine by me. Tate and I remain quiet, listening to a couple of the actors tell funny stories about their set experience. Some of them share how they got started in the business, and even Katrina tells a story about meeting a producer at the nightclub she used to work at, leaving out a few choice details.

Like how she slept with him. I only know this because I heard her say it to Tate point blank.

Spending time with all these people is making me think that this world isn't as glamorous as it portrays itself to be. And if you're young and don't have a strong sense of self, I can see how you'd become easily influenced by everyone surrounding you. The good and the bad.

Mostly the bad, only because it's always so tempting.

When we leave the restaurant, Tate keeps his hand on my lower back, just above my butt, as he guides me out of the building and toward our car. The moment we slide into the back seat, he pulls the door shut behind him and turns toward me, his expression full of relief.

"Thank God that's over."

I can't help but laugh. "You were the one who wanted to do this."

"Yeah, and it was torture." He leans back against the seat, his hand darting out to grab me and pull me closer to him. "I thought it would be interesting."

I go to him, resting my head against his muscular chest. "It was."

"With the exception of Katrina." When I glance up, I find he's already watching me. "I'm sorry if she upset you."

"You don't have to apologize. You didn't do anything."

"But I did. I messed around with her a few years ago." He grimaces. "And I barely remember it."

Thank God is what I want to say, but I remain quiet.

"I did a lot of shitty things, and getting back into the business is reminding me of all of those things I did. Stuff I'd rather forget." He presses his head against the seat, taking a deep breath. "I wasn't a good person."

"You weren't a bad person. You were just young and given way too much freedom," I point out.

"And I handled it all wrong. Not everyone completely messed up their careers. But I did. I screwed it up royally, and I had so much regret. But I also believed it was all done to me. Sure, I was partially responsible, but I also blamed other people. Circumstances. It's easy to point fingers when you don't want to face where you went wrong," he explains.

"A couple of years ago, I couldn't take full responsibility for my actions. Hell, even a few months ago I probably couldn't. But now? I see it. I see where I messed up. I see what could've been and how I threw it all away. I regret my choices," he admits.

"You've been given a second chance, though," I remind him, my voice soft. "And that's a good thing."

"I won't screw it up this time." His voice is fierce. The look on his face—determined. "Not after I lost everything before. I want to do this right. And while I regret what I did in the past, there's one good thing that came out of it."

"What's that?" I ask, my gaze returning to his.

"I have this second chance because of you. I met you." He reaches for me, his fingers streaking across my cheek, making me shiver. That and the sincerity glowing in his eyes. "And I'm not saying this because you're pretending to be my girlfriend and it's all helping out my career. I'm so damn grateful to you, Scarlett, for agreeing to this when you didn't have to. It's more that your dad sought me out and believed in me enough to hire me to perform at your party. Your family gave me an opportunity I would've never had otherwise, and I appreciate it. I appreciate you. For standing by my side. For believing in me."

I part my lips, ready to speak, but he presses his index finger against my mouth, silencing me.

"Your belief in me and my career gives me the strength to keep going. I have some ideas for the songs, and I think they're going to start coming together. We're going to start laying down the tracks next week. This album is going to get finished in time, and I feel really good about it."

I'm smiling when he removes his finger from my mouth. "That's great, Tate. I'm so happy for you."

"You're a big part of this." He cups the side of my face, his touch gentle, and I can't help myself.

I turn toward his palm and kiss it.

Heat flares in his gaze, and he tilts my head back, his mouth landing on mine. His kiss is hungry, his tongue insistent as it slides into my mouth, and I respond in kind, kissing him back just as intensely. His hands wander, touching me everywhere but where I want him the most, and a low groan of frustration leaves me.

He breaks away first, his breaths coming harder, his lips damp and swollen from mine. "What's wrong?"

"It's this dress." I tug on the slender column, showing him how fitted it is from the hips down. "The skirt is too tight."

He's smiling, looking rather pleased with himself. "What, you want to climb on top of me?"

"Well . . . yeah." I don't even bother trying to deny it.

Tate helps rectify the situation, gathering the skirt of my dress and helping me pull it up. Farther and farther until he can basically see my panties. Which I tell myself is no big deal, considering he's seen me in a bikini. Has felt me up when I'm wearing a bikini even.

But I see the interest in his gaze. The way his eyes slide over me slowly, making my skin heat. Like he's trying to figure out a way to get my clothes off while we're in the back seat of this car.

Thank goodness he hit a button and slid the partition up so our driver can't see us.

And why do so many moments happen between us while we're in a car?

"Come here," Tate murmurs, and I go to him, my dress carefully gathered just above my hips as I climb on top of his lap, straddling him. His hands slide beneath the bunched fabric of my dress, covering my ass, and a gasp leaves me when he yanks me closer.

I can feel his erection. Thick and heavy, pressing into my core, and I release a shuddery breath.

"See what you do to me?" He drifts one hand up my back, until his fingers are curled around my nape, pulling my head down so he can murmur against my lips, "I've been walking around like this for weeks."

"Weeks?" I squeak. We haven't even been here for that long.

"Feels like it." He tilts my head back, his mouth on my

throat. Delivering soft, wet kisses that have me straining closer. "You drive me fucking crazy. Your laugh. Your smile. The way you look at me."

I tilt my head back, my eyelids falling closed as he kisses and licks his way down my neck. "H-how do I look at you?"

"Like you believe in me," he whispers against my skin, pausing before he lifts his head.

I open my eyes, our gazes locking, and I see it then.

That's all Tate has ever wanted. For someone to believe in him, especially during those moments when he doesn't even trust himself.

"I believe in you," I say, my voice firm. "You can do whatever you set your heart on. Conquer whatever challenge comes your way."

His smile is faint. "Right now, all I can think about is conquering you."

You've already got me, I think to myself as his mouth returns to mine, our tongues stroking, circling each other. I bury my hands in his soft hair, holding him close, letting him devour me. Enjoying every single second, despite the trickle of fear running through me.

I want this. I want him. But I'm still a little scared. I've never gone this far before, and there are all these expectations in my head.

He probably has expectations too. Ones I'm sure I can't fulfill because I have zero experience and he's done so much more. He's lived a complete life before me, and what if—

"Hey." He ends the kiss, his deep voice making me open my eyes. "You're thinking too much."

I frown. "How did you—"

"I know. Because of this." He reaches toward me, lightly rubbing that crease between my eyebrows with his thumb. "I can feel you frowning, Scar. That brain is going into overdrive right now."

A breath leaves me, and he drops his hand, pressing his forehead against mine. "I can't help it. I'm a little . . . worried."

"Why?" His fingers thread through my hair, stroking it, lulling me into a trance. "Don't think too hard. Just . . . let it happen."

"You make it sound so easy," I whisper, envious of his experience. How he's acting like this is no big deal.

Maybe it's not a big deal to him, but this moment—as well as all the moments that have been leading up to it—feels life changing to me.

"It is. And then again, it's not. Here." He grabs my wrist and guides my hand so that it rests against his chest. "Feel that?"

His heart is pounding hard against my palm. I shift so I can stare into his eyes, and I see it. A hint of fear in his gaze. Maybe he's trying to play this off to ease my worry, but he's affected too.

Affected by me.

"Yes," I whisper.

"You do that to me too, Scar. I don't want to screw this up. I've messed everything else up in my life, and for once, I want to do it right. Everything. That includes you."

His sincere words have me lunging for him, kissing him with all I've got. My arms are wrapped tight around his neck as I shift closer, practically sitting on top of his erection, and when it brushes a particular spot between my thighs, a gasp escapes me.

"Feels good?" His mouth moves against mine, his teeth finding my lower lip and giving it a tug.

Another gasp leaves me, and I tilt my hips, his dick hitting that same exact spot again.

Oh God.

Pretty sure I just saw stars.

His hands go to my hips as our mouths remain fused, guiding me as I start to rub against him. It's like I can't stop myself. He helps me shift up and down, pulling me closer. Holding me tighter. I'm panting into his mouth, my breaths hitching, my skin tightening. He lets go of my hip, his hand sneaking in between us, his fingers finding my damp panties, pressing directly upon my clit.

"Tate," I moan, unable to kiss him any longer.

Only able to feel. The sensations racing through my blood, rolling over my skin. To focus on the throbbing between my thighs, the way he's touching me. As if he knows what I need and he's the only one who can take care of it.

"You're so wet," he murmurs, his fingers circling faster. "You're already close, aren't you."

I think I am. I've tried touching myself before but could never manage to experience any type of feeling when I experimented. Plus, I always felt a little ashamed. Like I shouldn't be doing it. Or a lot dumb because I seriously had no idea what I was doing.

Tate, though—he knows exactly what he's doing, and God, it feels . . . incredible.

When his fingers shift to slip beneath my panties, I stiffen, nervous. He can sense it, his lips seeking mine once more, his kiss gentle.

Almost sweet.

"Relax," he murmurs as his fingers work their way into my panties, lightly brushing against my sensitive flesh. I moan, clinging to him, angling my hips so he can touch me where I want him the most. "Oh fuck, Scar. You're soaked."

"Is—is that a bad thing?"

"Hell no," he says just before he savagely kisses me. I drown in his taste, the assured strokes of his tongue, not even realizing they match his thrusting fingers until I find my hips are moving with his hand.

My thighs tremble, my stomach tightening. I'm straining toward his busy fingers, seeking more of those foreign yet delicious sensations currently running through me. He presses his thumb against my clit, rubbing in tight circles until I'm practically bouncing on his hand, my entire body going still before I fall completely apart.

I'm . . . I'm coming. My first orgasm. Shivers steal over me, my mind going completely blank, my body consumed. It's like I'm floating, and I cling to him, as if I'll slip away and disappear forever.

His fingers slow their insistent rubbing, his thumb easing off my clit, and when I collapse against him, he holds me tight, his mouth at my ear, murmuring soothing words as my body still trembles.

"You're so pretty when you come, Scarlett." He kisses my neck. "I think I tore your dress."

"Wait, what?" I pull away from him slightly so I can look at the gathered fabric between us, spotting the tear in a seam immediately. "Oh no."

We borrowed it. Simon sent it over so I could wear it for the night, and we go and tear it.

"I'll pay for it," he reassures me, sounding amused. "It was worth it."

He's so right.

I'm smiling. "Totally worth it. But I have a question."

"What?" He kisses me, his lips lingering, and I nip at his lower lip with my teeth.

"Can we do it again? When we get home?"

He laughs, his hands gripping my butt once more, this time beneath my panties. "Did I create a monster just now?"

A sigh leaves me as I murmur, "I think so."

CHAPTER THIRTY-TWO

SCARLETT

I think I'm in love.

Okay, I'm getting way ahead of myself, but we've been spending a lot of time together, Tate and I. Yes, he's busy during the day, working on his album while I document bits and pieces of the process this last week, sharing it on my social media with the approval of Irresistible. Roger is loving every minute of it, sending me glowing reviews of my posts via text, rambling on and on about how good I am for the upcoming album and for Tate. How inspirational.

I have to believe Roger, because I secretly think the same thing. Not because I have a big ego or think the world revolves around me but because of one thing that's becoming more and more obvious as time goes on.

All the songs, all of Tate's lyrics, seem to be about . . .

Me.

He's used all the titles he told me he would. "I've Got You," "They Don't Know about You and Me," and the one that gets me the most, "My Untouched Girl."

When I hear him sing it, I sort of want to die of

embarrassment and melt with desire, all at once. It's a sexy song, all about me and my inexperience and how he wants to teach me . . .

Everything.

It's even a little dirty, and I can't think about when my family finally hears it, because that's an entirely new level of embarrassment that I'm not particularly eager to explore. But for right now, I can't worry about it. I don't want to worry about it.

I'm too busy spending time with Tate. Stealing every moment that I can with him. He's so busy—that brain of his never stops thinking, and he's working constantly. Which means he's always so tired by the end of the day.

But he's never too tired for me.

We've done all sorts of things over the last seven days. All except the one—actual intercourse. It's mostly my fault that it hasn't happened yet. I'm still nervous, a little wary, but perfectly willing to do everything else. Like give him a blow job, which I did for the first time last night.

I'm eager to do it again.

He's currently at the studio downtown, and it's late—almost eight o'clock. He's usually home by now. I glance around the empty living room, wishing he were here with me, and then my phone rings, indicating I have a FaceTime call.

When I check who it is, I'm surprised to see Rachel's name on the screen.

I answer, waiting for her face to appear, and the moment I see her, I'm hit with such a wave of homesickness I almost start crying.

"You suck," she tells me in greeting, even though she's smiling.

"What? What do you mean?" Leave it to Rachel to always have me hanging on the edge.

"You said you'd have me come out there so I could hang out with you, and I've barely heard a single peep from you! Just a quick text here and there." Rachel mock pouts. I can tell she's in her bedroom and it's dark. Like she's about to go to bed.

Considering she's three hours ahead of me, that's probably the case.

"I'm so sorry. I just—things have been happening so fast, and the days just fly by." My apology is lame. So are my excuses.

"Right. More like you're getting dicked every night and you've forgotten all about me." Rachel bursts out laughing when she sees my shocked face.

"I am not getting dicked every night." I glance around, like one of the security guys is going to pop out from behind a wall or lamp. I really hope they didn't hear her. Pretty sure they're currently outside. "But Tate and I have grown . . . closer."

Rachel grins. "Ooh, please do tell. And that happened fast."

"I know." I smile, remembering how I said I wouldn't stay here beyond two weeks. Thinking of all the time Tate and I have spent together and how I never want it to end. We're so much closer now, and I'm always eager to see him when he finally comes home from the studio. Tonight, I plan on smothering him with kisses, and hopefully we can take a late-night swim. Or we'll just go straight to bed.

The possibilities are endless.

"I don't hear you complaining," Rachel points out.

"There's no reason for me to complain. I'm having fun."

"Having fun. Is that code for getting naked with Tate Ramsey every night?"

I can feel my cheeks burn hot, and Rachel points at me.

"I knew it. You two are totally into each other, aren't you? I see the photos everywhere. All over the internet. On social media. Your social media. He's all you talk about." Rachel shakes her head, as if she can't believe it. "They follow you guys to every restaurant and place you go to, and I have to say, with all the photos I see—you two look like the real deal."

"That's because we are the real deal," I admit, my voice soft. Like I don't want to speak too loudly for fear that it'll break this magical spell Tate and I are both currently under.

Things are going so well. They have been for pretty much the entirety of our time here in California. To the point that I forget about everything else and just focus on him. On our life here.

I've FaceTimed with my parents a couple of times, and I'm always so vague in my responses when they ask questions like *When are you coming home?* and *How serious are you two?* Mom texts me all the time, asking for more details about our relationship, and I just brush her off or change the subject. I don't want to tell her too much. Our relationship feels so fragile still. I want to keep things private.

Just between me and Tate. No one else needs to know. Despite how popular we are online, that part of it still doesn't feel real.

I have no clue when we're coming home, and I don't want to rush the process. Tate is doing so well putting the album together, and I refuse to leave him alone and go back to New York.

He needs me.

"I knew this would happen," Rachel says vehemently, though I can tell she's not mad. More like she seems really happy for me. "From the way you talked, like you two were always snapping at each other, I figured it would eventually turn into an enemies-to-lovers situation. Looks like I was right."

"Enemies to lovers?" I'm frowning.

"Oh, you know what I'm talking about. Every great fake relationship in a movie or series or book starts out as an enemies-to-lovers story. They hate each other. Until they don't."

That's exactly how I feel about Tate. I couldn't stand him. And then I could.

Now I can't imagine life without him.

I'm thinking he feels the same.

"I think that's us. Well, me. He never seemed to mind me too badly."

"So you're telling me he's a boy obsessed," Rachel says, nodding.

I frown. "What are you talking about?"

My best friend sighs, rolling her eyes. "I've been reading, okay? Mostly romance books, and they have all of these tropes. Fake dating. Boy obsessed. Enemies to lovers. I don't have my best friend around to hang out with—and I'm not trying to make you feel bad, I'm just stating facts—so I need to occupy myself somehow. And that means I've been reading. A lot."

"I'll be home soon," I tell her, feeling bad even though she told me I shouldn't. "I promise."

"It's fine. I'm cool with it. Besides, I don't want you coming home. It's like you're living in an actual romance book. As if Tate is the ultimate book boyfriend of every girl's dreams. He's that good."

"He really is that good," I reassure her, breaking into laughter at the sly look on her face. "I just—I didn't think he would be this sweet. Or fun. Or . . . sexy."

"Sexy? Oh my." Rachel fans herself. "Scarlett, you never call any guy sexy. Not even Ian."

Ian. I haven't thought about him much lately.

I don't miss him. Not at all. I was chasing after someone who wasn't interested. It's nice to have someone chasing me for once.

"I hate to break it to you, but . . ." Rachel's voice drifts.

"But what?" I ask, panic hitting me when she still hasn't finished her sentence.

"I think you've hit the jackpot with this one." Her face is solemn, her eyes wide. "He seems like a winner. You're a lucky girl."

I smile to myself, unable to keep my joy contained. Rachel's right.

I am the luckiest girl in the world.

I'm dozing on the couch when I finally hear the door that leads from the kitchen to the garage open, indicating that Tate has finally returned. I sit up, pushing the hair out of my face, clad in an old Tate Ramsey Five Car Pileup T-shirt I found on Etsy that just arrived this afternoon. It's a little faded and completely oversize. The perfect thing to wear to greet Tate when he gets home.

I hear keys hitting the marble counter, and I watch Tate as he sets his wallet there as well, running a hand through his hair, a slow exhale leaving him as he stares unseeingly at the floor for a moment. I take him in, marveling at how handsome he is. How tall and broad and strong.

Oh, I've got it so bad for this man.

He glances over at me, frowning when he sees me sitting on the couch, no doubt looking drowsy.

"You waited up for me?" He makes his way to the living room.

"I sort of fell asleep." I shrug, my T-shirt slipping off one shoulder.

He comes to a stop in front of the couch I'm sitting on, his gaze dropping to my shirt. "What are you wearing?"

I sit up a little straighter, thrusting my chest out. "Do you like it? I found it on Etsy."

Tate is slowly shaking his head, studying the image on my shirt. "That's . . . wild. You look like a fangirl."

"I was a fangirl." I'm smiling. "I still am. I'm your biggest fangirl."

He likes me saying that. So much he reaches for me with a growl, hauling me into his arms with ease, his hands going to my backside, his eyes widening with surprise.

"You're not wearing panties," he accuses, though he doesn't sound too mad about it.

I lean in, pressing a soft kiss to his jaw, his stubble tickling my lips. "I'm wearing nothing under this shirt, Tate."

"Scandalous," he murmurs before he kisses me.

"You think so?"

"Definitely."

"So what are you going to do about it?"

He grins, his smile naughty. I'm throbbing just from the look on his face. "Let me show you."

Tate carries me into his bedroom—our bedroom now. We've given up all pretense of having separate rooms. I just use mine for a closet mostly. I sleep every night in his bed. Though most of the time we're not doing much sleeping.

Not that I'm complaining.

He drops me onto the mattress close to the edge and settles on his knees on the floor, directly in front of me. I watch as he runs his hands up my bare legs, pressing them open with his palms on the insides of my thighs, spreading me wide. I move with him willingly, all shyness having left me long ago, replaced by eagerness. All I want is to be with him. In every way possible. It's getting to the point that I can barely take it, I'm so completely taken with him. Obsessed with him, really.

Is there a girl-obsessed trope? Because I feel that way about Tate. Thoroughly obsessed with him in every way possible. Though I'm also fairly certain he feels the exact same way about me.

Tate stares at the spot between my legs before his smoldering gaze lifts to mine. "So pretty. And all mine."

A shiver moves through me at the heat in his eyes. His possessive words. "I missed you today."

"Did you?" He streaks his fingers across my thigh, making me jump in anticipation. "I didn't peg you as so damn needy all the time, Scar, but you've surpassed all of my expectations."

"I don't think you mind me being needy." Deep down, I think he loves it. He wants to be wanted, needed, appreciated.

But then again, don't we all?

"I like it." He rises up, kissing the inside of one knee, then the other. I'm already trembling, anticipating his mouth on me. I can't get enough of it. The way he makes me come with his lips and tongue. His fingers.

I'm addicted to the feeling. To him.

He shifts up, trailing kisses along the inside of my thigh, drawing closer and closer to where I want him, before he shifts upward, his mouth on my stomach. My ribs. He shoves the T-shirt upward, chuckling at seeing his younger self on the front of it, before his lips wrap around my nipple and he sucks it into his mouth.

I bury my hands in his hair, holding him close, lost to the sensation of his warm mouth and lashing tongue. I spread my legs and he settles in between them, my hands shifting to slip beneath his shirt so I can touch the hot, smooth skin of his back. I can't get enough of him. I want more.

I want all of him.

We kiss for what feels like hours, his shirt long gone, his jeans undone and my hand down the front, fingers curling around his erection. He's so hard for me, throbbing in my palm.

He finally breaks the kiss first, panting against my lips, "I want to be inside of you so fucking bad, Scar."

I go still, my fingers slipping beneath his boxer briefs so I can touch his silky skin. My fingers trace down the length of him. "I want it too."

His eyes light up, as if I just gave him the keys to the kingdom, and he glances toward the nightstand. "I've got condoms nearby."

I almost want to laugh. "You were prepared for this moment?"

"I'd hoped it was coming," he admits, dipping his head to kiss me, stealing my breath. My thoughts. My heart. "You're all I can think about, Scar. You consume me. This album. I'm sure you already realize this, but . . . it's all about you. You're my muse. My inspiration."

I blink up at him, trying to ignore the prick of threatening tears in the corners of my eyes. "Tate . . ."

"It's true. Every song. Every lyric. Every word. It all has to do with you." He glances down at the T-shirt that's currently bunched above my breasts. "And then I come home and you're wearing my face on your shirt, and that kind of blew my mind."

"In a good way or a bad?" I rest my hand against his chest, right in the center, so I can feel his thundering heart.

"A good way. The best way. I think you're just as obsessed as I am; you just show it in a different way." He grins, kissing me, and I can't help but think, *Yes*.

I'm completely obsessed with him. Just like he is with me.

"You should probably grab a condom," I whisper, noting the way his eyes light up at my unspoken invitation.

I'm ready.

Without hesitation he's scrambling, reaching over to throw the drawer open, his hand rustling around inside until he withdraws a condom packet. He leaves it on top of the night-stand and returns his attention to me, our mouths finding each other. Our hands wandering . . .

The T-shirt is eventually gone. As are his jeans and boxer briefs. Until the both of us are gloriously naked, our limbs entwined, his hands wandering, mapping every part of my skin he can touch.

"You're so soft, Scar," he murmurs at one point, running the back of his hand across my stomach. I'm trembling. "I don't want to hurt you."

"It's going to hurt no matter what," I say, trying to remain logical.

"Well, yeah, but I can try and make it better for you." He grins. "By giving you an orgasm. Or five."

"You make me come five times, and I might get too tired," I warn him.

"I'm taking that as a challenge," he murmurs, just before he dips his head.

CHAPTER THIRTY-THREE

SCARLETT

The moment his tongue touches my sensitive flesh, I feel like I'm about to shoot off the bed. It's like this every single time. The moment his fingers or mouth find me there, I'm lost. Overwhelmed.

Desperate for more.

He licks me from ass to clit, leaving no spot of me untouched. I shamelessly rub my pussy against his face, sucking in a sharp breath when he slides a finger inside of me, keeping it still for a moment. Letting me get used to it.

I'm already used to it. I want more. My whimpers make that obvious.

He adds another finger, his lips finding my clit, sucking it. Gently he thrusts his fingers in and out of me, his pace slow at first. Patient.

But I'm completely impatient. I want more. I want to come. And when he increases his speed, his fingers moving faster, his tongue circling my clit over and over, I draw closer to the edge.

Closer to bliss.

"Don't stop," I whisper, my voice strained, my hips lifting, seeking more.

He reaches for my hand, interlacing our fingers, our palms pressed close together, and I squeeze his hand, that now-familiar overwhelming sensation sweeping over me, sending me spiraling.

The orgasm rocks into me, leaving me breathless. Weightless. I'm shaking, his name falling from my lips, and too soon he's pulling away from me, reaching for that condom and tearing the wrapper off. I watch as he settles onto his haunches, rolling the condom onto his erection, and the remnants of my orgasm fade.

Replaced by a trickle of fear.

He's big. And he's going to somehow enter me? A couple of Tate's fingers don't compare to the size of his dick.

His gaze finds mine, and concern flickers in his eyes. "You look terrified."

"Sorry." I wince, and a relieved sigh leaves me when he settles on top of my body, covering me completely. He's so big and hard and warm, and I love lying with him like this.

I feel safe. Protected. Maybe even . . .

Loved.

I'm probably getting way ahead of myself.

"Don't apologize." He kisses me, his lips soft, his tongue teasing. "We can stop at any time if you need to."

"But what about you?"

"I'll be fine. I'm not going to push you to do anything you don't want to." His mouth is on mine once again, deepening the kiss, making me moan low in my throat. "But I think you're ready for me, Scar. You're wet and loose after your orgasm."

I nod when he lifts away from me slightly, taking a deep breath. "Let's do it then."

When I lift my gaze to his, I see he's smiling. Shaking his head. "You act like we're about to embark on this . . . tough project."

"I'm just trying to prepare myself. It might not be pleasant at first." I bite my lip, hating that I said that. I just want everything between us to be good.

Perfect.

"It'll get pleasant." His smile grows, and he kisses me yet again. "More than pleasant."

"I hope so," I say, sounding full of doubt.

He kisses me for long minutes. Slips his fingers between us so he can stroke me. He's right. I'm wet. Tingling with anticipation, the dread slowly going away the more he kisses me. When I feel his erection poking at my entrance, I tilt my hips up slightly, the head of his cock brushing against my clit.

Tate groans, pausing in his movements, like he needs to regain control of himself. I reach for him, running my hands down the front of his sweat-dampened chest, wishing I could rub my body all over his. I want to smell like him.

Okay, I am seriously in way over my head about this man.

"I'm gonna go slow, okay?" He braces his hand on the pillow beside my head, his other hand wrapped around the base of his erection. "Try to relax."

I exhale slowly and close my eyes, automatically tensing up when I feel him broach my entrance. He slips just inside of my body, stretching me wide, and I release a breath, absorbing the feel of him shifting deep. Deeper.

Until he's completely inside of me.

Tate is still, though I can hear him breathe. He's trying to keep it together, I can tell, and while it doesn't necessarily hurt, I do feel overwhelmingly full of him. I shift beneath him, making him groan, and he leans in, his forehead against mine, and I open my eyes to find his tightly closed.

"Are you okay?" I can't believe I'm the one who's asking that.

His eyes open, and he lifts his head away from mine. "Shouldn't I be asking you that question?"

"You seem like you're in pain." I run my fingernails up and down his back lightly, and he shivers.

"I just don't want to hurt you," he admits.

"It's all right," I whisper, wiggling beneath him. I'm not in pain, but it does feel different. In a good way.

He shifts, withdrawing almost all the way out before he plunges back in, and my breath hitches in my throat. "I want to move faster."

"Then move faster." I drift my hands down, sliding them over his ass and giving him a not-so-subtle push. "I'm not going to break, Tate."

That seems to be what he needs to hear, because he starts to move. Slow but steady at first, letting me adjust and get used to the sensation of him being inside of my body. His restraint is commendable. He's trying so hard to be gentle.

But I'm realizing that this doesn't hurt at all. The friction with his every withdrawal and push forward is delicious. I lift my legs, wrapping them around his hips, and we both moan when it sends him deeper.

"Jesus, Scarlett," he bites out, the corded muscles in his neck standing out as he strains against me. "You feel so good."

"Go faster," I encourage, and he doesn't hesitate.

We're moving against each other faster. Harder. Soon the sound of our sweat-covered bodies slapping against each other fills the room. He grunts with every thrust, and at one point, I crack my eyes open so I can just stare at him.

Only to find him watching me. His gaze is soft, his face is flushed, and when he dips down, his mouth finding mine in a tongue-thrusting kiss, I know.

I'm in love with him. It happened so quickly. Like an unstoppable force. And maybe I'm rushing things or I'm completely overthinking it, but I love him.

And I think he might be a little in love with me too.

"Are you close?" he asks me once he breaks the kiss, his gaze locked on mine. There's a glow in his eyes I've never noticed before.

I slowly shake my head, running my hands down his chest, fingernails drifting across his abs. "Not really."

"Shit." He reaches between us, his fingers finding my clit, and he rubs it as he continues to thrust, fucking me harder. Faster.

Tingles sweep over my skin, and he grabs hold of me with his other arm, adjusting my position so he somehow sinks even deeper. All of it is too much. Not enough.

Without warning the orgasm sweeps over me, my mouth hanging open but no sound coming out. My inner walls milk his erection, rippling along his shaft, and he groans, collapsing on top of me.

I hold him as he comes, running my hands over his shoulders, almost like I'm comforting him. Soothing him. Savoring the feel of him on top of me, crushing me into the mattress.

"Am I hurting you?" he finally asks when he finds his voice once more, making like he's going to lift off me.

I clamp my arms around him tighter, keeping him in place. "Don't leave yet."

"I, uh . . . need to get rid of the condom," he admits, chuckling.

"Just give me another minute." I sink my fingers into his hair, stroking the back of his head.

He lifts away just a little so he can look into my eyes. "Why?"

"I'm enjoying this." I smile at him. "Holding you."

Tate slowly shakes his head, the expression on his face almost wondering. Like he can't believe what I'm doing. "You are something else, Scarlett Lancaster."

"Is that a compliment?" I lift my brows.

He grins. "Definitely."

CHAPTER THIRTY-FOUR

TATE

I forgot to close the curtains last night—I was a little distracted—and the sun's early-morning rays shine through the bedroom window.

Right into my eyes.

Groaning, I roll over, my back to the window, a soft little bundle cuddled up right next to me.

A soft, naked little bundle.

Scarlett.

I tug her into my arms and press my face into her hair, breathing deep. Inhaling her scent. She always smells so damn good, and her skin is so soft. Everything about her is perfect.

Memories hit me, one after another of last night. She had at least three orgasms and I had two, and there was nothing fake about it.

I am 100 percent in this relationship. Like I told her last night, she's all I think about. All I write songs about. Every single song on that album is about her, and I have no problem telling that to the world.

My phone buzzes on the nightstand, and I crack open one

eye, wishing I could tell exactly what sort of notification I'm getting. Sounds like a text type of buzz. This early in the morning?

Scarlett stirs next to me, her ass brushing my cock, and just like that, it rises to the occasion, ready to do more of what we were doing all night.

"Who's texting you?" she murmurs, her voice sleepy.

"I don't know." I brush her hair away from the back of her neck and kiss her there. "Probably no one."

"Mm." Her ass brushes my dick again, and I rest my hands on her hips, keeping her in place. "You don't like that?"

"I like it too much." I slide my hand to her front, cupping her pussy. "If you aren't too sore, I'm going to show you exactly how much I like it."

"Promises, promises." She stretches, her body brushing mine, electrifying my skin everywhere she touches. "And I'm sore, but it's a good sore."

This girl is giving me full permission to go for it. I'm tilting my head, my mouth on her neck, just below her ear, when my fucking phone rings.

"Damn it," I mutter, rolling away from her so I can see who it is.

Roger. The fucker. At eight o'clock in the morning too.

The ringing stops, and I set my phone back on the nightstand. I'm about to reach for Scarlett when it starts ringing again.

"Just answer it," Scarlett encourages. "He won't stop calling until you do."

Knowing she's right, I answer the call. I'm about to ask him what the hell is going on when he speaks right over me.

"Number one."

Everything inside of me goes still. "What?"

"You're number one on the *Billboard* Hot One Hundred.

Number. One." Roger's voice vibrates with excitement. "Can you believe it? Number one, Tate. Number fucking one!"

"'Red' is number one?" I sit up, the sheets falling into my lap, and Scarlett does the same, pressing her head against my shoulder. I glance over at her, the inspiration behind the song, the album, everything, and I smile.

She smiles back, mouthing, *Number one?!*

"It's been riding up that top ten the last couple of weeks, getting higher and higher, and the chart updated today. You're number one." I don't think I've ever heard Roger sound so damn satisfied. "Enjoy your day, son. You're on top of the charts."

"Enjoy my day? What do you mean?"

"Take a break. A day off. It's well deserved. There's so much buzz surrounding you right now. You and Scarlett and this album. Just enjoy yourself. Take Scarlett out. Have fun. Congratulations."

He ends the call before I can say anything else.

I sit there stunned, absorbing what he just said. What it means. How I'll never forget this moment, when I found out that I hit number one on the top one hundred.

Holy. Shit.

"Tate." Scarlett's voice breaks through the fog, and I turn to her, blinking. "Your song is really number one?"

Nodding, I reach for her, gathering her in my arms, clutching her tight. She clings to me, her arms winding around my neck, her hands cradling the back of my head as we just sit there and hold each other.

"I just need to hug you for a second," I whisper into her hair, and she squeezes me closer. "You're the reason this happened."

"No, I'm not. Not really." She pulls out of my embrace, her gaze meeting mine. "You did this all on your own. You wrote that song. Sang it. Into your freaking phone. And look at you now." She throws her arms up in the air, her breasts jiggling with the movement, distracting me. "Look where you are! On top of the world!"

I tackle her, tickling her sides, making her squeal. I pin her to the mattress, continuously tickling her and not letting up until she's practically begging me to stop.

The next thing I know, we're kissing. Rocking against each other. My cock is hard. Aching. When I slip my fingers between her legs, she's wet.

Needy.

Rolling over and taking her with me, I devour her mouth, her ass wiggling against my dick, driving me out of my mind. Eventually I grab a condom, and she tries to help me roll it on but makes a mess of it and lets me take over.

"Ride me," I demand, and she does as I ask, straddling me, her breasts swaying as she lowers herself onto my cock. Until I'm completely embedded inside her.

She sits up, her dark hair a snarled mess, her hard little pink nipples teasing me. Her movements are awkward at first, slow and methodical, as she tries to find her rhythm.

I grip her hips, helping her. Guiding her. The morning light shines brighter, gilding her skin, making her golden, and I can't stop staring.

She's beautiful. Sexy.

All mine.

"You're so deep like this," she murmurs, her eyelids at half mast.

"Too much?" I tighten my hold on her hips, halting her from moving.

"No." She shakes her head, her teeth sinking into her lower lip. "It's perfect."

I let her do her thing. Silently marveling at her beauty, taking in the moment.

The morning I found out I have a number one song on my own. Not with the band but by myself. With a song I wrote.

About a beautiful girl who's smiling at me, my dick buried inside of her.

Life can't get much better than this.

It's lunchtime, and we've been lazy all day by choice. We're out by the pool, sunning ourselves. The security guards are on front door duty currently after I told them firmly that they're not allowed into the backyard for the next two hours at least. Maybe longer.

Glancing over at the lounger next to mine, I drink in the sight before me. Scarlett in the tiniest pair of white bikini bottoms I've ever seen.

And nothing else.

"You're a dirty girl, Scar," I drawl, smiling. "How'd I get so lucky?"

She's got a giant black straw hat on, which hides most of her face. "I would never do this for anyone else but you."

It took some convincing. She wasn't comfortable going topless, but I told her no one would see. The security guards wouldn't dare come to the backyard, not after I made my request. They're both cool dudes. Intimidating but quiet enough that they sort of blend into the background after a while, which I'm sure is the plan.

"I know." Reaching out, I streak my fingers across her stomach, making her jump. "You look hot."

"I am hot," she says. "It's stifling out here."

"Ha ha." It is August, and the sun is broiling. "You need more sunscreen?"

"No, I'm good."

Damn. I was hoping for an excuse to run my hands all over her skin.

"Want to swim?"

"Not yet." She wiggles her hips, like she's trying to get more comfortable. I wish I could see her face. "In a few minutes, though, yes."

"I'm going in." I climb off the lounger and don't even hesitate.

I'm in the pool in seconds, making a big enough splash that I hear Scarlett squeal just before I slip underwater. The moment I pop my head out of the water, I see she's sitting up, the hat on my lounger, a cute scowl on her face.

She's drenched.

"You should join me." I grin, cupping my hand and splashing her. The water lands on her calves and feet. "It feels good."

"Are you getting me back for that first day we were here?" she calls.

That day feels like a lifetime ago. When I didn't really trust her and we were circling each other like sharks. When I thought she was an uptight, spoiled little princess and didn't have any clue how I'd convinced her to do this with me.

Still not quite sure how I was able to finagle that. Not like it was about money. But I do know one thing.

Whenever anyone talks about Scarlett Lancaster now, her father's name is no longer attached.

"Maybe," I finally say, splashing her again. "Get in here."

She stands and slips her feet into a pair of black Gucci slides, then walks around the perimeter of the pool with her hips swaying and her breasts on display, seemingly comfortable in her skin, before she ends up at the shallow end.

I watch her, surprised my tongue isn't hanging out like

a dog's. She's so fucking sexy, and she doesn't even realize it. The transformation of Scarlett has been interesting to watch.

Can't help but think I have a lot to do with it.

When she kicks off her slides and dips her toes into the water, she gives a little mock shiver. "It's cold."

"It is not." I shake my head. "You can't just wade in, Scar. You gotta jump."

Pausing, she watches me as she swirls her foot in the water. "Sounds like a life analogy, Tate."

"Maybe I should make a T-shirt with that saying on it. Sell it on my merch store." I laugh when she rolls her eyes.

"Even on a day off you can't help but talk business." She's teasing me.

"Take my advice, baby. Just jump."

With a sigh she walks/hops over to the middle of the pool, the pavement no doubt hot on her feet. She sends me a look, holds her nose with her fingers, and jumps into the water.

I swim over to her so I'm directly in front of her when she pops out of the water, her dark hair slicked back from her face, water droplets clinging to her long eyelashes. She blinks at me, treading water, her shoulders dotted with goose bumps.

"You are cold," I murmur before I slip my arms around her waist. "Want me to warm you up?"

She kisses me before she ducks underwater for a second, swimming away from me. "Catch me if you can!"

I launch myself after her and catch her easily. Though she doesn't put up much of a fight, willingly letting me press her up against the tiled wall in the shallow end, her arms going around my neck the moment my mouth finds her.

"I wanna fuck you in this pool," I murmur against her lips long kiss-filled minutes later, my hand in the front of her panties.

"We need a condom," she murmurs back, her hand brushing against my cock.

"I'll pull out." I flick her clit, satisfaction humming in my veins when she wraps her legs around my hips, anchoring herself to me.

"Don't start that talk. That's how accidental pregnancies happen," she chastises.

Damn it, she's right.

"Then let's just feel each other up for a little bit." I tug at the waistband of her bottoms, trying to take them off.

She gently shoves me, freeing herself so she can swim away from me. "I'd rather swim."

Feeling dejected, I watch as she swims around the pool, laughing when she sees the disappointment on my face. I'm over it fast, though. We've got all the time in the world.

And I'll get my turn. I'll fuck her hard tonight. To the point that she'll be begging for more of my dick.

Wouldn't be the first time.

CHAPTER THIRTY-FIVE

SCARLETT

We took a day off only for Tate to jump back into work head-first the next morning, leaving first thing for the studio and not coming back until late at night. I spent the majority of my day making content, filming all day long so I'll have enough to post over the next week or so.

My follower-count growth hasn't slowed down. If anything, it's ramped up. I'm gaining so many followers across all my social media, it's still a little unbelievable. I know a lot of that is thanks to me being with Tate, but I'd also like to think I have something to do with it as well.

The comments on my posts are always positive. Always encouraging. Yes, there are a lot of questions about Tate, but I always try to give as much information as I can about him. Us.

There are haters too, of course. The more popular you are, the more criticism comes your way. I choose not to read those comments. Or watch the negative posts made about us.

And there are a lot of them.

A couple of days after Tate found out "Red" hit number one, he comes back to the house in the late afternoon, a big grin on his face when he walks into the kitchen. I'm sitting at the kitchen counter on my laptop, pleased to see that he's back earlier than normal.

"I booked a late-night talk show," he announces.

"Oh, wow." I shut my laptop, smiling at him. "Which one?"

When he says the name, I'm even more impressed. "That's a big deal!"

"I know, but it's a live one. Well, they end filming about an hour before it's broadcast. Simon pulled some strings and got me on Monday night's episode. He was able to get me on there because of the single going number one. He wants me to talk about the upcoming album," Tate explains.

"They'll probably want to know about us too," I point out, apprehension filling me.

It's one thing to pose for photos or have the paparazzi catch us. It's another thing entirely to go onto live TV and be interviewed by a professional who has no qualms about asking the tough questions.

"Yeah, Simon warned me about that." Tate shrugs like it's no big deal. "I'll be fine."

"You will be totally fine," I tell him, wanting to believe it. No, not wanting. I totally believe it.

I have faith in him.

"This is a big deal that he wants me as a guest, because last time I was on that guy's show, I was a complete asshole." Tate exhales roughly, shaking his head. "There were rumors he told everyone he could that he'd never work with me again, but I must've done something right. Or Simon eventually wore him down."

Tate's demons still follow him around, especially with people he's dealt with in the past in the industry.

"You'll prove to him that you're not the same person you

were," I say, my voice firm. "You're a new version of yourself. A better version."

"They want me to perform too," Tate adds, and I see it then. The worry in his gaze. "I've never sung that song live."

"I'm sure you'll be great," I say without hesitation.

He shifts closer, leaning in to give me a kiss. "No one else believes in me like you do, Scar. You make me feel like I can conquer anything."

Warmth spreads over my skin, leaving me a little dizzy. Or maybe that's from having Tate so close, seeing that particular gleam in his eyes. "That's because you can."

He kisses me again. "Don't ever leave me, okay?"

We both go still at his words, staring at each other. What he just said feels so . . .

Serious.

"This is real for you too, right?" His voice is the barest whisper. A rasp in the otherwise still room.

Slowly I nod, my gaze locked on his. "Yes."

His smile is slow. "I didn't think this could happen."

"Me either."

"I thought you were uptight."

"I thought you were a smug prick."

He rears back with a laugh, resting his hand on his chest. "Tell me how you really feel."

I shrug, laughing with him. "I'm just telling you my first impression."

His laughter dies, his expression turning serious. "I thought you were beautiful."

"I thought you were even better looking than you were in Five Car Pileup."

"That's not saying much." He grimaces.

"You were adorable back then. So cute with the floppy

hair." I reach out, teasing the ends of his hair. "You've still got it."

"Not as much as I used to." He dodges away from my seeking fingers, darting in for another kiss, this one full of tongue. "You make me feel like I've still got it."

"All of those fangirls leaving comments all over your social media doesn't prove to you that you still have it? Have you even searched your hashtag lately?"

He winces. "No. Sometimes I'm almost afraid to look."

I leave it alone, deciding to change the subject. "Are you almost finished with the album?"

His face lights up. He loves talking about his project. His songs. "We're so close. Putting a few finishing touches on it. I think you'll love it."

"I know I will."

"It's all about you." The solemn expression on his handsome face has my heart beating faster.

"You already told me," I whisper, closing my eyes the moment his lips touch mine.

He kisses me, gently pulling on my arms, so I stand before his hands go to my waist and haul me onto the marble kitchen counter. The moment I spread my legs, he's stepping in between them, his hands wandering, his mouth fused with mine. Like he can't get enough of me.

I feel the same way.

Our phones ding at the same exact time, but we ignore them, too wrapped up in each other. Tate is too focused on slipping his hands beneath my T-shirt, sliding them up to cup my breasts. He tugs on my bra like he's trying to tear it off me.

His phone starts to ring.

"Why are we constantly interrupted?" he murmurs against my lips, his hands still on my breasts.

My fingers are curled around the waistband of his pants. "You're a popular guy."

More notifications ding from both of our phones.

"Looks like we're both popular." With a reluctant sigh he removes his hands from my chest and checks his phone, frowning as he picks it up. "What's up?"

"Put the call on speaker. Scarlett needs to hear this." I recognize Simon's voice, but I don't think I've ever heard him sound so serious.

Tate sends me a look as he pulls the phone away from his ear and hits the button to switch to speaker, setting the phone on the counter. "Everything okay?"

"No, everything is not okay. Have you checked social media lately? Any gossip sites?"

I glance at Tate, who's already watching me. "No," he says. "Just spit it out, Simon."

"There's a rat. Someone shared all of the legal documents about your relationship with Scarlett. You've been exposed."

My heart hollows out, and I hop off the counter and start to pace the kitchen, my mind full of what he said.

What this all means.

"What do you mean, there's a rat?" Tate's voice is fierce. "And everyone knows about our fake relationship?"

"On that one gossip site, you know, the biggest one? Pages of the agreement are on there, including your signature page. Everyone knows the relationship is phony. And it came from either my office or Irresistible's. Considering the small staff I keep and the integrity of my lawyers and everyone else I employ, I have a feeling it came from Irresistible. Roger is about to have a coronary," Simon explains.

"What the fuck is this going to do for my album?" Tate asks, sounding furious.

His words are like a slap, leaving me breathless.

After everything he just said to me, after everything we just learned now, this is the first question he asks? About his album?

What about us?

"That's exactly what Roger said. He's already been in contact with his crisis-management team. They're also launching an investigation into everyone at the label to see who spilled this. Jesus." The frustration in Simon's voice is obvious. "This is a mess, guys."

"What should we do?" Tate glances over at me, but I avert my gaze, too hurt to look at him. I know this isn't his fault. I know the album is important to him. It's important to me too.

But what about our relationship? We only just confessed our feelings aren't fake. It's so real for me. Too real.

That's why this moment is so painful.

Grabbing my phone, I start checking my notifications. I'm tagged in a bunch of stuff. All articles blowing our cover about our legally drawn-up fake relationship put together only to sell albums and make us famous.

Ouch.

There are texts from my mom, Rachel, my dad. A couple of voice mails that I somehow missed. Oh, one from my lawyer's office.

It's a lot. Too much.

"Keep quiet. Don't leave the house. Roger is sending extra security over there as we speak. Don't say a word to anyone, not even security. What if they ratted you out?"

"They wouldn't. They probably believe we're real. We've given them enough evidence," Tate says wryly.

"I'll call you back. I'm going to reach out to Roger and see if we can put together a meeting with the crisis team." Simon ends the call.

The silence is deafening. I'm reading an article about us, the details becoming a blur because they're so awful. Full of triggering words like *bogus. Exposed. Trick. Fake.*

Fake, fake, fake.

"This is bad," Tate finally says, and I look at him, noting how pale he is, his phone open to one of the articles about us. "We look . . . really fucking bad."

"I know," I murmur, glancing back down at my phone, which lights up with a call from my dad.

I don't want to answer it. My heart is in my throat, and panic makes me sweaty.

I hit accept anyway, bracing myself for my father to start yelling.

"Scarlett, baby. Is this all true?" That's how he greets me.

I clutch my phone to my ear with trembling fingers, swallowing hard. "Well, it—it was."

"What the hell does that mean? And why didn't my lawyer tell me about this?" he roars.

"I'm eighteen. I hired my own lawyer," I tell him, wincing when he starts talking right over me.

"Your mother and I let you leave with this loser to go to Los Angeles to what? Play at a relationship so he can gain more fans for his upcoming album? Scarlett, he completely used you."

"He didn't." I turn so my back is to Tate, hating how my dad's words ring true. No matter how much I don't want to believe it—I'm living the experience; I know Tate cares about me—it still sounds awful.

"He did. Oh, I know you think you gained something out of it too, but he's the winner in this situation. Did you at least get financially compensated for this agreement?"

We never really talked about money. I never did it for that.

Originally I did it to get away from the very man who's currently yelling at me. I did it for attention.

I did it for myself.

"It wasn't about money," I start, but I'm cut off by my father's laughter.

"Oh, Scarlett. I always thought you were a smart girl, but you've handled this all wrong. That boy owes you big time. He can afford it. I gave him enough money for that goddamn performance. Or did he blow it all already on drugs and alcohol?"

"He's not like that anymore," I bite out. "And this is all your fault. You're the one who brought him into our lives. And now look what happened."

"I didn't tell you to run away with him and pretend to be a happy couple for public consumption! That's on you, Scarlett. Your mother is beside herself. She feels guilty that she let you go."

"There was no letting me go. I was going to do it whether you guys liked it or not," I tell him, throwing my head back so I can stare at the ceiling. I'm suddenly exhausted.

Overwhelmed.

"You think you know better because you're eighteen, and now you're finding out you don't know shit about life. Come home, Scarlett. We can call up the jet and fly you home so you don't have to deal with public scrutiny," Dad says.

"It's too late for that." I can literally hear the sound of car doors slamming outside. The low murmur of voices.

The paparazzi have arrived.

"Let us help you," Dad pleads. "You need to get away from him."

Slowly I turn around, eager to see Tate's face. To see the sympathy in his gaze. To know he's in this with me.

We're in this together.

But he's gone.

CHAPTER THIRTY-SIX

SCARLETT

There's a soft knock, and then my bedroom door swings open, revealing Rachel standing there, a worried expression on her face.

"Come in," I croak from beneath a pile of blankets on my bed. "And shut the door behind you."

She closes it softly before she approaches the bed, her eyes wide as she takes me in. "You look terrible."

"Gee, thanks." I love my friend's honesty, except in moments like this.

"I'm sorry. Just trying to keep it real." She settles on the edge of the bed, right by my feet. "Are you okay?"

"No." There is no recovering from this. The media hasn't stopped talking about me and Tate since our fake relationship was exposed Friday.

We had a meeting with the crisis-management team on the phone, and Tate was so withdrawn. So removed from the entire situation. He could barely look at me.

And I could barely look at him.

I talked to Mom, and she took care of my flight home. In

the early-morning hours of Saturday, before the sun was even up, I left the house in Calabasas and was whisked away to the airport, where I boarded a private jet hired by my family and flew home to New York.

Leaving Tate behind.

He wouldn't talk to me. Not really. He was in pure panic mode, and I don't think he knew what to say. I'm sure he felt as if he were watching his entire career go up in smoke, and I get it. His career, the album, it's all important to him.

But what about me? What about us?

I didn't talk to him about it. I didn't sleep with him that night. I went back to my room and packed my things. I lay in bed and cried, unable to sleep. He never came to comfort me. I don't know if he heard me, but how can I try to reason with someone who essentially turned into a zombie the moment things got rough?

I couldn't. That's part of the reason I left. If he wanted me, he'd call. He'd text. He'd chase me to the ends of the earth and let me know how much I mattered to him.

But he didn't do any of that. It's Sunday. I haven't heard a word. And the interest in our situation hasn't died down. I swear it's only grown. We're all anyone can talk about, and it's so weird.

Don't people have better things to do with their lives?

"I saw an article that said they figured out who did it," Rachel announces.

I sit up straight, pushing the covers away from my upper half. I'm sure I look terrible. I probably even smell. I haven't taken a shower since I've come home, which is kind of gross. Okay, really gross.

But I don't care.

"They did? Who was it?"

"Someone who worked at Irresistible. An intern with

nothing to lose. Supposedly he made a quarter of a mil for selling you guys out," Rachel says.

I fall back against my pillows, staring up at the ceiling. At the canopy that hangs above my bed. The same one I've had since I was fourteen and used to dream of getting together with one of the boys from Five Car Pileup. We could travel the world together, and I could watch him tour, all those fans screaming for him.

Screaming for Tate Ramsey.

But he would belong to me. Only me.

My fourteen-year-old girl's dreams almost came true. For a moment there, I felt it. I lived it.

And now it's gone.

"I hate this stupid canopy."

Rachel is quiet for a moment, probably shocked by my subject change.

"I'm serious. I need to redo my room. It looks like a little girl's bedroom," I explain.

"You should redo it then." Rachel's voice is gentle. I wonder if she thinks I've lost my mind.

I sort of feel like I have.

"I've changed, Rach." I sit back up again so I can look her in the eye. "Since being with Tate, I'm not the same person I was. I can't sit here in this bedroom and pretend that nothing happened. That my life will just go on and I'll be okay. It doesn't feel like I will ever be okay. I've lost him."

Rachel frowns. "What do you mean, you've lost him?"

I burst into tears, covering my face with my hands. I hate wallowing in my sadness, but I don't know what else to do. I can't change what happened. We've been exposed, and it's been such a humiliating experience. I feel like I can't show my face. Can't go out in public. Can't post on any of my accounts. I didn't take the coward's way out and turn off my comments, though I probably should've. I'm sure people are leaving all sorts of horrible comments, letting me know what they really think of me.

God, I don't care. I hope they forget me forever. I would trade all the followers, all the adoration, and all the free stuff companies sent me if I knew that Tate was still mine.

Once I get the tears out of me, I explain to Rachel what happened. How Tate treated me that day when we found out. How he hasn't reached out.

"Maybe he's trying to take care of a few things before he contacts you," Rachel suggests, trying to be . . . what? An optimist?

"Like what? What can he do? What's done is done. If he really cared, he'd already be putting together some sort of formal statement and announcing to the world that yeah, maybe we started out as fake, but we actually fell for each other," I say. "Unless he didn't actually fall for me. Maybe he was playing me all this time."

"No," Rachel starts, but I shake my head, cutting her off.

"He could've been. I got caught up in it all. He might've too."

"Are you saying that what you felt for him wasn't real?"

"No, but maybe those feelings weren't as intense for him as they are for me." I grab a tissue from the box on my nightstand and blow my nose. "If I don't hear from him by tomorrow, I'm blocking him."

Rachel frowns. "Are you sure that's a good idea?"

"I refuse to sit around and wait for him. He can reach out. He needs to say something to me, Rach. I feel like I'm dying over here," I practically wail.

"He's an asshole," Rachel says fiercely, scowling.

"He is." I close my eyes, fighting off the tears that want to fall. "But I think I'm in love with him."

Rachel is quiet, and when I open my eyes once more, I find her peering at me. “Really?” she asks, sounding shocked.

I nod, misery coursing through me. “Yeah. Why else would I feel so awful? So . . . alone? I just spent a few glorious weeks with him in Los Angeles. We were together constantly when he wasn't at the studio. Everything between us grew so fast, and our experiences together, our feelings, it was all heightened. Overwhelming. We were in it together. No one else would understand what that was like. Just him.”

And just me.

“Maybe you should reach out to him,” Rachel suggests. “Maybe he's scared you're mad at him or whatever.”

“I'm scared too,” I confess. “What if he doesn't want to talk to me? What if he's freaking out? He's watched his career disappear before.”

“That was his fault,” Rachel points out. “This situation is a little different.”

“Still his fault, though. Mine too. Everyone involved knew the risk. We just didn't think we'd get exposed.” I cover my face with my hands, hating how my head is spinning with too many things. “I don't know what to do.”

“What does your mom say? And your dad?”

I drop my hands. “Dad says I should forget Tate Ramsey for the rest of my life and put this entire thing behind me. Mom just offers me comfort and lets me cry on her shoulder. She's given me no real advice besides letting me know it's going to get better eventually.”

“What if he never does anything? Never reaches out, never makes a public statement, just . . . disappears. What then?”

I ponder her words for a moment, hating how my stomach churns at the probability of Tate doing exactly that.

It could happen. I wouldn't be surprised if it did fall out that way.

"Then I know he never cared about me in the first place, and I'll let him go. I've already let him go. If he wants to come back to me, he can." I glance out the window, at the bright-blue sky with white puffy clouds.

That's the weird thing about sadness. About losing someone who was so important in your life, even for such a short time. Life goes on. Nothing stops, while you feel as if your world just ended. It might've stopped for me, but everyone else is carrying on like nothing happened. To them, nothing did happen.

I'm the one suffering. And it feels like I'm doing this all alone.

I hate that most of all.

Monday night. It's late, past eleven, and I still haven't heard a word from Tate. The gossip seems to have died down somewhat. It helps that there's another scandal already happening. Another singer getting in trouble for saying something rude about his ex-wife, who's also famous.

I don't know how celebrities manage keeping up this sort of thing for years. I can barely handle what just happened to me, and Tate and I were together for almost a month. That's it.

My parents have tiptoed around me, and I know that's my mom's doing. Dad would be in here giving me a lecture on the daily if she hadn't told him to leave me alone. It's been nice. Peaceful.

A little lonely.

There is a rapid-fire knock on my door, and before I can

say anything, it's opening, my mother sweeping into the room clad in a pale-blue silk robe, elegant as ever.

"Darling. You need to come out to the living room and watch TV with me," she declares, standing at the foot of my bed.

I haven't left it much since I came home, and I'm starting to get sick of it. Sick of myself.

"Why?" I've been trying to avoid any sort of media at all costs, except for bingeing a bunch of movies. All of them romantic comedies full of the tropes Rachel told me about. They're comforting. Though they probably also leave me with too much hope. Like everything between Tate and me is going to work out in the end.

My rational mind says no way is that going to happen, but my hopeful heart?

It's holding out for a miracle.

"There's something coming on that I think you should see." She clasps her hands together in front of herself, watching me. "Just . . . come out and watch it with me."

"Is Dad out there?" I really don't want to hear it from him. I love my father, and for the most part he's been leaving me alone since I came home, but I know he's dying to give me a speech.

I'm not ready to hear it yet.

"He fell asleep about an hour ago. It'll just be me and you. Come on." She waves a hand. "Join me."

"Okay, give me a minute," I grumble as I throw my covers back and slide out of bed.

"Don't take too long. It's going to start soon," she tells me before she leaves my bedroom.

I brush my teeth and pull my hair into a topknot. I don't bother changing, though. I at least took a shower today, and I'm wearing a silky pajama-shorts set that's a pale-pink color.

A step up from the old ratty clothes I had on for the previous twenty-four hours.

When I enter the living room, I see Mom is perched on the edge of the couch, hunched over and staring at the TV. The moment she notices me, she aims the remote at the screen and pauses the commercial, a faint smile on her face.

"You look good."

I shrug, settling into an overstuffed chair. "What do you want to show me?"

"It's coming on right now." She hits the remote again and fast-forwards through the little bit of commercial that she can. "Just watch."

I wait, bored as the commercials drone on. The eleven o'clock newscast says goodbye, only to launch into more commercials. I'm checking my phone, but there's not much to see, since I'm avoiding social media like it's the plague, and I set it on the chair, my eyes going wide when I see what's coming on next.

When they list the special guests.

Tate's name flashes on the screen, and I realize . . .

He never canceled his talk show appearance.

"I don't know if I want to watch this," I say.

"You should," Mom says, and when I glance over at her, I notice there's a strange look on her face. "Just . . . let's see what happens."

Nerves chew at my stomach, and I sit up straighter, bracing myself. The talk show host performs his usual monologue at first, and I'm over it almost immediately. I just want to get to Tate. I want to know what he's going to perform. What he's going to say. I'm sure he's nervous. Afraid the host is going to ask hard-hitting questions, and after everything that just happened, I know those questions are going to be all about us.

The host rambles for a solid ten minutes, maybe longer, and when it goes to a commercial break, I'm halfway out of the chair, unable to take it anymore. "I'm going to bed."

"But darling, you have to watch Tate's performance." Mom leaps to her feet, rushing toward me, her hands landing on my shoulders as if she's going to push me back onto the chair. "It's important."

"Why? Are you trying to make me even sadder? He hasn't contacted me since I left, Mom. Not once. Not a single call or text or anything. Which is making me realize that what happened between us when we were together meant nothing to him." The tears are back—I am so sick of crying—and I blink hard, trying to stop them.

But it's no use. They're streaking down my cheeks, and I feel like I'm on the verge of a total mental breakdown.

"Oh, darling. You really love him, don't you?" When I nod, she pulls me into a crushing hug, holding me tight. "Can you trust me? Just for a little bit?"

"Why do you want me to watch it? Do you know something I don't?" I pull away from her, staring into her dark-brown eyes, which are so much like my own. "Tell me."

Her head shakes slightly, her lips parting, and I wait in anticipation.

"I can't tell you. Just know that you need to see this." Her expression is somber, and with a reluctant nod, I settle back into the chair.

And I wait.

CHAPTER THIRTY-SEVEN

TATE

I feel like I'm going to throw up.

Tonight is more important than anything else I've ever done in my life. More important than any public appearance I made with Five Car Pileup. More important than the night I performed for Scarlett's birthday party.

I'm going to reveal the truth tonight. And I'm going to sing—not the song they think I plan on singing either. Not even Roger or Simon know about that. I discussed it with the talk show host, and Jimmy's good with it. Once I explained my situation and pleaded my case, he was totally down for it.

"This is probably gonna go viral, huh," Jimmy said to me before the show started.

"I won't complain if it does," I told him. "I just hope I can follow through."

"You've got this, man." Jimmy clasped my shoulder and gave it a shake.

He's probably not going to go easy on me, and I'm prepared for that. Somewhat. I'm waiting backstage, about to walk out on set, and when they announce my name and the crowd claps and cheers—I'm shocked—I head out, smiling and nodding, my heart sitting in my throat.

"So Tate, what have you been up to lately?" Jimmy asks, making the audience laugh.

I chuckle too, glancing out at the crowd, though I can't make out any of their faces. The stage lights are too bright, and actually, I'm grateful for it.

"Not much," is how I answer him. "You know, the usual."

"You're having a comeback moment."

"Indeed I am."

"And already finding yourself embroiled in scandal." Jimmy says it with relish, and I remind myself he's only doing this because this is what people want.

"Yeah, didn't mean for that to happen." I shake my head, rubbing my fingers along my jaw. Hating how uncomfortable I feel.

But I need to do this. I need to say it. Spill it all.

"We hear about fake relationships all the time in Hollywood. But no one ever cops to them, you know? This is a first." Jimmy watches me, his eyes sparkling, and he gives me a little nod of encouragement. "The relationship started out fake between you two, right? Did it eventually turn into something real?"

"It started out fake." I sit up straighter and clear my throat. This is do-or-die time. "I can't lie about it. Those documents that were leaked? They are one hundred percent real, and we were victimized by that Irresistible employee leaking everything. But yes, Scarlett and I signed a contract, and we were involved in a fake relationship for publicity purposes through my record label."

"The publicity surrounding you two after the kiss photo was completely wild. Like, everyone was talking about it. Your comeback. How you two made such a great couple. She's got such a huge audience on social media, and people still love you from your Five Car Pileup days. It was a big deal. People were rooting for you two, so to find out it wasn't real is just . . ." Jimmy shakes his head. "Man, it was a little disappointing."

The audience groans its agreement.

"I let everyone down. I know I did. Including Scarlett. But believe me when I say my feelings for her the last couple of weeks, before everything came out?" My gaze goes to the camera, and I say, "They were authentic."

The crowd claps, and my face flushes. I'm not looking for approval, but hearing their applause makes me feel a lot better.

I hope Gloria Lancaster comes through and gets her to watch this live. It'll mean so much more.

"What are you saying, Tate?" Jimmy asks.

"I'm saying that I'm in love with Scarlett." I turn toward him to see the smile on his face. He's eating this up. "I know people might think I'm just saying this to save face, but I'm being real right now. I love her. The new album is all about her. Every single song. Every word I wrote."

"I hear you wrote all the lyrics," Jimmy adds.

I nod. "I did. Every song is from my heart. For Scarlett."

"Including your latest number one hit, 'Red.' Congratulations on that, by the way. Pretty cool to go from a former rebel in a boy band to having the number one single on the *Billboard* charts."

"It feels amazing," I agree. "I still can't believe I've been given this second chance."

"All thanks to performing at Scarlett's birthday party. How did you get that gig again?" Jimmy asks.

I tell the story, and then we go to commercial break. As soon as the cameras are off, Jimmy's leaning over his desk, his gaze on me. "You're doing great. Keep it up."

"Thank you." A makeup artist darts out, dabbing at my

forehead with one of those puff things. I'm sweating thanks to what I'm saying and the hot lights.

"You're really in love with her?"

I nod. "Hope she watches. This is the first time I've told her."

Jimmy's mouth drops open. "Seriously?"

"Yeah. Bad move?"

"We'll see," he says with a broad smile, just as the cameras turn back on.

We talk about the album some more. He asks a few questions about my troubled past, but they're more like gentle lobs than heavy slams on top of my head. I express my gratitude to the fans for loving the song and say I hope they'll enjoy the album. I offer up hints about an upcoming tour.

And then it's almost time for me to perform.

"You were going to sing 'Red,' but you came to me with a special request, right?" Jimmy's brows shoot up.

Nerves eat at me again. This is where it gets tricky. I never ran the idea by Simon or Roger. "Yeah. I was hoping I could sing my new song for your audience tonight."

Lots of cheering and yelling in response to that statement.

"Looks like they don't have a problem with it. What's the song called?"

"Its title is 'Lonely for You Only.' It's a play on Five Car Pile-up's song 'Lonely for You,'" I explain.

"That's the only song that went number one for you guys, huh?"

"Yeah." I nod. "I literally just wrote it."

Jimmy frowns, his expression wary. "Wait, so it's not recorded for the album?"

"Uh, not yet."

"Can't wait to hear it." Jimmy's smile is brittle, and I can tell this isn't what he expected.

Shit.

There's another commercial break, and I go to the side of the stage, where the band waits. It's the guys I used while recording the album, and we've been going over the song all damn day, me trying to get it just right.

They sound great. The music is solid. It's me I'm worried about. I don't want to choke. Or look like a fool.

That's the biggest one. Looking like a fool.

Okay, scratch that. The worst fear is that Scarlett won't see me perform. Or she will and won't give a shit. That I've already blown it.

All I've done since she left is work on this damn song. I wanted to call her, text her, but this is such a bigger declaration. It might be a mistake, but I had to do it this way. Show her that I love her in front of the whole damn world.

And fuck the consequences.

It was a risk, me coming on this show. Simon didn't want me to do it. Roger was all for it. He's trying to salvage the album, while Simon is trying to salvage my reputation. Both feel like they're in the toilet, but maybe . . .

Maybe not. The audience's reaction has been positive all evening. Now that I'm about to perform, though, I'm full of nerves.

Worry. Plenty of worry.

Jimmy announces me and the song, and the guitar starts, a melodic, almost melancholy sound. I grip the microphone and close my eyes, telling myself it's going to be all right.

I'm going to kill it.

The words flow from me without thought. About longing and need. About meeting a sunshine girl with flashing brown eyes and a laugh like a song. How I fell in love and can't think about anyone else.

Nothing will do
Only you
I'm lonely for you only
Missing you so bad
You're the best I've ever had
In love with a girl who feels the same
Do you feel the same?
Are you lonely for me only, or is it all a game?

I run through the rest of the song with ease, giving it my all. My voice sounds good. The audience is swaying to the music. Even singing along with the chorus the second time around. Hell, even Jimmy is nodding his head to the beat, a faint smile on his face. And when the final note hits and I pull away from the mic, the audience erupts into overwhelming applause.

Jimmy runs up and gives me a hug, a grin on his face as he murmurs, "If she doesn't respond to that performance, then something is seriously wrong with her."

I nod and laugh, the sound nervous. I can't stop smiling. The crowd keeps cheering, and I wave a hand at them, bowing before I turn to the band and bow to them as well. These four guys have kept me sane over the last few days, even when I was tempted to give it all up.

I didn't, though. I couldn't. I had to do this. For me.

And for Scarlett.

For us.

CHAPTER THIRTY-EIGHT

SCARLETT

I'm . . .

Stunned.

"What did you think?"

I turn to look at my mother, who has a vaguely smug look on her face. As if she knew all about this and had all the faith in the world that I would be floored. Which I am. I can't believe he said what he said.

Tate is in love with me.

And he just declared it on national television.

"He sounded so good," I say, my voice small.

But he didn't look . . . great. He seemed nervous. Worried. Tired. His face was a little pale and he was unshaven. Oh, he didn't look *bad*. He's still incredibly handsome and charming, but I know him well enough. Spent a lot of time with him, especially lately.

He seemed stressed. Worried about his performance?

Worried about me seeing it?

"He wrote that song for you, Scarlett," Mom murmurs. "He called me and we spoke earlier."

"You talked to Tate?" I squeak.

She nods. "He wanted to ask me for forgiveness for duping us, and he wanted to thank me and your father for giving him the opportunity to perform at your party. It changed his life, he said."

"Because of his career?"

"Because he met you," she says gently. "He's in love with you. And when he told me those exact words, I swear I thought he was going to cry. His voice was brimming with emotion. He misses you so much."

My eyes fill with tears. I miss him too. "Why didn't he call me?"

"He wanted to make sure you believed him. What better way to make a declaration of love than on late-night television?" Mom laughs.

"He didn't need to make it such a public spectacle," I murmur, loving that he did, though.

I think of the lyrics. How he's lonely for me only.

I feel the same exact way. There's no one else for me.

Just him.

"Do you love him?" Mom asks.

I nod, the tears starting to fall.

"You should call him."

"But why won't he call me?" I'm repeating myself, and maybe I'm being ridiculous. He's made a move.

I suppose it's my turn.

An exasperated sigh leaves my mother. "Just call him, Scarlett. Tell him how you feel."

Grabbing my phone, I watch as she crosses the room and drops a kiss on my forehead, smiling down at me. "You're so lucky."

"Why?"

"To be so young and madly in love. You found a good one, darling."

Before I can say anything in response, she exits the room, leaving me alone, and I stare at the phone for a moment before I bring up Tate's number. I stare at the contact page, his name becoming blurred the longer I look. My nerves paralyze me completely. I want to call him.

I do.

But what if . . .

What if what? All my worry is futile. He won't reject me. He's probably waiting for me. Anxious.

Giving in, I hit the button, and the phone begins to ring.

Tate answers on the second ring, breathless when he says my name.

"I saw your performance," is what I greet him with.

He's quiet for a second. "What did you think?"

"I loved it." I pause, taking a deep, fortifying breath. "I love the new song."

His laugh is full of relief, and I smile, wishing I were with him. "I wrote that for you, Scar. And I meant every word I said. I am lonely for only you."

"Did you mean what you said to the host before you performed?" I clutch my phone tighter, needing to hear him say it.

"About being in love with you?" He exhales roughly. "I wish you were with me so I could say it to your face."

"Well, you're not. So say it now to me over the phone," I demand, then realize how awful I sound. "Please," I add, my voice a raw whisper.

He actually chuckles, and the sound washes over me, reassuring my chaotic thoughts.

"I love you, Scarlett. I fell in love with you, and I don't want you to ever leave my side again. Come back to Los Angeles. Come back to me," he says softly.

I close my eyes, exhaling with relief. "Tate."

"I can't stand not having you here with me. I miss you too damn much. And before you say something about photographers and reporters or whatever, just know they've left the house. They're gone. They've moved on to the next scandal. Besides, how scandalous can we be, if we actually love each other? Because we do love each other, right?"

Oh, he sounds worried.

He's so silly.

"I love you," I whisper into the phone. "And I miss you."

He's smiling. I can hear it in his voice when he speaks.

"I love you too, Scar." Only the slightest hesitation before he says, "Come back to me."

Less than twelve hours later, and I'm in Los Angeles, having just landed thanks to my dad pulling a few strings that allowed me to use the Lancaster family jet to fly to California.

He didn't even protest when my mother asked. I think they've both known this was going to happen. And I'm sure Tate redeemed himself in their eyes with last night's performance.

I exit the plane, carefully walking down the steps, and I'm surprised to see a sleek black sports car waiting for me. The driver's door swings open and Tate steps out, tall and handsome, clad in all black with sunglasses covering his eyes. He whips them off and our gazes connect, a giant smile curling his lips.

I drop the bag I was carrying on the tarmac and run toward him, throwing my arms out at the last second just as he swings me into his embrace. I cling to him, pressing my face against his chest and closing my eyes. Breathing in his familiar delicious smell, absorbing his heat and strength.

When I pull back slightly, he kisses me, stealing my breath. My thoughts.

My heart.

His hand shifts to cup my face as he stares into my eyes, never looking away as he murmurs, "Don't leave me again."

"I won't," I promise.

He kisses me again, like he can't help himself. "You're beautiful."

"I missed you."

"I love you," he returns, the words so much more meaningful in person. When I'm staring into his eyes. Hearing his voice.

I'm smiling and crying at the same time. "I love you too."

"Come on tour with me?" He raises his brows, his expression expectant.

Please. As if I could ever turn him down.

"Yes." I nod, sniffing. His thumbs streak across my cheeks, wiping the tears away, his touch gentle. "I would love to."

"We're really going to do this, huh?" His smile is bright and blinding. Like the sun.

"Yes," I whisper, leaning my cheek into his palm and closing my eyes for the briefest moment before I open them again, loving the way he looks at me. "We really are."

ACKNOWLEDGMENTS

I'm incredibly lucky I get to do this writing thing for a living. And I'm excited to be working with a traditional publisher again. It's definitely been a while . . .

I want to thank my editor, Marilyn, for taking a chance on Scarlett and Tate's story. And to everyone at Blackstone Publishing—thank you for all that you do to make this book shine!

To my agent, Nicole Resciniti, thank you for always being in my corner and taking care of me. When we embarked on this journey together, I had no idea where it would take us. I don't know about you, but I'm shocked and surprised in the best way at where we're at now. I appreciate all that you do!

Nina, you have been by my side since 2016, and I will never forget when you approached my table at that signing in Los Angeles and said, "I'm a publicist now—want to work with me?" I'm so glad I said yes. You have stood with me through the down times and the good times, and I feel like we just keep growing together. And now that you're one of my agents? I feel like we could conquer the world! Thank you for being my person.

And finally, to all the readers. Thank you for reading me, for leaving reviews, for talking about my books online or to your friends. I absolutely cannot do this job without you, and having your support means the world to me. I appreciate all of you.